A Dance of Fates

The Veiled Fates Series
Book I

Eevy A.

For the quiet dreamers,

✦.　+　.✦.　+　.✦

Because your dreams deserve to be heard, too.

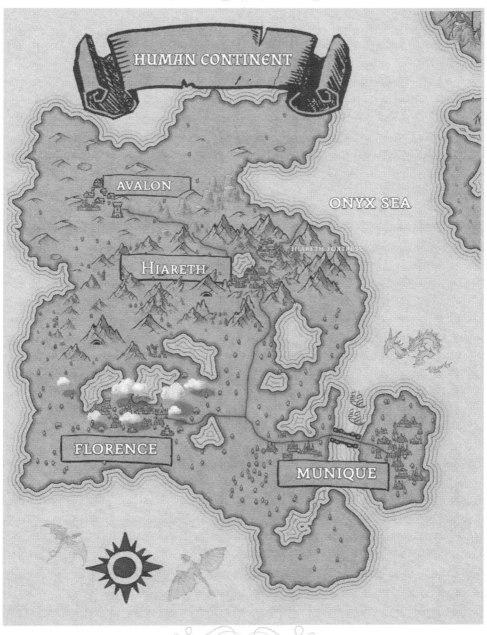

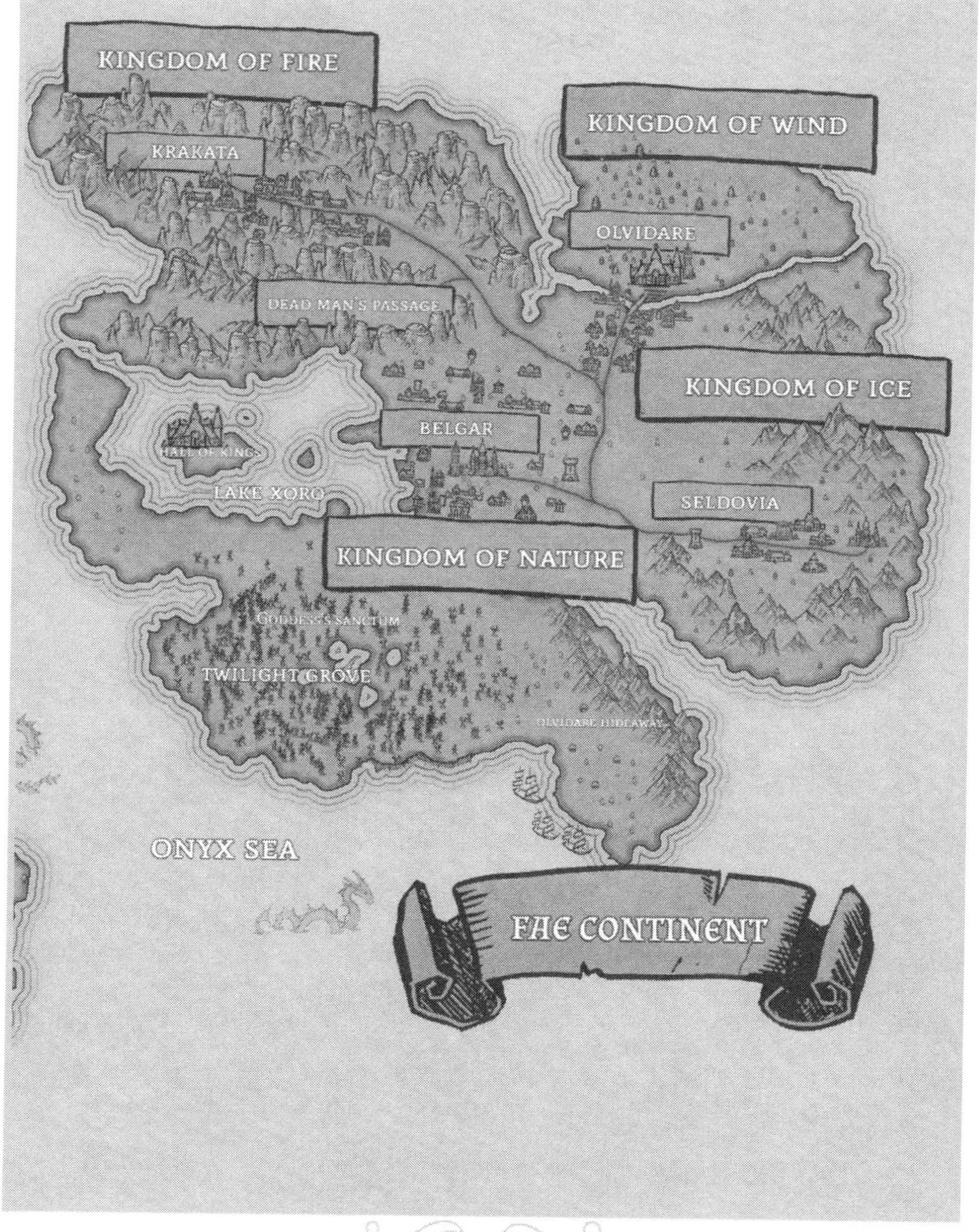

KINGDOM OF FIRE

KINGDOM OF WIND

KRAKATA

OLVIDARE

KINGDOM OF ICE

DEAD MAN'S PASSAGE

BELGAR

HALL OF KINGS

LAKE XORO

SELDOVIA

KINGDOM OF NATURE

GODDESS'S SANCTUM

TWILIGHT GROVE

OLVIDARE HIDEAWAY

ONYX SEA

FAE CONTINENT

Part One

The Chains of Fate

Chapter One

Selene

WHEN THEIR WELLS RUN DRY AND TONGUES BECOME PARCHED, they'll think of me. When there's no ice to numb their pain or cool their drinks, they'll think of me. Today, I kneel before them, a cool blade resting on my throat. Was it sorrow or guilt that shone on some of their faces? I spent eighteen years facing the reality of this day, yet nothing could prepare me for the moments that lay before me.

Would it hurt when the Goddess claimed me?

The blade on my throat, while wholly deadly, was never intended to cause my death. No, this lethal relic was just a precautionary measure to ensure that I don't doom my entire kingdom by escaping.

"In yielding to the Fae Goddess, we offer Princess Selene of Avalon," The man who spoke was sweating profusely beneath the baking sun of the Avalon Desert. I recognized him to be my father's herald. Despite the situation I found myself in, I couldn't help but snort a laugh as he stood there, trembling, while my knees dug into the gritty sand. A sword scraped my throat, and *he* got to shake? He wiped his balmy palms against his tabard, which gleamed with shades of gold and ruby.

"In yielding," I whispered, "not in honor." My kingdom would yield to the Fae bitch Goddess who cursed Avalon over a military dispute.

Eevy A.

"As requested, she stands before you on her eighteenth birthday," the sweating man continued.

Eighteen years, I thought. Eighteen years to decide who I hated more. The Goddess who forced my existence, or the father I was forced to have. I didn't need to look behind me to know he shed no tears.

My mother remained behind us in the sprawling sandstone castle, casting shadows over us. I wondered if she watched from above, but I would likely never know. Unsurprisingly, I was only offered a brief farewell with her, a simple embrace that gave me no strength—no courage for what was to come.

I shifted on my knees, the gritty sand biting into my skin. The king had ordered a spectacle out of this, forcing the city of Avalon to stand before us in the too-small dusty courtyard. It was a round space, with many familiar faces looking anywhere but at me. Most of the crowd remained as far as they could away, nearly pressed against the sandstone walls at their back. Some people spilled into the alleys and archways connecting into the round courtyard as if preparing to leave the moment the Goddess claimed me. Would they watch when she did?

"Goddess, we only await you to take her as your sacrifice, to spare our lands," he spoke, eyes darting between me, the king at my back, and the crowd before us.

Imbecile.

Allowing my head to roll back, I stared into the dull, cloudless sky. Shades of cream and tan melted into each other, the bitter, lifeless air allowing for no vibrancy. I nearly smiled at that sky. A sky that promised to punish this kingdom with more draught. A sky that would avenge me after years of torment, years of being used. A single tear rolled down my cheek. I crystallized it into a small frozen bead with a blink. I listened for the delicate sound of it shattering on the rocks below me—a behavior I picked up as a child. Only when the soft shattering of ice was replaced with the sound of cracking stones did my head snap back to the crowd before me.

Goddess—

Several bodies were propelled towards me as the towering sandstone wall tumbled, forcing them to fall forward. The wall fell atop several familiar faces, pinning them to the sandy ground. An enormous wind surrounded us, causing

4

the sand to whip wildly through the air. Screams shattered the thick tension that had built only moments ago. I took an uneasy breath, choking on a sandy gulp of air as I shifted from where I knelt. I winced at the sharpness of the blade that remained resting at my throat despite the commotion. I blinked, trying to see through the haze of sand. There was nothing—it was as if some enormous wind had blown down the castle walls. Wind shouldn't be strong enough to—

Another gust of wind ripped through the courtyard, forcing more sand and dust to hang in the air. Screams echoed around me as more and more sandstone walls fell. Everything around me stilled as if I had frozen time and space. The sharp blade at my throat clattered to the ground with a deafening thud. The swordsman that was wielding it now lay in two pieces at my side, his blood inching toward where my knees met the sand. A shadow consumed me a moment later; no doubt the king—my father—had risen from his throne of sandstone and ruby.

"*Now,*" he growled at no one in particular. I understood. He was talking to the Fae Goddess. He was telling her to take me now—to claim my life *now*.

"If you don't take her *now,* then you—"

Before the king could finish threatening the Fae Goddess, he was blown forward, nearly toppling over my kneeling body. Once the dust cleared, the remnants of the sandstone and ruby throne lay in a pile before me. A metallic scent filled my nostrils, the unmistakable smell of fear. I wasn't sure if that scent was radiating from me or the people of Avalon, who continued peeling away from the courtyard before more walls were sent toppling upon them.

My hands began to tremble, creating a jingling sound with the chains that kept me bound and attached to the ground—to this place. My father, or rather the king, was unconscious a mere two feet from me, a thin line of blood dripping from his nose down his tanned cheek. I watched, in a half-dazed state, as one, then two drops of blood hit the sand beneath his face. My lungs clenched at the sight of him—the king, lying so helplessly on the sandy floor of his own courtyard—his own kingdom. I glanced at the sword that now lay inches from me, then at the king's exposed throat. I looked down to my chained wrists and ankles, feeling a wave of relief crash over me. Had I not been chained, I wasn't entirely sure I would have refrained from the opportunity to use that sword on the King of Avalon.

"Get. Up. Now." A harsh, unrelenting voice boomed above me.

I snapped my gaze away from my father's bleeding face to behold a man whose face remained shrouded behind a dark cloth. His hand was outstretched as if I could grasp it.

"Does it look like I can?" I spat, surprised at both the rasp and lethality in my voice.

The man rolled his eyes at me. The way his brows furrowed gave me a sense that he was scowling behind that cloth that concealed his face.

Before I could register what was happening, he ripped a golden blade free from its sheath and snapped the chains binding me to the floor. He wrenched me upwards by my elbow and cut through the chains between my wrists.

"Who are you—"

"Let's save the pleasantries for later, *princess*," he barked, eyes scanning behind me.

The man lunged for me; a flash of vibrant blue light paired with an other-worldly scream echoed around us before I was plunged into a fleeting darkness.

Chapter Two

Selene

"What... what the hells was *that*?" I spat at the masked man standing before me. He was leaning against a dripping cave wall. The air was thick and wet, reeking of grungy mildew. The man stood tall and rigid, expecting me to lash out at him. Now that there was no dust to cloud my vision, I could tell he was Fae, but his mask still concealed most of his face.

"I didn't know princesses were allowed to talk like that," he said with a scoff.

"I'm allowed to talk however I want." My heart was still pounding, my body shaking from fear... or perhaps from shock. I was supposed to be dead by the hand of the Fae Goddess. I looked around, taking in the intricacies of where I stood, feverishly hoping I could find a way out of here. But to what? I had no idea where this cave was or how the hells we got here. I hesitated, eyes still scanning the small, damp room that had no way in or out. Only rocks and darkness surrounded us in the space that already felt too small for one, let alone two.

"Don't you think you should be a little more grateful to your savior?" His voice was low and taunting.

"I was ready to go," I snarled at the stranger, teeth clenched tight. "You've just damned them to who knows what. If you don't take me ba—"

"Shut up," he lunged forward, crouching before me, his still-masked face inches from mine. Out of fear, my breath hitched at the sudden proximity of him. He blinked his green eyes, the same shade as the evergreens of Hiareth.

"You will come with me. You will not see Avalon in the next twelve hours, and if you want," he snapped his fingers, the same cuffs I had on my wrists only a moment ago appearing in his hands, "I can put these back on to make things easier on us both." Watching me, he took up a place leaning against the cave wall furthest from me. It still only offered a few feet of distance between us.

Twelve hours. My shoulders slumped. He wanted to keep me through my eighteenth birthday so my sacrifice wouldn't be completed and the Fae Goddess's curse would fall upon Avalon. This ending... it was my father's—the King of Avalon's—greatest fear in life. Avalon was already losing sway with the other human kingdoms; no doubt a curse would push the remaining citizens into Hiareth and beyond. I scowled at the man who took me. I didn't hate the people of Avalon, nor my mother, even if I was only allowed brief encounters with her. If he kept me here, I would doom them all.

"Considering escaping?" he seemed to coo at me, yet his eyes were soft and examining.

"How did we get here?" I replied, trying to leash the anger that rose within me. I remembered standing in Avalon, and a blink later, we were here.

"I flexed us here," he examined some dirt under his nail. I let out a sound that was almost a laugh. Almost. He rolled his eyes at the sound. "I'm Fae," he started, gesturing to his body.

I ground my teeth together, waiting for him to give more information.

"Some of us have... special magic," he spoke hesitantly as if deciding how to explain this foreign concept to me. "All humans and most Fae must walk from place to place. I, however, can flex reality for a moment." I looked up at him. "A moment is not finite. Depending on how much energy I've used up, I can flex reality for longer or shorter."

"So you decided to transport us into a tiny wet cave?" My voice bordered on acidic.

"Flexed, but, yes, I did, princess. I know it isn't quite up to your standards, but I'm sure that—"

"What is your name?" I barked, surprised by the intensity of my voice.

White-frigid anger started to spread through my veins, the leash on my demi-fae magic becoming longer and longer with every passing moment. I would not allow him to act like I was ever privileged to be the Princess of Avalon. I blew out a frigid breath, magic sputtering within me. Shards of ice began falling from the cave ceiling, crashing around us. I looked around and realized the cave was no longer gleaming with condensation but ice.

The still-masked Fae man—no, Fae *male*, eyed me closely as if considering chaining me up again. "Dayne, High Fae of Olvidare," he smiled, "at your service."

I blinked at him, almost not hearing his words beneath the icy waves that roared in my head.

Growing up demi-Fae with humans offered few things, but Fae history was something we were forced to study. Not because it's intriguing but because knowledge is power, and when you are a human against a Fae, you need all the help you can get.

"Olvidare," I repeated the name of his city, "The Kingdom of Wind, then."

"Smart girl," he winked. "We've got twelve hours to kill," He slid down the cave wall, plopping into a sitting position atop the slick stony ground. "Get comfortable."

I noted the subject change but ignored him and pulled my knees to my chest into an all-too-familiar fetal position. Dayne swiped the mask from his face, stuffing it into his pack. I looked away as if I wasn't supposed to see him. I allowed my eyes to creep back. He leaned his head against the now-melting cave walls and closed his eyes, his large frame rising and falling with each breath. His easy synchronous breathing made him seem at ease. I nearly scoffed at the easiness of that breath—at the irony of it because I sat here waiting for my kingdom to burn.

Bastard.

I scanned him, eyes catching on the fighting leathers he wore. Even from across the cave, I could tell they were some of the best quality. *High Fae of Olvidare*. He would have to be closely related to the king, possibly a nephew or son. His face was peppered with small, very faint scars. He wasn't small in any way; his prominent brow bone and jaw were rich features of his face. His lips were firm and straight, indicating he was not asleep. I looked away at the thought of him waking to find my eyes upon him.

I forced my eyes shut, not to rest but to think. My life was spared by someone close to the King of Wind, no doubt operating under his direction. Why would he want me alive? I chewed on my lip. Perhaps I didn't matter at all. Perhaps the King of Wind wanted my kingdom to fall under the Goddess's curse... Which meant I was no more than a pawn like I had always been. I was no use to the male that lay before me once twelve hours was up. *Dayne of Olvidare.* Would I be sent back to Avalon? Set free to do as I please, or possibly killed? I shook at the uncertainty of my circumstances. For eighteen years, I knew what would happen; for eighteen years, I waited, never unsure of my destiny. I was always meant to die. I opened my eyes, gaze falling on him. And while this male may not have good intentions for me... I still made it out of there—of Avalon. I touched my chest, just to be sure I was here, alive and breathing. I began trembling, not from the cold but from the small flame of hope that ignited within me.

Chapter Three

Selene

"GET UP, PRINCESS," DAYNE GRUNTED WHILE SHUFFLING ITEMS around.

I opened my eyes and rubbed my face. How long had it been? I blinked, Dayne's figure coming into view. He had changed clothes at some point, and I shivered at the thought of the male stripping naked while I was sleeping a mere few feet from him. I glanced at the pack he was shouldering. The leathers he had on earlier peeked out from the top of it.

"Wow, you uh... look disheveled," he cracked a smile that seemed genuine.

"Disheveled? You *flexed* me into this freezing, disgusting place and made me sleep on the floor," I spat back, not feeling as chipper as he was.

"To be fair, you're the one that froze the cave," he shrugged, shoving a gleaming dagger of gold into his pack.

"How long was I asleep?" I rolled my eyes, feeling the familiarity of rage slip into my veins.

"Over eleven hours, I bet you would've pushed past twelve if I let you."

Goddess, eleven hours. I shifted from where I sat on the pebbly ground of the cave. The dress I wore from my execution ceremony was covered in wet spots and dirt. While enraged I had slept that long, I wasn't surprised. One doesn't sleep particularly well the week leading up to your execution. Apparently, all I needed was to be kidnapped and shoved into a dark cave.

"So what? You're going to flex us out of here and then what? Watch my kingdom burn?"

"Aren't you tired of this... What did you call it? *Freezing disgusting place?*" He eyed me, one brow raised.

"Dayne," I whispered, disgusted by how pleadingly I spoke his name. I was desperate for information, desperate to be anywhere but here. The cave suddenly felt smaller—darker—and wetter.

Dayne's face morphed from playful to curious as he took in my desperation. A heartbeat later, the look vanished and was replaced with a slight smile. "Let's get some fresh air. How does that sound?"

I watched his face, waiting for something to give away his intentions. He was annoyingly pleasant. "How long until midnight?"

"A few minutes," he shifted on his feet, eyes dropping to the floor between us.

Guilt panged through me. There hadn't been a way out of this cave to help any of them... but had I really *slept* at such a dire time? I replayed the curse on Avalon's King. 'For your role in the slaughter of five hundred Fae soldiers, I force a Fae male onto your wife. She will bear a demi-Fae child who you will raise and love and offer to me in ultimate sacrifice on their eighteenth birthday. Only then will your kingdom be absolved of its crimes. If you do not succeed in this task, or your wife can not bear a child, your kingdom will be cursed and doomed to fall before my hand.'

I knew the curse by heart. I had repeated it over and over, wondering, why me? I never understood why the Goddess cursed only Avalon. The other kingdoms, Hiareth, Florence, and Munique, played similar roles in the death of those Fae males. I was the only demi-Fae forced to live just to die.

"So, what's the *plan?*" I spoke through gritted teeth, my attention falling back upon the male who took me.

"Sounds like you already know the plan," He was hesitant but took several striding steps toward me. "Here." He handed me a knife, the blade smaller than my hand.

I looked up at him. He was much stronger than me, tiny blade or not. He didn't want me to be defenseless. Why? I reached out and took the knife. He would be leaving me, then. He would flex us out of here and leave me with a miniature blade.

Great.

"We have a long walk today. You should keep it on you." His half-smile made me shrink in on myself. I was used to scowls and furrowed brows. I was the walking, breathing reminder that the Fae Goddess would curse us all if I failed them.

Yet... I still let out a breath of relief. This mysterious male, who had somehow handed my life back to me... wasn't planning to leave me to fend for myself in a land I only planned to live in only until today. If I returned to Avalon after the curse was placed, the king—or perhaps even the people— might kill me anyway.

"Can I have a bigger one?" I instantly winced at how unnatural it felt to make a joke.

"No," Dayne grunted, "And if you think about trying to use it on me, just know that you're literally half the Fae that I am, and I can snap you like a stick," he finished with a smirk.

"Well, okay then." I turned the golden-bladed knife over in my hand, "When do we go up?"

"Down," he said before wrapping an arm around my waist.

A fleeting moment of pure darkness before dry air slammed into my face, and I found myself at the mouth of a cave overlooking a bottomless ravine. It didn't take my eyes long to adjust; it was nearly as dark out here as inside the cave behind me. Dayne and I stood near the edge of the cliff, the grey, jagged rock wall of the ravine so steep they were barely visible from where we stood. I looked beyond the canyon, only to find more grey, jagged rocks and mountains surrounding us. There was no doubt in my mind where we stood. The Hiareth Mountains are just east of Avalon.

"Not long now," Dayne said, looking out on the horizon as if he could see something I couldn't. I knew what he meant... Not long until the Goddess unleashed herself upon Avalon.

I swallowed hard, accepting the unknown fate of my kingdom. I trailed to where Dayne's eyes roamed and locked on them on the dark, hardly visible

13

horizon ahead. An enormous crack sliced the air, making me flinch at how sudden and loud it was. I knew that within the city walls, the sound was deafening. I shuddered at what that sound could mean—what the Goddess was unleashing upon them.

Dayne took a small step in my direction, but he didn't move any closer. I couldn't peel my eyes away from the dark horizon, even though there was nothing to see. What was this curse?

Very faint flashes of light, invisible to the human eye, peppered the dark horizon. I had no doubts that my demi-Fae eyesight allowed me to see such a faint and distant light.

I narrowed my eyes, thoughts and ideas swarming in my head as I tried to figure out what was happening to them. What had the Goddess done? More lights flickered and flashed, followed by an enormous cracking boom. My shoulders sagged, if only slightly. It was lightning.

"Storms. It's just storms." I started. "They... they need easier access to water now anyway with me gone... I think they will be okay; they will-"

My exhaustive rambling was cut short as the tears started streaming down my face. Dayne didn't say it, and he didn't have to anyway. It wouldn't be *just* a storm; this was an angry Fae Goddess we were talking about. This would be the storm of all storms; it would last an eternity if the Goddess felt like it.

"I hate you," I said before letting my knees buckle beneath me.

"I know," I heard Dayne whisper.

The world blacked out.

Chapter Four

Dayne

THE PRINCESS WEPT UNCONTROLLABLY ON THE ROCKY SURFACE OF the Hiareth Mountains. I considered consoling her, but she was pulsating with a frigid white rage. Her hair seemed to glow an even whiter shade of blonde. Her rounded golden eyes shone with intensity, amplified by her tears. I studied her face then, the faint freckles that adorned her cheeks, her pouty full lips. She was beautiful, even in sadness. I stood by as every tear froze mid-air before falling to the rocky surface below into a million tiny pieces. I forced myself to watch... To not look away. I was privileged—the King of Olvidare's only son. I was given everything I could ever need or desire. What lay before me—who lay before me, it was beyond her heart that was breaking. It was her soul. The Princess of Avalon wept, and I stood by like a fool, allowing her cold fury to cool me to my core.

Chapter Five

Selene

THE SUN WAS BEGINNING TO PEEK OVER THE HORIZON BY THE TIME I got myself under control. I spent hours consoling myself on the rocky mountainside. He watched me the entire time.

Dayne cleared his throat as I sat on a nearby rock, brushing off pebbles and dust stuck to my bare knees. "We move northeast to the Fae lands. I have a small camp on the edge of the continent once we—"

"I am not going *anywhere* with *you*." I finally spoke to him after telling him I hated him. I did hate him.

He smiled. "You don't really have a choice, princess."

"Like hells, I don't." I spat, now standing. I took several strides from him with no apparent direction other than to distance myself from him. To be anywhere but here, near him.

"Perfect, that's the way we're supposed to be going." Dayne drawled from behind me. Without hesitation, I twisted my toe in the dirt and turned in a different direction, now headed deeper within the Hiareth Mountains.

"Now you're *actually* walking the way we have to go."

I flipped, stalking back towards him, seething with a familiar white rage that had gotten me through so many excruciating days. It was blinding—numbing—my free drug that never lost the strength of its high.

"You," I jabbed him in the chest with my index finger, "can tell me exactly why you took me yesterday." I plopped myself down on a nearby boulder, "or I will not be getting up." I crossed my arms. "I will starve to death, you know. I'm not afraid." I knew my options were limited. Where did I have to go? I sat straighter, eyes pinning him.

Dayne chuckled but shifted awkwardly on his weight. "I truly can't tell you, princess. But why do you need to know? Is it not enough that I came to save you?"

"You know, you have a lot of arrogance to think just because you saved me, you get to keep me as your pretty little pet."

"Who said you were pretty?" He winked but dropped his eyes from mine a heartbeat later.

"I am this close," I pinched my fingers together, "to freezing you into a block of annoying Fae oaf."

"Okay... You're sort of pretty, I guess." He held his hands up as a sign of truce. "If I give you some information about me, will you come with me? If I can prove you can trust me at least a little, would that help?"

"I want a bigger knife," I said, tossing him the small one. He caught it and laughed. "And... I'm waiting for your life story, but please take your time." I knew whatever he had to say would likely not be enough to change my mind about him. He was *Fae*, after all. But... I was, too, sort of.

"I said *some* information," he eyed me with furrowed brows. I gestured at him to continue. "I am Dayne, son of the King of Wind. I can manipulate wind and air and flex reality—to move myself, others, and objects through space, but not time." He flicked out his hand, and a delicate white flower from who knows where appeared in his palm.

"I already knew most of *that*," I said, seething at his arrogance. If I went anywhere near the Fae lands, I truly hoped all of them weren't this bad.

"I'm not done yet. Do you ever relax?" He began pacing before me, stones crunching beneath his feet with every step. I had half a thought to shove him off the cliff into the ravine below. "My father tasked me with saving you from the Goddess."

"And?" Bile rose in my throat. I was not meant to be alive. I touched my chest as if making sure my heart still beat there.

"And, so I did. Save you, that is. Now, we go to my camp on the edge of the Fae continent to rest properly before we head to Olvidare." He crossed his arms. "If I knew what my father had planned, I would share it, but I am not privy to all the information."

I studied him, allowing the events of the past twelve hours to swim within me. I spent eighteen years wishing, dreaming, to be something—anything other than who I was. I had looked into the stars every night, picking out my favorite constellation and memorizing it so that I could one day share those memories with someone—anyone who truly cared. My cheeks heated. Of course, I wanted love. But I was desperate. I craved any form of companionship, yet I always found myself alone, staring at the same exquisite constellations, tears streaming down my cheeks. It was always just me and the stars. I clenched my jaw at the memory of those hopeless dreams I had. Yet I still had them, despite it all. I still dreamed.

I narrowed my eyes upon Dayne, feeling uncomfortable by his curious, watchful eyes. I now found myself in a situation where my dreams actually held hope, didn't they? The flutter in my chest was a testament to that. I could actually *have* a dream that I could do something about. My heart tugged in two directions, guilt again ripping through me. Was the price of my dreams worth an entire kingdom's destruction? Was there anything left to do for them?

"I..." I started, stopping short.

"What is it you want then, princess? Now that you get to live." His words speared me, staking through my chest, into my soul. Something within me forced me to answer without thinking.

"Purpose," I breathed, eyes dropping to his feet. My mind was slower than my mouth as my thoughts came spewing out.

"I'm tired of being a shell of myself." I twisted my toe into the dusty ground. I had nowhere to go, but going with him... maybe it could offer something. Perhaps I wouldn't be left to crawl back to Avalon, beg for forgiveness, and endure the eternity of storms the Goddess had unleashed. I shivered, imagining myself in that life. Perhaps I deserved to suffer with them, but... I would not go back there. I wasn't sure my body would even allow it. Choosing not to go with Dayne would leave me no choice but to do just that. To walk back into Avalon and see those same disapproving faces. To continue living beneath my father's disapproving eye, a demi-Fae in a kingdom of humans. The living dead girl that no one cared to even glance at unless it was to gawk. My throat tightened, my body realizing what it was I would do before my mind registered it. I couldn't go back there.

"Fine," I whispered. I didn't want to go with Dayne… But finding that companionship—that purpose… I knew I would not find it within the walls of Avalon. I knew that my already rotting soul would fully perish the moment I stepped back within those sandstone walls.

"So you'll come with me?" he sounded a little too excited, most likely because going back empty-handed would mean he failed his father.

I stuck out my tongue and then my hand. "Bigger knife, please."

"Of course, princess," he dug around in his pack to retrieve a more normal-sized but still small blade. My body felt tight after voicing my decision out loud. I rolled my shoulders, relieving only half an ounce worth of stress.

"And would you stop calling me princess?" I spoke with a bitterness that seemed to have no effect on the arrogant male.

"Never." He winked.

Dayne walked behind me, allowing me to set the pace, considering I was not dressed for the occasion. I wore the ceremony dress that was picked out, especially for my execution. It fell just above the knee and was too tight around my torso. Years ago, the dress may have been more extraordinary. After years of a failing economy, a simple white dress with fake stones of ruby and gold beading was all the king would spare for his pitiful demi-Fae daughter.

"Here's a good spot if you need to go to the bathroom," Dayne spoke with indifference as he inclined his head toward a group of dense bushes that appeared on the path ahead of us. We had been traveling up a rocky path through the Hiareth Mountains. I wasn't positive, but I thought we were traveling east.

"I don't have to go," I shrugged.

I grew up in a desert wasteland. My kingdom—my home, was founded atop mounds and mounds of sand. I learned not to drink much and rarely had to relieve myself. When I was young, I remember the king—my 'father' assessing me for magic. A Fae from the Kingdom of Ice had sired me. My father could only hope that some of the male's ice magic was passed down to me, hoping that their affinity–*my affinity,* would be powerful enough to save the parched kingdom. Around my eighth birthday, lingering signs of this water affinity started rearing.

It was one of the hottest days at the peak of summer in Avalon. Our kingdom of rock and sand got overwhelmingly hot during the day but deathly cold at night. None of the buildings could keep up with the temperature changes. This particular day began cool, so the people of Avalon were not worried about conserving the cool air in their homes from the night before. A sudden heat wave struck. The temperature kept climbing, and within minutes, the whole city was barricaded within their homes or cowering in any shade they could find. The king and I sat together in the sandstone castle, trying to keep cool. I remember I was near panting. It was so hot sweat streamed and glistened on my body. I remember standing, anger rising in my body, and exclaiming that I couldn't take the heat. At that exact moment, the entire room suddenly cooled. The king looked at me, then down to my frosting fingertips.

From that day forward, the king put me to use. I was only eight, but my purpose became healing the city of sand and stone. And so I did. Every day, I was forced to test my magic further until I was eventually given daily tasks. Each morning, I would tempt the rain to come; if it did not, I would travel to the only well within the kingdom to bring water back to the city. In the afternoon, I would cool the houses of the smallest children only after tending to the king's quarters first. Eventually, I didn't mind having things to do, but it was an empty, soulless life. I was the Princess of Avalon, the girl with the heart of ice. But I knew it wasn't made of ice. My heart bucked and throbbed for someone else to notice it, too. No one ever did.

I stumbled over a rock, forcing me back to reality. We had moved on from the clearing with the bushes, now coming upon a path curving to the right, which, if I wasn't turned around, wasn't the direction of the Fae continent. I looked over my shoulder to ensure I was headed in the right direction when a loud cracking sound sliced the air.

Dayne lunged out in front of me in response to the sound, scanning around us. There was nothing but pines and rocky mountains.

"Have you ever been in the Hiareth Mountains before?" he whispered, focusing on one shorter peak on the horizon ahead.

"No." It came out as a squeak. I was terrified, no doubt about that, but somehow, as I felt my heart race beneath the icy adrenaline that coursed through me, I felt alive. I willed my breath to remain steady, focusing on the latter feeling. I was alive.

"We're nearing the eastern edge, closest to the Twilight Grove of the Fae lands. *Things* tend to slip into this part of the mountains."

I shuddered at his emphasis on 'things.' I've had enough history of the Fae lands to know that I never want to encounter any of the said *things*. "Well, what *things* crack like that?" I shuddered, wrapping my arms around myself to warm my icy body.

A blast of putrid air propelled us backward, toppling over each other. Dayne scrambled to his feet and had twin swords out in an instant. Both were made with a hilt of gold, iridescent opal stones set within it. The blade shone a metallic silver color, flashing in my eyes as he stood with them readied.

The sound of talons against stone ripped through the air. Dayne's swords sagged ever so slightly as a creature I could only describe as a cross between a giant scorpion and a centipede crawled its spindly legs over a small, saw-toothed mountain. Its segmented body shifted with horrifying grace as it moved, the tough outer shell making a slight clicking noise as it crawled hesitantly toward us. My blood ran cold as the creature raised its scorpion-like tail, momentarily pausing to snap it like a whip. Then, it began its rapid descent toward us.

"Run," Dayne said while sheathing his twin blades and turning on a heel. I didn't need to be told twice.

We sprinted in the opposite direction of that *thing*, struggling over the rough mountainous terrain. Dayne was by my side; he looped his arm through mine and flexed us forward. I stumbled and realized we only made it twenty feet from where we were. I gritted my teeth. It was better than nothing. I risked a glance over my shoulder at the giant scorpion closing in on us. Up close, I could get a better idea of its enormity. One of its spindly legs looked as if it could crush me alone. Dayne panted beside me, looking around before looping an arm through mine and flexing us again. This time upwards, clinging to a nearly dead evergreen tree. We were on either side of the trunk, one of Dayne's arms grasping the tree trunk, the other over my mouth as if he could sense the scream trying to rip from my throat. The fragile tree swayed at the addition of our weight, but it would hold... for now.

The scorpion creature now crawled around at the base of our tree. Did it know we were up here? If it could climb trees like it does mountains... I allowed my thoughts to taper off as I took in the creature from above. I could see spindly hairs poking out of the creature's rigid armored back. It snapped its tail once more, making me jump, and crawled faster than lightning, returning to the direction we had run from.

Dayne and I both slumped at the same time, his enormous hand uncupping from around my mouth and jaw.

"What—"

"A scuttler," Dayne cut me off. "They're faster than the Goddess but dumb as stones." He was still panting from the unprepared flexing he had done. He noticed me watching him. "Flexing up is, well, it takes even more energy than flexing forward or back, especially with another person," he spoke between pants.

"How about flexing down.." I said as the trunk swayed beneath our weight, letting out small splintering sounds.

"It's not as bad, but..." he stopped to catch his breath. "I'm going to need a minute."

I allowed myself to slump against the tree while Dayne caught his breath and waited for some energy to refill. It felt uncomfortable to be so close to the male, but I shoved it from my mind.

"The Hiareth fortress is nearby. They keep one in the mountains to fend off creature attacks from the eastern side. We can't go back that way." He pointed in the direction we had just come from. "And the only other way through these mountains puts us near the sea after dark. We have no other option than to head to the fortress for the night." He looked grim and annoyed.

I didn't know what to say. It didn't matter to me; What sort of timeline was I on? I was supposed to be dead yesterday. None of this mattered. "Okay." I shrugged, inching my body away from his slightly.

Wiping the sweat built up from his face, Dayne said, "I can get us there in an hour once we are down from this damned—"

My heart sank as another cracking sound sliced the air. My body tensed as I looked down, searching for that *thing* that had chased us up here.

Nothing. It hadn't been the scuttler this time, but the tree.

We were down in a flash; Dayne doubled over, catching his breath from another unexpected flex. I looked up at the tree. It stood proud and tall, even though it was half dead.

"Dramatic much?" I barked at the tree before slumping against its base. A bead of sweat formed on my upper lip.

I wrapped a gentle vortex of cool air around myself, allowing some of it to reach Dayne. He whimpered at the relief the air brought him.

"How much more walking?" I asked, hoping for as little as possible. I glanced around, seeing nothing but rocks and trees. The scenery may have been bland to some, but after only having *sand* to look at, I was mesmerized by this.

"None," he said. "I need an hour to rest, and I can flex us right into the fortress."

"Thank the Goddess." I slackened even further into the tree, still wrapping crisp air around the both of us.

"How do you do that?" Dayne raised a brow at me, still doubled over.

"Do what?"

"Move the air. You should just be able to cool it, not move it, right?" His features were hardened, his tone even more severe than his face.

"I... I don't know... I never thought of it before; I thought it was just part of what my father passed on to me," I said, keeping it to myself that it was something I had picked up during my many bored nights in Avalon. He didn't need to know anything more about me.

Dayne stared at me for a moment before tersely nodding. He groaned as he lowered himself to the needle-covered floor, resting his back against a large rock and stretching his legs out forward. "Can you wake me up in an hour, or if anything happens?" He looked at me, but the seriousness he wore moments ago had vanished. Now, he looked exhausted.

He trusted that I wouldn't leave then. "Sure, your majesty." I rolled my eyes.

"Thanks, princess." He crossed his arms over his chest and closed his eyes.

I allowed the wind of cool mountain air to die around us now that our breathing was under control. I searched for any beads of sweat to form on Dayne's face, but none appeared. He was already asleep, face relaxed from its natural hardened state. The harsh lines and scowl marks now softened, leaving a peaceful, handsome face. I looked away, searching for a shadow to track when an hour would be up.

I soaked in the sun, allowing the mountain air to envelop me with its cool touch. No wonder people left Avalon for Hiareth. The weather is exquisite here. I became drowsy while basking in the sun and slowly slipped into oblivion.

Chapter Six

Selene

"Remind me to never let you keep watch again." A taunting voice woke me from a less-than-comfortable sleep. My eyes shot open. I took in my surroundings, barely illuminated by what was left of the sun. The darkness enveloped us; the crisp air from this afternoon now had a harsh bite to it. I became suddenly too aware of the scratchy bark of the tree jutting into my back.

"I... I'm-" I started, looking to the ground in shame. I could feel my cheeks blush and was suddenly thankful we were under the cover of darkness. "It's fine," Dayne said. "I needed the extra time anyway." He shrugged and extended a hand out to me. I grabbed it, and he heaved me up to my feet.

I watched him out of the corner of my eye as I attempted to brush off bits of bark from my backside. He kept one eye glued to me and the other scanning our surroundings. I couldn't help the chill that made its way down my spine at the memory of the scuttler—and the reason Dayne kept an eye on the darkness around us.

"Ready?" He stepped forward, about to wrap a too-easy hand around me.

"Wait." I stepped away from him. "They won't let you into a human fortress as a Fae," I looked him up and down, "they might not even let me in." I cocked my head, trying to understand why he thought this plan would work.

"They'll let us in, princess," he said, stepping toward me. I echoed his steps but away from him.

"How are you so sure?" I spoke as he stepped forward again, like a predator and his prey. I wanted to bare my teeth at him—to prove to him that I was far from anyone's prey.

"Hiareth contracts the Fae to hunt creatures in the Eastern Mountains. We've always stayed in the fortress. It's half of the reason they keep it separated from their city walls."

I stopped backing away from him. "Really?"

"Really," Dayne said with a wink. "Can we go now? I'd like to sleep in a bed."

I rolled my eyes and outstretched my arm in answer. He ignored it and stepped forward to grasp around my waist. "More secure," he said before the fleeting darkness surrounded us.

The Hiareth fortress was illuminated by firelight and bustled with people. I had to blink several times to adjust to the humming life around me. I looked around, one brow raised high. It was like its own city with women and their children, little shops, and more. I had been to Hiareth before. It sits in an almost perfect circular valley with the Hiareth Mountains surrounding it. I looked to our right, toward the steep rocky drop-off that led down to the city. All I could make out was its faint glow from far below. I didn't look around too long before Dayne grabbed me by the elbow, hauling me toward a building with a shaggy straw roof. He half-dragged me through the dusty dirt paths toward the quaint building. It had a slight glow like the rest of the humble buildings of the fortress. A Fae female stood behind a small counter open to all passersby. Anyone could easily walk to the building and get a room without entering the small straw hut.

"Two rooms," Dayne grunted to the thin, black-haired female behind the counter. She was pretty, with glowing ashen eyes. Seeing Fae work in the fortress surprised me, given we were on the human continent. I wondered how I never knew of this place. Dayne flicked four coins at her, stuffing his hands into his pockets with such an immediacy that I glanced back to the dark-haired female in wonder. She, too, was looking between us with a similar inquisitive stare.

"Of course," she cooed at Dayne, her voice not as sweet as she must think it is. I could've sworn he blushed.

She took the coin and returned two delicate copper keys with a slip of paper that read 201 and 308.

"Next door to each other," Dayne said through gritted teeth, his hands still shoved deep within his pockets. I shifted on my feet, uncomfortable by the exchange, uncomfortable by being here... with him.

"Oh—well, why didn't you say so." The black-haired female exclaimed enthusiastically that only a feywit would be deceived by. It made Dayne clench his hands into fists. She dug under the counter for an extended moment, eventually handing Dayne two keys with a piece of paper that said 409 and 410. She smiled at him as he finally pulled his hands from his pockets to snatch the tarnished copper keys from her before grumbling a clipped thanks.

"Do you know her?" I asked him as we walked around the edge of the straw hut to the back of it. I realized it was just a tiny office space for the inn.

"Old... friend." He shrugged.

It grew darker around us, making it impossible for me to read his face, even while squinting. "409 and 410. So we've got to go up?" I asked, looking ahead at the barely illuminated open-concept inn with no upper floors. The inns were all connected, each with their own doors. I squinted at the small numbers hanging above each door; I read 100, 101, 102.

"Down," Dayne grumbled as we approached a flight of stone stairs leading into the darkness below. I swallowed and looked down the dark shaft. I had half a thought to go back and demand a room on ground level. Putting myself back between Dayne and the dark-haired female had me sighing and taking the first step downward.

We went down each flight of stairs in a hurry. Dayne was hard to keep up with, even though it seemed like he was taking each step slower as I fell behind. Once we reached the last stair, we faced a long, unlit hallway that smelled musty and wet. It was hardly illuminated, but the faintest flicker of firelight offered just enough to keep you from tripping over the uneven stone floor. I resisted the urge to pinch my nose shut as we wandered through the musty hall. Even Avalon had been well-lit and clean. But Avalon had been built by humans for humans. This inn had been made by humans for the Fae. It wasn't surprising that it was kept in such conditions, regardless of any truce Hiareth may have with the Fae.

After what felt like an eternity, we reached two doors that read 409 and 410. We stood before the doors, nowhere else to go but in or back where we came from. The dark-haired female from the inn's office had given us the two rooms deepest within the underground inn. The farthest walk in and back up. A faint flicker of ice pulsed beneath my skin at her blatant pettiness.

I turned to face Dayne, who was already handing me the key to room 409; I turned back to my door, which stood on the left of his room. I shoved the key in the hole, and with a bit of a struggle, I twisted it into its unlocked position, allowing it to swing open. I hesitated before stepping into the room. I glanced up at Dayne, again taking in his solid features. I didn't want to be with him, but being alone in the strange place made me equally unsettled. I turned back to the dark room ahead, my eyes falling on the bed. The sweet release of sleep beckoned, forcing any thought of discomfort at being alone from my mind. I stalked into the room, listening for my door swinging shut behind me. When it didn't, I turned to see Dayne resting against my door frame, one hand gripping it above his head.

His eyes were dark, "Let me know if you need anything," he lingered for a moment for my reply. We stood and watched each other, only the sound of our breath swirling between us. My heart rate quickened as his darkened eyes hovered over me. I knew he heard it, too, as his eyes flicked down to the spot my heart thundered beneath my chest. I finally broke the silent stillness between us with a shallow nod. He closed the door without even a nod back, and I was alone.

Goddess.

I let out a shaky breath and began looking around my room. It wasn't lavish like I was used to in my living quarters in Avalon, but it wasn't terrible. I realized there were two beds, so we could have shared a room. I thought of the four coins Dayne had paid for the rooms. It was cheaper than a desperate wench, and he was high Fae. I knew he had the coin to spare.

I walked into the washroom and stripped down naked, preparing to scrub away the filth and horror from the past twenty-four hours. I ripped the curtain back, hoping there would be a shower, not just a tub. About half of the citizens in Avalon had showers if they were lucky. I sighed in relief as I saw it. I turned the knobs up as hot as it would go, and thank the Goddess; it steamed up the bathroom within minutes. I breathed in the warm steam for a moment before stepping into the hot water. The heat fogged my brain but offered a means to relieve the tight tension around my core.

There was a singular bar of soap in the shower; I grabbed it and scrubbed every inch of my body with more pressure than was necessary to clean myself. I scrubbed so viciously that it began to hurt. I bit through the pain as I desperately tried to clean deeper than my skin. By the time the bar of soap had dwindled in half from my scrubbing, the shower began to grow cold. I allowed it. I let the cool water run over my body. The now cooling air filled my nostrils and mind. It sparked my senses, making me feel alive. I turned beneath the freezing water, allowing it to consume me. My body wanted to tug away from the cold, but my mind was alive and thriving beneath it. I grappled for a towel, and thank the Goddess, one was within reach. I stepped out of the shower and wrapped it around myself. Given the low cost of staying here, I wasn't all that surprised by how tiny the towel was.

"Hells," I said aloud when I saw my dirty white dress on the washroom floor. I had nothing clean to put on.

I walked into the sleeping quarters of my room. I threw open all the drawers and closets to find them empty, other than a few extra towels as small as the one I had wrapped around me. Icy annoyance popped within me. I threw myself onto the bed, my towel falling off my body and heaping into a pile around me. Rubbing my temples for a moment, I stood and tightly bound the towel back around myself. I walked to the full-length mirror, finding it hung almost comically crooked on the wall. The towel fell to my upper thigh but had enough coverage... Barely.

I sighed and peeked out of my room, glancing down the long hallway before stepping out. I stood before Dayne's room, water still dripping off of me onto the stone floor beneath me. I reached up to knock, but he swung open the door before my knuckles made contact with it.

"I heard you; what's wrong?" he scanned me, his eyes widening as they trailed to my bare legs and feet.

I suddenly felt entirely naked and blushed. This time, there was no cover of darkness to conceal my reddened cheeks.

"Hells," he cursed. "I can go to town and grab you something. The shops might be closed, but I'm sure I can convince someone to let me in... or I have clothes in my pack?" He shifted on his feet as he rambled.

"Anything *clean* will be fine," I spoke through gritted teeth.

"Give me a moment. Or do you want to come in?" He opened the door further in question.

"I'd rather not stand naked in the hall for much longer if you don't mind." I didn't wait for his response this time as I pushed past him, swallowing my nerves. I plopped onto the armchair in the corner of his room. In the room's soft, ambient glow, various pieces of his equipment were spread across the worn wooden floor as if he were organizing them. As my eyes roamed, absorbing the details, he mirrored my line of sight as if tracking my thoughts. My attention fell upon an impressive array of blades, ranging from gleaming short daggers with ornate hilts to longer, more menacing swords. I couldn't be sure where he had kept such blades in our time traveling.

"I was just rearranging my packs."

"I see." My eyes fell on a stack of clothes sitting atop a table. "Is that..." I pointed at the clothes.

"Yeah, here," he nearly tripped over to the stack and pulled out an oversized white long-sleeve shirt and some thick navy pants meant for battling something... maybe scuttlers. He walked to the chair I was sitting on and handed them to me.

"We should probably find something to eat," Dayne said, walking away from me toward the washroom. "I'm going to wash quickly; I'll come get you when I'm out?"

"I'll just stay in here," I said, waving a casual hand at him to shower. He didn't question it and closed the door behind him.

I slipped out of my towel and into the shirt first. It clung to me in awkward places, falling mid-thigh.

"The shirt is longer than the towel," I grunted to no one other than myself. I huffed a strained laugh and pulled on the pants. I clasped a hand over my mouth at seeing my reflection in the mirror. At least it was clean. I shrugged and sat back in the armchair, swinging my legs over the side of it.

"Sleeping again?"

I jumped from the chair as Dayne stood above me, dripping water from his shower. I looked away faster than I shot from the chair. I allowed my head to swivel back to him a moment later, if only out of embarrassment that I had looked away with such intensity.

"You look ridiculous," he chuckled, using one towel to dry his hair, the other around his hips.

"Well, they're *your* clothes." I snapped, feeling myself blush. I'd never blushed so much in my life. He tossed the towel he was using on his hair into a corner and stalked over to me with a casual sort of grace only a Fae could have. I kept my eyes on his face, resisting the urge to take all of him in. I had been around men before... even shirtless ones—but being in the presence of a Fae male was *much* different. They were, or he was... not hard on the eyes. I chewed on my lip, annoyed at how jumpy I felt.

"Here," he said while taking my wrist in his hand with an equal amount of ease and grace. I would have pulled away if I weren't shocked at the gentle way he grasped my wrist with one hand and the end of the too-long sleeve with the other. He wordlessly rolled both sleeves up on my arms, then kneeled to roll each of my pant legs. I chewed on the inside of my cheek as he knelt before me, the muscles in his back shifting as he finished rolling my pants.

"How's that?" he asked, patting my leg as he rose to his normal height again.

"Fine," I crossed my arms, again keeping my eyes trained on his face and *not* his dripping wet torso. Goddess, if I was going to be around Fae males, I would have to get a grip on myself.

"You're a hard one to please," He furrowed his brows at me before disappearing into the bathroom.

Good. Let him disapprove of me. I would not give him any satisfaction.

My stomach growled. I hadn't even realized I was hungry until Dayne mentioned getting food. The pounding in my head was likely due to just that — a lack of any sort of proper meal over the past day. Dayne walked out of the bathroom in a nearly identical outfit to the one he gave me.

Great, we match.

"My lady." He extended his arm to me in beckoning.

Eevy A.

I only stared at him for a long moment, this stranger who came into my life twenty-four hours ago to save me from my fate–from death. My eyes fell on his outstretched hand, one he had outstretched once before as I knelt shackled within that sandstone castle—within my 'home.' I knew I couldn't trust him entirely, but something about him had me stepping forward to meet him. Maybe it was his calm and gentle nature or the unabashed pet names. Still, I linked my arm to his anyway, shivering at the first unnecessary touch between us.

We unlinked arms to jog up the several flights of stairs to exit the underground rooms but wordlessly relinked upon emerging. Arm in arm, we strolled past the main office of the inn, the pretty female attempting to burn a hole through us with her fiery gaze.

"Where to, princess?" Dayne spoke while looking down at me. "There's a ton of options. We've got the Tavryn, or the Tavryn."

"The Tavryn it is, then," I said, feeling amused and almost too giddy to have something to do that wasn't walking circles in the same sandy castle.

We picked a half-circle booth in the back that was intended to fit a large group. I slid in first, and he followed, keeping a reasonable distance between us. I glanced around at the entirely wooden pub called the Tavryn, finding both human and Fae, yet none intermingled. I squinted through the dim light at a particularly rowdy group of human men laughing and sloshing their drinks together.

"If you thought the tavern options were limited, just wait until you see the menu," Dayne chuckled as a busty human woman who looked in her forties approached our table. She tossed the menus to us and set down two giant blood-red drinks, allowing them to slosh together slightly and spill atop the already red-stained wooden table. I looked at Dayne with a brow raised. He winked as if he knew some secret way to order drinks here that I didn't.

"What'll it be," the waitress said in a nasally, disinterested voice.

I glanced down at the stained and ripped menu, reading the two options listed:

Roasted goat leg and potatoes: 1 coin

Creamed goat stew: 1 coin

"I'll have the goat stew," Dayne glanced at the drinks on the table, "and

32

another bootlegger for me and the lady." The waitress and I raised an eyebrow at the same time but said nothing.

I reread the meal options and then once more. It wasn't a hard decision... it was almost comical that I was having such difficulty deciding on this simple meal, yet somehow it felt important. My first meal... freed from the chains of fate.

The woman tapped a finger against the table while impatiently waiting for my order. "Ummm. I guess I'll try the stew." I followed Dayne's order, hoping it would be the right choice. The waitress only grunted before walking away from our table.

Dayne leaned back into the booth, swiping one of the red drinks from the table's edge. I echoed him, relaxing against the cushioned backrest.

"Bootlegger?" I said with a raised brow, watching his shoulders slump. He was comfortable here. It was easy to know why. The atmosphere was inviting and cozy.

"Try it," he reached out his long arm and scooted the other glass toward me. I crinkled my nose at the thought of drinking something that not only would dull my senses but would most likely taste atrocious.

"Oh, come on... Just give it a sip," he inched the drink closer to me. I leaned over to sniff it. It wasn't enticing, but it wasn't putrid either. I stuck my tongue out and dipped it into the red liquid, quickly retracting it back into my mouth. Dayne let out a booming laugh at the sight.

"What in the sodding Goddess are you *doing*?" He clutched his stomach in laughter with one hand as he struggled to hold his drink stable with the other.

"I'm trying it." I snapped, my face reddening at the smirk he wore on his face.

"It's *'wine'* but with a little extra Faerie kick," his smirk deepened in a challenge.

I picked up the giant glass in both hands and gave it a real drink this time. The taste was like the wine I've had before, but stronger—richer. I took two more sips and set the glass down. It went straight to my head, making me feel instantly lighter.

"Why would you order me a second? I will pass out drunk in an alley after half of this one." I couldn't help but scowl with genuine annoyance at how light and airy I was already feeling from the three sips.

"Oh, I won't let you pass out in an alley, princess." Dayne scooted closer to me so he could nudge me with an elbow. "And the third drink is for me too; she'd never bring me that many at once if I had said that." He took two huge gulps, clearing half of his drink. "You know, us Fae bastards and our drinking habits."

I snorted. At least he was self-aware.

I watched as he guzzled more bootlegger, wondering if there was something he was trying to forget–or perhaps a feeling he wanted to bury deep inside of him. I'd likely never know.

Dayne set down his drink, stretching his legs out and crossing his arms over his chest. I suppose Dayne was the first Fae I had ever met, other than myself, which I'm not sure counts. I wasn't human, but I wasn't Fae, either. I had been around humans my whole life, learned from them, walked like them, talked like them. Dayne was... like them, I suppose, but different in ways that were hard to place.

"Can you show me your wind magic?" I asked, watching Dayne flinch in surprise. I knew my own magic, not particularly well, but... it was the only magic I had ever seen.

He observed me for a long moment, lips set in a firm line as if deciding why I was asking. He didn't break eye contact with me as he created a gust of wind and sent it toward me. The breeze felt like hands as they wrapped around my wrists and unfurled the sleeves he had rolled up before we left the inn. I stared down at the unfurling sleeves and shivered. Then, in a swift motion, the sleeves were rolled back up, even tighter than they were before.

I snapped my head up from my wrists to gape at him in complete awe at the complexity of what he had just done. It was simple, yes, but to twist and morph the air to *feel* like fingers moving along my arms... was impressive.

"Normally, I would've used it to remove the entire shirt rather than sleeves, but uh... I didn't think that would be appropriate here," he spoke brazenly, the wine fueling his words.

I blushed deeper than when I stood in a towel before him in the inn. Wanting to change the subject, I asked, "How long did it take you to learn?"

He shrugged, "Fifty years or so."

I spit out the sip of bootlegger at that. "Fifty years? How old *are* you?" I knew how Fae aging worked for the most part. Every year older, they age at a much slower rate. He looked twenty, which meant he had to be multiple hundreds of years old. My eyes widened at the realization, even though he hadn't yet told me his age.

He took a long drink, finishing off the first of his three glasses. "I'm 348 years young," he winced as if somewhat ashamed of who or what he was.

"You look it," was all I said to lighten the mood, unsure why it made me so uncomfortable to see him so somber. He chuckled as the waitress dropped off more bootlegger drinks and our bowls of goat stew. Too famished to waste time speaking, we ate and sipped silently until our bowls were clean.

"I can't tell if that stew was amazing or if I was close to starving to death," I said while stretching out on the booth.

"Probably the latter," he mused, slurring his words slightly.

He had finished off two drinks, his eyes now glazed and lingering. I'm not sure I was much better off after making it a third or so into my drink. I hadn't wanted to drink it—to allow my senses to dull... but that floating feeling... the feeling of the weight of everything drifting off of me was too tempting. My head floated through the clouds, light as a feather. I had never been drunk before, only tipsy from sneaking into the cellar to try the king's private stash of wine one night. It was safe to say I never drank again after being caught by one of the servants.

"You're staring," I told Dayne, realizing his eyes were fixed upon me.

"Why doesn't your skin tan like the others in Avalon?" he asked, taking me by surprise. I looked down at my creamy pale skin spattered with light-honied freckles. "Does it surprise you? I'm demi-Fae to an ice-wielding Faerie. It's more than just my skin that remains different from those in Avalon." I pinned him with a hardened but not harsh look.

He shook his head. "You'd think you would still tan."

"Do you not like my pale skin, your royal highness?" I said with a sweet bite. He choked on his drink at that.

"I'd like to-," he started, "I like it."

"You'd like to like it?" I teased him, and he scooted closer once more to

35

bump me in the shoulder with his.

We sat like that for half an hour, shoulder to shoulder, sipping on our drinks and enjoying letting our heads float through the clouds. My thoughts, unsurprisingly, drifted to my kingdom. The kingdom where everyone knew my name, but no one cared to even converse with me. I was the living dead girl, literally. Ghostly pale and condemned to death. I might as well have been a ghost, the way people treated me. Yet I still cared for the people of Avalon; I couldn't blame them. I had a ticking death sentence; who would want to befriend someone like that? I cocked my head to the side, watching Dayne's chest rise and fall in steady rhythm with mine. I found myself more grounded just then. He might be Fae, but he walked like me—talked like me—*breathed* like me. I turned from him then, wincing at the bitter taste that filled my mouth. I was too trusting, too desperate for a companion. Was I befriending this stranger? A stranger who was dragging me along to who knows what? At this thought, I pushed away from him, not wanting to trust him too much too fast.

"What is your father going to do to me?" I spoke, embarrassed by how meek my voice sounded. The first words I had said in half an hour.

Dayne went rigid at my question as if suddenly sobering up. "I don't know," he sounded sad and wholly genuine.

"I can't go with you," I said, surprising myself even. His head slumped at that, but he turned to face me anyway.

"Selene." He spoke my name for the first time, but I didn't react, couldn't —or rather, shouldn't react. "Selene," he repeated with more strength in his voice. I turned to meet his eyes.

Despite the desperation in his voice, I couldn't help but feel as if he was desperate for himself... for what the King of Wind would do to him if he failed to bring me to him. I couldn't go... I couldn't—

He reached out to place his hand on my forearm, eyes searing into me. "I promise I won't let anything happen to you. I have a lot of sway with my father. I wouldn't have saved you from the Goddess to damn you to him." His ever-green eyes pierced me with swirling emotions of sorrow and guilt.

I pondered his words—his face and whatever was aching behind those eyes. I allowed his statement to roll inside my head. What was the worst that could happen if I went? I die? I nearly snorted at the thought. I should have been dead already. I glanced back at the bootlegger drinks on the table before us. It was sad... but somehow, the past day had been more fun and full of promise than any other day of my life. I couldn't even remember a day that didn't involve me waking up and being instantly reminded of my destined fate of death. Yet this morning... for the first time ever, I did.

I looked back to Dayne, his hand fully gripping my forearm, eyes scanning me. Oh Goddess, it was a bad idea to go with him for so many reasons but... but I had nothing to sodding lose, right?

"Swear?" I was holding back tears by this point; trying to conceal them would be impossible, considering how closely he watched me.

He squeezed my forearm. "I swear it."

* * *

WE RETURNED to the underground rooms only to stand in front of them silently once more. I glanced up at Dayne, his eyes still dark and sad. Before I could ask, he spoke, "I'm sorry."

I didn't dare move; I didn't dare take a breath.

He continued somberly, "You didn't deserve to grow up in a city where no one wants to be your friend." He spoke softly but continued, "Believe it or not, no one wants to be friends with you when your father is not only a prick but the King."

I remained deathly still, Dayne hovering at my side.

"I know my father tasked me with saving you," he paused. "But if I would have known.. could have known... I'd like to think I would have gotten you out anyway." He waited only a heartbeat before finishing, "You don't need to say anything. I just thought you should know." A warm wind brushed my cheek ever so slightly. I didn't realize I was crying until I noticed what the breeze was doing; it was drying my tears before they fell.

"Tears don't count unless they fall," Dayne said in a quiet but not meek voice before unlocking his room and disappearing before me. The warm breeze persisted, curling around my body like a warm hug. I was certain the wind would remain if I stood there all night.

37

Chapter Seven

Selene

I woke to a knock at my door.

"One minute," I croaked out.

I threw the blankets off me and swung my legs off the bed. I trudged over to the door and swung it open. Dayne was fully dressed in the fighting leathers I had seen him in before. His hair was still damp from a morning shower. His eyes trailed to my bare legs. I had discarded the horrible pants and slept in the oversized shirt instead. "What?" I grumbled, still groggy from being woke. I couldn't help the flash of heat that sparked within me under his gaze. It wasn't that it was him, but rather that *someone*—anyone—looked at me longer than a glance.

"You didn't think to put on pants before opening the door?" His voice was flat and deflated as he stared at me in his shirt.

I rolled my eyes. "The towel was shorter than this."

Dayne's chest heaved upwards as if remembering, forcing that flash of heat from earlier to glow within me. "I went to a shop this morning." He tossed a large canvas sack at me. I opened the bag to see boots, a top, pants, and under-garments.

"How'd you know my size?" I held up the brassiere from the bag with a finger, half teasing—half genuinely curious.

Dayne's cheeks flushed. "Lucky guess," he shrugged. "Change. Now."

I winced at the harsh tone. "Oh. Kay." I mocked him and shut the door in his face.

I emptied the contents of the canvas bag onto my bed and slipped Dayne's shirt off. To my surprise, the undergarments fit fine. I pulled the plain black shirt on, examining it in the mirror. I slipped into the black pants that felt made of waterproof fabric. The shirt had a slight crop to it, and the pants a bit of a low rise, leaving a sliver of my abdomen exposed. I tried yanking on the shirt to stretch it down, eventually giving up. I laced the ankle-high brown leather boots and stuck my knife in my waistband. I glanced in the mirror one last time. My hair had curled and kinked after not brushing it when it was still wet. It fell in long, swooping golden white waves down my back and over my shoulders. I shrugged at my reflection and stuffed Dayne's shirt and pants into the canvas bag he had given me. I grabbed the copper key to the room and hurried out the door, locking it behind me.

"Got everything?" he asked while scanning me from head to toe, eyes catching on the exposed skin of my waist.

"I think I forgot my cheek powder and hairbrush," I said a little less genuinely, winning me the continent's longest eye roll.

"I need you to listen and not talk for five minutes. Can you do that?"

I made a zipping motion across my mouth, followed by a click of the lock with my room key. Then, for dramatic effect, I handed him the key. Somehow, he managed an even bigger eye roll than before.

"We have to survive three major treks today." He paused. "The first will be getting through and out of the Hiareth Mountains without coming across another scuttler."

I held my hand up in invisible cheers as if saying, 'I can drink to that.' I was feeling better this morning. The hope of my new future lifted some of the weight of Avalon's curse that still remained upon me. While it hurt my chest to consider, I still felt better—lighter.

"The second," he continued, "will be crossing the Onyx Sea."

I stumbled on a step as it sank in that I would be leaving the human continent. I'd never ventured beyond Hiareth into the other two human kingdoms.

"The Onyx Sea is too wide for me to flex us over, but if we can manage a quarter of through the waters, I can get us across. That is only if I don't have to flex us anywhere before we make it to the coast." He was deadly serious now.

"Once I have flexed us from the sea to the Fae continent, we have to make it to the Olvidare Hideaway. I will only be able to flex us so far, so if we can't make it over a quarter of the way into the Onyx Sea, I will only be able to flex us to the coast in the Twilight Grove." Dayne paused, checking to make sure I was following. "*If* we can make it halfway across the Onyx Sea, we can skip the Twilight Grove altogether, and I should be able to get us right up to the Hideaway."

"What's worse, the Onyx Sea or the Twilight Grove?" I asked.

"It depends on who you ask, although most would say the Twilight Grove is worse."

I tapped a finger on my lower lip, "So we need to get as far into the Onyx Sea as possible to avoid the Twilight Grove?"

"Correct..." he said, prompting me to continue.

"But that is only if we can manage conflict-free until the coast?" I said, crinkling my nose. He nodded.

We bounded up the last flight of stairs, sighing simultaneously as the sun hit our faces.

"All you have to do is follow, princess," he patted my back while saying. I had never been so relieved to hear that all I had to do was follow. No expectations.

We returned to the small straw-roofed hut where the pretty black-haired female was still working. She wore the same clothes, but it was as if she had yanked her top down low and applied powder to her cheeks since we saw her last.

"Dayne," she spoke in a voice dripping with honey.

"Shaina," Dayne replied, avoiding eye contact with her.

"How was your stay?" She spoke to him, and only him. It made me feel small and insignificant. I was used to the feeling, so I shrunk into it—embraced it. Dayne turned to me then and repeated Shaina's question, forcing my involvement in the conversation. I winced, unsure if I was thankful or annoyed at the small act.

"Oh, um..., it was fine, thank you," I said, nodding at Shaina, who now looked irritated. Dayne set the keys on the table as Shaina reached for his hand, asking, "Can we talk?"

He pulled his hand away before she could touch it, grunted, and said, "We're in a hurry." He grabbed me around the shoulders and stalked off. I heard a distressed huff sound from behind us. Dayne was still leading me forward by my shoulder when I noticed the blush on his face.

"Okay, you have to tell me who that is," I poked him in the ribs with a finger.

He dropped his hand from my shoulder and said, "I told you, an old friend."

"Do you sleep with all your old friends? Or just the pretty dark-haired ones?" I meant it jokingly, but it came out harsher than I intended. He grunted and ignored my question entirely before pushing past me to lead us into the mountains.

As I followed, I remembered last night's conversation. He told me he was lonely. How much of his life has he been lonely? I've made it eighteen years, and it felt unbearable. I skipped ahead to walk next to him. "Do you want to play a game?"

"A what?" he said as if he wasn't sure he heard me right.

"Do you not know what a game is?" I bumped into him, smirking. He bumped back twice as hard, forcing me to stumble on the rocky path we walked.

"What game?"

"I used to play this in Avalon... when I got bored. You think of a color or object, like an animal. Then you have to find ten of those objects."

"So, how do the two of us play?"

"I was thinking of making it a race. Whoever finds five first wins," I said, stepping hesitantly over some loosely stacked rocks.

Dayne grunted again before saying, "Bird." He began counting before I realized what was happening. "Four and five. So what do I win?" Dayne raised a brow at me.

I gave him a wicked grin. "Another round.... Green things, go."

Together, we played the game I used to play alone for many years growing up in Avalon. Neither of us tired of the game, even after the hours it took us to

Eevy A.

make it through the Hiareth Mountains. While the walk felt long, it was relatively easy, even for me. Only the monstrous waves of the Onyx Sea crashing onto the shore halted our game.

"The Twilight Grove is... worse than that?" I gestured to the rippling black waves crashing onto the beach before us. I swiveled my head to take in the vast coast that was the edge of the human continent. Our rocky path would lead us down to the shore where those menacing black waves crashed against sharp, jagged black rocks that already glistened with salt water. The sand and pebbles at our feet were not the golden hue of typical beaches but a deep gray, almost mirroring the sea it bordered.

The rhythmic crash of the waves echoed like thunder, an overwhelming symphony that dominated all other sounds. Despite the ominous ambiance, there was a mesmerizing allure—a beauty in the raw power and relentless nature of the Onyx Sea.

"Much worse than that." He frowned.

We worked our way down the last slope and began our walk toward the rocky coast.

"I wish I could get us all the way across," Dayne ran a hand through his dirty blonde hair. "There's a small dock I had prepared with boats depending on what the weather was looking like for the day," he strained his eyes. "It's up ahead there," he pointed and began walking, so I followed.

"You call those boats?" I wished I was joking as I took in the small wooden dock and accompanying boats.

"We have to be inconspicuous, sorry princess."

"Right, I forgot I was a part of some grand secret mission," My words were joking, but pain flashed in Dayne's eyes. I resisted the urge to reach out and touch him, instead wringing my hands in front of me.

"Should we wait out the storm?" I asked, unsure if my question was naive or not.

"This is a decent day. I have seen the Onyx Sea so much stronger than this. We go now."

I swallowed my fear as we approached the wooden salt-stained dock. It creaked and groaned as the obsidian waves smashed against it. Dayne tossed his bags into the largest of boats before turning to me. He got down on one knee and gestured toward my foot.

"Weird way to propose, but yes," I mused, standing before him, arms crossed.

"Your *foot*, princess," he said with an outstretched hand. I glanced down to where his knee connected with the groaning wooden dock, then back to the lip of the boat a few feet above my head. He beckoned me over one last time before I huffed and stalked to his side.

I rested one hand on his shoulder and placed my left foot in his palm. "On three," he said, "One, two, three." He hoisted me up by my foot, and I swung my right leg over the boat's edge and climbed on board. It was larger once I was on it, but it still didn't seem all that safe, considering the enormous waves that crashed against the dock. Dayne grabbed the lip of the boat and hoisted himself up in a swift motion.

"I'm offended you didn't think I could do that."

"You can hop down and show me if you'd like?" His eyes were blazing with playful challenge.

"I think I need to conserve my energy," I stretched my hands above my head and yawned theatrically just as a huge wave crashed against the side of the boat, throwing me off balance.

Dayne chuckled before turning to pull and unravel an assortment of ropes so we could pull away from the dock. I looked at the raging sea before us and felt my playful mood disappear. I scanned the horizon, seeing nothing but endless monstrous waves. The waves near the edge of Avalon were always calm and lapping, but these... these were angry waves. Each crash was seeking some sort of violent vengeance. I turned back to watch the jagged rocks of the shore grow smaller as we pulled away from safety, right into the belly of a beast. I slid my hands together behind my back to hide how hard they were uncontrollably convulsing. I had barely seen the world. I had been in the same sandy shithole for eighteen years, and now I was setting sail straight into a storm that looked like it would snap this boat in two. The water was rough already, but it still didn't compare to what lay ahead on the horizon. The further we sailed into those waves, the more rigid my body became. My shakes became more pronounced against my already taut muscles and bones.

Eevy A.

Dayne sat behind the boat's wheel, watching me from the corner of his eye. He stood up. "Why don't you come sit over here." He gestured to the bench he was sitting on behind the wheel.

"Where will you sit?" I tried and failed to say it without my voice shaking.

"I usually stand for this, more control," I sensed he was lying. He patted the bench behind him, a gentle smile pasted on his face. The sudden smash of a wave that tossed the boat to the side had me slithering to the spot behind him without another word. There was no concealing my shaking body. I scooted as far into the corner as possible, pulling my knees up to my chest. It didn't leave much room for him, but he sat beside me anyway as the boat drifted further into the crashing waves. He draped an arm over my knees and grabbed my ice-cold hands. If I hadn't been paralyzed by fear, I would have pulled away.

"I'm going to control the winds as much as I can. We're going to be okay." He squeezed my hands. The grimace on his face told me that my hands pulsated at a temperature even colder than ice.

He hadn't asked me to try and calm the waters with my affinity; I wasn't sure I could manage much on these waves, even if I was practiced in magic. As if sensing my thoughts, he whispered, "Do it if you can." A giant black wave crashed into us. The boat groaned in protest as it fought against the massive waves. Dayne launched from sitting beside me, using his entire body weight to whip the boat back in the right direction.

Another wave crashed, and another. The boat tossed left, then back to the right. A colossal wave started ripping from beneath the nose of the boat, sending us flying down. It felt as if we were in a forward free fall until the nose of the boat smashed back into the water. I was sent flying forward, slamming my face into the wheel. Blood began to gush from my lip. I heard Dayne yelling, but I could barely make it out over the ringing in my head.

"Hold on..."

The words barely broke through to me between the rushing blood and blinding pain. It wasn't my lip that hurt; rather, it felt like my brain had been jostled loose, every thought scraping against my skull. We began to dip again, nose first. I grabbed Dayne around his left leg, clinging to him with both my arms and legs. If I had a tail, it would've been tucked between my legs in shame at how I cowered at his feet. The boat crashed into the wave, jostling my every thought. My blood leaked into Dayne's pants as it streamed from my face. We were going to die. This boat would snap in two. How did he think we would survive the Twilight Grove if it's worse than this? I put a hand to my lip, pulling away to see bright red blood covering it.

How was I *still* bleeding? A flash of angry ice writhed within me as I remembered what I was capable of–the magic that thrummed within me. The painful ice that probably numbed the bones in Dayne's leg from how hard I gripped him. I stopped the blood from running out of my lip with a single thought, frozen before another drop could fall. With that, ice and, power, and fury began spreading through my veins like wildfire. I released my grip on Dayne's leg.

I am not helpless.

Another massive black wave hit the front of the boat, sending Dayne toppling over the steering wheel. He scrambled to get back behind it and control the direction we were moving.

Beyond the immediate onslaught of waves that drenched every part of this boat and us, the horizon painted a terrifying picture of an icy, violent death. The Onyx Sea was preparing its killing blow. A monstrous wave, its crest rising to a chilling height of at least ten towering pines, was gathering strength and momentum. The scale of it dwarfed everything else in sight, casting a vast shadow that seemed to darken not only the already black waves but the sky itself. The patterns in its churning face told tales of its fury and promise of death. I felt the weight of its impending assault, the tight knot of dread coiling in my stomach. A quick glance at Dayne revealed his wide eyes reflecting the same terror. His breath grew shallow and rapid as his gaze remained locked onto the looming wave that was still somehow growing, the gravity of our situation making his limbs tremble and face blanch.

"I can flex us back," he yelled, still throwing his whole body weight around to keep the boat moving in a not-so-straight line.

No amount of wind control would stop that wave from splitting this boat in two. If we fell into this sea, we'd be swallowed alive in seconds. No one would miss us.

The wave loomed closer, growing taller and taller by the second.

"Grab onto me." Dayne started screaming. I knew he wanted to flex us back to the shore and safety. A part of me nearly listened. But the other part of me—the magic raging beneath my skin, begging to be unleashed, won out.

Icy rage coursed through my veins as I vowed to stand firm. I would not yield to my fears. I would no longer be confined by weakness.

I would not be helpless.

I stood but walked past and ahead of Dayne. I barely made out the sound of him yelling to grab onto him. My hair whipped around me as I allowed my feet to freeze in place with every step I took toward the boat's bow. I dug down deep within myself like I had done when working for my father. I dug deeper than I ever fathomed I could excavate within this Fae gift of mine. I dug so deep that it threatened to consume my whole being just for attempting. The monstrous wave began to crash down on us. I heard Dayne abandon the wheel, and the jerking motion of the boat confirmed he no longer stood behind it. I stepped forward three more paces and ripped out of the hole I had dug within myself. I flung my hands and body forward as my magic erupted from me.

I was not helpless.

Cold enveloped me. Ice cold, and then darkness.

Chapter Eight

Selene

I SHOOK BACK INTO CONSCIOUSNESS, FINDING MYSELF CURLED IN A ball on the floor of the boat's deck. I was encased in ice and had to shake myself free to get up. I tried but failed to get both feet beneath my weight. Dayne rushed over to me, grasping my shoulders to hold me steady as I swayed and fell back to a sitting position on the slatted wooden floor.

"We're.. we're still on the boat?" My voice was so raspy it was nearly a whisper.

"Look," Dayne said before I beheld the calm black lapping waters around us, a twin to the waters I knew.

"What?" I croaked. My head swiveled to take in the eery scene. It didn't look right; it didn't *feel* right for such dark and looming waters to be... calm.

Dayne scooped me up and carried me over to the bench behind the steering wheel. I allowed my exhausted body to settle deeply in his arms. He slid me from his arms onto the bench; I barely felt strong enough to remain in the sitting position he placed me in. He crouched on the floor before me, keeping one arm on my shoulder to keep me from collapsing.

"I was about to flex us out of here. I have never seen a wave like *that*; it was like your presence..." Dayne paused, scanning my face. "The presence of you angered the waves." I took in his words but could hardly comprehend them as I fought the temptation to allow my body to slide into a lying position atop the bench. "You walked out there and crouched into a small ball, and... it looked like you caught on fire. But it wasn't fire; it was something else. You stood straight up emitting a light so bright I had to look away, and the next thing I knew, I watched the waves around us be vaporized into mist." He explained. "Do you know how you did that?" His eyes pinned me. He wore a hundred emotions at once: questioning, concern, fear...

"I... I just dug into my magic like I always did in Avalon, but I dug deeper... I didn't do any of that on purpose... I—"

I barely had the energy to think, let alone talk. Dayne noticed and looked from me to the open waters ahead.

"I should be able to dock the boat on the Fae continent rather than abandoning it and flexing us in." He scratched his head. "Remind me to show you the Twilight Grove sometime, though." He winked, trying to lighten the mood.

I tried to manage a small smile through the exhaustion that coursed through me. I felt like I could lay on the floor and pant like a dog. "How much—"

"An hour tops," he interrupted and rose from his crouched position to settle beside me.

I nodded, allowing my head to roll to the side and rest on his shoulder.

"We don't tell anyone about that," he said in a taut, strained voice.

Confusion coursed through me at his words, but exhaustion won out as my body fully relaxed against him before succumbing to it.

* * *

I AWOKE with my head in Dayne's lap, the rest of my body curled in a ball on the bench beside him. His arm draped around me, keeping me from rolling off the bench.

I stirred, stretched, and pushed from his lap. "Did you really just let me sleep like a lap dog?"

Dayne's laugh was nice to hear, given the events of the past couple of hours. "What did you expect me to do? Tell you to go curl up on the floor?"

I shoved him with my shoulder and squinted at the horizon. The Fae continent was in view now, the edge of it packed with trees that were consumed by an eery twilight that only persisted within the thick of the woods. I pointed. "Is that the Twilight Grove?"

"The one and only. Always twilight, always creepy. I'm going to dock us close to the Hideaway. It'll be a five-minute hike, then we can get you settled... and washed." He pinched his nose as if I smelled.

I rolled my eyes and brought my hand to my lip after remembering I had split it open.

"I cleaned it up for you. No more scary bloody face, sorry." He smiled.

We didn't speak for the rest of the trip to the shore, even though I wanted to ask what those horrible screeching sounds were coming from the Twilight Grove.

As we neared the weathered dock, more and more distant cries of strange creatures from the Twilight Grove filled the air around us. The wooden planks of the pier, aged by sun and salt, groaned beneath the weight of time. I squinted at the dock. Nestled amongst scattered barrels and coiled ropes, a male with a thick, tangled beard, sun-kissed by countless days on the sea, began energetically jumping up and down. Each leap caused his worn boots to thud against the wood, and with every descent, the bells on the fishing net he wore on his back jingled. He flailed his arms with exuberance, trying to catch our attention amidst the backdrop of bobbing boats and fluttering sails. "That's Belzhar. He lives at the Hideaway and helps with all the day-to-day tasks like taking care of the ships. He gave me a lot of grief that I'd be leaving this boat behind to get us here."

"I see," I said as I examined Belzhar from a distance. I had no idea what to expect at the Hideaway, but it wasn't worth asking; I would see soon enough.

Laughter broke the silence, and Dayne stood triumphantly for Belzhar.

"My baby. You made it," Belzhar exclaimed, clasping his hands to his chest.

"What did I tell you about calling me your baby, Belz?" Dayne joked with his friend.

"Ah sod off, wontcha'," Belzhar called back to Dayne, but his gnarly grin remained on his face.

Dayne began scooping up his items and headed for the boat deck to throw

49

Belzhar the ropes. I sat in exhausted silence as the males worked to get us secured to shore. Dayne hopped out of the boat first and embraced Belzhar in that half hug that men do. I began dismounting the boat on my own, swinging a leg over the side and hoisting the rest of my body. I made it halfway down before Dayne gripped his hands on my hips and hauled me the rest of the way.

I turned in a fury. "I could've done it myself," I said and pushed past him off the dock. I wasn't sure why I snapped, but exhaustion overwhelmed me.

"Now, now, who is this pretty little feisty lady?" Belzhar started. "The others you brought were all—"

Dayne cut him off by grabbing him into a headlock and rubbing the top of his head.

Exhaustion weighed heavily on my shoulders, pulling my gaze downward. Every step was a battle, the soles of my feet feeling like lead. The aroma of something savory wafted in the air, beckoning my empty stomach. Dayne reached my side in a swift stride. Without a word, we ventured deeper into the Fae continent. Around us, the landscape shimmered with otherworldly hues; every plant and flower seemed more saturated with color, and every whisper of wind felt as if it carried some hint of ancient magic. I yearned to explore this land and take in more of its heightened beauty, but for now, the simple act of placing one foot in front of the other demanded all the strength I could muster.

"When we get there, it will be kind of a whirlwind." Dayne kept a good distance from me, his mood seeming colder all of a sudden. "We're not going to stop to talk with anyone. I'll get you straight into your living quarters, okay?"

I made a grumbling sound, which must've been a good enough response for Dayne because he pressed forward.

The distant echoes of mirthful laughter drifted on the wind long before the revelers came into view. As we reached the crest of the hill, the panorama that unfolded was both wild and enchanting. A multitude of Fae were sprawled throughout a grassy meadow. Fae males, their chiseled features accentuated by the play of dappled sunlight, roared in hearty laughter, clashing their goblets in boisterous toasts. Fae females, their long, ethereal gowns trailing behind them like wisps of clouds, danced with grace and abandon, their laughter harmonizing with the evening songbirds. I would never get over the bewitching way that Fae were like humans, only heightened in the most ethereal ways.

At the meadow's edge, an ancient, moss-draped cave yawned open, its entrance framed by tendrils of ivy and luminescent fungi. It seemed to hold secrets as old as the continent itself. Around it, approximately thirty Fae formed a riotous circle, their antics ranging from soulful ballads to playful wrestling on the dew-kissed grass.

Dayne, his eyes alight with mischief and merriment, shot me a roguish grin, his sharp features softened by the spectacle before us.

As we approached, a thin but tall male snapped his head to Dayne. He started hollering and ran up to us. He slapped an arm around his back. "Dayney boyyyy." The dark-haired male exclaimed. "You're back. You brought such a fine lady—"

Dayne interrupted him in a deathly serious tone. "We need to get in quickly. Go in ahead of us and tell everyone to clear a path."

The male straightened at the tone. "Yes sir," he spoke with steadfast loyalty. He ran up ahead, and the hollering died down.

"You didn't have to ruin their fun," I said, glaring at Dayne, taken aback by the unusual way he was acting. I knew I hadn't known the male long, but—

"Everyone will stop us if I don't send him ahead; it'll be easier this way." He shrugged.

Everyone smiled or bowed to us, well to him, as we passed by. They were all beautiful. Their faces each looked like it was crafted especially for them. One foxy-faced female with red hair stuck out to me as extraordinarily beautiful. She wore a velvet dress in shades of green that clung to her curved body. We headed inside the cave entrance. I was surprised to see the inside bustling with even more activity than in the clearing outside the cave. It was mostly an open-concept design. The main area had tables and an open floor for camaraderie and dancing. Around the edge of the cave lay stairs that spiraled up and up, leading to several doors along the way. I pitied anyone who had to stay on one of the upper floors.

"I'm the room closest to the top," Dayne said.

"Of course you are," I sighed and began walking up the steps, not realizing Dayne had stayed behind me.

"Princess," he said with amusement from the base of the stairs. I whipped around to behold his devilish smirk and outstretched hand. Oh, right.

My legs protested as I jogged back down the few steps to him, and he flexed us up to the top of the cave. There was a protective stone railing that I leaned over to watch the Hideaway from above. I took in the bustling but humble ambiance. It was quaint. I liked it here.

"I thought you were taking me to *my* room?" I said, now turning from the ledge toward Dayne. His face grew nervous, and his eyes darted from mine.

"What is wrong with you?" I snapped, instantly feeling guilty for the tone I had used.

"What? Nothing is *wrong* with me," he sounded defensive.

"Did my whole ice thing on the boat freak you out?" I asked, exasperated, shoving my hands into my pockets with a scowl.

He shifted on his feet before the time-faded wooden door to his room, "No," he said. "Here, just come inside."

I followed him into his room. It was a humble room with stone floors and walls like the rest of the cave. It had quite a large bed and washroom, which I doubted the other rooms had. Shades of ivory, maroon, and gold were a common theme throughout the quarters as I took in the various decor and furniture.

"Look," he said as he started casually kicking off his shoes and removing his jacket and weaponry.

"I don't know how to tell you this without looking like a sodding prick," he continued removing items from his body until he was down to his pants and shirt. I remained wholly frozen, back rigid against the stone wall of his room. I couldn't tell if the cold sandwiched between my back and the wall was from me or the stone wall itself. All of my fear of him, of the circumstances, came flooding back. He noticed the change in my stance, in my face. He rubbed the back of his neck and took a step towards me.

"Don't," I said, tears already welling in my eyes. "Just tell me."

"Selene, can you sit down, please?" he asked.

This was going to be bad. So very bad. I traveled from the human continent to this unfamiliar Fae world. The second we got here, he had some terrible news for me?

"You're disgusting," I spat and slunk to a nearby ottoman to sit on while he broke whatever news to me.

Dayne sighed, and it somehow *sounded* sad. "There's more demi-Fae." He paused, watching me. "One for each human kingdom."

Other demi-Fae? What was he saying? I am the only demi-Fae... I—

"What do you *mean?*" I spoke with fury bubbling in my throat. I couldn't help but twist in discomfort and confusion from where I sat atop the stiff ottoman.

"This lie, this story... it goes way beyond me, Selene. I..." he searched for words he thought might make this better, finding none.

"My father, the King of Wind... he has some of the best spies on the continent. So good that they were able to breach the Goddess's wards." Dayne looked at the ground as he spoke. I began to tremble. "He learned of demi-Fae children. Four of them. Gaia of Munique, Aeryn of Florence, Idris of Hiareth," Dayne paused before finishing, "and Selene of Avalon."

The world began to spin around me. I was going to vomit. I ran to Dayne's washroom and shoved my head into the tub, bracing my hands on the edge. I barely felt it when Dayne touched my back. "Do you want me to keep going?"

Then it all came up. I began vomiting so violently that I couldn't contain it within the tub. I hadn't eaten much the past few days, so it quickly turned into violent retching. I retched for what felt like hours. Dayne left only to get towels and a change of clothes for me.

Belzhar's words hit me like a ton of stones. He had said something about 'the others he brought.'

"They're here, aren't they?" I choked and looked up at him. He nodded his reply.

"And you," I pointed at him with a shaky finger, "brought them here." I was seething with an icy rage I didn't care to contain as I allowed frost to form on my fingertips. He knew more, and he... he didn't tell me. I clenched my hands into fists.

"All but one," Dayne's face dropped into such a deep frown that I thought he might cry right before me.

I waited for him to continue, but he didn't.

"Who?" I croaked out before I started retching again.

Dayne rubbed my back. I had no energy to swat him away, so I became colder than ice, too frigid to touch. He never stopped rubbing circles on my back, even as I pumped my frozen fury through my veins. After a few minutes, the retching stopped, and my temper tapered off.

"Who," I repeated quieter this time.

"Aeryn of Florence. He was the first to turn eighteen. I couldn't get to him in time. The Goddess claimed him and..." he trailed off. "The demi-Fae curse was only supposed to be between the humans and the Fae Goddess. She never intended for any Fae to learn of the curse. My father is a skeptic. Once he learned of it, he ordered me to interfere. After failing Aeryn, I went after Gaia, Idris, and you. You know the rest."

Dayne was ripping my world out from under me for the second time. My thoughts spun in my head. "Is that why you took me so late?" I croaked.

"What?" Dayne asked with genuine confusion.

"You came for me at the last second. I was the last to turn eighteen," I prompted him further.

"I tried to get Aeryn before the day of his eighteenth birthday. I failed him. So, I got Gaia out long before her execution. We had to stay hidden far longer, of course. Idris was complicated, but I ultimately got her out the morning of her eighteenth birthday. The Goddess had to know at that point what was happening. I chose to wait until the last moment with you because it was unexpected. The Goddess had nothing left to worry about. You were bound, a sword to your throat."

"You don't have to remind me," I spat. He winced.

"I'm a pawn in this just like you are, Selene. I don't know why the Goddess kept her curse so secret; I don't know why my father wanted the demi-Fae." Tears welled in his eyes. "I just did what I was told like I always have," he said softly. "I wouldn't take it back either. I hate myself for lying, but I'll never apologize for saving you, Gaia, and Idris." A moment of silence hung in the air. "You will love them, by the way."

"That is quite enough," I spoke, rising to my feet. "Show me my room," I said, staring not at but right through Dayne. He didn't shift a muscle. "Show. Me. My. Room," I said again. Dayne bowed his head and handed me a towel to wipe the vomit from my clothes.

"You won't run?" he asked, trying to get me to look him in the eyes. I snorted a breath of air out of my nose. "Take my room; I'll stay somewhere else." He took a step toward me.

I began grinding my teeth to keep my head from imploding.

"I'll call someone up to clean this. You can stay in here, Selene." He was near pleading for me to stay.

"Then get out," I said, pointing to the door. He hovered before me for a long moment before bowing his head and leaving without another word.

I crumpled to the floor. I was tired of crying. Tomorrow, I promised myself. Tomorrow, I will fight.

And with that, I allowed myself to weep. I wept for Avalon. I wept for Gaia and Idris... for Aeryn. I wept until I was too exhausted to do anything but stare blankly at the wall.

Tomorrow, I'll fight.

Chapter Nine

Selene

I WOKE TO HUNGER PAINS SO INTENSE THAT THEY ECHOED through the depths of my being. My entire body swayed beneath me as I pulled myself from Dayne's bed. Looking around the room, I could see my mess had been cleaned, and last night's dinner sat atop an intricate golden platter. I had half a thought to eat it even though it looked stale from sitting there all night.

I took a shaky breath in. I'd take my life back today. No more following. I got a second chance at life, a second chance that the demi-Fae from Florence never got. Aeryn. I had murmured his name countless times last night, weeping for him. I never met him or even knew he existed until he was gone. Still, it felt like a part of me was fractured. I had also wept for Gaia and Idris. I let their names sit on my tongue until they were no longer unfamiliar. Did they do the same with my name? Would they want to hear what I have to say? I wanted to avoid every pathetic Fae bastard in this camp, Dayne included, and get to them, see their faces—learn their stories. I needed them to leave with me, to figure out what to do or where to go. I thought of Dayne. An uncanny mix of emotions flooded me as his face flashed in my mind. We weren't friends, so it wasn't as if he betrayed me, yet it felt like he had. Would I have stayed back in the human continent if he had told me before we left? I let out a sharp breath. I doubted I would have stayed. I spent years wondering why the Fae Goddess only punished Avalon with my existence. I spent years wishing for someone like me while being thankful there was no one else enduring the kind of loneliness I was. Having learned that others like me existed and that they stayed where Dayne wanted to take me... I would have found myself here either way. I winced at the realization that, for some unknown reason, I *wanted* a reason to hate him.

I let out a long sigh, rolling my neck as the empty pit in my stomach groaned. What Dayne had done felt like a betrayal, but it did not alter my path. For that, I could put one foot in front of the other today. I would find Gaia and Idris, and I would hear their stories.

* * *

SODDING HELLS.

I groaned dramatically as I remembered how high up I was and that I had *no* idea where Gaia and Idris were staying. Dayne had flexed us up here, and if I wanted to get to Gaia and Idris, I needed him to show me where they were. The thought of Dayne wrapping an arm around me to flex us left a bitter taste in my mouth.

I walked around the room, taking in the utter bareness of it. It was spacious with only necessary furnishings such as a small round table with chairs, a bed, a loveseat and ottoman, and a humbly sized armoire. It made sense. He lived in Olvidare, and his belongings would likely be there. I thought for a moment of the four Fae kingdoms: Olvidare, Kingdom of Wind; Seldovia, Kingdom of Ice; Krakata, Kingdom of Fire; and Belgar, Kingdom of Nature. Crinkling my nose, I struggled to recall the many maps I had studied of the Fae continent. To be near the Twilight Grove meant we must be on the edge of Belgar. Given the name *Hideaway,* I wondered how secret this place was to the other kingdoms.

A faint knock sounded at the door, forcing me to halt my meandering around the spacious stone room. If it was Dayne, I wasn't sure I had much to say to him. I panicked momentarily, looking around like someone else would decide what to do for me. Another faint knock. Nervously, I slithered my way to the door and rapped three times faintly in reply.

Eevy A.

"I don't know what that means," Dayne whispered through the thick oak door between us. My breath caught upon hearing his voice.

I nudged the door open a crack as if in silent answer that he was, in fact, allowed to come into his bedroom. He came in, closing the door behind him, his somber eyes on the ground. I stood near the foot of the bed, still wearing the same outfit from the Hiareth Fortress. Even though I recoiled at his presence, I didn't shrink within myself. I forced myself to stand tall and watch Dayne's face as he turned to meet me. He looked different from the first couple of days I was with him. He seemed relaxed but had a pained expression on his face.

"I can send them up here if you'd like," He spoke with ease as if he had his words already planned. I knew who he was talking about.

"No," I said. "I'll go to them." I waited.

Dayne looked around the room, eyes catching on the uneaten food platter. "You must be starving." He gestured to the untouched food, his eyes widening in surprise.

"I didn't even know they brought it in," I said, happy to be talking about something trivial.

"I told them to wake you," Dayne grumbled, shifting awkwardly on his feet. His eyes darted from my relentless gaze to the floor. I bit back the urge to look away.

"I can go if you'd like. We don't have to talk. I figured I'd at least offer to flex you down from here and..." Dayne trailed off.

I studied his face, which seemed to make him uncomfortable as he again broke free from my eye contact. I considered my options. I could remain unattached to the male who uprooted me yet spoke to me and treated me like something that perhaps resembled a friend. Something I had never experienced in my eighteen years of life. Or, I could allow him some grace. My mother always warned me of falling into trust too quickly. She knew I led a lonely life and taught me it would be my greatest weakness. I wanted so badly to return to the annoying jokes or sipping on wine, but after learning other demi-Fae sacrifices had been saved... there were bigger things at work.

I started slowly. "I'm sorry I called you disgusting." The least I could do was create a neutral ground between us. We didn't have to be friends.

58

"Well, you're not wrong; you've smelled me after a day of travel," he tried to lighten the mood, but it only made me feel an immense sorrow. He took a small step forward as if noticing the sadness that consumed me. I considered stepping away but didn't.

Silence hung between us. It was as if neither of us knew how to proceed with the other. He was looking at me like a snowflake bound to shatter at any moment. Fragile. Maybe I was weak, but I would not be anymore. I would not be stagnant like I had been for eighteen years. I would make something of myself. Something within me told me that Gaia and Idris were the first step in that direction. They had to be. I straightened my spine and slipped a neutral look back onto my face.

"Can you bring fresh food?" I asked, keeping my tone cool and airy.

"Of course." He was gone in an instant. I blinked; I hadn't seen him flex before. I had always been with him during it.

Ten heartbeats later, he returned with a golden platter of steaming eggs, hotcakes, sausages, and colorful berries.

"That was fast."

Dayne brought the platter to the bed and placed it atop the sheets still strewn about from my restless night of sleep. I climbed into bed, sat cross-legged next to the platter of food, and began picking at some of the unfamiliar-looking fruit.

"I assume this isn't all for me?" I asked through a mouthful of deliciously juicy orange berries. It was a gentle nudge in the right direction that Dayne wasted no time in accepting. He swung a chair around from the corner of the room, placing it next to the bed.

The bed was so tall that I sat above eye level with him. He rested an arm on the bed, seemingly uninterested in the food. I popped fruit into my mouth, then grabbed a hotcake and bit into it. Dayne's brow furrowed as he watched me. He seemed to be having an internal battle on what to say. I focused my energy on the food.

"Selene," he started in a pinched tone.

"No." I didn't want to talk about anything serious. I didn't want to think about Dayne or the King of Wind. My focus was on Gaia and Idris and figuring out where we belong.

"Okay," he said. "What would you like to do today?"

"Show me around?"

"Of course, my lady," he said with a sad smile. I felt I wouldn't be seeing much of Dayne after today. I wasn't entirely sure how that made me feel.

"When do we leave for Olvidare?"

His eyes sparked at my question. "We have a crew that has to finish some work in the Twilight Grove, and then we'll leave as a group. I would guess ten days if everything goes to plan."

Ten days. I allowed my body to sag with a small amount of relief. I could do much within ten days, starting with meeting Gaia and Idris.

"Can you take me to them after breakfast?" I tried to keep my voice neutral and calm.

"Of course."

"What are they like?"

Dayne pondered my question for a long moment. "Gaia is incredibly reserved. She walks and talks like royalty. She is like mother nature herself, sired by a Fae from the Kingdom of Nature." He scratched his head before continuing. "Idris... she was sired by a male from the Kingdom of Fire, and well... let's just say it shows. She didn't speak to me our entire time traveling together. I swear she used that time to allow her burning rage to build inside her. She had basically bit the heads off of half my crew when she arrived."

I found myself smiling. "They sound amazing."

"If by amazing you mean murderous, then yep, amazing." Dayne joked. I smiled as if he was joking about people I already knew and loved.

"How would you describe me to them?" I asked nervously, keeping my eyes on the platter of food.

"That's easy... I did that this morning—"

"They... they asked about me?"

He nodded. "I said that Selene of Avalon was like a walking diamond in the rough. That you care deeply, love fiercely, and likely would've beheaded me by now if I had given you a larger knife." I blushed at his words. "For what it's worth, princess, I hope you never spend another day lonely. I think Gaia and Idris will be the start of healing that heart of yours—"

"My soul," I interrupted.

"Your soul." He nodded, watching me more intensely than ever. His green eyes were shining, even in the dimly lit cave room.

I finished some ham from the platter and heaved myself off the bed. I looked down at my disheveled hair and day-old outfit. Before I could register my next thought, a few stacks of clothing appeared on the bed. I whipped my head around to Dayne, who was smirking against the wall. "Let me know if you need more," he said.

My eyes narrowed upon him. "Are you going to lean on that wall all day, or are you going to let me change?" I began rifling through my options, thankful to see a large assortment. Dayne held his hands up and walked to his washroom, closing the door behind him.

I stripped down, realizing I should have bathed. "Too late now," I mumbled.

I fumbled through the undergarments, noting that every choice was a lacey matching set. I rolled my eyes, grabbed a black set, and threw it on. I picked out a dark maroon top that clung to me. It was long enough to tuck into the black pants I slipped on. I stared at my reflection in the mirror for a moment, deciding it was as good as it would get. I sighed and turned from the mirror to rap twice on the washroom door to notify Dayne he could come out.

"Good choice," he said, smiling at me but keeping his eyes on my face.

"So, you like lace?" I tried to joke, but it came out awkward and hoarse. His eyes dipped to my collarbone before darting back up to my face. Oh, sodding Goddess. I didn't want him to look at me like that. It made things so much more... complicated.

"Which one did you pick?" he asked, taking a discreet step toward me.

"Wouldn't you like to know?" I shoved past him to the washroom to rinse my face. Dayne leaned on the door frame behind me, contemplating something.

"We normally eat in the common spaces; if you'd like to join my crew there for the rest of the meals? Unless you'd rather it be brought here," he stumbled through saying.

"Sure," I replied, drying my face off. "You can have your room back. Just show me mine."

"You're already settled in here. It's just ten days; it's no bother."

61

Eevy A.

I elbowed past him out of the washroom, shoving him aside like a curtain. Fine. I didn't have it in me to argue.

"Ready?" he asked me.

I took a deep breath, surprised by the lack of shakiness in it, and straightened my back. "As I'll ever be."

With that, he prowled towards me and wrapped his arms around me in an embrace. I was so surprised that I couldn't even react in time to hug him back if I wanted to. I hadn't wanted to. I stood there so rigid that I thought he might snap me in two despite the gentle way he held me against him. I wriggled at the uncomfortable way my arms remained pinned at my sides.

"I'm sorry," he whispered in my ear.

I would have cried if it weren't for the promise I made myself yesterday. "They're going to love you," he whispered even closer. A shiver ran down my spine at his breath in my ear. I didn't understand why he was hugging me. I didn't understand why this male even sent a second glance in my direction. Yet here I was, in a haphazard embrace with him. He shifted me to his side and flexed us in front of a door many levels lower than his room. I blinked, and he was gone just as fast as we had arrived here, flexing off to Goddess knows where.

I looked at the door in front of me, sucked in a long, deep breath, and went in.

* * *

I SAW who I assumed was Gaia first and was nearly knocked to my knees at how breathtaking she was. Her skin was of molten dark chocolate. Her eyes shone the color of sweet, calm waters, a deep, majestic blue. Her hair, though, had me gaping at her. It was a nearly metallic silver mixed with onyx black at the roots. Her maroon-stained lips parted slightly at the sight of me, and I couldn't help but drop to my knees.

"Get up, child," she cooed at me, even though we were the same age. I looked up to her, the beautiful demi-Fae female with a hand stretched out to me. I took it, and she led me up and over to a beautiful ivory couch. Although I could tell this room was similar to Dayne's, I didn't have the urge

62

to analyze my surroundings—to map escape routes or possible weapons. I was safe here.

She took me in her arms and began stroking my hair. I allowed her to hold me. The scene might be awkward for anyone watching, but it felt far from it. I breathed her in deeply. She smelled of sage and spring rain.

I leaned out of the intense embrace to look at her. She took my hand. "Tell me everything."

"I..." I choked, fighting against the emotions that swelled within me. Gaia's calming eyes were the only thing keeping me grounded. "I was young the first time I realized I had been born dead." The silence in the room was deafening, only my pinched, quivering voice slicing through it. "I was just a child when I fully grasped it." Without thinking, I found that my hand had shifted to my inner thighs, tracing the delicately raised scars that were a memory of the day everything clicked into place. Gaia rubbed gentle circles on my back as if coaxing me to tell her.

"I was nine when I tried to take my... end into my own hands..." I trailed off as I felt Gaia's hand hesitate rubbing gentle circles on my back. I bowed my head, "I wanted the scars hidden in case it didn't work."

Silence hung in the air, a moment of grief and knowing. "Each time after, my father—" I winced at my own words, "the king punished me for my selfishness." Gaia's steady, circling hand gripped my shoulder in solidarity and understanding. "Maybe I was selfish. After all, I am only one being. Ending myself that way... it cursed them all." I frowned. "Putting the entire Kingdom of Avalon at risk for something so... trivial—"

"Your life is not trivial, child." Gaia interrupted her once calm eyes, a now brewing cerulean storm. "Every person has a right to dream," her eyes settled only slightly. "What is yours?"

I chewed on my lip at the question. The irony was comical, yet I knew deep down that I had dreams only the night sky knew about. The ones I had whispered to the stars as I stared up at them, eyes set on that same constellation. If I closed my eyes, I could picture it and feel its pattern burned on the inside of my eyelids. The shape was of three interlocking links, the brightest star dotted in the center.

"To love and be loved," I whispered. It wasn't as simple as it sounded, of course. There were no rules or stipulations; I wanted every kind. The kind that exists between friends, the kind that forms between a leader and her people, the kind that unfolds between teacher and student, man and woman, woman and woman... Somehow, I felt I didn't need to explain that to Gaia. She knew all too well. I relaxed into her at the utterly comforting feeling of her wordless understanding.

"Idris," Gaia sang, snapping my now glazing eyes to the short brunette standing idly in the corner listening. Had she been here the whole time?

I looked at her, our gazes falling lightly upon each other. Idris was beautiful, too. She was small, probably under five feet tall. Her brunette hair was cut so that it barely touched the top of her shoulders. Her eyes were gray like ash, her lips pouty and round. Everything about her was angular and sharp, other than those lips. She stood, arms crossed, simply watching us.

"Come," Gaia purred, drawing out the m. Gaia extended her arm out to the short, fiery woman. As she got closer, I noticed the scars that peppered her entire body. In horror, I began to break my promise to myself. I wept ever so slightly at the sight of her scars.

"Do not weep, girl," Idris spoke. "This is the skin of a warrior. I am proud to wear it."

"I... I'm sorry," I choked out, wiping the tears from my face with the back of my wrist.

"I don't hug," she said, looking between Gaia and me, still in a half embrace. "But I am happy you are here."

"It is our turn to share our stories." Gaia gestured to Idris.

"You know mine, you tell it," Idris said while crossing her arms, not breaking eye contact with Gaia.

"It is not mine to tell," Gaia countered. Idris uncrossed her arms and let out an exasperated sigh.

"Fiiine. But no crying," she said with force while looking at me. "You water affinity Fae are all the same." I wanted to look away, ashamed at my weakness, but held her gaze. I would be strong for her while she told her truth.

Idris began. "From the moment I was born until Dayne arrived, I was treated as a prisoner by 'my kingdom,' Hiareth." I stifled my gasp. "I was not told my purpose in life," she spat the word 'purpose' as if it were poison. "I only learned of it when I arrived here." She gestured to the room around us. "I assumed I was tortured and abused for being half Fae. It turns out the person who hated me most was my birth mother. Her favorite thing to do was chain me in iron to suppress my magic, slicing my skin slowly with a hot blade that glowed red."

"How... how are you coping with this new... information?"

Idris raised an eyebrow. "I've been here three weeks. It's hardly new anymore. I might have burned a few rooms to ashes before coming to grips with it, but I came out on the other side." Gaia patted Idris's leg, pride shining in her eyes.

"She isn't exaggerating; this really is our third room since coming here," Gaia chuckled sweetly.

I wanted to shake my head as I beheld them. They were both so beautiful; I almost couldn't believe they were only half-Fae.

"I didn't realize you had been here so many weeks," I raised an eyebrow.

"I guess that just makes you the baby of the group," was all Idris said in reply.

I waited for Idris to continue her story but realized that was all she had to tell. It was so simple, yet so complex. She lived eighteen years of torturous hell and stands before us proud and strong. I became ashamed of the self-inflicted scars on my inner thighs. Her scars... hers were real.

Gaia broke the silence. "I was honored to live a fruitful and fulfilling eighteen years in Munique. Once, I felt I was broken. The people of Munique, my friends and family, pieced me back together." Gaia smiled pleasantly, her eyes shut as if remembering their faces.

"When Dayne took me from Munique, we had many... discussions," Gaia spoke the last word with an edge, "about the outcome of our arrangement. You see, my family and the people of Munique were willing to pay the ultimate price. They were willing to let the Fae Goddess force a curse on their lands to spare me. It was decided by a nearly unanimous vote that I would not be offered up to the Goddess. Of course, I had other plans. I would not stand by while these people suffered the great losses I knew would befall them." Gaia paused. I was in awe at the way she spoke. She spoke as if she had the wisdom of hundreds of years of life. Then I thought of how

Eevy A.

Dayne spoke so casually, being nearly 350 years old. I found myself smiling at that.

Gaia continued. "I planned to offer myself on my eighteenth birthday. I had spent my entire eighteenth year writing letters to every resident of Munique. I love every one of them. I was weeks out from my birthday and still finishing the letters when Dayne appeared in my room. He, of course, didn't explain before... what do they call it? Flexing? Before flexing us into a small room built beneath one of our many great lakes." Gaia sighed and squeezed my hand. "I am sure my friends found my notes and felt deep sorrow. When the curse befell them, I know they rejoiced that I was alive, even if they did not know where I was."

The curses. I had forgotten. "What was Munique cursed with?" I asked Gaia.

"Infertility," she said. "Of both land and womb." She bowed her head. "All those with midterm offspring suffered greatly."

We all bowed our heads. Idris broke the silence. "I've been told that a centuries-old disease fell upon Hiraeth, starting with the king." She didn't hide the smile on her face.

I considered my time with Dayne in the Hiareth Fortress. "What of the mountain fortress to the east?"

Idris cocked her head. "It seems you know more of 'my kingdom' than I do."

I blushed, ashamed at my question. Thank the Goddess for Gaia, who asked, "You were within the fortress, then?" I nodded.

"I heard of the curse that befell Hiareth. I imagine the fortress would be safe with only three weeks to infect, assuming they're quarantined from the city walls." Gaia pondered.

"Sod em'," Idris cursed and stood. Gaia and I both watched her. "I want to show you around," she said, smoke and flame dancing in her eyes.

"Please," I mused, standing to follow her.

Idris had only meant to show me around their small space, yet we spent the next three hours going through the room. I learned that Gaia had a girlfriend in Munique that she hoped would move on. I learned that Idris would like to burn down this cave and all the 'Fae sodheads' within it.

66

I was wholly at peace with the two of them before I realized we hadn't spoken of the future–our future. Idris was putting away some papers she had burned the edges of as a gift to Gaia, who loved to paint with berries and ash.

"Are you going to Olvidare with the group?" I asked, unsure of how else to bring it up.

Nothing seemed to break Gaia's calm composure, so she replied, "Do *you* plan to go to Olvidare, child?"

Somehow, it was comforting to hear Gaia speaking to me as if she was generations older than me. "I... I don't know... I don't think so." I looked between the two.

Idris tossed her petite body onto the couch, unfazed by the question. "We were waiting for you," Idris started. "But we have spoken on the matter," She shot a heated glance toward Gaia. I got the feeling the two didn't agree.

"It doesn't seem like the choice is ours to make."

"Like hells, it's not." Idris shot back.

I looked between the two, hoping not to be involved in the argument. Idris's hair grew darker as she became more upset at the topic. I thought she might begin smoldering if the issue became more heated.

Gaia turned to me, "I have not met King Theon of Olvidare but have heard a great deal of him..." I chewed on my cheek, anticipating poor news based on Gaia's hesitant tone. "I have it on good authority that King Theon does not stop until he gets what he desires." Her eyes danced with challenge.

"And he desires us," I looked between Gaia and Idris blankly. Idris rolled her eyes, but her smoldering hair returned to its usual brunette color. "Let him try," Idris hissed.

"Idris." Gaia warned calmly, motherly, "Would you prefer to run your whole life avoiding the king?"

The question was loud—deafening. It rang true for the Goddess as well. Would she seek us, too? Would we spend our lives hiding from King Theon *and* the Goddess? My stomach clenched into a tight knot.

"Then we go," I used a strong voice, both demi-Fae's attention snapping back to me. We would deal with the king... together.

"We go," Gaia repeated, pinning Idris with pointed yet endearing eyes. They had only known each other three weeks, but their loyalty already ran so deep. I felt a prick of jealousy at their time together without me. Idris rolled her eyes, annoyed at us both before changing the topic.

"Shall we go down for lunch?"She tossed her hair slightly. I wanted to talk about Aeryn... about how his human kingdom would be the only one without a curse. We had time, though, so I answered, "Sure."

The three of us wandered out of the room and to the bottom of the stairs in just a few minutes. I took some time looking around the common space, as I was rushed through it when I arrived here just last night. The vaulted ceiling went so high I couldn't see the top before disappearing. I thought about how I would need to find Dayne whenever I wanted to go up or down and considered asking to move rooms again.

Everyone around us was drunk and jolly. Idris seemed to think they were all drunken buffoons; she wasn't wrong. At the back of the space was a long counter filled with food. Behind it was a kitchen where four females were scrubbing the dishes, which I assumed were used to prepare the lunch. Many of the males and females watched us. Some went as far as whistling in delight as we walked past. It made me wonder why we got so much attention, but I settled on the reason being that we were new guests to the group. A particularly burly male sent an invisible kiss to Gaia. Idris sent a gush of heat his way in a warning. It seemed to do the trick as he suddenly found his goblet of red wine and turned from us.

I scanned the room and spotted Dayne sitting at a long table amongst several males and females. His eyes lit up as I watched him from across the room. He had already spotted me. He waved me over to him, but I just shook my head. He looked disappointed but shrugged and returned to conversing with the table. He was sitting across from the foxy-face red-haired female I remembered picking out from the crowd yesterday. She wore a crimson shirt with a sweeping curved neckline, making her hair look even more red.

"Selene," Gaia called from a few feet away. Idris was nearly sprinting for the food counter. I jogged to catch up with them. We filled our plates with too much food and found a table to sit at. Gaia and Idris sat on the same side, across from me. Idris, of course, warned all the males around us that if they got too close to her, she would, and I quote, 'burn them to their bones, and then burn their bones to dust.'

I sat facing Dayne's back, but it didn't stop him from checking over his shoulder every five minutes. Eventually, I caught his eye and mouthed, 'Stop looking at me.' he mouthed back, 'Hells no, princess.' I just rolled my eyes, tucking my wringing hands into my lap. Did he watch me because he thought I was flighty and unpredictable? Perhaps I was.

"Do you two come down for all your meals?" I asked Gaia and Idris.

"We don't have a pretty prince to bring us food to our room," Idris said with a bite.

I laughed, appreciating her honesty.

Gaia shoved her with an elbow. "We do. We stay mostly secluded the rest of the time, so it's nice getting out of the room."

"How do you spend most of your days?" I asked, scanning around us.

Gaia answered. "We go on walks or nap. Sometimes, we will find a game to play or get drunk off of their Faerie wine." Idris giggled at that. My cheeks heated at the jealousy that pricked there. I wished I could have experienced those moments with them.

"I'd like to learn to fight," I said. "Do you think they'd teach me?" I inclined my chin to the males brawling in the grass just outside the lip of the cave.

Idris laughed. "I'm sure they would, but the real question is, do you really want to learn from those oafs?" She pointed to the males, who were now spanking each other on the rear.

"Good point." I sighed but felt the disappointment swell within. "Hey, I'll be right back," I got up to return my plate to the kitchen. As I swung my leg from the bench, the two fell into easy chatter.

It was somewhat unnerving walking around the common space alone. I suddenly felt incredibly self-conscious, wishing I had asked Gaia or Idris to accompany me. I considered the look Idris would have given me if I had and shivered. Dayne was right; I loved them both. I felt like they were the friends—the family that I was always meant to have.

I was scraping my plate into the garbage when a 'boo' sounded only inches from my ear. I jumped nearly a foot in the air and whipped around to Dayne, who was already reaching out to steady me.

"Shit, sorry," he said while rubbing the back of his neck.

"Can you stop staring at me?" I tapped my foot in annoyance.

"Can you stop staring at me?" He countered with a coy smile. "How else would you know I'm staring at you if you weren't staring at me?"

I rolled my eyes, taking my time to do so.

"Will you sit with me for dinner tonight?" His eyes sparkled in tune with his question.

I swallowed the hope that I could eat in my room one more night. Still, after experiencing Idris mocking me for it, I forced myself to say, "I suppose I can make an appearance." I still wondered why he cared to ask me or why he cared if I liked him or not.

Dayne beamed at that. "You know, we take dinner very seriously around here." I raised an eyebrow.

"Males in their best trousers, and the ladies can't wear pants."

"So you're telling me, not only do I have to leave my room for dinner, I have to come down in my black lace panties?"

I wasn't surprised when Dayne blushed.

"Ah, so you picked black, then?" He asked eagerly, his eyes dipping to my neckline for only a moment.

I ignored his comment, "So what do I wear?" My mind skipped to the red-haired female clad in the pretty velvet dress.

"I'll leave you some options." He smirked.

"You do realize I have to come find you *every* time I want to go up to that damned room?"

"I'm easy to find," he countered. "I'll look forward to bringing you to my room later, princess."

"Creep," I shoved past him to head back to Gaia and Idris. I could feel his lingering gaze watching me the whole way back.

With only a few sly comments from Idris, we fell back into conversation easily. We sat and talked for an hour before Gaia wanted to nap, Idris following after her loyally. I wondered if I would always feel slightly singled out in this trio. I shook the thought; even if I did, I wouldn't care. I had *friends*.

I waved the pair off at the foot of the stairs and sighed, looking around the common room. Everyone was so happy; a massive culture shift coming from the quiet and depressing Avalon to this barnyard.

I began looking around for Dayne so that he could bring me back to my room. I spotted him talking to the red-haired female; he leaned against the food counter, popping miniature desserts into his mouth as they spoke. She kept her hand on his bicep, occasionally squeezing it when they laughed. I didn't know how it hadn't crossed my mind sooner, but I wondered if that was Dayne's romantic partner or... what was the word the Fae used? Mate. I watched them closer now, trying to decide. I considered walking over to be introduced; it would be the easiest way to learn. When I felt myself shrinking from the inter-action, I forced myself to walk over and say hello.

I stood tall, forcing a straight back as I walked up to the two, keeping a neutral face as I approached.

"Selene," Dayne said to me, prompting the red-haired beauty to turn and look at me. She smiled and dropped her hand from Dayne's arm, allowing me to fill the space between them. She was sickeningly stunning, with her sharp, pointed features peppered with freckles the same shade as her cherry-red hair.

"This is Mairda. She organizes all of the military affairs for Olvidare," Dayne told me. Mairda's steely glance toward Dayne didn't go unnoticed by me.

"It's great to meet you, Mairda," I said, extending my hand. Mairda looked down at my hand, a quiet, mocking laugh escaping her lips.

"We don't shake hands here," Dayne said to me, a half grimace on his face. I could feel the blush bursting into my cheeks. I tamed it as much as possible, cooling it off slowly with the ice within me. I dropped my hand to my side. "Well, it's still great to meet you."

I shrugged and turned to Dayne. "I need to go up."

"I'll be right back," Dayne said to Mairda, which annoyed me. He grabbed me around my arm and flexed us up to the room. I considered making a joke but decided against it.

"Do you need anything else?" he asked, seeming impatient to return to his conversation with Mairda.

"I'm fine," I huffed.

"Alright, I'll send some dresses and see you for dinner?" He was hurrying through his words.

I realized that meant I would be stuck up here until he came to get me later, but I didn't have the energy to mention it. The second I nodded to him, he was gone. I walked around the room, wanting to nap but not entirely wanting to wake up groggy and annoyed before dinner. I caught a glimpse of myself in the mirror and realized I needed a bath. I walked to the washroom and ran a hand along the gleaming porcelain tub. I shook the memory of myself doubled over, vomiting into it. It now glistened; someone had been here to clean it while I blindly wept in the other room. I turned the golden knobs slightly, and warm water began rushing into the tub. I undressed slowly as the tub filled.

I allowed myself a moment before the mirror, taking in my thin and frail body. I pressed firm fingers against my arms and legs, feeling the lack of muscle. There was a chance the three of us would die in Olvidare, but with this lack of strength and absence of training... it was inevitable we'd die on our own in the unfamiliar Fae lands. Where would we go anyway? If we went to Olvidare, Dayne would keep us safe... right? I sighed and turned from the mirror to slip into the warm water. I rested my eyes and thought of absolutely nothing. It was just me and this heavenly-smelling citrus and cinnamon soap. I breathed in deeply and then let out a long breath. For the first time in my eighteen years, I felt not alone, even sitting in a room by myself.

Chapter Ten

Selene

DAYNE SAUNTERED INTO THE ROOM, WEARING A PLAIN WHITE button-up shirt revealing part of his chest and a pair of creased black pants. I couldn't help but blush. Kidnapper or not, he wasn't hard on the eyes. He studied me longer than I was comfortable with, "I hoped you'd pick that one."

"It was a hard choice, "I shrugged. "You look nice."

"I'm very nice." He grinned.

He swayed as he took a small step toward me. "Sir, I need to know how much you've had to drink." I joked, but there was a tinge of curiosity in my voice. His eyes held a glazing sheen to them that told me he had spent a good while drinking. I was proud of him, even if only a little, for not being more brazen about my dress choice. I glanced down at the dress I wore. It had a high neckline and thin straps, but the back of the dress was where the beauty lay. It plunged low, so low that if it were an inch deeper, my backside would be exposed. The lilac fabric was loose and draping. It swung against my back and ribcage as I moved. It was the most exquisite dress I have ever had the chance to put on my body.

"Only two drinks." He winked.

"Two behemoth glasses?"

"Two ultra-behemoth glasses," he grinned crookedly. "So, are we going down or what?" He extended his hand.

"Only if you behave," I took a half step toward him. I was in a particularly exquisite mood after soaking in those delectable oils.

"Always," he took several striding steps toward me and started to reach for my waist. I extended my arm instead, remembering how he had flexed me when that foxy-faced Mairda was around. He raised a brow.

"It seems safe enough to do it this way," I kept my face neutral but felt a flash of annoyance bubble inside.

"Fair enough." He grumbled, looping an arm through mine to flex us to the base of the stairs.

The common room was full of commotion, as usual, bustling with live music from a joyous fiddler. I couldn't help but smile as I watched the male jump, clicking his heels together, all while keeping perfect tempo with his jaunty tune. I sniffed the air. The whole room was filled with decadent smells from whatever they were cooking. I struggled to find anyone without wine in their hand. Many drank and danced, seemingly not caring that their wine sloshed on the floor around them. I scanned the empty tables, noting that everyone, and I mean *everyone*, was up moving around and mingling with others.

"So is it that the more hours tick by, the more drunk people get? I said, not really asking.

"You catch on quick, princess." He winked at me, "Want a drink?"

I eyed him, taking in the intensity of his stare, the way he kept every shred of his attention on me. I swallowed the curiosity, "I suppose better late than never."

We walked over to the large table where the seemingly constant supply of Faerie wine was kept. Dayne filled a glass three-quarters full for me, which was plenty considering the size of the glass goblet. He bent over and whispered in my ear. "I've actually had four ultra-behemoth glasses."

"It's a miracle you're behaving yourself," I said as he poured himself a fifth glass. "You've got to at least make it through dinner, Dayne." My gaze turned pointed as I looked between his relaxed face and the brown barrel he emptied further into his goblet.

"Are you worried about me, princess?"

"No," I was quick to answer, "I'm worried about me. You're my ride up there, you know." I glanced upward to his room that lay far above our heads.

He waved a hand at my comment and placed it on my bare back to lead me to an empty table. The feeling of his rough palm on such a tender part of me had me shrinking in on myself as we walked. I was hardly used to having eyes on me... so having a hand in that spot was... unfamiliar territory to my senses.

"It's nice to see you in something like that," Dayne plopped beside me at the table. I just rolled my eyes at him.

"No, I mean it. You look..." he searched for a word, "radiant."

Goddess.

That hand on my back... those lingering eyes, and now this? I didn't know how to respond. I wanted to hide my face, scared that it showed just how naive I was.

Radiant.

My stomach clenched, sparking with nerves. "Thanks," I looked to the ground, unsure how to respond to such words. My eyes eventually fell on two males brawling inside the common space on what was supposed to be the dance floor. I looked around, taking in everyone in the room. Despite the odd sight of it, I was impressed by how well-dressed everyone was... All these beautiful Fae tucked away in a humble rocky cave.

My eyes fell back upon the brawling males. "Can they teach me to fight?" I tipped my head toward the brawl.

He followed my gaze and burst into hearty laughter. "What, you want to learn how to bar fight?"

"No." I was annoyed now. "I want to be able to defend myself if... I don't know... if I ever need to."

"Plan on going somewhere?" His voice had an edge to it.

"I just think I should be able to protect myself if I need to." I scowled. "Never mind."

"I can teach you, it's better than those two buffoons."

"Who taught the buffoons?" I asked, now turning to face Dayne.

"Well... me," he said, realizing the all too easy joke I could make about his training abilities. "I can show you the basics."

"Alright." I turned to stare at the table before us, not really expecting he would actually show me anything about fighting.

"I'll grab us some food. Be right back," He said before flexing himself to the front of the line at the food counter. I shook my head at the sudden way he vanished. He hovered over the options, hesitating. A second later, small portions of what looked like every item at the counter appeared before me. I glanced back over to him; he was waiting for my approval. I gave him a thumbs up. At that, he proceeded to make his plate of food. He hurried back over, apparently deciding the best time to be slow was after placing food in front of me without a fork.

"Thank you," I said as he handed me silverware and slipped into place beside me. Others filtered into the tables around us as we wordlessly ate, taking in the boisterous laughter and immaculate fiddling tunes that wafted through the space.

"Will you dance with me later?" Dayne broke our silence through a bite of roasted carrots. His tone was playful and unserious.

"Absolutely not."

He nudged the wine my way. "I've learned that I'm a much better dancer when wine is involved."

I reached for the glass and took a huge gulp but maintained that I would not be dancing tonight.

"Drunk bastard," Dayne said. I looked at him, confused, until he started counting to five. "That's two drinks for you." He nudged my arm.

"*You* are the drunk bastard, using my own game against me." He just shrugged and started scanning the room again.

We played the game until I finished my wine, and Dayne had already gone up for another and drank part of that one. Our table was now entirely filled with others, but everyone kept a slight distance from us. The weight of Dayne's title became excruciatingly heavier as I noticed more nuances from those near us. I stared into my empty glass, shoving the heavy thoughts from my mind. I found it easy to do so as the wine began swirling throughout me.

I hadn't planned on getting drunk, but something about the atmosphere here begged me to keep going. I wasn't sure if I felt safe or if I simply wanted—needed to have a break from life. "Another one," I shoved my glass at Dayne.

"Interesting, interesting," he slurred. "I'm to take commands from you now?" His grin was utterly devilish, but the grittiness in his voice had me wondering if there was some truth behind those words. Perhaps the male was a little too used to taking orders from his father.

My head was soaring above the clouds, so the somber thought drifted away as fast as it came on. I stuck my tongue out at him and swung my leg from the bench to go fill my glass. When I was halfway to the barrels of wine, I looked back to again stick my tongue out at him. His eyes darted up from the arch of my exposed back the moment he realized I had turned. A flash of heat bubbled within me, not from the wine... but from those eyes. I turned back to the barrels, hoping he couldn't read my face at that moment. I filled my goblet, and by the time I turned around to walk back, Mairda was speaking with Dayne. She leaned over the table so that even from here, I could see her generous cleavage. She wore a tight red dress cut in a deep V at the front. Her beauty left even me at a loss for words. Dayne wasn't *with* her... was he? He wouldn't look at me the way he did if... I bit my tongue, not allowing the thought to continue. I strolled toward them leisurely, hoping they'd finish their conversation by the time I made it over. Mairda eyed me first, glancing up from Dayne to me. Her peachy, lush lips spread into a smile as I returned to my spot beside Dayne.

"Anyway, if you could just make sure you have the weapons report for me tomorrow, that would be just perfect, darling," Mairda sang before patting his hand. "I'll see you soon," she glanced between the two of us, but my eyes were on her fingers. Her fingertips traced the top of his knuckles in an almost loving way. My stomach curled, but I forced myself to give the female a curt nod goodbye.

Dayne turned to me, taking another swig of his wine. "You didn't fill it much," he raised a brow, glancing at my glass.

Oh, Goddess. I *had* filled it much. It was another three-quarters full glass that I must've awkwardly drank while slowly making my way back to the table. Shit. My pulse rose, the wine using my quickening heart rate to pump through me angrily.

"I didn't think I needed much more," I said, trying to sound unbothered, yet it came out as messy and slurred.

Eevy A.

"Someone's drunk." Dayne jabbed me in the ribs with a finger. I swatted him away but missed his hand.

"Maybe I should take that one from you." He began pulling my drink toward him with a playful smile.

I snatched my drink back, making it slosh slightly on the table. I covered my face with both hands, not out of embarrassment, but overwhelmed at the spinning feeling within my head. Every emotion swarmed me as the wine lifted my head higher and higher, forcing anger, sadness, and every other feeling to weigh down on me. I couldn't recover from the wine I had just drank, so I leaned over the table and kept my face entirely concealed as the unusually intense feeling consumed me.

Dayne leaned into me, pressing his cheek to mine. "Are you okay?" he whispered. I felt his lips brush against my cheek as he spoke. The action had me recoiling, especially with the knowledge that *everyone* in this room kept a portion of their attention on him—on us both.

I shook my head, starting to feel tears well in my eyes.

What the *hells*.

Why was I crying? My head was floating and spinning as the tears poured down my cheeks. I tried to call on my magic—to force them to stop from spilling out, but nothing helped. I dropped my hands from my face for only a moment to wipe away some of the tears, still trying to conceal my face from Dayne. He shifted back, and the feeling of fleeting freefall came over me the second he saw the tears.

I was suddenly standing. I shoved both of my palms against his chest hard, forcing him away from me. I knew by the sensation he had flexed us. I blinked and took in the new location. He had flexed us up to his room.

"What's wrong?" he asked with concern sparking in his eyes. He stood towering over me but did not touch me.

"I don't know," my voice was pinched and nearly wailing. I stood awkwardly, covering my face. I had no idea why I couldn't stop this overwhelming sensation of crying. My chest rose and fell in quick, shallow breaths. My mind danced, a weightless thing within my skull, but my body... it felt like lead. I wanted to sleep it off—go for a swim—do anything to get away from this feeling consuming me.

78

Dayne shifted awkwardly before me until my tears turned into full-blown sobs. I couldn't stop the crescendoing sorrow. I doubled over, my lungs pinching tight and gasping for air. My head was flying, sending my thoughts tumbling around in my brain. The tears and sobs became violent as my entire body began to shake. I hardly had the ability to feel embarrassed that Dayne was witnessing all of this. I clutched my chest as if I could reach in and pull out whatever was making me feel so much dread—so much rage, and sorrow and grief.

One moment, I was bent over, everything consuming me, and the next, Dayne was pulling me to the floor. He lowered himself onto the cold stone floor, back resting against the foot of his bed. He shifted my trembling, rigid self into a half-lying position between his legs, face buried in his torso. I didn't know how long I sobbed into him, but by the time the sobbing finally turned to only tears, the tears finally drying, his shirt had several wet blotches adorning it.

I breathed, hot and heavy, into his abdomen, finally feeling the prick of embarrassment set in. Dayne pushed the hair from my face, struggling to shift some strands that adhered to my cheek from my tears. I kept my eyes squeezed shut, wholly embarrassed by all of this. I felt terrible for pulling a drunk Dayne from the boisterous common space below. My head was still buzzing and spinning from the drinks, but my once-leaden body felt... a bit better.

"Are you okay?" he asked. I nodded quickly, feeling the wetness on his shirt beneath my cheek. He held me firmly against him, his stomach rising in easy, deep breaths.

"I promised myself I wouldn't cry anymore... and Idris wouldn't let me cry while she told me about her life in Hiareth." My voice cracked when I spoke Idris's name.

"You do realize you have an affinity for water, right?" Dayne said, a chuckle in his voice.

I finally opened my eyes and shifted to peer up at him. I wasn't sure what his words meant. His face was soft as he looked down at me, green eyes meeting mine.

"When Fae suppress their magic, especially when they have to try extraordinarily hard to suppress it, it tends to find its way out, one way or another. It is part of you, you know?"

"My tears aren't my magic," I snapped.

He shrugged. "It makes sense to me why that would happen, especially after a few drinks," he added with a wink as if he was trying to lighten the mood. It only made me feel worse for tearing him from the party that roared below us. "How about no more suppressing our tears... I can speak with Idris if—"

"No. It's fine." I said, still embarrassed and still very much sprawled on the floor between Dayne's legs.

"Thank you," I said, realizing what he had done for me without hesitation. "You can go back to the party if you want."

"I want to be here," he spoke a little too quickly.

His words made my breathing stutter. My brain, heart, and body all reacted differently to those words. My body stiffened from where I lay between his legs, yet my mouth—my mind loosened. He had fractured it just the tiniest bit with those words. The wine coursed through my veins, fueling my thoughts. I wanted him here, too. I wanted... Oh, Goddess, what did I want? I became all too aware of my body against his. The way my cheek leaned against his hardened abdomen. While his words fractured a barrier, a question remained in my mind. I thought of Mairda... Of the ignorance I bore. I knew nothing of this male... his life back home... the foxy-faced female who allowed her fingers to linger on his skin. The too-heavy feeling of jealousy pulsed through me, fracturing that barrier I put up with Dayne even further. I didn't want to be ignorant. My lips parted. I found my voice, fueled heavily by not only the Faerie wine, but that fracturing barrier... by those simple words he just spoke.

I want to be here.

"Who is Mairda?" The words came tumbling out as that barrier I built began to crumble.

A long, heavy silence hung between us before Dayne spoke, "You... know who she is?"

"No. *Who* is she?" I asked again, emphasizing the who. I held my breath for his response, finding it impossible to look him in the eye.

"Ahhh." he took a deep breath, forcing my head to rise in sync with it, "You mean, who is she *to me*?" I was thankful for my positioning against him as a wave of sickeningly sharp embarrassment pricked my insides.

Thank the Goddess he couldn't see all of my face right now.

Dayne picked at another strand of hair on my face, crusted to my cheek from dried tears. "She's—"

"An old friend?" I interrupted. I wanted to know more, but I couldn't stand the near-painful humiliation that burst within me. I shifted now to watch his face.

"Yes..." he hesitated, eyes relaxing as if he was trying to soften the mood.

"Is there..." I hesitated for the right words.

Dayne didn't need them. "No. There's no one."

"Okay." I breathed out a shaky breath, feeling relieved he didn't make me ask it. I wasn't all too sure why I needed to know, but I did. I removed my face from his abdomen and shifted into a sitting position, still between his legs. Dayne scooted back from me and hovered near the foot of his bed before sitting on the edge of it. The covers were still strewn from the night before.

"How are you feeling," he asked me with an eyebrow raised.

I shifted from where I sat on the floor before him. "Great."

Dayne snorted, but I understood why.

I wasn't lying. I did feel good, better than good. In that short time, my head was back to the happy, floating feeling I had before. Maybe he had been right about the magic. Maybe having let all of *that* out left nothing but that wine to fill me with flutters.

"Do you want to go back down or... Do you want me to help you into bed?" He cocked his head at me, pressing his lips into a firm line.

I couldn't help but drop my eyes to his lips.

I want to be here.

I wanted him to repeat it. I wanted to hear it again. I flicked my gaze from his lips to his eyes, breath catching in my throat. He looked cautious, curious even, but those deep green eyes that were set on me drove my words.

"No," I said, wholly unable to look away from him. If it wasn't his eyes forcing me to speak, it was the floating, dancing state of my intoxicated mind, "the bath, though..." I held my breath, not entirely sure that those words had come out of me. The firm line of his lips faltered.

"You want me to help you... into the bath?" The muscles in his neck flexed.

"I do." I rose to my feet, never breaking eye contact with him. I ignored my faint, spinning thoughts of logic. It wouldn't win out against the feeling brewing inside of me. A feeling that left me unsatiated every damned time. A feeling I rarely felt, one that meant heartbreak, as I was never able to act on it. A feeling that was never reciprocated—never acted on. Desire. Dayne's face contorted from confusion into something I couldn't quite interpret.

"Selene," his tone was warning, that much was clear.

I walked toward him, allowing the feeling in my head to drive my every action. Every step forward felt almost like an out-of-body experience. I leaned into it as if it were a play... As if I was acting out one of my many hopeless dreams from my time in Avalon. I flicked one of my dress's straps off of my shoulder. The left side of my dress sagged only slightly.

Dayne's eyes didn't leave mine. "Stop," he said.

"Why?" An all too familiar pit began forming in my stomach.

"You're drunk. I'm drunk. I uh—"

"Don't think it's a good idea?" I asked, still standing before him, one strap hanging off my shoulder. Heat bloomed in both my body and cheeks.

"It's not a good idea... maybe I should go," He shifted from where he sat on the foot of the bed.

I crossed my arms, feeling the pit within me widen at the all-too-familiar feeling of rejection. I felt far too sober to continue standing before him, the blush burning throughout my face. I pulled the strap back onto my shoulder with an aggressive flick of my wrist. Dayne's eyes widened, but he didn't shift from where he sat on the bed. I turned from him then and stomped into the washroom, slamming the door behind me. I was so stupid.

What the hells, Selene?

I began furiously ripping out the hundreds of pins I had meticulously set throughout my hair, allowing them to fall wherever they fell. Some bounced off the tops of my feet as I threw them aimlessly onto the cold stone floor.

Dayne knocked on the door. "Can I come in?"

"No," I snapped, pulling the pins out more furiously than before. I didn't care that I ripped several strands of hair out with every motion.

I heard the door crack open anyway. I glanced at him through the mirror. His eyes roamed the pins all over the stone floor.

"No one," I said, unsure if my voice shook from anger or shame. "No one ever wants me. I will always be unwanted, no matter who it is or what I do. I am never enough." I threw more pins onto the ground. This was beyond desire... beyond friendship. It was pathetic, really, how intensely I craved connection. "Even now, I don't have an *expiration date*, and I'm still not wanted." I felt the familiar feeling of tears pricking my senses.

Dayne walked over to me and grabbed both of my wrists to keep me from ripping more pins out. I fought him hard, even flaring ice to my wrists. He held them firmly and stared at me. His face remained soft but concerned.

"Just go. I'm already going to have to deal with this—with you in the morning," I stopped fighting his grip on my wrists and slumped.

"I need you to know, it's not that I don't want to..." he trailed off, shifting his weight between his feet. "Selene, have you ever kissed anyone?"

His question took me by surprise. The shame, the pitifulness of all of this, was overwhelming. I hadn't kissed anyone. People in Avalon barely wanted to hold a conversation with me, let alone kiss me.

"I don't want to answer that," I mumbled, keeping my eyes set on anything but him.

"I'm not shaming you," He shook his head, relaxing his tight grip on my wrists. "I'm actually asking."

I looked up at him, holding his gaze for only a moment.

"Well then, no," I snapped my wrists away from his loosened grasp.

"How drunk are you right now?" he asked, rubbing the back of his neck with a hand.

"Not." I spat at him. I turned back to the mirror and picked at another pin in my hair.

"Swear it?"

I snorted a puff of air out my nose, pretending to be focused on the pins in my hair.

I flinched at the feeling of Dayne's hand suddenly pressing against the bare arch of my back. I went rigid and still at the touch, eyes finding him through the mirror. We stood like this for many moments, his hand on the arch of my back, our eyes locked on each other through the mirror. I found it hard to breathe—hard to look at him, But it was even more challenging to look away. He tugged me towards him gently, forcing me to shift. I allowed it—allowed him to rotate my body to face him. Our eyes remained set on the other as his hand gently stoked up and down my back. I knew I was shivering beneath his touch, but it hardly registered in my mind. His other arm shifted at his side as he brought it up to my face, gripping his long fingers around the base of my jaw. My heart stuttered a beat beneath the touch—beneath the moment itself. What was he doing? Was he... I suddenly became self-conscious about how I stood... How I let my arms hang limply at my sides. I tried to refocus on the fingers trailing up and down my spine or the hand gripping my jaw, but I couldn't. This was too new, and I was far too nervous. It took everything within me to keep from collapsing. Dayne's neutral lips quirked into a slight smile, sending embers throughout my core.

"I'm waiting for you, princess," he spoke. I realized he was trying to kiss me, or he wanted me to kiss him. Between the nearness of him and the finger he trailed up my spine, my mind was a heaping wet mess. I willed ice to my mind in hopes that it would ground me. I stepped into him, hesitating again on hand placement. I decided to put them both flat against his chest. He took a clumsy, ragged breath beneath my palms. I rose on my toes, closing the distance between his face and mine. He pulled my body tightly against him. Goddess, the feeling of our chests against each other...

"Now?" I asked, and he huffed a quick laugh.

He wrapped the hand on my back around my waist further and lifted me off my feet to be at eye level with him. His other hand remained cupping my jaw, his thumb stroking my cheek. I wrapped my arms around his neck and leaned my face in slowly. If there were warning bells in my mind, their ringing was entirely masked by desire. I needed this. I needed to know what it felt to have lips against mine. Our mouths had only a fraction of space between them for a moment. I knew he would wait for me to close the distance. He would give that subtle act to me. I couldn't help but smile as I pushed to close the distance. Our lips finally met in a lush, inviting moment. He was warm and gentle but kissed me deeply. His tongue slid across my teeth momentarily, and I opened from him. Our tongues mingled for half a breath before he broke free, keeping me lifted against him. I couldn't help the loud, labored breaths that escaped me. We watched each other, mouths still only a fraction of a distance apart. My eyes flicked from his back to his mouth. I leaned back in slowly, parting my lips ever so slightly to connect with him. A heartbeat later, my feet connected with the stone floor as Dayne plopped me back into a standing position before him.

"One kiss?" I raised a brow, looking up at him. His jaw was clenched tight, but he wore a soft smile.

"One kiss," he gave me a shallow nod. I crossed my arms, pinning my brows together.

"Well, what is the point of that?" I huffed.

"Excuse me?" Dayne let out a pretend offended laugh, crossing his arms to mimic me.

"Stay with me," I stated, eyes glancing to where the bed was in the other room.

"Absolutely not." His tone bordered serious now.

I frowned at him and furrowed my brows even deeper.

"Yes, it's cute, but it's not going to work on me," he reached out to fix a piece of my hair that was half pinned and falling in my face.

"No more kissing," I said and mimicked, tracing an X over my heart in promise. "I don't want to be alone." It was the truth, yet we knew I would be more than welcome in Gaia and Idris's room. I held my breath for his answer, unsure why I needed this.

He sighed and took my face in his hands. "I don't want you to be alone. Thinking about your past... spending all that time alone..." He tightened his grip slightly so I'd meet his eyes. I looked up at him, his eyes glossy, if only slightly. He was so much more like me than I had realized.

He pulled me into his chest and wrapped his arms around me. I couldn't help but collapse into the male. He was still a stranger in many ways, yet he was my first friend. Dayne released from the embrace, steadying me with a hand. The glossiness in his eyes was gone, and only a grin remained on his face. "It was an honor to kiss you, princess," he bowed theatrically. "'I'd uh... like to find myself doing it again sometime."

Heat flashed within my core. "Not too bad for my first time?" I nudged his foot with mine.

"Not too bad," Dayne agreed, keeping his feverish eyes locked on mine.

Dayne left the washroom to change his clothes as I picked the remaining pins from my hair. My golden white locks fell in beautiful silken ribbons around me. A pale blue sleep dress appeared on the stone counter before me. It was entirely sheer, with white lace trimming the edges. I choked on a laugh, but the dress was suddenly gone, replaced by one of Dayne's massive long-sleeve shirts. I shimmied off my dress and slipped the long-sleeved shirt over my head. The sleeves fell inches past my fingertips, and the bottom of the shirt at mid-thigh.

"Figured that one was more comfortable," Dayne spoke from the doorway. He was now *entirely* shirtless, with black undershorts that fell a couple of inches above his knees. This was the second time that I found myself with him shirtless. I allowed myself to actually take in his body this time. He had a slight tan, which, next to me, looked more like a deep tan. His broad shoulders connected to those large arms that he had just wrapped around me. His chest was moving up and down with quick breaths beneath my lingering eyes. His torso was toned as it led to the muscled V shape that disappeared into his undershorts below. I looked back up to meet his eyes, which were still trailing back up my body.

"Do you have anything under that?" he growled, now looking me in the eyes. His sweet, evergreen eyes shone with delight yet seemed to remain cautious.

A flare of heat bubbled within me as his shining eyes forced my playful mood. With a flick of my hand, my panties slid down my legs to the floor beneath me. "No," I said, pushing past him into the bedroom, leaving my undergarment on the washroom floor. Dayne remained wide-eyed, staring at the panties I had left on the floor. I climbed into bed, scooting until I reached the exact middle of it. Dayne finally peeled himself away from the doorway and stood before me at the foot of the bed.

"I'm going to need you to scoot over, princess," his eyes were completely and utterly wild upon me.

My eyes dipped to the slight bulge in his undershorts, now more accentuated after my teasing. I shifted a half inch to my left and patted the bed next to me on my right. I was thoroughly giddy right now. I had never known what it felt like to have a friend until these past few nights. Sleeping was one of the loneliest times for me in Avalon. While my room was magnificent, it likely didn't compare to having a warm body beside you. Dayne hesitated as if he was still contemplating climbing into the bed with me.

"No kissing," he reminded me as he strode over to the side I had beckoned him. He lifted the edge of the covers, revealing my right side slightly. My shirt was now hiked up, nearly exposing me. Dayne sucked in one of the sharpest breaths I'd ever heard and climbed into bed beside me. We laid like this for a moment, him on his back with his hands interlaced atop his chest, me on my back looking over at him. My head still danced amongst the clouds, but I could feel it coming down from its temporary high. My actions were, no doubt, a result of that. I wondered how I would feel tomorrow... but I let the thought slip from my mind. I turned my body in his direction, now propped up on my side. I wriggled closer to him until the front of my body collided with his side. My mind spun with emotions and awe that I had almost never got to experience these feelings. I had gone eighteen years with various love interests who always laughed in my face when I built the nerve to talk to them. I wrapped my arms around Dayne's bicep and rested my chin on his shoulder. My heavy breathing caressed his ear as I nuzzled into him further. I felt him shiver, but he did not move otherwise.

"One more kiss," I begged in a whisper. He turned just enough to look at me pointedly. "I swear, just a kiss." I wouldn't know what... or even how to do anything else.

He shifted, now rolling onto his side to face me. He wrapped a hand around my waist and pulled me flush against him. I fought the heat, knowing that I would beg for more than a kiss if I didn't keep a leash on it. It was an unusual feeling, but I wanted to succumb to it. I rolled my left shoulder into him harshly, flipping him to his back, bodies still flush but mine now atop him. My heart rate rose, continuing to pump that wine-laced blood through every part of me.

"This is *not* a kiss," he growled in my ear with uneven breath.

I felt him beneath my body. My chest to his, the spot beneath his under-shorts that thrummed against me. My shirt had shifted above my waist, yet his

87

hands remained only as low as my lower back. Heat flushed through my cheeks and coiled in the spot below my abdomen. It was such a deep, burning sensation that I was almost taken aback by it. I began moving my hips in slow motions against him. He allowed it, I think, only because he seemed paralyzed. It confused me how stunned and hesitant he was to touch me. The hard part of him that I ground against told me enough about how he felt. I rotated against him again. He was three hundred years old and had shared a bed with many females. I shouldn't be any different... this shouldn't be any different. His eyes were wide and wild, hands only moving with the rotation of my hips. I started grinding against him harder and faster. I wanted to see his face better, so I rose above him, arms fully extended on either side of his head. I kept circling my hips against him, with added pressure in my new position.

"Selene," he said in a breathy voice as we met eyes. It was a warning. Raw instincts took over, my body reacting to the heat, moving me. I brought my hand to his throat and wrapped it around the base of his jaw. Dayne's eyes rolled into the back of his head for a moment. The next breath, he flipped us hard and fast, him now above me but no longer flush against me. I wriggled, bucking my hips forward in protest. His eyes were wild, sweat pricking his forehead. Our breathing, both unnatural, somehow seemed to sync up. He rotated his body off me and back to the bed beside me, flipping me to face him again. Now, face to face, he wrapped a hand in my hair and kissed me deeply. We stayed like this for minutes, our tongues tangling in each other, lips like fire and ice. Dayne broke free from my lips, trailing kisses down to my chin and cheek and beneath my jaw. He dragged his teeth against my neck and nipped slightly. Then, he twisted my hips. In an instant, I was facing away from him. He wrapped his arms around me as I nuzzled my back into his warm body. It was amazing how perfect I fit into the grooves of him.

"Sleep," Dayne grunted while unwrapping an arm from around me to trail a finger up my back into my hair. I shivered as I felt my skin grow hot at the touch. He twisted his hand into my hair and gently rubbed and massaged my head. I allowed the heat within to die down fully until I succumbed to Dayne's gentle touch—succumbing to the feeling of safety from having him at my back. I found myself drifting off as he continued to draw those delicate circles and lines against my skin.

Chapter Eleven

Selene

I WAS SMILING THE MOMENT I WOKE. HAVING SOMEONE... HAVING him next to me all night was... almost surreal. I carefully wriggled out from beneath Dayne's protective arm that lay draped over me. Even though he slumbered peacefully, my cheeks still flushed at the imprinted memory of his lips on mine.

I stretched, needing to roll away from Dayne's warmth. That heat that radiated from him made me think of the blistering sun in Avalon... Of always escaping its heat. My stomach churned. It was odd to think about Avalon... about how things were a mere week ago. Even more peculiar was the thought of having a future—my own path in life.

I glanced at Dayne, sleeping motionless next to me. My eyes shifted to his lips, a bubble of heat bursting at the sight of the soft, peachy hue of them. Goddess, I barely knew him... but the way he treated me, the way he spoke to me... I had never met anyone like that until coming to this ancient continent. He was more than a breath of fresh air. He was a gust of life, sweeping through the stagnant corridors of my being. A whisper of promise rode on his every breath. I thought back to the underground inn we visited after the scuttler attack and how he had kept a comforting wind around me the entire night. He had done that, even though he didn't know me. The thought had my chest tightening. To be so *nice* to a stranger... I'd never met that sort of kindness before. I had never known it could exist in a person—in a Fae. He still barely knew me, and I him, yet... I found myself smiling–shaking the urge to climb atop him and beg for another kiss.

I slipped out of bed, making sure Dayne didn't stir so I could take a quick bath. I braided my hair down the center of my back before walking back into the sleeping quarters of the room, Dayne still dozing. I rifled through the clothes options he had left for me, picking a simple white blouse with a brown bustier and tan pants for the day. I contemplated waking Dayne. I had nothing to do without him but couldn't bring myself to.

Instead, I cracked the door open and slipped out of the room. I leaned over the stone ledge, looking at the common space below. I hadn't seen it so quiet since I had arrived. It was early, but not that early. Perhaps the drunken nights were enough to keep them in bed into the late morning hours.

I slowly walked down the steps and allowed my hand to run against the smooth stone railing. I planned to descend towards Gaia and Idris's room, but I knew it would take me an hour to get there. I hoped they wouldn't be out for breakfast by the time I arrived. About fifteen minutes into my descent, I realized I should have woken Dayne. I continued anyway; it wasn't *that* bad. I passed by a few males on my journey down; some seemed hungover and angry, and others just gave me a nod and moved past. I went by about ten more rooms before a door swung open and a flash of red hair whipped out in front of me. The female nearly bumped into me at the suddenness of her arrival into the stairwell.

"Oh," she exclaimed, covering her mouth in surprise.

Mairda.

A flash of angry jealousy pricked my senses as I beheld the female who looked devastatingly beautiful, even in last night's red dress.

She's an old friend.

I ground my teeth together, refocusing on the female. Given her clothing, I doubted the door she came from was hers. Thankfully, I had no idea whose door it was, nor did I care.

"Selene," Mairda said with a smile. "How are you? Where's Dayne?"

I blinked at the two questions she had asked me. "Oh, I'm fine. He's still asleep; I figured I would venture out alone today." I eyed her and the beautiful freckles that spattered her face like paint. She eyed me back.

"Did he take his room back yet? I thought he would set you up with the other two girls..." Mairda trailed off.

"Umm, it was just a little crowded in there."

She frowned, not even caring to disguise it for something else.

"It's a little embarrassing bumping into you like this." She looked down at what she was still wearing, then back up at me.

"Oh, don't worry about it," I waved a casual hand at her. She shrugged and bid me a good day before heading up the stairs behind me. Thank Goddess.

I practically jogged the rest of the way down to Gaia and Idris's room. It didn't take me as long as I thought, but I was more than winded when I knocked on the door.

"Coming," Gaia's sweet, sing-songy voice chimed out. She opened the door. "Selene." She pulled me into their room by hand. Idris was sprawled out on the couch, sending small balls of fire into the air until they puffed out into balls of dissipating smoke. I took up an open spot in an ivory armchair, crinkling my nose at the smoke that filled my nostrils.

"I'd like to walk to the dock if you two want to join me?" I fidgeted in my chair, glancing between them. They seemed too happy sitting here idle—stagnant. Somehow, seeing that state of contentment left me yearning for *more*. More for myself, but more importantly, for them both... For us all.

"Of course," Gaia said, shooting Idris a pointed look.

"Yeah, sure, sounds fine," Idris said, glancing my way.

I tried to contain my excitement by looking around the room casually. "Well... would you like to go now?" I shifted in my seat.

Idris stood up and went to her room without a word. I sent a confused look at Gaia, who only shrugged back at me. Idris returned a few minutes later in different clothes; she wore black from head to toe. "Let's go, ice wench." She playfully shoved me and started walking out the door, myself and Gaia following closely behind.

The three of us managed to exit the cave conflict-free, but we seemed to gain a guest on the way to the dock. Gaia noticed the male following behind us from a distance. I did my best to ignore him, taking in the salt-kissed breeze that fluttered through the tall grass around us. The meadow was beautiful, particularly when the Onyx Sea came into view. The serenity of the lush green colliding with the angry waters echoed what my life had become. That scene— that chaos crashing into serenity, we were one and the same.

"Figures, we can't be trusted even down to the dock that's five sodding steps away," Idris hissed loud enough for our guest to hear. I glanced over my shoulder to watch him hang back a couple more paces. I shrugged. At least he seemed polite enough.

Once we arrived at the dock, we walked to the edge overlooking the Onyx Sea. The near-obsidian waves at the shore lapped against the dock in soothing patterns that reminded me of my mother. She used to tap her feet again and again, over and over, in this mesmerizing lyrical way. I shook the thoughts of her, and the home I found I did not miss, looking past the somber waters at the shore. Enormous waves built and crashed into each other, one after another, after another. I thought back to the day I had... well, what *had* I done? I hadn't allowed myself time to grasp the display of magic that day Dayne and I crossed the sea. It wasn't the magic that disturbed me but rather the look of shock on Dayne's face. Three hundred years of life, yet he still swam with concern at how I shattered those roaring waves.

"Show us something," Idris broke the silence but was looking at me. I stared at her for a moment, the salt-tinged wind nipping at my face. I looked back to the sea and understood precisely what she meant.

I lifted both hands, more for show than anything, and with a curl of my finger, I forced an enormous spritz of mist at all of us, sending Idris into a blinding rage. Gaia and I clutched our stomachs in laughter as Idris screamed some choice words directed at me. Our laughing eventually subsided, and I found myself curious about Gaia's magic.

"I'd love to see yours..." I trailed off, holding Gaia's sweet blue eyes in mine.

She nodded and walked from the dock to a small grassy patch of land. Idris and I followed closely behind. Gaia knelt on the grass, brushing it gently as if caressing every blade with her fingertips. She pressed her palms into the grass and began glowing a soft hue of gold. She remained in this position for many moments before removing her hands and whispering something inaudible. She pushed off the ground and took a few steps back. I kept my eyes locked on the grassy ground she had been touching. The ground shifted slightly. A branch punched its way through from the dirt. poking out slowly as if it were bashful. The grass parted ways as the singular branch thrust itself up and up, twisting and spinning toward the sky until it was an enormous, spindly ancient tree. A breeze shook its leaves, each rustle holding a story of its own. Idris and I gaped at it and at the Nature Princess striding forward to wrap each arm around the trunk of the tree in a gentle embrace. How Gaia of her.

"You can grow trees?" I asked, stepping forward.

"Not exactly," Gaia countered. "If given the time to speak, the land will tell you her story. The tree you see before you has been restored; it fell over two hundred years ago." She finished with a smile while admiring a leaf. The tree looked ancient and old, yet somehow, it glowed with restored health and life.

"That is amazing, Gaia." I reached out to run a finger along a branch. "How long will it stay?"

"Until Mother Planet claims her once again," she spoke with her eyes closed as if in prayer.

"Watch this," Idris said, not waiting to be asked for her display of magic.

Idris stood unwavering, her silhouette framed against the backdrop of the blue morning sky. Her eyes, pools of molten intensity, bore into the depths of my soul as she chewed on one of her pouty lips in concentration.

In a sudden, explosive burst, her ethereal form transformed into a writhing inferno, and the world around us erupted in a blazing crescendo. Flames roared and crackled, their scalding tongues reaching skyward in a torrent of crimson and gold. The sight was nothing short of awe-inspiring, an otherworldly spectacle.

The air grew thick with the acrid scent of singed earth and burning wood, a pungent reminder of the elemental power Idris commanded. It mingled with the unmistakable aroma of scorched grass, creating an almost intoxicating blend that hung in the atmosphere. It wasn't a delightful smell but one of rich, raw power.

Gaia and I instinctively stepped back, the ground's warmth still lingering beneath our feet, as Idris raised her hand with an elegant flourish.

With a wave, she sent an oversized fireball hurtling in our direction. The air hissed and crackled as the colossal orb blazed toward us, casting a frenetic light in every shade of crimson. Then, the fireball imploded in an instant, vanishing into a swirling ball of smoke mere inches from us, leaving behind a ghostly, lingering scent of charred embers. The stark contrast between the inferno's fury and the enigmatic wisps of dissipating smoke carved an indelible memory, an unforgettable moment etched in sight, smell, and sound, forever etching the power and enigma of Idris into our souls.

Gaia clapped enthusiastically as Idris bowed deeply at her display of magic.

"We should come here every morning," I said abruptly to the two powerful demi-Fae before me. I somehow knew there was something richer—rawer swimming within each of us. Everything in me yearned to grasp onto that power and yank. "We should show each other something new each day, maybe learn from each other or—"

Idris interrupted me, "I'm in." She was beaming still from her fireball. She may have surprised herself, even. I was beaming, too, at these two beautiful friends of mine.

"Every morning until Olvidare?" I asked not in question but in promise.

"Every day," both Gaia and Idris repeated.

We had skipped breakfast that morning to go to the dock. By the time we returned to the mossy cave entrance, it exploded with smells of roast beef and potatoes. We indulged in both lively conversation and mirthful laughter as we filled out plates. The weather was particularly lovely today, so we decided to settle down with our plates of food just outside the lip of the cave entrance beneath the lush canopy of ivy. Once we were stuffed full of roast beef, carrots, and potatoes, I offered to take all the plates back. I needed to stretch my legs and hopefully happen upon a dessert or two... or three.

I shoveled the uneaten food into the bin while eyeing a delectable-looking miniature pastry when a voice sounded from behind me. "Selene of Avalon," a male voice purred. I froze at the unrecognizable, sturdy voice. Turning, I peered up at the male that towered above me. I willed myself not to shrink but to straighten and look directly into the male's green eyes. I took in his facial features and couldn't help but cock my head at him. He was a much older version of Dayne. My throat tightened. Was this... the king? He cocked his head back at me, an easy smile creeping onto his face.

"I was told I could find you with my nephew," the male paused, watching me.

He wasn't the king, then.

I didn't shift a muscle in my face, fighting to keep it neutral. "It seems as if my sources were wrong." The longer I stood before him, beneath his unrelenting gaze, the more I was certain I did not like him. He sure looked like Dayne, but everything else... his smell, aura, and sneer... was nothing like Dayne. I considered his words.

Find *me* with his nephew, not the other way around.

"Well, I'm here, aren't I?" I pinned the male with a glare. His gaze sharpened momentarily before he cracked into a broad, beautiful, yet sinful smile. My heart skipped a beat. There was no question that he wore Dayne's same playful smile.

"Nicodemus," the male said, extending a hand.

"Is that supposed to be your name?" I asked, unsure why I felt drawn to be so cold and distant with this male. If his aura bore a color, it would no doubt be a deep onyx black.

He began to step toward me, hovering his foot before placing it on the ground slowly. I swallowed the sensation to draw back and focused my gaze on him. How I responded to this male's every move felt important, somehow. He wasn't the king, but... he seemed important, perhaps more so. Despite the importance of this male, my mind screamed at me not to stand down. I lifted my chin a fraction higher. His smile broadened further at that like I was playing into some sick game in his mind. He raised his hand to my cheek, brushing a long strand of hair behind my ear before leaning in to whisper, "It is so lovely to finally meet you, my dear."

A shiver ran down my spine. If not for the slithering breath in my ear, but at that word.

Finally.

I dug within myself to find that familiar icy force within my veins. I created a frigid vortex not only within me but around me. While it was not visible, the nasty coolness of the swirling frigid air was enough for Nicodemus to recoil.

A twisted grin bloomed on his face despite how hard I tried to get the male to look disgusted, annoyed, or shocked. It seemed everything I did made his eyes light even further. "I think I like you." He reached another hand toward my face, stopping just before my cheek as if waiting for something. Without breaking eye contact with him, I concentrated on the finger that nearly caressed my cheek. I allowed the presence of it, the closeness of it, to call more and more ice to roil within me. I ground my teeth together, annoyed by his audacity to stand so close. While my eyes blazed into him, my peripheral vision speared into that finger he held near my cheek. In a sharp exhale, I forced my magic onto that finger. I broke eye contact with him to watch his finger drain of color and curl unnaturally away from my cheek. I exhaled my remaining breath as color returned to his finger a moment later.

"She bites," Nicodemus said while examining his still-extended hand and finger. "Interesting," he purred but looked at me now with feral eyes. I took a half step back, finding a hateful vengeance swirling there. I didn't understand it... but it was unmistakable. I swallowed hard, forcing the bubble of fear in my throat to bob back down into my core. Nicodemus's eyes flicked to my throat —to the fear I had just swallowed and shone as if he recognized what that action was. As if he could sense my fear from the subtle movement of my throat.

"Nic," Dayne's voice broke the tense moment, examining us closely.

"Nephew," the male turned to embrace Dayne. "Your father sent me to assist with the peglin removal in the grove." I watched as the two embraced in what seemed to be a genuine interaction.

"He is... rather impatient to meet our new friends here," Nic gestured to me. "He hoped I could help move things along." Dayne clapped his uncle on the back, strategically leading him away from me.

"I will set you up with Mairda to go over our progress thus far," Dayne updated his uncle. "She will have more information for you than I."

Nic nodded, elbowing Dayne in the side, "You've had more important duties to keep up with, I see." He inclined his head ever so slightly in my direction.

Dayne shoved his uncle's elbow away playfully as they strolled just out of hearing range from where I stood. I let out the quivering breath I held during that interaction. I returned to where I knew my friends lay, spotting Gaia resting her head in Idris's lap. While Idris looked far from amused, she allowed

Gaia to continue resting atop her legs. I sighed, tossing the plates into a tub of sudsy water near the kitchen. I took a deep, quivering breath, forcing the interaction with Dayne's uncle far from my mind.

Unsure of what to do with my time, I wandered over to where Gaia slept atop a grumbling Idris. She shot me an unamused look, rolling her eyes at the situation she had found herself in. I only smiled and curled up on the grass, resting my head atop her other leg.

"Would you two like a blanket too? I'm sure I could get one of these twits to fetch you some," Idris scowled at me, gesturing to the males near us. Gaia didn't stir, and I snuggled into Idris's lap further.

"I was thinking," I started, "Our kingdom's curses—"

"Hiareth is *not* my kingdom," Idris spoke in a seething whisper through gritted teeth.

"I—Okay, the kingdom's curses... I find them to be very particular to their strengths." Idris cocked her head at me. "Munique is the most fertile land on the human continent. Don't you find it strange their curse is infertility of land and womb?" Idris was listening but didn't speak. "And Avalon, well, it may be more that the downfall is accessibility to water. They find themselves now cursed with what is likely an eternity of it."

"What of the people of Hiareth?" Idris asked.

"They are some of the healthiest, heartiest people on the land. The people of Hiareth are known to live the longest—"

"And the Goddess curses them with a long forgotten disease, damning the lucky to their beds, and the unlucky to death." Idris finished for me.

"Exactly," I said, "I find the curses to be... oddly specific."

Idris shook her head. "The Goddess is a cruel wench who allowed me to be burned alive for eighteen years. Of course, she spun such curses." I felt the heat begin to ripple off Idris at her words. Gaia stirred only slightly.

"Do you think she will try to come after us if she learns where we are?" I asked. I didn't particularly want to spend my life in hiding after finally getting a second chance at it. Would she care to seek us out? After all, she upheld her part of the deal by damning three human kingdoms. All debts should be paid. Shouldn't they? I stared up at the blue sky, allowing the thoughts of the Goddess to trickle away as my eyes fluttered shut.

"Can we talk?" Dayne's voice sounded in the near distance. Idris shook her leg to jostle me.

I only sat up, not wanting to feel like I was keeping anything from Gaia and Idris. "What's up?"

Dayne's mouth tightened. Idris shoved me with a hand as if silently saying, 'Go on, it's fine; we trust you.' I pushed myself off the grass and brushed my pants off as I walked toward Dayne. I took a shaky breath as I strode forward. His face was neutral as if we hadn't shared any of those moments last night. I chewed my cheek, feeling my cheeks flush at the memory. He gave me a curt nod before turning to enter the Hideaway, ducking beneath a low-hanging vine of ivy. I followed with peaked curiosity as he took a spot at an empty table. Given the awkward time between meals, most of the tables had been cleared out, with only a few lingering males and females sprinkled throughout the space.

"What's so important you had to disturb my beauty sleep?" I slipped into a seat across the table from him.

"You didn't seem to be doing much sleeping," he replied with a forced smile.

My neutral face dropped to a frown. "What's wrong?"

"I'm sorry you had to meet my uncle without me." He watched me with a furrowed brow.

I replayed the interaction in my head. "It's not a big deal," I decided to say with a wave of my hand.

"Did he want anything?"

"No," I said a little too quickly. "He introduced himself, and then you walked up. That's pretty much it." I tried to keep my voice uninterested to ease Dayne's mind. The interaction had been... odd but still uneventful.

Dayne watched me for a moment, his shoulders finally sagging and face softening. "He has a way of finding people. An odd character, but he means well."

"I see."

Dayne leaned forward, dropping his voice into a low growl. "You didn't want to wake me this morning?"

I clenched my jaw at the sound of his low, rumbling voice. "I... You looked peaceful; I didn't want to disturb you." I shrugged.

Dayne reached across the table to rest his hand atop mine. I pulled my hand back in surprise. A moment of hurt flashed in Dayne's eyes at my reaction to his touch. Dayne and I had an unusual relationship, to say the least. His touching me in front of anyone else didn't seem like a brilliant idea. He seemed to understand the sentiment and returned his hand to his side of the table. I stifled the apology I wanted to give and chewed on my lip instead.

"You could never disturb me," he eyed me, upper body still bent over the table. "Next time—"

I interrupted him, feeling my cheeks warm with whatever he was about to say. "Next time, wake me, blah blah blah."

Dayne cocked his head at that. "You're in a mood today, princess."

"Dayne, what am I supposed to do for ten days? I'm going crazy, and it's hardly been two full days. I just really—"

"You're bored?" Dayne interrupted.

"Take me to the Twilight Grove," I blurted out before realizing what I was saying.

Dayne was so taken aback by the comment that his mouth dropped open slightly. He watched me closely, waiting for me to go on, but I had no more to say. I wanted to experience this world. While every moment out of Avalon had been an experience on its own... I got a taste and now I needed more. I didn't care if that made me a glutton for life. We only get one; shouldn't we all be?

"So let me get this straight: you are so *bored* here with me that you want to go on a suicide mission?"

I flinched at the word suicide and rubbed the inside of my thighs where faintly raised scars could be found. "I need to see this land; I need to do something to feel more prepared about being here."

"I'm not taking you to the Twilight Grove, Selene." He crossed his arms.

"You don't need to," I was starting to feel upset now.

"You won't be going to the Twilight Grove, with or without me, unless you wish to perish a slow and painful death."

My annoyance was starting to turn to anger. "Maybe I do," I spat.

Dayne's eyes narrowed to daggers, assessing my face carefully. I swallowed, realizing how attractive he looked while he glared at me in that way. Heat bubbled, waging war against the angry ice that roared at my annoyance with him. I shifted in my seat, unprepared for such intense, conflicting feelings.

We sat in heated silence for many minutes before Dayne spoke, "We go to the edge, no deeper than fifteen trees. Be prepared to see and hear distressingly more dreadful creatures than the scuttler we came across in the mountains."

"Gaia and Idris will come too if they want," I stated.

"No. Only you. If they want to come, we go separately. I won't be responsible for multiple inept demi-Fae at the same time within *that forest*."

I flinched at the word inept. He was right, though; we were wholly undertrained to do much of anything.

"Tomorrow then?" I asked. Dayne nodded reluctantly, a pained look plastered on his face. "You're hard to say no to."

We sat for many more minutes, watching the room eb and flow with jolly drunk Fae bastards. Two males tapped their glasses of Faerie wine together in cheers, sloshing the red liquid everywhere. The sight of the wine brought me back to last night. My cheeks flushed, remembering the moments shared between Dayne and myself. I hadn't allowed myself to think much of it today, driving the fresh memory down until I was ready to confront it. I had wanted to kiss him, do more than kiss him. Heat rushed to my stomach as I watched him scan the crowd before us with a stern face. I wanted to know what he was thinking... if he thought of me—of last night. I blew out a too-loud breath. I needed to think rationally about my future and about Olvidare. What would it bring? Was it wise to give in to these new feelings? I spent eighteen years seeking this kind of companionship—*any* companionship. I deserved this; didn't I deserve to have fun?

"No drinks today?" I cut through the silence in question.

Dayne brought his eyes back to mine, his face soft and neutral. "I have meetings with Mairda all day, and after last night, not a bad idea to give it a rest today."

I stifled my wince, unsure of if he was implying something about last night... about all we had done. His composure suggested he hadn't thought twice about it. I chewed my cheek, feeling entirely too young and naive to be anywhere near this male, given his experience. To me, what we had done *was* a lot. It meant a lot. I hadn't contemplated it yet, but did he regret our shared moments last night? We didn't *do* all that much to regret, but... I suddenly became self-conscious and began picking at my nails in my lap.

"Unless you wanted to fill me with wine and try to kiss me again," he whispered, "only then could I make an exception."

Heat coiled in my stomach in an instant. I wanted to shy away from his banter, even though moments ago, I wondered where it was.

Feywit. I was nothing but a melting, naive feywit.

I tried to control my breathing patterns and replied, "So you'll only kiss me if I fill you with wine first?" I stifled the cringe I felt from speaking.

His gaze deepened, gripping me so tight I knew I couldn't look away. "Absolutely not, princess."

The coil of heat began bubbling and roiling even louder within me. No part of me knew how to continue bantering with him, yet he awaited my reply.

Sod.

I sucked in a shaky breath. "Cool."

Dayne snorted through his nose the moment the word left my lips. Apparently, 'cool' was not the best thing to say at that moment. Dayne sighed, breaking the tense eye contact we had been holding, and went back to scanning the crowd. I was officially, very, *very* embarrassed.

Goddess, damn it, Selene.

"I'm not good at this," I found myself saying with genuine sadness, allowing the thick cloud of embarrassment to lead my words. "You have so much experience, and you know what to say, and I—"

"Who said I have so much experience?"

"I just assumed with... your age and all," I trailed off, the female from the Hiareth fortress and Mairda's faces flashing in my mind. Goddess, they were both so exquisitely beautiful. There had to be more females, too.

Dayne sighed. "If there's anything I can tell you to put your mind at ease... I'll tell you anything."

"No, no, there's nothing," I replied, not meeting Dayne's eyes. "I just... I don't want to do something stupid." The statement meant so much more than I could tell him right now. I wasn't so sure allowing this coiling heat to persist was smart. I wasn't confident going to Olvidare was smart. There was *so* much I wasn't sure of. Dayne's face softened. I stifled a groan. I wasn't so sure there was anything I could do but succumb to the coiling heat that blistered between us.

"Nothing you ever do will be stupid, Selene." He shifted his face, trying to get me to meet his eyes. "I promise."

His words softened the burning embarrassment in my cheeks, but not enough to look at him. I was so damned new at this. I didn't even know what *this* was. But I knew I liked it. Oh, hells, I liked it.

"This isn't great timing, I know, but I have to meet Mairda. Would you like to come with me?" Dayne cocked his head, still trying to get my eyes to meet his.

I considered the offer. "No, I shouldn't be involved in that kind of stuff. You go, I'll be fine." I tried to reassure him, annoyed at myself for making him feel like he had to offer that. They'd have official Olvidare business to discuss. It wasn't appropriate for me to be there. It would likely bore me to death anyway.

"I'll find you again for dinner," he said, flexing away before I could respond.

That damned flexing.

Chapter Twelve

Selene

DINNER WAS UNEVENTFUL FOR THE MOST PART. DAYNE HAD YET TO show, but Gaia and Idris were as good of company, if not better. I could let my guard down around them and breathe. I had told them about my plans for the Twilight Grove in the morning. They promised me they would still meet at the dock and wield their magic together as we had planned to do each day. I made Gaia swear to force Idris to go, even if she was moody that day. 'When isn't Idris feeling moody?' was all Gaia had to say in response. She wasn't wrong. The two eventually retired to their rooms for the night, leaving me sitting alone.

I waited an hour after Gaia and Idris left before I started considering the walk up the spiraling stairs for bed. The common room was alive and thriving, yet I sat uninvolved, unsure of how to join in on the camaraderie or if I was even welcome to.

I didn't mind watching; in fact, I preferred it that way. It was interesting watching all of them interact. While not all that different from humans, the Fae seemed more lively, and of course, none were hard on the eyes, making it that much easier to sit by and watch. I spotted Dayne's uncle Nic across the room. The males at the table were all reserved but looked at him with the highest respect. I swallowed hard. Maybe I had the wrong idea about him.

Eevy A.

"I am so sorry," a voice spoke from behind me. I turned to see Dayne. He wore a slight grimace on his face as he shifted on his weight. I wasn't surprised to see him running a hand through his dirty blond hair. He seemed to always be doing that when he was uncomfortable.

"Don't be." I shrugged.

"I said I'd be here." His gaze turned almost longing as he studied my face, eyes bouncing over every feature.

"Really, it isn't a big deal. You were busy," I reassured him. "Did you get food?"

"Mairda had some brought up for us."

I nodded and looked away from him to scan the crowd. Dayne quickly took up a spot next to me, resting his back against the table. I leaned my elbows in front of me, propping them up on the table, watching him curiously. He sat so near that the sides of our legs touched.

"I know you said you don't dance..." He trailed off. I filtered through the hundreds of sounds in the common room for a moment before the sounds of merry strings broke through to me. I looked over at Dayne, a grimace already forming on my face.

"I'll lead every step." He shifted closer to me, pressing his leg harder against mine.

"Is it a good idea..." I looked around at the bustling room. These weren't just his comrades; they were his people, his kingdom in many ways.

"Why should it matter to them who I dance with?"

I forced an utterly dramatic look onto my face, "The pretty Prince of Wind, dancing with a demi-Fae," my tone was mocking, only because I mocked myself.

"The Prince of Wind, dancing with a pretty demi-Fae," Dayne countered with a playful smile that made my chest lurch. I looked down to my lap.

"One dance. I promise I won't let you fall."

I looked from my lap to him, finding his eyes to be full of hopeful delight. Even though I wanted nothing to do with that wine-soaked dance floor, dashing that light from his eyes would hurt worse than falling would.

"Fiiiine," I groaned, watching the delight in his eyes grow from a hopeful twinkle to brilliant exuberance. He grabbed my hand and lifted me from where

I sat before leading me to the overly boisterous dance floor. I trailed behind him, his hand extended back, clasped with mine. The fiddling tunes grew louder the closer we got, just as the floor grew stickier beneath our feet.

"Doesn't anyone clean?" I laughed but was genuinely curious.

Dayne reached the edge of the dance floor before I tugged him to stop. He turned on a heel, accepting that the edge was as far as I would go. He closed the distance between us, grasping my hand tighter, his other hand finding its place on the small of my back.

"Belz does, but he does an awful job at it," Dayne smiled as he thought of his friend—of the bearded male I met when first arriving on the continent.

"I see," I spoke shyly now, my free hand finding its place on Dayne's shoulder. We swayed gently, even though the music was more of a cheerful gallivant. I wasn't particularly bad at dancing; rather, I didn't enjoy having so many eyes on me.

I looked up at Dayne to find him already smiling down at me. I glanced around, finding the exact reason I *didn't want to dance* occurring in every corner of this damned place.

"I thought you said they wouldn't care..."

"*I said,* why should it matter to them who I danced with, not that they wouldn't care," Dayne winked.

Handsome sodding prick.

I squeezed his hand tight, forcing a flash of ice through it. Dayne raised his brows, "Two can play that, princess." A sudden gust of wind took the shape of a hand and began tickling my ribs.

I wriggled away from that wind, and Dayne entirely, stepping away and dropping his hand. He let the wind die down and stood with both of his hands extended as others spun and danced around him, gleeful melodies filling the air. I shook my head and sighed.

Sod him.

I stepped forward, and we continued our slow swaying once more.

"How was your day?" Dayne asked, giving my hand a single quick squeeze. I swallowed at the easiness of his question. So simple, yet so out of the ordinary for me to hear.

"It was fine, how was yours?" I forced a neutral voice, yet all of me roared beneath his touch.

"Exhausting," he released a remarkably long sigh but kept his eyes on me and me alone. That kind of intense attention had me wondering what it was like to love and be loved. I knew what this was between us wasn't love... We just met. Yet I still wondered what it was like... How did it compare to what I felt in this moment as this male held me against him, watching me with every ounce of his being?

"Tell me something about yourself." I suddenly asked, an urge to know more about him overcoming me. He picked up the speed of our swaying as if my words ignited something within him.

He leaned his head closer to mine, hovering his lips before the top of my head, "Where would you like me to start?"

I wriggled beneath the nearness of his face, suddenly unable to just sway.

"How about something funny?"

Dayne pulled back, straightening as he continued leading our rhythmic sways. I kept my eyes on him as he spoke, the rest of the room's noises fading into the background.

"One time, when I was a teen learning how to use my magic, I accidentally sent a vortex of wind upon myself and my classmates. It pulled down my pants and everyone else's too." His eyes were dancing with a bright, amused light. "Even the instructor's."

I giggled, finding school being about magic to be an enigma to me. "I'm sure your lessons were much different from mine."

"And that we were both taught to hate the other?" Dayne's face softened into a somber look.

I nodded. Dayne began turning us slightly now. We swayed together, side-stepping slightly into a small circle. "Being demi-Fae is... well, it's strange." I looked down at our feet, stepping in sync. "I don't really belong anywhere. I'm taught to hate you, but I am half *you*. You're taught to hate the human half of me. What does that leave?" I frowned, "There are no parts left *to love*."

A moment of silence flittered between us, only the ironically joyous music bouncing through the air between us.

"Look at me," His voice was so steady and firm that I did just that.

106

His mouth was tightened into a line, and while he looked like he struggled for the right words, his eyes spoke all the right ones.

"It's okay. You don't have to say anything." I forced a smile, squeezing his hand once.

Dayne suddenly stopped our swaying and sidestepping, unclasping his hand from mine. His hand remained on the small of my back while he trailed a finger of his now free hand down my arm, watching the goose-bumps form in its wake. "I think there are plenty parts of you to love, princess." He smiled softly, eyes tracking his finger on my still-extended arm. After a moment, he threaded his fingers through mine once again but did not start swaying again. We just stood there. In the middle of the sticky, wine-soiled dance floor, drunk bastards were spinning all around us; we just stood there.

I swallowed the tears that threatened to fall, forcing a swift subject change as his eyes bore into me. "What is the Kingdom of Wind like?"

The intensity of the moment fizzled out at my words. Dayne began swaying once more, to a slow, somber song that finally matched the tempo of our movements. "It's quaint, sort of like here..." he trailed off in thought. "The city of Olvidare stretches down a long stone path that leads to the Olvidare manor."

"Where you live," I breathed, still astonished that I danced with the King of Wind's *son*.

He nodded.

"Do you like it there?"

A grimace flashed on his face but vanished a moment later.

"Be honest," I whispered.

He cleared his throat and began rubbing his thumb against the small of my back, "It's lonely, but my family is there."

"Why don't you have..." I chewed my lip before finishing my sentence, "A partner?"

He let out a clipped laugh, snorting air out of his nose in my direction. "I guess I just haven't found the right person," he shrugged. "Why don't you have one?" He held my gaze with an intensity that made me want to squirm.

My turn to snort. "You know, the whole dead at eighteen thing kind of kills the mood for most people," I forced a half smile onto my face, but my insides stung from the topic.

"And now you have all the time in the world," He grinned at me but seemed to be holding back words.

I hadn't yet considered the immortal nature of being Fae and how it would affect a demi-Fae. Perhaps I *was* immortal. I shivered at the thought, or rather, the unknown. Either way, I remained grateful that I was saved from death. However, an eternal life seemed—

Dayne cut off my thoughts, "Have you ever considered being with someone that was..." he trailed off in thought, glancing away before finishing, "Fae."

I watched him, taken aback by both his words and the clear discomfort on his face. He scanned behind me as he waited for my reply. Growing up with humans meant that was all I knew. Growing up with a death sentence meant that I didn't consider anything long-term for myself, so I answered, "No."

Dayne's body went rigid, but only subtly so. He nodded but said no more on the topic. I found myself racking my brain on what else to say but came up with nothing. We continued our swaying for more minutes, but it all felt different now—more rigid. Our steps faltered now, not syncing like they had before.

"We should head to bed if you still plan on me taking you to the grove tomorrow," Dayne dropped my hand without warning. I nodded and stepped back from him.

"Sure, we can go," I forced a smile but knew it had to look more like a grimace. I didn't understand why the shift in mood had been so dramatic.

He reached out, wrapping an arm through mine, and flexed us to the top of the Hideaway just before his door. I shook my head slightly as I adjusted to the entirely new location. Somehow the silence between us was louder than the raucous common room below.

I turned to face the door, cocking my head in confusion. Dayne shifted on his feet awkwardly. I didn't understand what was happening right now.

"Should we... go in?" I chewed on my lip as I strode toward the weathered wooden door.

"I wasn't sure you wanted me to?" He cocked his head at me in question.

I hesitated now, my nerves spiking. The notion of sleeping alone after last night... feeling so safe—so whole... I wasn't sure I could ever sleep alone again, but I couldn't tell him that.

"Please, will you come in?" I wasn't sure why it came out in a whisper.

Dayne's rigidity loosened, if only slightly, before he nodded and strode into the room with me.

More clumsily than the night before and less fueled by wine, the two of us found our way into bed. While this time we shared no kisses, he still pulled me tightly against him and traced lines down my arms until I drifted into a safe slumber, dreams guarded by him.

Chapter Thirteen

Selene

"I can hardly walk," I groaned at Dayne as he continued strapping an assortment of golden armor to me. He ignored my cries of discomfort as he cinched a shin covering to my leg. "Is this necessary?" I shook my leg free from Dayne's grasp.

He stood back to admire his work. I gleamed in the morning sun, clad in gold from head to toe. Dayne sent a gust of wind to brush my hair from my face. "Here," he grunted, handing me a golden sword longer than my arm.

"You do realize I have never swung a sword in my life?"

"It's better you have it, unpracticed even," Dayne threw a day pack over his shoulder.

I let the sun and breeze caress my face, tilting my head back in satisfaction. I wasn't sure how I felt about Dayne fussing over me. Since our dance in the common room, things had been tense between us—formal almost. I'd weighed my answer to his question countless times, wondering if I had in some way shut him down with my answer.

Have you ever considered being with someone that was Fae.

While it might've come out harsh, I had good reason for answering no. Why would I have considered it? I spent my life on the human continent, surrounded only by humans with a predestined fate of death. Of course I never considered it. I now felt it wasn't the right answer, given the way Dayne conversed more formally with me, a rigid aura about him. I twisted my boot in the dirt as I watched him pretend not to be watching me.

He had prepped me all morning on what to expect in the Twilight Grove. I wasn't thrilled to learn that some of the worst creatures patrolled the edges of the grove, looking for a passerby to sink their teeth or claws into. Another tidbit I learned was that, *apparently,* many of the creatures killed people for sport. Given my demi-Fae heritage, I would be an unusual scent to them.

I turned the golden sword over in my hand, shoulder sagging at its weight. Dayne said we would be aiding in the peglin removal process if I was forcing them into the grove. He told me, 'No one should enter that forest without reason.' I found the peglin removal process to be quite interesting and had pressed him on it. He told me peglins were hog-like creatures with the ability to reproduce on their own. They are incredibly invasive as they constantly reproduce, creating armies of more of them. We wouldn't be going near any dens but taking out more solitary targets: Peglins traveling alone or in small groups. Each year, the peglins needed to be culled to prevent them from reproducing too rapidly and ultimately traveling beyond the Twilight Grove, where they most definitely were not wanted.

"If we see one peglin, we see one peglin. We won't be traveling deeper than fifteen trees." He eyed me until I nodded.

Dayne and I walked thirty minutes from the Olvidare Hideaway to the eastern edge of the Twilight Grove. He wouldn't flex us there to conserve energy. "You are not safe anywhere you stand, from above or below. I take out the peglins, and you watch. From a distance, but not too far. Understood?"

"Aye, aye," I mocked. I put on a confident face but was disturbed about what we may encounter inside the Twilight Grove. Still, it felt right to experience the ancient place firsthand.

We walked to the woods while Dayne continued repeating warnings and suggestions. I kept the eye-rolling to a minimum as we approached. We had to be getting close. I smelled it before I saw it, the stench of old rotting food and death. "They say that smell is the smell of fear," Dayne started, "but I've smelled my crew's fear before; it smells nothing of the grove." The smell was so putrid I had half a thought to pinch my nose closed. The only thing keeping me from it was the thought of breathing that horrid stench into my mouth.

A few minutes later, the trees came into view and grew taller and taller as we approached. I squinted into the trees, noting that the deeper into the woods you went, the darker it was. Spindly grey trees erupted from the ground; none bore a single leaf or berry. It was as if the soil itself was cruel, keeping these trees alive, but just barely. Dayne stopped walking only briefly to look over his shoulder at me, waiting for a sign to continue forward. I nodded.

"Stay close," he whispered before stepping forward past the first tree of the grove. I kept close to his side, swiveling my head from around as the darkening twilight surrounded us. As my nose got used to the horrid stench, I found the soft glow of twilight to be somewhat peaceful despite what I knew lurked.

We strolled, keeping our footsteps as quiet as possible to avoid alerting any creatures of our presence. We were about eight trees into the grove when we were wholly enveloped in twilight. It was as if the moon was stuck in a near-rising position for all of eternity. I pitied the sun and the moon either way; their neverending efforts to make man wake or sleep without even a thanks. Perhaps here, the moon got to rest.

Various pitches of croaks and far-from-ethereal humming echoed around us. They entangled with so many other horrible sounds that it was hard to hear any one of them at once, but rather, it was a cacophony of terror. I took in the trees around us; their branches were gnarly and twisted as if stuck amid a haunting dance.

A slight rustling sounded ahead of us, and Dayne stopped, holding a hand out to signal me to do the same. I swallowed but kept my attention on Dayne and his movements rather than sliding my eyes down his muscled back. He suddenly crouched, and I followed suit. I wanted to scan the area around us, but I felt I was safer watching him and reacting when he did. He signaled the direction he thought the sound was coming from and began crouch-walking in that direction. I followed, attempting to mimic the awkward waddle he was doing. We went through some thick fern-like bushes that opened to a clearing. We hung back, placing ourselves in the thick of the ferns, but could see into the clearing beyond the thick foliage. A shallow puddle, no bigger than a large bed, separated the clearing in two. Twilight reflected off the pool, making it look like liquid metal. I scanned for the source of the sound, eyes falling on two hog-like creatures that were nuzzling their snouts through thick black muck on the glittering puddle's edge. Peglins. They looked a lot like hogs, but they had a faint green hue. They were mostly skin-covered with haphazard splotches of coarse fur on their bodies. Their irises were blood red, a harsh crimson line rimming each iris. Their tusks grew out of the side of their mouth wildly, reminding me of the gnarly tree branches around us.

We remained tucked within the thick bushes, watching the two peglins. I had to remind myself to breathe—to keep my attention more on Dayne than on the creatures in the clearing. Dayne held up a hand signal that I assumed meant 'stay sodding put.' He began inching closer to the peglins without leaving the cover of the bushes. I raised my brows, shocked at the enormous male's silence as he shifted through the thick ferns. He unsheathed the sword behind his back, opal gemstones flashing in the twilight. He took one and then two silent crouched steps beyond the bushes and paused. Nothing. The moment was too tense to breathe. My lungs burned in defiance, but I would not risk a sharp breath.

Dayne rose into a standing position in a slow, deliberate manner. If the peglins were facing us, they would see him and likely charge him upon first glance. Dayne told me that hunting peglins was easy; you don't have to chase them down. They come right to you. Dayne raised his foot to step toward the peglins when a wholly unnatural sound sliced through the air, stopping his foot mid-air. The sound was screeching as if the insides of my ears were made of ceramic, and a talon was being scraped down them. My eyes widened at the sound as I tried to control my breathing. Dayne had told me over and over again, 'The ones who panic are the ones who don't make it out.' The sound seemed to approach and soon felt like it was being directed straight into my ears, yet it sounded distant at the same time. I wasn't sure where to look or how far away the threat was. I stopped scanning around, feeling my heart rate pick up as my sense of hearing failed me. This is what these creatures did. Disorient. Approach. Attack. My attention fell on the peglins as their heads snapped up, looking directly to their left.

I watched Dayne extend his foot behind him a half step, retreating into the bushes. Before his foot could contact the ground, a large black feline-like figure leaped into the clearing from the left. I sucked in a breath at the sight of the peculiar beast. It was entirely mesmerizing. Its body was fully fluid as if it was made of pure black oil suspended in the air. The liquid form changed into four-legged shapes resembling large cats as it walked casually to the peglins. Every second that passed, the black figure shifted into a new feline shape. One second, it was a thin and limber house cat; the next, a stocky beastly thing. There were no pronounced features on it. No eyes. Only flowing black oil. There seemed to be no rhyme or reason to the shifts, just that it was ever-changing—ever-flowing. Dayne was still retreating into the bushes with me, taking silent steps backward. My heart was thundering at the mesmerizing creature as I glanced between it and Dayne. How dangerous was it? The peglins, still stunned and watching the beast approach, turned on a heel and ran from it. The black creature then rocked back on its haunches, shifting from small to large, strong legs, and launched onto them.

Dayne took the opportunity to leap back into the bushes to my side. His hand was on my knee, grabbing it hard, but he kept his eyes on the clearing—on that feline thing. The black creature gracefully closed the distance between it and the peglins. It reached out a feline paw and swatted at the slower of the two peglins. I stifled a gasp as the once hog-like creature vaporized beneath its paw, turning into a thick puddle of black. The vaporized peglin hovered in liquid form for a moment before collapsing to the ground in a shapeless black puddle. The black beast wasted no time in swatting at the other peglin. It, too, turned into a shimmering puddle of liquid darkness. The beautiful flowing feline bent lazily to lap up both pools, its flowing body still morphing into different forms.

Dayne braced a hand on the ground. I could *feel* his nervous energy radiating from him and seeping into me. I couldn't peel my eyes from the shifting feline until I heard Dayne's breath stop. My eyes snapped to him. He crouched in a position that made him look spring-loaded, as if all it would take was one movement to set him off. I held my breath, too, but it felt like my thundering heart could be heard a mile away.

The beautiful flowing cat finished lapping up both dark liquid puddles. I squinted, fixing my eyes on it, and could've sworn it seemed to grow in size just slightly. Its face remained away from us, giving me a fraction of hope that it wouldn't sense our location. The cat was still until its right ear flicked back in our direction.

Dayne was standing faster than my brain could interpret what was going on. He grabbed my arm, hauling me up. "Run," he said in a low growl that made every internal part of me sink into a deadly free fall.

We both took off in a hard sprint back in the direction we had come. Our feet pounded hard into the ground, sending painful shock waves through my armor-clad shins. We were not deep within the forest; if we could manage this pace for five minutes, we would be out of the grove. That thing wouldn't follow us out, would it? My ears began ringing with fear, my legs burning with pain, but by some miracle, I kept Dayne's pace. The terrible screech we heard earlier sliced the air yet again. It was a haunting sound that had no directionality; it was so far from us, yet somehow still sounded like the beast would pounce upon us at any moment, turning us into a puddle of liquid darkness. I pushed through the feeling of terror that was pulsing not only through my body but rippling off of it. If there were creatures in here that sensed that rippling fear... I shook the thought.

With each lunge forward, I willed my gold-clad legs to push off the ground harder and faster. I kept close to Dayne's heels out of fear that if I fell behind... Oh, Goddess, I didn't want to think about that either.

I suddenly found myself slamming into Dayne's back. He had dug his heels into the grimy black mud, forcing me into him. I shook the confusion that clouded my mind as the flowing black creature leaped over our heads, meeting the ground before us. It knew we were trying to leave. It knew what direction 'leaving' meant for us. Dayne grabbed my arm and wrenched me to the right. We hurdled ourselves in the new direction, away from the creature that was no doubt following us.

My brain was such a blur I had no idea what way we were running now. Why were we running? Why hadn't he flexed us yet? What was the point of—

Another screech scraped down the insides of my ear, so deafening that I let out a yelp. Another screech, somehow even louder, ripped through the air, piercing my ear canals like a glowing hot spear. I felt a drip of warm liquid slide down my cheek. I didn't slow my pace, ignoring the pain that ripped through not only my legs but also my entire head. Dayne was somehow able to track the creature through all of the mayhem. I was lucky to get one foot in front of the other, let alone be aware of much else. He grabbed my arm and wrenched me slightly further right as the creature leaped into the position I was in mere seconds ago.

Sodding Goddess save us.

Still charging ahead, Dayne flung a hand toward the creature, sending a monstrous wind in its direction. The flowing feline creature split into a million tiny onyx orbs suspended in the air. I allowed my eyes to remain on it only a second longer than necessary, mesmerized by how it avoided Dayne's wind attack. Clever little wench, wasn't it? I blinked, and the orbs began regrouping into their familiar feline form, already launching at us. It may have avoided the attack, but we still had a way to slow it.

We were crashing and panting through the grove away from the creature when the familiar scent of seawater hit me. We were running towards the sea. Another screech pierced the air, forcing more drops of blood to stream down my cheek. We weren't going to make it. We were already slowing. It was close, but it wasn't close enough. Why wasn't Dayne flexing us? We were close enough to the edge just then. He could've flexed us all the way back into the Hideaway.

"Dayne," I shrieked, hoping he would look my way. "Sodding flex us."

Dayne sent another blast of wind behind us. I didn't turn to look at the creature I knew would only be stopped for a few moments. We continued through the trees, pushing through the fear and exhaustion. Dayne made no movements to suggest he had heard me. Or rather, that he wanted to listen. Perhaps he was using this as a lesson to me. Angry ice flared in me at that. Was that why he wasn't flexing us?

The trees began thinning slightly, and a rocky ledge appeared before us. Dayne had sent many more winds at the creature, allowing us the time to reach the ledge. He was a few paces ahead of me. Were we jumping? He launched his massive body off the ledge as if in answer. I wasted no time doing the same.

We fell for a long while before crashing into the Onyx Sea below. I looked around, panicked for Dayne, choking on violent thrashing seawater. Salt stung my eyes, and the minor cuts I knew now peppered my arms and legs from running through the grove. I willed the water around me to calm, and it did ever so slightly. Dayne burst above the surface in a violent choking cough. I focused hard on him as my own head bobbed up and down with the waves. He was being thrashed farther and farther out to sea. The waves threatened to pull me under just as I again fought with them to calm. They, of course, listened. I dug within myself and beckoned the waves surrounding Dayne to shift their movements in my direction. Dayne slowly thrashed back toward me into the calmer waters by the rocky edge. I remained soothing the waters by me as I tugged on those waves to bring him closer. It was challenging to do both simultaneously, but I would not let him be tossed out further. Once I managed to get him close enough to me, I willed the rough seas to wrap around us, floating us to the edge. We were able to drag ourselves ashore onto a jagged rocky surface. I choked up seawater before ensuring Dayne's entire body was safely ashore, then released my grip on the sea. It began thrashing violently around us the moment I allowed it to. Dayne was panting even harder than I was, although my energy felt nearly depleted. My body wanted to slump against the sharp rocks. Instead, I shoved a finger in Dayne's face.

I choked out in anger and confusion. "Why didn't you flex us?"

Dayne remained lying, hardly propping himself up on his elbows. He stared at the rock beneath him as he tried to get his breathing under control. I watched him choke up seawater and pant for many minutes before he finally controlled his breathing. We were both thoroughly soaked and reeking of salt.

"Fury," he choked. "Once they begin tracking you, they don't stop. Returning to the Hideaway would have meant leading it right into the front door." I waited for him to continue, still not understanding fully. "The water broke the tracking bond the fury made with us."

"Why didn't you flex us to the cliff's edge?" I asked.

"Furies are smart... and fast. If I had flexed us there, it would have likely redirected us away from the cliff's edge anyway. I needed to conserve my energy for more attacks."

I thought back to the spiraling wind attacks that Dayne had thrown in the fury's direction. Dayne finally regained enough composure to pull himself into a sitting position.

I bit back my questions about the fury and how it naturally flowed through the air while shifting into different shapes and sizes of felines. For such a lethal creature, it sure was beautiful.

"Now that you and the grove are acquainted, will you ever be going back?" I didn't miss the acidic bite in his voice.

"Not anytime soon," I whispered and turned to look at the raging sea before us. The waves crashed against our rock, peppering us with water. My cheek had been washed clean from the salt water, but my ears still throbbed from the horrible screech of the fury. Dayne leaned his back against the tall cliff behind him. I thought he could flex us from here as I peered at the rocky edge we would otherwise have to scale.

"Do you need time?" I asked, unsure of how his wind magic affected his ability to flex.

"No," he closed his eyes and ran a hand through his wet hair before heaving himself to his feet. His mood was off, but I didn't want to press him on it. I had put us in this situation after all.

I looked at him, feeling guilty I had even asked to come here. If he had gotten hurt... I looked away, hot shame filling my cheeks. He approached, watching his footing carefully. He looped an arm through mine, and we were standing in his room in an instant.

We looked at each other, dripping salt water all over the stone floor, and nearly died of laughter.

Chapter Fourteen

Selene

I SAT CROSS-LEGGED IN FRONT OF THE FULL-LENGTH MIRROR IN Dane's room, brushing out my hair. It had been a week now since arriving on the Fae continent, which meant, we would be heading to Olvidare in only a matter of days. Gaia, Idris, and I had kept our word and met at the dock each morning. Idris had the least control of her magic, as she had been suppressed from it nearly her whole life. Gaia and I helped her each morning despite my own naivety to my magic. Coaxing that angry inferno from her was the easy part; leashing it... that was another story. Our bond had only grown stronger in the days we spent here. Somehow, I felt once we left this place... we would be an inseparable trio and a force to be reckoned with. We all felt uneasy about going to Olvidare, but we would not be helpless there.

I paced Dayne's room, waiting for him to retrieve me for dinner after I had decided to take a post-lunch nap. We had expended a lot of energy experimenting with our magic this morning. By lunch, Gaia, Idris, and I were ready to sleep the rest of our day away.

I rose to my feet and smoothed the shimmering metallic silver dress I wore for dinner tonight. It clung to my body through my hips and fell naturally to the floor. We had been dressing lavishly for dinner most evenings, but I hadn't touched the Faerie wine since the first night. Dayne hadn't either.

Eevy A.

I cringed, thinking of how awkward it had become between me and Dayne. While Dayne stayed with me each night, we only spoke and interacted casually. There was the occasional shared touch between us... but I could tell he was distancing himself from that other kind of connection with me... The kind that melted my icy core. I felt both guilt and annoyance that one conversation ruined so much. I was happy to have him near me, a friend I needed so deeply, but now... instead of heat sparking at the thought of our lips touching, I cringed.

Today had been busy for the both of us, myself with Gaia and Idris, and him in meetings with Mairda and Nic. I looked back to my reflection, wondering if Dayne would like the dress. Despite how things felt, I still craved being around him. I craved that feeling that lit within me as his eyes roamed my face or body. I craved the sense of calm he brought just by being something warm and safe next to me while I slept. I had yet to find such peace in anyone else, even in Gaia and Idris, whom I loved with my whole being.

As I strode around the room, flashes of light danced about the space as my dress caught in the streams of flickering firelight. I spun around, forcing the beautiful twinkles of light to explode around the room in a fitful dance.

"Lovely," Dayne's voice sounded from behind me. I jumped at the surprise and turned around to push him away.

His neutral face dropped into a frown. My eyes dropped from his face to his hands. He held a platter of food and a small, oddly colored box. "I thought we could stay up here tonight?" He shifted, and instead of dropping his eyes from me like he had the past several days, he held my eye contact firm.

"Oh." I strode toward the armoire and began shuffling through some comfier clothes. My insides clenched.

"Leave it on," the commanding tone sent an explosion of red hot embers down my abdomen. Something was different with him right now.

I turned around from the armoire, eyes flicking to the box in his hand. "What is that?" I tilted my head at the odd-looking box.

"An echo box," he smiled while setting the food platter on the bed and examining the box. "It captures sound that can be replayed. I purchased this particular one back in Olvidare. I haven't used it yet, but the shop owner said she recorded a lovely string quartet." He pressed a small button on the box, and

120

a beautiful symphony of strings began to sound. The song was slow and melodic, the noise relieving an ounce of tension in the room. The shop owner was right; It was lovely.

Dayne moved the platter to the small round table in the corner of his room. Goddess, I was nervous. We barely spent any time together the past few days; his bantering nearly stalled out. Right now felt... different. I cocked my head at him, studying his face and movements. He gestured for me to join him at the table. I drank him in as I took cautious steps forward. His tousled, dirty blond hair fell in waves around his forehead and ears. His mouth was quirked in a gentle, beckoning smile. He looked excited but serene, a face I hadn't seen in days. I lowered myself into my chair without breaking eye contact with him before he found his seat across from me. We sat and picked at the potatoes and pork in front of us. I fidgeted, wishing he would come up with something to discuss. I considered bringing up the other day... the conversation that made all of this so strange.

"How was your day?" He broke the near-awkward silence.

"It was good. Idris set Gaia's tree on fire, so we had to deal with that. I'm sure you can imagine how that went over."

"Oh, I'm sure Idris had everyone to blame but herself," Dayne joked.

"She told Gaia she shouldn't have put the tree there." I laughed at the recent memory and the look on Idris's face. Dayne laughed with me for a moment before silence fell across the room once again.

I cleared my throat in an effort to break the tension. Dayne glanced at me, waiting. Oh sod. I had nothing to say.

"I," I started, but my mind ran in circles. "It rained today," I blurted out. I bit my tongue the moment the words left my lips.

Dayne raised his brows high. "It sure did," he shot me a look that I knew meant, 'Are we really talking about the weather?' Dayne speared a potato with his fork, keeping his eyes on me.

Well, now sodding what?

"Do you..." Dayne narrowed his eyes, "like the rain?"

Shit.

"I uh," I scratched the back of my neck, "I hate it," I watched for his reaction, but there was none. He only watched me with a blank face. Gaia and

Idris had much more to say when they learned about my deep-rooted hatred of rain.

"You're not going to laugh and say, 'Water affinity Fae can't hate rain'?"

Dayne raised a brow now, setting his fork down on his plate, potato still speared. "I can't say it didn't cross my mind," he smirked, but something about that smile was sad and knowing.

My insides churned. Both at the thought of the overwhelming emotions that course through me when it rains, but mostly... because of that smirk.

"It has to do with Avalon?" He settled back into his seat, crossing his arms over his chest.

I nearly shook my head in surprise. "How did you—"

"The land that never rains. The water Fae that's forced to make it..." His smirk was replaced with a soft frown.

I thought of Gaia's words.

Once upon a time... there was a girl who watered her kingdom with her tears.

"I never brought enough rain." I frowned back at him. It had destroyed me. Countless days—weeks—*years* coaxing the rain to come. It was never enough for them.

"Sod them," Dayne shrugged, shifting the tone of the conversation.

He was right. Sod them. Sod them all. I had Gaia and Idris now. I had... him.

Once upon a time... there was a girl who watered her kingdom with her tears. But no more. That girl is no more.

Another bout of tension-filled silence hung between us like a sopping wet rag. It weighed down on me, pushing the air from my lungs.

"You look... so beautiful tonight," Dayne said, gesturing across the table at me. I blushed at the compliment and looked away. My mind fizzled with confusion. I thought he was distancing himself these past few days. I didn't understand. I could feel that he kept his eyes on me, so I forced a neutral face. Neither of us continued eating as if the weight of the tension made it impossible to move.

"You make this hard, you know."

"I make what hard?" I continued avoiding his eyes, still soaking in his compliment and fighting against the confusion that pricked my senses. Apart from my family, no one ever complimented my appearance. I wasn't sure I had ever been called beautiful before. Maybe by my mother, but—

"Just..." Dayne trailed off. A light, jaunty song hummed from the echo box.

I couldn't take the silence between us and changed the subject altogether. "We leave in three nights?"

Dayne sighed and sat back in his chair. I hoped that I appeared neutral, but my insides were set ablaze by him. He was so near I could smell his aspen and honey scent. I wanted him to reach out and touch me; I... I had no idea how to say it. But if I just—

"So I take it you still plan on coming with us?" Dayne crossed his arms now. I began sweating. I was upset at myself and the many wasted days since we had kissed. Going to Olvidare would change so much. Would I even see much of him once we were there? I tapped my foot as the realization set in. I more than wanted more–I needed more. But what if I couldn't have more?

The creeping sense of doom slid throughout me, gutting me. This... this... whatever this was between us lit me aflame. My mind buzzed with excitement each day when I got the chance to interact with him. I swallowed hard, finding it impossible to sit beneath his hardened gaze.

I stood from the table, suddenly uncomfortable in my dress, uncomfortable with. All of this. "I don't have a choice," I finally answered his question. "I'm going to change into something more comfortable."

Dayne gave a slight huff. We both knew his father—the King of Wind—would not accept anything short of what he wanted. If his son couldn't bring us to Olvidare, someone else would.

I shuffled through the stacks of clothes in the armoire. I knew changing out of my dress would kill the mood.

Feywit. I was a sodding feywit.

Who am I kidding? There was no *mood*, just an unnatural concoction of emotions that neither of us wanted to talk about. Or perhaps more accurately, we didn't know *how* to discuss them. We didn't know if crossing that line was okay. Goddess, I wanted to cross that line. I wanted to leap over it. But... He made me nervous—*this* made me nervous. I was tired of ruining every conversation we had. I was too damned new to this. Too damned new at having anyone look my way twice. I blinked, remembering that I was searching for something to change into.

"Let me know if you need any help," Dayne spoke in a quiet, testing voice. My upper body was leaned over inside the armoire. The clothing around me muffled his voice, but I could still hear him rise from his chair. He was being helpful, wasn't he? He was... Sod. I repeated his words in my head, but the heat that bloomed in my gut gave me the answer to the weight of his words. I thought of his soft lips against mine. I thought of the way they felt, the way they tasted. I wasn't just hungry for more of that feeling. I was starving.

Be brave.

I closed my eyes for a moment and shut out every weak thought. Every warning bell or nerve that pinched me. I swallowed them, burying them so far within I could no longer feel them. Breathing slowly, I turned to him, allowing the heat building inside me to feed my words.

"I would love some." I breathed, locking eyes with him.

His evergreen eyes lit; they roamed my face, checking for any sign that I was joking. When he found none, he stepped toward me slowly. One foot after the other. So slow, I began counting his steps to keep from melting into the floor.

Oh, Goddess.

The look in his eyes as they swept over my silhouette. I willed my knees to stop shaking. I wanted him to touch me—kiss me—and hear my name on his lips.

"Selene," he growled, sensing what I wanted. "Turn around," he cocked his head. I nearly whimpered at his voice but turned, facing the armoire once more.

He stepped closer until I could feel his hard frame against my back. He traced a finger over my shoulder and down my arm, then wrapped his arm around me, pulling me tight against him. I could feel the entirety of him hard against my back. My breathing became jagged as my lungs lurched beneath the heat that built within me. He pressed his lips against my ear, wrapping a hand around my throat. If he wasn't holding me against him, I would've fallen to my knees beneath that touch. I had *never* been touched that way. I never could have thought up something like this. Every sensation, every ounce of pressure that he placed upon my body, burned with desire. His warm breath curled around my ear, sending a violent shiver through me. He chuckled, sending a second round of chills down my spine. I needed to be facing him, my aching, burning part against his. I fought against his grip to turn, but he held me firmly against him.

"Where are you going?" he said as his lips brushed against my neck. My whole body trembled. I tried to turn and face him one more time. He gripped my throat tighter in answer while tracing down my shoulder with his free hand. He trailed that finger down my arm until he found my hand, balled in a tight fist.

"Relax," he said into my ear, this time his voice pricking with concern.

How could I relax? I was about to burn from the inside out. I swallowed and allowed my hand to unfurl for him. He sighed in my ear at my obedience. His hand left my now relaxed fist and began roaming my abdomen. He traced lines and swirls near my belly button.

Lower. Please lower. While I didn't know what I wanted, my body did. I was wholly rigid from need but somehow also relaxed because it was *he* who was touching me. I willed his hands to roam lower on me. As if in answer, his fingers began tracing beneath my belly button. I tipped my head back, and a slight whimpering sound escaped me. An icy storm of embarrassment coursed through me at that sound I had made. I fought against covering my mouth with my hand so I wouldn't make it again.

"Whimper for me again, princess," He began rubbing closer to where I needed him most.

Goddess. I whimpered again. This time, I felt no shame in the noise. Only heat flushed me as I noticed how feral the sound made Dayne.

"Lower," I breathed out loud, feeling my nerves begin to melt away. It was as if anything I said or did fueled him.

"Oh?" He replied in my ear, his breath heavy and hot. He allowed his finger to graze the aching spot between my legs. Another whimper escaped from my lips at the explosion of heat that burst through me from that damned touch.

I started shifting, pulling at my dress to feel more of him. Goddess, if he didn't get this dress off of me... Dayne's gentle finger pressed harder against me, sending me into a near-dizzying spiral. I needed more of it. His fingers were so delicate, too delicate. Goddess, we hadn't done as much as kiss since the night of the Faerie wine, and now... I think I would crumple to the floor and beg for him if he stopped touching me.

He raised his hands to grip my shoulders, holding me in place as he backed away. If it weren't for his hold on me, I would've been turned around and against him in a heartbeat. He kept one hand firmly on my shoulder as he traced the other hand down my back to where the zipper of my dress was. My breath caught in my throat. If he kissed me right now, I would probably erupt into flames.

"You want help?" Dayne said in a voice smoother than silk. I tried but failed to say 'yes.' "Say it," he purred in my ear.

I tried again; "Mhm" was all I could manage. I wondered if Dayne felt as wholly rabid as I did.

I sensed the devilish smile on his face as he began unzipping the back of my dress. His hand approached the top of my brassier. He unzipped slightly past it, letting out a loud, jagged breath that made me want to crumple to the floor. He continued unzipping until he reached the bottom of the zipper that lay just above the matching black panties. He allowed the back of my dress to hang open as he released the grip on my shoulder, finally giving me full range of motion. I turned slowly to face him, finally able to make eye contact with him. I was unsure how I stood upright as I beheld him. His chest rising in uneven breaths, he stared back at me. We remained a few feet apart, still drinking each other in.

Goddess, his face. I wanted to touch every groove and line of him. How did he... I steadied my breathing... how did he want *me?*

I brought both hands to where my shoulder straps lay. They were the only thing keeping my dress in place. Dayne's hands squeezed tightly into a fist. A flick of both wrists would drop my dress into a pool of silver beneath me. He waited, staring into my eyes, devouring me. I took my time, teasing him by flicking one of my straps. My dress held firm, supported only by my right strap.

"If you don't do it, I will," Dayne spoke in a breathy voice.

I stifled a sigh upon hearing his voice and flicked at the remaining strap. My dress fell to the floor in a plume of silver. Dayne sucked in a quick breath as he beheld me in the black lace set he had added to my wardrobe. He took several backward steps until he bumped against the bed and fell into a sitting position atop it. He sat there and took me in, eyes roaming from my face feverishly.

He trailed his eyes down to my collarbone, then to the gentle curves of my breast peeking out from the black brassier. They roamed down my abdomen and stopped at the spot I knew he wanted, hidden only by a mere sheet of black lace. His eyes were aflame, burning nearly emerald at the sight of that spot. He broke free and continued his gaze down the length of my body, then back up to my face.

"Come here," he nearly growled.

I took a shaky breath and stalked to where he sat atop the bed, craving his hands on my body. If I had any ounce of nerves left within me, they were entirely masked by a burning desire. He threw his shirt off in a quick motion as I approached. His muscles glistened in the dimly lit room. I ached to touch every inch of him. I would feel every part of him.

I made it to the edge of the bed, nearly face-to-face with him now that he was sitting.

"You are... a treat," he smirked, eyes roaming me up and down again. I swallowed the desire that consumed me from watching him look at me. I hesitated for a moment, unsure of what to do next, as he remained in a seated position.

I shuffled forward an inch until his bent knees brushed against the fronts of my thighs. I took a trembling breath and climbed atop him, wrapping my arms around his neck and my legs around his middle. I wasn't exactly sure where to touch or what he might like, but I allowed my bursting desire to lead me. We sat facing each other, wholly still as our most tender parts lay atop one another, only a few layers of clothes between. I began rotating my hips like I had the first night we kissed. I rubbed that part of me against him, feeling how hard he was beneath me. His eyes rolled into the back of his head, yet he kept his hands off of me. My head was spinning, the feeling of him against me... it would undo me. He gripped his hands around my waist, still allowing my hips to rotate and shift freely. He let out a moan that forced an uncontrolled whimper from my lips. I didn't care about the sounds that escaped me now; They made him wild.

"Come here," he said in a soft but demanding voice. I knew he meant my lips.

I continued rotating my hips against his length as I hovered my lips a hair's distance from his. He moved forward to break the distance, but I leaned away just enough so our lips never met.

"Teasing me?" he breathed. We kept our eyes locked on each other. Dayne removed one of his hands from my hips and wrapped it firmly around my jaw.

He brought my face to his again, his eyes lighting with fire as he plunged into a hot, wet kiss. Our tongues mingled immediately as if they had missed each other. The taste of him, the feel of him against my body, it was all so much at once. The closer we got, the more I craved. I began rotating harder and faster against him, his kisses becoming rougher and deeper in sync with my hips.

I shifted my hips back and began fiddling with the button of his pants. Dayne pulled away from the kiss, his eyes wild and commanding.

"Not tonight," he said, watching me. I continued fiddling with the button anyway, finally freeing it. Dayne flipped me from on top of him to beneath him. I now lay atop the bed, Dayne hovering closely above me. I glanced to where I had just unbuttoned, his hard length now exposed ever so slightly. My eyes slid along that bare exposed skin, only the girth of him in view. My eyes rolled to the back of my head at the pleasure of seeing him, seeing that. I had dreamed of this moment many times in Avalon. Wondering if I'd ever experience something like this... knowing that I wouldn't with my death sentence.

Hells.

I flicked my eyes back to his face, in awe that I was actually experiencing the intense desire and pleasure I had dreamed of. Dayne laughed heavily and leaned closer to me, kissing me sweetly. I was burning. I needed the heat to be released. I bucked my hips towards him, but he shifted away.

"Who's the tease now?" I whispered as I nipped his lower lip.

He rolled from above me to beside me, making me scowl at the change in position. He nipped at my ear and neck while trailing a gentle finger down my throat. He grasped one of my breasts in his hand, careful not to expose them from beneath my brassiere. He could rip it off of me for all I cared. His finger trailed further and further down my body until it reached the scalloped edge of black lace. He flicked at the fabric slightly while licking a line up my neck. I shivered.

"Please," I begged him, unsure of what I was asking for. I just knew I needed more of his touch.

He allowed his finger to dip below the edge of the lace. They hovered around but not against where I needed them to be. I threw my head back in agony that he would not press his fingers onto that part of me.

"Please," I spoke now, too eager to keep my voice in a whisper.

He kissed my cheek and ever so gently and pressed his fingers against me. We both gasped at the same time at the wetness of me. He rubbed it between his fingers.

"Mmmmm," he whispered in my ear.

"Please," I begged again with more urgency. It was the only thing I could say.

"So polite today, princess."

Sod.

I clenched my jaw at his voice—at the name. Hearing him call me that while we did *this*? It shredded me... Wholly shredded me into molten ribbons of desire.

He continued kissing my cheek and neck with urgency. He placed his fingers back against me. I couldn't help the moan that bubbled out. The sound fueled him as he began rubbing in small circles. My hips threatened to buck as he pressed harder and with more urgency. I could feel my breasts peaking further at the pleasurable touch. Dayne flicked and rubbed me before plunging two fingers inside of me. I gasped, and Dayne made a growling sound in my ear. He worked his thumb against me while pumping his fingers in and out. My hips bucked in the air uncontrollably. I needed more. He continued rubbing and pumping until I was panting heavily. It felt so good that I was grinding hard against his hand for more. I felt the edge near and began running, sprinting for it, begging for release. He stopped abruptly when I needed him most. I tossed my head back in frustration. He wore a devilish smile as he leaned in to kiss me deeply before resuming with his hand.

"More," I breathed into his mouth, biting his lower lip. He flipped his body on top of me again, only removing his fingers from inside of me for a moment. He was able to go so much deeper in this position. I needed the release. I needed this heat to die down before it consumed me.

"Dayne," I moaned up at him, keeping my eyes locked on his. He rubbed harder and faster, fueled by the sound of his name on my lips. A sudden euphoric feeling ripped through my entire body. My hips bucked and rotated forward as a series of whimpers and moans escaped from my lips. He didn't stop or slow until my legs had halted their twisting and writhing. He pulled his fingers from inside of me. I let out a gasp from the sensitivity of it.

Holy—

I lay there as my insides fluttered with pleasure. The heat dissipated slowly, and the temporary high wore off. Dayne had nuzzled his face into my neck, allowing my body to come down from the euphoria. I turned to look at him in awe at the feeling of him inside of me–the pleasure that he had created for me.

"Don't you—" I began reaching for him.

"No," Dayne interrupted me, pulling my hand away from his pants and up to his lips. He pressed a gentle kiss on the back of my hand.

I wanted him to have that release, too. I reached back to where his pants were still unbuttoned. Dayne grabbed my wrist before I could touch him. He remained silent until I allowed my wrist to relax and fall.

"That was... Goddess... I think I need more," I admitted with a nervous chuckle.

Dayne laughed. "You are absolutely stunning, Selene," he peered at me with those beautiful evergreen eyes.

"You are breathtaking," I said back to Dayne, trailing a finger up and down his muscled abdomen. I was surprised at how natural it felt to compliment the male.

We stared into each other's eyes, no words shared between us for many moments. It didn't feel awkward this time to lay here without speaking.

"I'm sorry I've been weird," Dayne frowned before pressing a kiss against my shoulder.

I poked him in the ribs gently before resting my hand atop his muscled abdomen, stoking it softly. Dayne's jaw clenched between every stroke up or down.

"It took me a few days to understand what you meant," he followed up. I knew what he meant. He meant the night we danced when he asked if I'd ever considered being with someone who was Fae.

"Of course, you hadn't considered it," he whispered, eyes studying me. I halted my hand, allowing it to rest on his chest now.

"I've considered it now," I whispered back, eyes falling to his lips.

His chest lurched at my words and stopped rising as if he was holding his breath for me to continue.

"I don't think we have a choice who we fall for," I paused to think, watching his curious eyes. I thought of how *human* he was—how human they all were. "You're Dayne," I smiled at him, "Not Fae. Just Dayne." His eyes sparkled at my words. "You're Selene," He echoed my words. "Not demi-Fae, just Selene." He smiled back at me before nuzzling his face into my neck.

We lay like this for many minutes before he broke free to wash, offering me the washroom first. I declined and let him go. I couldn't stop thinking about him, those fingers–that feeling. I got the release I needed so badly, yet somehow, I needed it even more than before. I lay in the bed, utterly consumed by what had just happened. A smile spread across my face. I was happy. I was happy for my future; for once in my life, I had a chance, a fighting chance to be someone, to be *happy*.

Chapter Fifteen

Selene

It took Dayne and I an hour to part ways this morning. His shy, sleepy kisses quickly filled with desire, turning deeper and more passionate. It took every ounce of self-control not to lie in bed with him all day. Once we managed to tear our lips and limbs apart, we readied for the day slowly. It seemed we were bringing our lips back together every other moment as we shuffled around the room, finding clothes. The taste and feel of him lingered on my lips, even hours after parting from him.

Gaia and Idris had begun packing their limited items into bags that Dayne had supplied them with. We had two nights left in the Hideaway before the two-day trip to Olvidare. Dayne said we would be traveling on foot. He knelt before me, pressing kisses atop my feet as he promised to find me more comfortable walking shoes.

My uneasiness about Olvidare was almost entirely gone. It was replaced with excitement to see Dayne's home and learn everything about him and where he grew up. I knew I hadn't known Dayne long, but I couldn't help but let the novel feelings lead me. I was deprived of this my whole life, and now, I would make every moment with him count. My mind swirled back to Olvidare... I daydreamed about what his room would be like. I imagined it to have tall vaulted ceilings with everything made of light and airy white. I wondered if his bed frame was made of gold and if his sheets were of warm ivory. I swallowed the desire that filled me as I pictured the two of us tangled beneath those ivory sheets. I shook the sleepy daydream from my head as I threw random articles of clothing into a bag. Dayne would bring me down for dinner soon but would have to meet with his uncle about traveling expenses during his meal. While I wanted to spend every fleeting moment with him, I would enjoy my dinner with Gaia and Idris. The two of them also played a role in easing my mind about Olvidare. We would all stay together. We would all be okay. And for now, being okay was just enough, despite not knowing what the King of Wind wanted from us.

I looked at myself in the full-length mirror, leaning against the wall. It had a golden frame set with stones of opal. I wore a simple flowing white dress, a dark leather bustier cinched tightly around my waist. Dayne appeared behind me. I watched his reflection in the mirror, a smile twitching on my face at the sight of him. He flipped me around to face him, leaning down to press his lips against mine. He kissed me as if he hadn't seen me in years. He released his mouth from mine, pulling me into a tight embrace, resting his lips against my forehead. I breathed him in, mind flashing to the first time I laid eyes on him. I was in a similar flowing white gown. I squeezed him around the center. He had saved me. I owed so much to him.

"I missed you today," he whispered against my face.

I ignored the need that raged within me. "It was only two hours," I poked him in his hardened abdomen. I had missed him too.

Dayne scooped me up in his arms, carrying me over to sit with him on the foot of the bed. He held my hands in his and peered into my eyes. "I can't wait for you to see Olvidare."

My eyes dropped to his lips, craving them against mine yet again. A strange feeling overcame me then: The weight of my desire for him... it was heavy and made me think. But I pushed the thoughts away. I deserved to be rash. I deserved to give in to my need for this beautiful male who had rescued me. So much was stolen from me, but this... this would not be.

I smiled at him and leaned in to kiss his cheek. His face warmed under my lip's touch. I still felt nervous around him, feeling that pull to let him lead—to wait for his kisses or touch. Each time my stomach lurched, telling me to sit back and wait for his caress, I reminded myself that I deserved this. I had already lost too, too much time. I pressed slow and deliberate kisses from his cheek, trailing to his mouth. I placed one then two kisses on his lips before he opened for me. I allowed my tongue to slip gently into his mouth. His tongue swirled against mine in answer. I broke free first but kept my lips brushing against his ever so slightly. His hands began roaming my body. He stroked my back up and down before wrapping around to my front, bringing a hand to one of my breasts. I was aching for him to touch them—taste them. He grappled at them roughly but never dipped his hands below the top of my dress. He leaned his head to my collarbone and kissed up until he reached my ear. He nipped at the lobe of my ear playfully.

"Dinner," he said in a voice that made me want to skip dinner entirely. I could skip every meal for a week and stay in this room with him, still only hungry for one thing. This feeling he brought out within me... It was intoxicating.

I pressed my palm firmly against his chest and shoved. He fell backward against the bed. I climbed on top of him, orienting my body so that our faces aligned. My actions had become less skittish over the past few days. My mind drowning in thoughts of him. He wrapped his strong hands around my waist and pulled me tight against him. I nuzzled my face into his neck, pressing my lips against him. Dayne let a soft moan escape from his lips.

We lay like this for minutes, body against body, legs intertwined. I never wanted to break loose, to *not* feel his body against mine. How in the hells had I gone so long without this?

"I want to give you this," Dayne said, fishing a hand into his pocket. I was confused but intrigued. He sat up, pulling me along with him. He pulled my legs atop him, and I slouched against him lazily. He pulled out a golden chain, fiddling with it for a moment. He propped the chain on his hand and turned it to me. It was a delicate chain of gold with an opal set pendant. I sucked in a breath, taking in its radiance.

"I know someone here... he's great with this kind of thing..." Dayne trailed off as I brought a finger to touch the opal pendant.

"I had him take a stone from my sword to make it. I want you to have this," Dayne blushed then, "if you want it."

The necklace was breathtaking. The iridescent stone glittered from Dayne's palm as he held it before me. Dayne brushed a thumb against my cheek, wiping away tears, I realized.

"I..." I choked, "I've never been given a gift before."

Only the gift of death.

Dayne continued wiping tear after tear away until no more fell. "I will make up for it," He whispered. "For every gift you never got, for the days and nights you spent alone, for the punishments you endured. I will do everything I can to make it better." Pained fury danced in his eyes.

He removed my hair from my back, swiping it to one side. He slid the delicate chain around my throat, allowing the opal pendant to fall into the hollow space between my collarbones. I reached up to touch it. "Thank you."

He took my face in both hands and kissed me. It felt different from our other shared kisses. It somehow felt sad and somber; it was a kiss of promise–of the promises he made... To make up for it. Not for anything he had done to me but for everything I had missed out on—the childhood and life I never had. I would make up for his heartaches, too, I silently promised within the kiss. I let the tears stream down my face, mingling in our kiss. The salt, a bite of reality through the euphoria of his taste.

He broke free from the kiss to look at me, "I will spend every day making up for it."

"Me too," I promised back. A light shone in his eyes at that. That someone —that I cared to mend him too.

"Dinner," he whispered again in my ear.

I wiped the remaining tears from my face and straightened. "Dinner," I repeated.

* * *

IT WAS pork and beans for dinner tonight. Dayne had left me at the table with some friendly-looking females when we realized Gaia and Idris were nowhere to be found. He grabbed a large plate of food and flexed to wherever the meeting with his uncle was. I still wasn't sure how I felt about Nic. He hadn't bothered me since we first met, so I could've been wrong about him.

Eevy A.

I devoured my food quickly, hardly speaking to the friendly females to my left. They were a little gruff but very kind, nothing like that overly feminine red-headed female, Mairda, who wore that same sickeningly fake smile. I watched everyone around me, the Fae I had deeply hated for so long. I had despised the Goddess and the entirety of this Fae continent. Movement caught my eye. A male grabbed someone short and scraggly around the neck, locking him in a headlock only to mess up his hair and release him. I giggled at the sight. They were just like humans, only prettier and more powerful. I was taught to hate magic, too, yet the King of Avalon preyed upon mine. It never made sense to me. I learned to harness that magic these past few weeks–to love it. I felt stronger each day I met Gaia and Idris at the dock. Some days, we would spend hours controlling our magic, allowing it to burn brightly and fizzle out slowly. I attempted to freeze one of Idris's toes like I had done to Dayne's uncle's finger. I was never able to recreate it.

Gaia knew the most about how magic worked. She was lucky enough to have grown up in a land that wanted her. She taught us more about the hierarchy of magic. There were high Fae, like Dayne, who were of the immediate family to any kingdom ruler. The kings of each kingdom were of the highest Fae, not necessarily more powerful than high Fae, but more practiced. Then, there was the rest of the Fae, which varied in magic and strength. Lowest on the magic totem pole, apart from humans, were demi-Fae. I thought to the day I froze the monstrous waves of the Onyx sea. That was powerful... wasn't it? I shivered, not wanting to know what a king was capable of—What Dayne was capable of.

I looked down at my fingers and formed a thin layer of frost on each tip. I had been sired by an ice-wielding Fae with a water affinity. My mother, an ordinary human, told me my father was a beautiful male with hair the color of ice and bright, glowing golden eyes. It was the only thing she would say to me about him. It was likely the only thing she knew. I wondered if I could find him–to learn who he is. Would he want to meet me? Do *I* want to meet him? I never allowed these questions to enter my mind, but I now let them wander freely. None of this mattered before. It was all outside the realm of possibilities. But now... I'd have to think about it. I knew Dayne would make it happen if I wanted it.

The clanging of dishes and glasses sounded around me. Confused by the commotion, I spotted a handsome blonde male standing on a table near the center of the common room.

"Do you hear me, Kingdom of Olvidare?" he bellowed.

"We hear you." The whole room echoed together. I sat back to watch and listen to the display of camaraderie and loyalty.

"Cheers to you all. Another successful undertaking," he paused, allowing the crowd to hoot and holler excitedly.

"But not all of us will return to Olvidare," the handsome male allowed his voice to drop many octaves. The room grew entirely silent.

"This calls for seventeen moments of silence, one for each soldier fallen."

I counted seventeen moments.

"Lan Borski," the male bellowed. "Cane Havernache."

He read all seventeen names. Everyone in the room had their eyes locked on him. Upon the final name, the blonde male bowed his head for seventeen more moments–for their families.

"For Olvidare," he shouted.

"For Olvidare," the entire room yelled back. I swore the cave shook at the strength of their conjoined voices.

The room slowly picked up its usual chatter, silverware scraping against plates and glasses being sloshed together all around me.

I dropped my emptied plate into the wash tub for the kitchen crew and wandered to the lip of the cave. It was twilight out, a perfect match to the grove I knew lay so close. A shiver went down my spine at the memory of our encounter with the fury. I swiveled my head, taking in the clearing. A few males were playing a game of 'who can kick the other the hardest.' I rolled my eyes at them before taking a short stroll to the dock. My mind was spinning with thoughts and feelings. It was unusual to feel happy and to have the promise of purpose. Thinking of my future was intoxicating, but I felt a pull to clear and settle my thoughts. I longed to hear the crashing of the sea, so I set out for the dock. I was able to easily slip away from the cave unnoticed. At least one male followed Gaia, Idris, and me each morning. Being alone, I was able to slip away. The scent of the sea hit me seconds before the sight of it. Its angry waves looked beautiful in the twilight. I allowed the roaring of water and the scent of salt to cool my mind.

Eevy A.

It didn't take long. I stood on the dock and closed my eyes, allowing the sea mist to caress my cheeks. I welcomed the cold. It calmed the roaring inside of me.

"Selene," an urgent voice sounded behind me. I froze at the unfamiliarity of the voice and the hushed tone he was using. I whipped around and faced a slender Fae male with hair and a beard of deep auburn red. I had never seen this male; how could he know my name? I assessed my situation; he stood before me, my heels nearly against the edge of the dock. I could feel the soft misting of water on my ankles as the onyx waves slapped against the weathering wood beneath my feet.

He held up his hands and backed away from me a step. I narrowed my eyes at him, forcing him back two more steps. "I need to talk to you." I studied his freckle-splattered face, searching my mind for any memory of him. His eyes glittered the same deep auburn red as his hair, and his jawline was as if it was carved from stone.

Ice began forming on my fingers. I let a few shards sputter out the tips of them. He glanced down, watching my subtle threat. He turned to walk from me, allowing his back to be exposed for five paces. He turned back to face me, now a reasonable distance away from the dock I stood upon. I didn't trust him, but he was making an effort to show that he trusted me. I could've sent shards of ice through the delicate vertebrae of his neck.

He sent a gust of wind toward me, picking up the bits of ice that had dropped from my fingers to the dock around me. He floated them up to my face, letting them hover there for a moment as if saying, 'I could kill you, too.' He then allowed the breeze to curl around the ice and drift them over to the Onyx Sea behind me. Wind magic.

"Are you from Olvidare?" I asked.

"I... Not exactly," the stranger replied.

I stalked toward him and stopped when only five steps remained between us. Somehow, his silent threat of death soothed my nerves about him.

"Talk then," I spat.

"I'm Aeryn."

My heart stopped beating, his words freezing it into a solid brick of ice.

I gritted my teeth. "Aeryn is dead."

138

The auburn-haired male smiled, soft and sad. "I can prove it." He reached into a bag that lay against his back.

My chest became tighter and tighter. It didn't make sense... what kind of trick was this? My mother's voice rang in my ears. 'Don't be so trusting, you pretty little thing.' I had trusted Dayne, and it worked for me, but...

I watched him, taking in his deep navy clothes and how he moved. How could he *prove* who he was? He removed a handful of messy, creased papers.

"Can I come to you?" he asked me.

"No," I snapped. "Set them down. Back up."

The male set the papers on the dusty ground and backed up. I hurried to the papers, gathering them in a neat stack. I looked at the top piece. Was it a letter? I began reading.

My dearest baby,

I noted the deep wrinkles and stained splotches all over the sheet. Dried tears? I continued reading the letter.

How does a mother say goodbye to her only son? How does she not only say goodbye but lead him by hand to the mouth of a beast? My son. My sweet Aeryn. I love you so much. I spend every day thinking of you, and I will spend every moment mourning you. Every memory we made, I treasure deeply. You were brought into my life when I could barely breathe a moment longer. You gave me eighteen more years of breath. I am forever grateful for the extra years I got with you, my sweet, sweet boy. You must understand why Florence needs to obey. We must obey. You say you understand, but even I have spent eighteen years trying to understand it. Why must you be taken from us? The Goddess commands it. Not my Goddess, but their Goddess. Your Goddess.

Do not be afraid; she will be gentle, she promised. She will caress you and put you into a deep, endless slumber. My only peace is from the knowledge of this, how gently she will claim you. My dear boy, I will see you, I will watch you fall, and I will fall with you. Forever and always, Mama.

I was shaking, wholly and thoroughly shaking. I shoved the top note to the back of the pile and looked to the next. Another goodbye letter. I shoved it to the back, glancing over the next. "I will see you in the next life. Love, Papa."

Tears streamed down my face. I shoved the note to the back, looking at the next. Aeryn approached me slowly until he was only a pace away.

"She killed herself," he said flatly. I knew he meant his mother. The papers made swishing sounds as they shook in my hands.

He took the papers from me, shoving them in the pack behind him. He reached out and grasped my quivering hands, squeezing them tightly.

"Will you listen?" he asked me, gripping my hands. I barely managed a nod. He led me toward the rocky mountains behind us. I tried to control my breathing as he found a rock for us to sit on. Aeryn kept my hands in his, steadying me slightly. He took a long, drawn-out breath. "So, I'm not dead."

I couldn't help but breathe out a jagged breath at the light-hearted joke.

"When the Goddess came to claim me, she did just that. But she didn't kill me. She had never intended to kill me. On killing... us."

I knew who he meant by 'us.'

"Of course, I was furious with the Goddess. At the promise my mother had made to fall with me. I never fell." Aeryn looked down at our hands, grasping each other. His eyes started welling with tears, but none fell. "I learned weeks later that she had slit her throat the moment the Goddess wrapped her arms around me and met my lips in a kiss of death." Tears now shone on Aeryn's freckled face.

I kept still and silent, allowing him time to continue.

"She never intended on killing us, Selene," he said.

"I don't understand," I tried hard to keep the scowl off my face.

"The Goddess wants to tell you herself." He wouldn't look at me; he just kept a tight grip on my hands.

"I..." I choked. "What more can you tell me?"

"Not much." He frowned. "She has a plan for us, Selene; she has always had one."

A dam broke within me. I couldn't discern what I was feeling. The Goddess was never going to kill us? Everything I knew and felt growing up was minimized to nothing in an instant. Had I suffered for... nothing? Ice filled my veins, cooling my hands. Aeryn only slackened his grip on them slightly. Then I thought of him. Of Dayne, and Olvidare. Of our plans—our promises to make up for the lives we were dealt. Ice thrummed within me. My body threatened to shatter at any moment. Where would I go? Where was I supposed to go? This was *my* sodding life.

"I don't think I can..." I started but was cut off by Aeryn.

"You really don't have a choice," his face hardened now, the sadness entirely wiped away.

I took a step away from him, pulling my hands from his. Why didn't I ever get a say in things? I was forced to die. I was forced to go to the Fae continent and Olvidare. Now that I want to go, I'm forced to seek the Goddess.

"This is *my* life," I spat.

Aeryn gave me a sad, knowing smile, "I wish it was that way, too." His tone wasn't defeated but understanding. He had gone through all of this already. Months ago, when the Goddess 'claimed' him.

"So what? We are all just puppets, then?" I squeezed my eyes shut and began pacing in front of him.

Aeryn sighed, tracking me with his auburn eyes, "Someone had to be us."

Someone had to be us. It hit me like a ton of stones upon my chest. This was never, and *would* never be, my life. This happiness I felt over the past few weeks, it was just borrowed sodding time.

"What if—"

"What if you won't come?" He interrupted me. "Let me put it this way,

Selene. I am the nice one. If you don't come with me, the next will haul you off, biting and screaming."

Goddess sodding, damn it.

It wasn't fair. I tilted my head back, looking up at the stars. It didn't take long for me to spot it. The three interlocking links, a bright star shining in the center. The hopes and dreams, the sorrows and pains I had whispered to her —to that constellation. It was pathetic, really. I tore my eyes away from the starry night I had stared at for more time than I'd like to admit, finding Aeryn's face.

"I need time," I whispered meekly.

"No," he said. "You can't keep the Goddess waiting."

"Tomorrow," I breathed, nearly begging.

"Tonight," he countered. "I won't come back, and I won't speak about her location aloud. You wouldn't make it there alone, anyway." His words sounded smug, but his tone was far from it.

A crushing weight consumed me as I realized my time with Dayne was reduced from a lifetime to an hour in seconds. I rubbed my face, sorrow building in my chest. How would I bear this? How would he... My head lulled to the side, suddenly incapable of staying upright.

"Three hours," I managed to croak.

Aeryrn glared at me through the hazy darkness between us but nodded. "Find me here in three hours."

I wasted no time skittering away from Aeryn, jogging back to the cave. I felt drunk off Faerie wine, my head spinning, my chest filled with ice. I scanned the common room for Dayne. I had to get to Gaia and Idris first. No sign of him. I wobbled up the cave's stairs and stood before Gaia and Idris's room. My hand shook as I reached for the handle and turned. I nearly fell into the room, both females gaping at the surprise. I shut the door behind me, Gaia and Idris instantly at my side. Gaia gripped me.

"You're pale, girl," She stated with immense worry flooding her face.

"You are..." Idris said, looking equally concerned. "I don't know *how* one could get more pale, but you are."

The shaking in my hands reverberated throughout my entire body as I collapsed onto their ivory armchair.

"I just met Aeryn," I said, feeling as if I was about to vomit my dinner all over the burgundy rug beneath me.

"You what?" Idris scowled at me now.

Through bouts of nausea and trembling, I recounted the events that had just occurred. Everything spilled out of me in a tumbling whirlwind of breaths. I told them about Dayne and the relationship we had formed. I shared every detail about my feelings for him, the sorrow I felt in leaving him, and the pain in my chest at telling him. I told them of Aeryn's mother and the Goddess's mysterious plan for us. I told them that the Goddess had no intentions of letting us walk free, whether we went with Aeryn or not. We sat in silence after everything was done spilling out of me. Not only did the king of wind seek us, but so did the sodding Goddess of Fae.

Gaia spoke first. "I've changed my mind on Olvidare."

"A feywit could've told me that," Idris spat toward Gaia. Gaia brushed her off with an elegant wave of her hand.

"We may need Dayne to..." Idris started and stopped at the sight of my trembling lips. I knew she meant we may need him to get us out of here. I don't know how I could ask him that after breaking the news–breaking the promise I had made mere hours ago.

I realized every second I spent here was less time to explain myself to Dayne. I wasn't even sure I could find Dayne right now. The reality of leaving him was crushing me. My first friend... he would never forgive me. I looked at the females before me. My friends, my sisters. Seeing them fueled me with strength, but nothing eased the pain. I stood.

"I have to find him." Gaia and Idris embraced me tightly, filling my bones with abundant strength and courage. "I will meet you back here as soon as I can." They nodded to me.

I stepped out of the room and skittered down the cobbled stairs to the common room. It was the time of night when every Fae in this place could be found in this very room. I rubbed my temples as I scanned the rowdy crowd, searching for him. My eyes slid over several groups of brawling males, dancing females, and those having boisterous conversations. I took several steps into the crowd, ducking to avoid being elbowed in the face by a drunken, dancing buffoon.

Where was he? A jaunty fiddle played, forcing my steps forward to echo its beat. I forged deeper into the crowd, stopping occasionally to raise to the tips of my toes in search of a head full of dirty blonde hair. His meeting would have to be done soon, right?

"Oh, sod, sorry," I shook my head at the accidental impact with a scowling female. I briefly touched her on the arm in apology before turning from her. I rubbed my own shoulder, annoyed at how much it hurt from the impact.

Where the sod was he?

I scanned the room again, eyes falling on two tall males with dirty blonde hair. My chest collapsed in relief.

Dayne clapped his uncle on the back, a glass of Faerie wine in his hand. At least ten people stood in my path to him. I swallowed hard and drew in a deep breath before twisting through the crowd. I forced myself to walk as slowly and casually as possible. I still had at least six people to weave through when Dayne sensed me. He turned, keeping one hand on his uncle's back to take me in. His smile was fleeting, dropping into a frown as he surely saw the look on my face. Daggers of ice pierced through my heart at that face. I controlled my movements, but the fear in my eyes... I knew he could see that.

I wove through two more people before Dayne excused himself from his uncle. The few people between us cleared out of the way as he strode toward me. We met in the center of the room a moment later. His arm was around me, nestling me into his side the second we were in touching distance.

"What is it?"

"Room," I choked. We appeared in the room an instant later. Even though nothing had changed, everything about the room felt dimmer—sadder. Even the lack of the jaunty fiddle tune seemed to feel depressing. The world began greying. It wasn't fair. My world had always been grey. I looked up at Dayne, the male who colored my world for me, and began crying.

"Kiss me," Not caring that my tears streamed down my cheeks into the corners of my mouth. Dayne didn't hesitate. He grabbed my face in his hands and kissed me with all the love in the world. We continued kissing and embracing until I broke free.

"Can..." I choked. "Can you sit over here?" I suddenly felt guilty for asking

144

for that kiss. It felt selfish, but I needed one last kiss before I tore down each promise, one by one.

Dayne took up a chair, never removing his eyes from my face. I could only imagine how I looked. I hadn't had time to plan my words–how to break this news to him. I had been standing before Aeryn less than thirty minutes ago.

"I just met Aeryn," I said, stalking closer to Dayne but unsure how to position my body. I scooted a chair before him, sitting knee to knee with him. The concern lessened on his face, but confusion blossomed.

"Aeryn is dead."

"He isn't. He... he isn't."

"Where is he?" Dayne cocked his head at me, concern taking up his face yet again. He didn't mock me. He only gently nudged me for more information. But who Aeryn was... where he was... it didn't matter.

"I can't go to Olvidare." I fought through the words. No matter how much I wanted to shamefully look away, I forced my eyes to remain on him. His ever-green eyes dulled at the impact of my words. His face slackened, becoming white as a ghost. He swallowed hard, fighting the tears I could see swelling in those dulled green eyes. "The Goddess... she took him, she didn't kill him. She has a plan for us all."

"We have a plan," Dayne interrupted with force. The tears started spilling down his cheeks as he looked at me with devastation.

All I could think to say was 'had.'

A small sob bubbled out of Dayne. My heart wrenched in a million directions, folding in on itself. I couldn't take this. The opal pendant around my neck suddenly felt heavier, as if burning a hole through my throat. We sat in silence, tears staining both our cheeks.

"I will see you again," I said.

Dayne shook his head over and over and over. Looking at him was excruciating. The time we wouldn't have together gone so quickly. I stood, needing to touch him. I rotated around to stand above him but at his side. He kept his glossy eyes trained on the now-empty chair before him.

"I've spent years asking the Goddess why I couldn't find my light–my reason to live..." Dayne choked. "I thanked the Goddess yesterday. The Goddess that was going to *kill* you. I thanked her... Because I had found my light." His chin dipped in sorrow. My heart snapped in half at the words. I touched his cheek, trying to turn his face to mine. He fought against the pressure, keeping his head straight and unmoving. I climbed atop his lap, our noses inches from each other. I looked into his eyes, but they were cold and distant. He wasn't looking at me but rather through me.

"I will see you again," I said, taking his face into both of my hands. I cradled that beautiful face, stroking his cheeks with my thumbs. He allowed his eyes to unglaze slightly, now looking at me, at my face. He looked so sad. So horribly sad. My heart was slowly being chipped away each moment I looked at him.

"I've never loved anyone," he said, looking into my very soul. "And I think..." he started, hesitating. "I think if we had more time... I think I would have loved you." Just like that, the chipping of my heart turned into large chunks and pieces being ripped from my chest. Love. One word. Two hearts. A million possibilities, shattered to none. Just like that.

"I will see you again," I repeated for the third time.

"Don't promise that, princess," he smiled ever so slightly, but my heart kept on breaking.

He wrapped his arms around my waist, pulling my body against his. We sat there momentarily, allowing our hearts to thunder against each other. Our chests rose and fell in the same uneven way. Our cheeks, hot and stained with tears, flush with one another.

Dayne squeezed me against him as if trying to attach me to his body so I could never leave. I hoped it would work–I could be forced to go with him instead.

"I'm thankful for our time together," Dayne breathed into my ear. "I will see you again," he finally told me. "I will see you again.... I will see you... again." His voice cracked hard on the last word. I realized he had spoken it three times, an echo to each time I had promised it.

"How long do we have?" he asked in a shuddering quiet breath.

"Two hours," I whispered so faintly I wasn't sure he heard me. The hitch of his breath confirmed that he had.

"The stars will align, Selene. If it is meant to be, the stars will align," he took a shaky breath. I thought of my constellation—the three aligned links. It had to be a sign... it had to be.

"If they take too long to align, by the Goddess, I will take the stars, all of them, and align them myself," he breathed out. "I will see you again."

He released his tight grasp on me, allowing me to lean back from him and meet his eyes. They were full of sorrow and regret but had regained their true evergreen color. I kissed him. It was a sorrowful kiss, a kiss of apology–of regret. He kissed me back, the softness becoming rougher with each fleeting moment. The sorrowful kiss grew and grew into some kind of hungry beast. An urgent beast that could never be satiated. His tongue slid across my lips in beckoning. I opened, and our tongues danced together in a beautiful but tragic symphony. I would miss him—miss this. He stood, grasping me to keep my face to his, my legs wrapping tightly around his waist. He took me to the bed and dropped us both atop it, tongues never losing sight of each other. Our kisses became wild, wet, and messy. Dayne bit my lip, a growl escaping from his throat and into my mouth. I flung my hand down to grasp below his belt. I was ready for him.

I rubbed against his hardness with pure, urgent need. I fiddled with his belt and then the button, removing both easily. I grappled for the zipper of his pants and unzipped. It took everything in me not to break free from Dayne's kiss to look at what had now fully emerged from his pants. I grasped it, wrapping my hand around the hefty girth of it. Dayne moaned in my mouth at my hand around him. I began pumping him as Dayne slipped a hand beneath the top of my dress. He pinched one of my nipples between his fingers, and I writhed in pleasure.

Dayne flipped me. He settled himself in a sitting position on his bed, propped up against the wall. He pulled me atop him, straddling him. I shuddered at the feeling of his bare length against the sheer layer of lace beneath my dress. We locked eyes while rotating our hips against each other. His eyes were wilder than I had ever seen them. He leaned in and kissed my throat, trailing his tongue up to and then in my ear.

I whimpered and started grappling at my lace panties, trying to shove them aside to be skin-on-skin with our most tender parts. Dayne grabbed my wrist before I could fully shift them aside. He didn't speak, only moved my hand up to his chest and away from where I wanted him most. Confusion sparked but was quickly masked with desire. We kissed with ferocity, yet it still remained tender. His hips ground into me, heating me so intensely that I thought I might release myself right then.

I shifted, ever so slightly, to the left. The wetness of me allowed the lace to slip to the side. We both remained still for a moment, sucking in a breath at the feeling of my bare slickness against his length. He remained motionless while I slowly rubbed my wetness up him. I could feel the tip of him against me. He let out a throaty moan at the feeling. I picked up speed, rubbing and rotating against him, becoming wetter and wetter.

I trailed my hand down his body and grasped what I wanted inside of me. I lifted my hips slightly in preparation to allow him to slowly sink into me. He again wrenched my hand up and away. I broke free from his mouth, looking at him in confusion. I needed this—he needed this, didn't he?

He surged his lips back to mine, rocking his hips thoroughly against me. We both picked up speed. Dayne was rubbing both of my nipples now but through the top part of my dress. I had half a thought to rip the top of my dress down so he could put them in his mouth, but I was too focused on the sensation flowing through me, rubbing against me. All I could do was rotate my hips against his hardness. Faster and harder, we thrust against each other, the bare wetness of me sliding up and down him. I wanted him to slip inside of me; I needed him to.

"Dayne," I spoke his name, tossing my head back. His lips were on my throat a heartbeat later, kissing down to my chest. My mind exploded into a cacophony of wild lust and fear. Fear that these were our last moments. The emotions were a bizarre cocktail that fueled my rotating hips and the thoughts on the tip of my tongue.

"I'll find you," I whispered, continuing to rub hard against him, feeling more hot sparks detonate in my core.

Somehow, those words... words driven by fear and sorrow, not lust or desire... those words sent Dayne into a frenzied state. He grappled at my hair, pulling my face to his. He pressed his forehead against mine, planting gentle kisses against my lips as we continued to twist and rotate against each other. So much hung in the air between us. Rage. Lust. Fear. Shame. Sorrow.

I opened my mouth, a whimper escaping my lips at the weight of that tension and the burning need coursing through my center. He opened then, too, and we breathed each other in.

He picked up speed as the sensation became overwhelming, bucking his hips forward into me.

"I will not lose you," he snarled into my mouth. I squeezed my eyes shut to keep the tears from spilling out. I could hardly handle everything that swam through me—through us—between us. It was as if we were one. We were nothing but the same heaping mess of raging lust.

A whimpering sound escaped him as he rocked hard against me. I knew he was close... I knew he was close because I was, too.

His length began flickering and pulsating beneath me as he paused his thrust in a sudden halt. A deep moan rumbled from his chest as he throbbed beneath me. The quivering feeling of him—of that, sent me into an instant release. I threw my head back in pleasure, nearly panting as my legs spasmed around him. We released in sync. I met his mouth, and we breathed heavily into each other. We stayed in this position for a moment, allowing our breathing to slow. Dayne slumped into the wall. I could feel the stickiness between us, our fluids intermingling against our skin.

He wrapped his arms around me in an embrace. We hugged for a moment, the smell of him the only sensation on my mind. Aspen and honey.

He pulled away then, kissing me. "The stars will align," he whispered, stroking his thumb against my cheek. Deep within me, I hoped that they would.

* * *

WE EACH TOOK turns washing up before climbing into bed again. We spent our final hour locked in each other's arms. I asked Dayne to describe his home for me. His bedroom, his garden, anything. He stroked my arms sweetly as he went through each room of the Olvidare Manor, describing it in as much fine detail as possible. I clung to him desperately, breathing him in, feeling his chest rise and fall. The ache in my chest had only been masked by desire. It returned now, after our release. I didn't want to leave this male... This beautiful, lovely, and strong male. My savior. I didn't want to, but I had to. I didn't have a choice, and we both knew it.

The time approached two hours in what felt like seconds. We were clinging to each other by the end of our time, neither of us speaking. We held each other in silent heartbreak.

He broke the silence. "Do you need me to take you three to the dock?" He managed to keep his words steady.

"Just outside of the cave, away from the others, would be fine," I said, thankful that he offered instead of me asking. He patted my arm.

I took a deep breath, imagining Dayne walking through the manor's halls. Empty-handed. It all hit me as I remembered. His father... the king. My heart sank.

"Will you be punished?" I asked him. I felt stupid for not thinking of it sooner. Dayne just traced circles and swirls along my arms. "Dayne," I said, forcing him to look at me. He continued tracing the swirls. His silence was answer enough. "Will it be physical?" I barely managed to whisper. He nodded while continuing to draw those damned swirls on my arm. I whimpered softly and gripped him tighter. "I'm sorry." I choked back the sobs that filled my throat. I remembered my recent promise to myself. No more tears. That was a joke. I would spend every night crying, sobbing for this male—for whatever his father would do to him.

He stopped tracing swirls and tilted my chin up so he could look at me.

"It doesn't compare to the unknown of what will happen to you."

I realized it then. I at least knew where he was going, what would happen to him, where I could find him. He would be left in the dark, with no way to me and no way to know if I was okay.

"I'm sorry," I said again. He kissed me. "It's okay." We both knew it wasn't okay.

Our time was running out, and we both knew it. He kissed each of my cheeks and my forehead before shifting us from the position we lay against one another. He scooted off the bed, leading me by hand to follow.

It was silly, but with every fiber of my being, I wished he would refuse to let me go, to hold me hostage. I wanted him to keep me locked in a box as long as every moment could be spent with him. I wished that would be enough. He reached out and gently touched the opal stone that hung between my collar-bones. I stood on my tiptoes, and he leaned into my kiss.

"I don't know where you're going, but I won't let you leave without a pack." He said once he broke from the kiss.

I forced myself to roll my eyes at him, but it stung to see again how caring this male truly was. He began stuffing things into a bag and flexing an assort-ment of items from Goddess knows where to the room.

"Change," he said to me while handing me clothes. I had him help me out of my bustier and dress. He took me in with a heavy breath as I stood before him in my lace set. I started unhooking my brassier, and he turned to give me privacy. It made me laugh, the privacy he gave me after all we had just done. I slipped both the top and bottom lace pieces off of my body and threw on the items of clothing he had picked out. He turned back, watching me finish buttoning and zipping in various places. I was clad in a white top with a protective leather coat. My pants felt waterproof and insulated, as well as my laced-up boots.

Dayne strapped a gold sword to my back and shoved three knives in assorted places across my body. He took a step back and breathed in with a nod.

"Ready?" he asked.

"Never," I replied.

"Me either."

We both stepped forward to embrace each other in a tight hug.

"You were my first friend," I told him, embracing him tightly. To my surprise, he said, "You were mine too." I allowed one single tear to fall before stepping back from the embrace.

Dayne wrapped an arm around my waist and flexed us into Gaia and Idris's room.

The two females were sitting on the couch, packed and fully prepared for the traveling ahead. It would take a decent amount of energy to flex the three of us, but it wasn't far, so he would recuperate quickly. Gaia and Idris looked solemnly between us before rising to meet us by the door. We wordlessly grasped each other and allowed Dayne to flex us outside. He brought us to where I had asked, just outside the cave, only far enough to be out of sight.

Gaia and Idris walked ahead slowly, giving us a moment of privacy. Neither of us had tears left to cry. He took my hands and leaned down to kiss me one last time.

"When we meet again," Dayne breathed, "I will still make it up to you. A gift for every day you've been alive." He tapped the opal stone around my neck. I reached my hand up to stroke his face. "I can't wait to see you again, Dayne."

He smiled. "Go kick some Goddess ass, princess." I smiled back at him as he pulled me into a tight embrace. I breathed in the smell of aspen and honey. It wrapped around me in a gentle caress. We pulled away and met eyes.

"I will see you again," he stated.

"I will see you again," I repeated, squeezing his hands in mine.

And just like that, we parted ways.

Part Two

Yielding to Fate

Chapter Sixteen

Selene

My hands thrummed with raging ice as I jogged through the shadowy twilight to catch up to Gaia and Idris. I swallowed the sorrow, the grief, and the pain, allowing both rage and curiosity to fuel me. The three of us crept into the shadows beyond the dock, hugging the rocky mountainside where I knew Aeryn would be waiting. Aeryn. An iron fist gripped my stomach. He had come here, ruining everything, yet... I exhaled, finding relief in the thought that he had survived. His shadowy figure was illuminated by moonlight as he leaned against the rocky edge of a mountain. I felt Idris warm from beside me, heat rippling from her as she, too, beheld the male. I placed an icy hand on her shoulder, assuring her—cooling her.

"Gaia, Idris," Aeryn spoke with what sounded like relief. He shoved from the position he leaned against the rocky mountain wall and strolled toward us. Gaia extended her arms first, greeting him in a tight embrace. Aeryn stood stunned for a moment before wrapping his arms around her in answer. Idris and I watched from a few paces away as Gaia pulled back and took Aeryn's face in her hands. Aeryn looked uncomfortable by the touch, but Gaia proceeded anyway. She kissed his forehead for a long moment and mumbled something to him. He grasped her shoulders tightly as she whispered. The two held each other until eventually breaking free and turning to look at us.

Idris strode forward, sparks trailing behind her, filling the air around us with energy. She grasped his hands with hers and bowed her head deeply to him. Aeryn bowed back even deeper than she had. I knew the unspoken words, the trauma that flittered between them. It made my life–my trauma feel inconsequential compared to the two that joined hands before me.

I closed my eyes and pushed Dayne deep within me, into the stomach of my soul. It didn't compare, not in the slightest, to the anguish-filled lives before me. I looked to the sea. The lapping waters of the Onyx Sea made the wooden docks around us groan. I wanted to walk to it, to dive beneath the frigid waves to numb my pain. I turned back to Idris and Aeryn, who had now dropped each other's hands.

I studied Aeryn's grim face. His features were harmonious, the deep auburn of his hair, beard, eyes, and freckles all the same hue. He reminded me of the male version of Mairda.

"You follow me closely," Aeryn said with intensity, speaking to all three of us. "The trip should take us four hours—five if we have... issues."

I don't know what I expected, but such a short trip was not it. The Twilight Grove extended over a ten-hour walk along the southwestern coast of the Fae continent. Mountains remained at our backs, which meant we would be traveling the barren valley between the mountains and grove or into the Twilight Grove itself.

Sodding Goddess, save us.

My fear was solidified as Aeryn stalked straight for the grove. Idris, Gaia, and I scampered along behind him. None of us spoke as we took hesitant steps toward the gnarling trees and the not-so-sweet beckoning of twilight.

Aeryn swaggered ahead of us, not a hint of fear shining on his face. I worked to keep my face neutral as I glanced at Gaia and Idris. Both of their eyes darted around them, but their breathing was steady. I had downplayed my exchange with the fury from the grove when I told them about it. I hadn't wanted them to worry about me. Now, as we strolled back into the horrifying place, I fear I left them underprepared by minimizing the horrors of it.

Aeryn walked ahead while the three of us tiptoed forward, side by side until we reached the grove's edge. The air itself seemed to shimmer with an ethereal silver glow. I hadn't yet seen the magical forest at night, and with it lit by twilight for all of eternity, it glowed amidst the cover of darkness of the rest of the world. The light beckoned us as the gnarled tree branches danced upwards in a weary waltz, a promise of the danger to come. A shiver pulsated through me as we strode closer to those forever-dancing trees. I wished I knew what magic made the moon such a companion to this place. I blinked, the hazy glow of the Twilight Grove blurring in my peripherals.

Aeryn halted just before the edge, scanning the trees before us. I watched his head swivel back and forth, back and forth, standing tall and composed. I looked past him, deep into the timeless grove. Was it timeless? I cocked my head. It was as if time didn't pass; It was stuck in a single moment of perpetual darkness. My eyes refocused on Aeryn; his brave stance and composure were far from an echo of my own self. I hoped that wherever we were going... whatever the Goddess had in store... that it would allow me to stand just as tall.

Aeryn flicked his hand, a swirling wind spinning around his wrist like a bracelet. He rotated his wrist repeatedly, the vortex of wind growing larger, sending gusts of wind at all of us. My hair whipped around me as Aeryn forced the wind to grow until an orb surrounded us. The eery forest before us grew quiet as only the sound of whistling and spinning wind remained in my ears.

"It will allow us to move in silence," Aeryn began in a whisper. "But many predators like to watch for their... victims. So keep a keen eye out."

Gaia, Idris, and I only glanced at each other and swallowed.

Aeryn pressed us forward into the Twilight Grove, his wind whirling around us. He picked up a slight jog, the three of us following without command. I noted that he didn't even care to glance back at us.

The trees grew thick quickly at this pace, and my heart began thundering as I counted how deep we were. 6...7...8...9... trees deep. I remembered what Dayne had said, the common misconception about the grove. Some of the strongest and most wicked prowled the edges while it remained minutely safer deep within.

10...11...12...13

While the wind helped mask our sounds, it made it hard for me to hear the sounds of the grove. I wasn't complaining, though; they weren't particularly pleasant.

14...15...16...17

Eevy A.

We made it deeper than Dayne, and I had gone, still jogging ahead without problem. Twilight coursed through the space around us; only the gnarled bark of the decaying trees snuffed out its silver hue.

18...19...20...21

How have we not seen—

"A meal of four delivered right to meeee," a voice slid inside my head, making me pull my shoulders to my ears in a wince.

Gaia, Idris, and I all halted. My body wanted to move ahead, but a sensation beckoned me to stay.

"Move ahead," Aeryn snarled at the three of us.

His command had us jogging ahead despite the otherworldly pull to stay. There was nothing around us but darkness and the same haunting trees.

The voice slithered through my head yet again, as if it was my own thought, "How pretty, I love blonde hair... It has such a refreshing feel."

I cringed at the disturbing voice. I was sure now that it, whatever it was, wasn't speaking out loud. It was talking to us within our minds. Aeryn picked up the pace, but only slightly.

"What's wrong, you don't want to play?" The voice spread within my head, seeping into my thoughts, drawing out every ounce of fear. I wanted to run fast or fall to the ground in a heap of frozen fear. The words were... well, they were horrifying, but it was the feeling... the feeling of the words scraping against the inside of my skull—my brain, with slimy, greasy fingers.

The fingers gripped tighter as it hissed. "Stop running, my pretties." The burning sensation to halt, to allow the greasy fingers to squeeze me until I popped, came over me. Aeryn took off, now sprinting ahead with much more vigor than before.

"Keep running, my dear, Aeryyyynnn," it hissed inside our heads. Aeryn dug his heels into the mucky ground beneath us. The three of us, panting from fear, nearly toppled into him. What was he doing? Aeryn breathed heavily, his body heaving up and down in quick motions. I looked around, everywhere I could. There was nothing but trees, hundreds of them, thousands of them.

"Now," the horribly greasy fingers clenched on my thoughts tightly. "Bring me the blonde one." I froze at that. No. I thought. No. No. No. "No?" The fingers caressed me now, sliding a single finger around my skull. "Then come to

158

me yourself." It pressed on a thought, a horrible memory, pressing it deeper and deeper until I couldn't remember what memory it was even pressing on. "Come along," It crooned, swiping its greasy fingers against every part within me. I felt my foot begin to rise off the ground, to step forward.

"No," Aeryn hissed but didn't look at me. He remained doubled over, panting with his hands resting against his knees.

I let my foot hang in the air for a moment. "Pretty, pretty girl, do come to me," The fingers found another memory and plucked at it. It was a recent memory from only hours ago. My mind played the images. I was back in the Hideaway, Dayne's pained eyes pinned to the empty chair before him. They were drained of color as I broke my promises. The greasy fingers plucked on this memory like a taut fiddle string. The memory reverberated through my skull as those fingers kept strumming the strings to my mind. My foot remained hanging mid-air as it continued playing.

I scratched at my face—my eyes to make it stop, but it just kept repeating... Dayne's empty stare and the color vanishing from his eyes. The exact moment his heart fractured. The fingers kept plucking the strings, over and over, replaying until I was screaming. I shrieked at it and begged it to stop. The creature laughed slowly. It was deafening from within my head. It wrapped its finger around that string, threatening to snap it, but it plucked again, replaying the memory. It slid a slimy finger down the string as I watched the memory morph into something it wasn't... Dayne stood and turned to me, "I hate you. For all of eternity, I will hate you," Dayne spat in my face. My whole body began to shake, my foot still suspended.

It wasn't real. I dug into my mind, searching for the truth, the actual memory. I couldn't find it. The thing continued, allowing its horrible, greasy finger to slide down the strings of my memories.

"Get out," Dayne pointed at the door. I fell to my knees in the memory. *Hells*, maybe I was on my knees right now. I shook my head, trying to shake out the sight burning into my eyelids. I grasped at him, pleading with him to love me. To just love me and to forgive me.

I screamed again. I clawed at my eyes and couldn't see anything. All I could see was Dayne before me. His eyes were full of hate and disgust. "No," I screamed at Dayne, but my mouth did not move. The greasy fingers that tormented my mind began pressing on the strings—on my memory. It pressed and pressed until Dayne's face faded ever so slightly. With gentle strokes, it began strumming my mind once more. Then, without warning, the feeling emptied my mind. A moment of bliss—of quiet.

But the moment was short. The fingers hovered above the strings of my mind as Dayne's fuming face faded. Suddenly, it pressed against those strings so intensely that they all snapped at once. And then it was gone. The entirety of the memory vanished. The pain, the urgent unrelenting grief, washed away at the snapping of the string. The fingers caressed me again in beckoning. All I could see was darkness. All I could hear was that beckoning, the promise of sweet release. The promise to snap every horrid memory within my head—to leave me with nothing but good memories, even through my state of transfix-ion, I winced. Didn't I have any good memories? The fingers groped and groped for a memory to play... A sweet memory of love or happiness. But the fingers found none, leaving my mind an empty void of nothing. I blinked, the grip on my mind wavering beneath the surprise of what it saw within me. I shook my head, grinding my teeth together as reality reared its ugly head. It wanted to lure me with the promise of an eternity of sweet memories. I blinked again, and my vision started to return. Instead of stepping forward with my foot, I brought it backward, planting it onto the mucky floor of the grove.

"Run," I whispered, eyes finally focusing on Aeryn, Gaia, and Idris.

"You," the voice hissed. The greasy caress emptied my mind the exact moment I took a springing lunge forward. The four of us took off, leaving the hissing being behind us.

"Where are you going," the thing hissed, but we kept running until the greasy caress of its fingers faded far into the distance. We didn't stop running after the thing was gone. Aeryn wrapped a cloak of wind around us again, keeping us stumbling forward.

I brushed my thoughts against my memories as if questioning what remained. I allowed my thoughts to replay the memory that the thing kept plucking at. I sighed in relief at the memory that was restored, the true memory. I wanted to vomit at the thought that my miserable life had just saved me. Had I any pleasant memories for it to play, would I have succumbed to the creature's beckoning? I wondered then why it didn't play any of Dayne...

perhaps because it snapped all the memories of him. I brushed my memories once more, just to be sure they remained, and sighed in relief.

Aeryn allowed our sprint to slowly return back to a jog. No one dared speak, but we glanced at each other often as if in questioning, 'Are you okay?'

Idris looked as if she had seen a ghost, which we had... well, at least heard one. Gaia was composed, a face of stone, somehow looking collected. Aeryn was also stone-faced, forging ahead, taking specific turns, and ducking under deliberate branches. We ran like this for hours, ducking and running from sounds and glowing eyes.

It wasn't until a beautiful glittering pool of water appeared that Aeryn let the wind barrier fall. I shuddered; the last time I saw twilight sparkle off the waters within the grove, a menacing feline beast tried to kill me.

Aeryn stalked to the large pool of water. The closer we got, the more I could make out the smaller bodies of water surrounding the main pond.

Aeryn slowed to a walk as we approached the pool-filled area. The open space was sprinkled with trees but wasn't nearly as thick with them as the area around it. The moonlight glittered and bounced off the still bodies of water. I narrowed my eyes upon them. Something about those pools felt off... They were too still... too depthless. Our strides became more casual as we approached the clearing. We dodged the smaller bodies of water, weaving through them to reach the largest pool. Somehow, the air felt cleaner here. I breathed in deep, filling my lungs so full it became painful. There was no stench clinging to the air around us.

The eery-looking pools seemed to cool the air, providing a refreshing sanctuary as we approached. Aeryn turned to look at us, giving us a slight nod. I looked back at him and allowed myself to slump slightly at the realization. We were here. Wherever it was, we were going... this was it. Aeryn held my gaze for a long moment. It felt as if unspoken words were flowing between us. This was difficult for us both. I stepped toward him the exact moment his face morphed, eyes widening. I cocked my head, then realized he was no longer looking at me but behind me. I twisted around to check Idris, scanning her body, then to Gaia. My throat kinked, a choking sound escaping me as my eyes beheld her. Gaia stood before us glossy-eyed, a long black, bloody point protruding from her gut. Her blood quickly saturated her shirt at the site of her injury.

Eevy A.

Idris's scream pierced the night as I beheld the creature behind Gaia. It was human-esque, with arms that came to a sharp point, one of which was protruding through Gaia. Not my Gaia. I took a hesitant step forward, unsure of how to help. Aside from its horrible arms, the rest of it looked human. It was larger than a normal human, larger than your average Fae. Its skin looked as if it was made of dark metal, yet it still appeared flexible and skin-like. A smile crept across its beautiful face as it began twisting its pointed arm from inside of Gaia. She dropped to her knees, her face already losing color. I thrust forward another step before I was pushed to the mucky ground by Idris, who flung herself at the creature.

She propelled her arms forward with fury, her whole body burning with a glowing red light. Heat rippled off of her and into the core of the creature. The smile didn't fade from the creature's face as it began to glow red hot. Realizing her mistake, I shot a blast of cool water at it before it burned Gaia from the inside out.

The beast then allowed Gaia's limp body to slide off its pointed iron arm. She fell to the ground in a pile, blood pooling slowly by her abdomen. Idris screamed again, releasing endless fireballs at the creature. It advanced on her with smooth, deliberate steps as it again glowed red hot. The acrid scent of smoke filled the air as she hurdled more and more glowing balls of fire. She wouldn't melt it, I realized. It was too dense, too strong. Aeryn sent wind toward Idris's fireballs, feeding them until they tripled in size. The creature glowed so bright I almost had to look away. I scanned around us frantically, wondering how to stop the beast from advancing on Idris. We needed to get out of here.... We needed to save Gaia and ourselves. Aeryn and Idris poured their magic into the creature, its red-hot heat bending and rippling the air around it. They stood now, side by side, pouring their magic into it.

It kept advancing. They couldn't get it hot enough. The iron creature clanked its metal arms together threateningly, blood staining one of them. Idris stepped forward with force, the flaming balls turning into an endless stream of blinding metallic topaz. The stone of her people. It didn't matter; the creature advanced. I looked to my hands, then to the man of iron that approached us. I delved within my magic, pulling the ice from its slumbering state. I looked at Gaia, who lay with weak breath on the forest floor, icy rage filling me.

162

Before I knew what I was doing, I screamed, "Stop." I sent two spurts of my magic towards Aeryn and Idris. It froze their hands together for only a moment. A moment was all I needed. I succumbed to the ice cooling my core and propelled freezing cold water at the glowing creature. The water wrapped around the beast, quenching it deeply. The iron body instantly popped and sucked in on itself, turning a dark black color. It contorted in odd, unnatural ways but continued trying to inch forward as if programmed to do so. I sent a single shard of ice in its direction. The shard impaled the now brittle iron creature right through its center. The moment the shard connected with its core, the beast exploded, shattering into tiny black bits that showered us.

None of us wasted any time in the following seconds. Aeryn ran to the largest pool of water, kneeling at the edge, chanting in a language I had never heard before. Idris and I were at Gaia's side, Idris attempting to pick Gaia up in her arms. Idris let out a guttural scream as she tried and failed to heave Gaia up.

"Let me," I said to Idris, who backed away and allowed me to gently cradle the limp Gaia in my arms. She was heavy, and I was small, but I would manage. I brought Gaia over to Aeryn, who was now parting the glittering pool in two down the center. I wanted to balk at the sight of it but knew that time was already not on our side. A set of opaque iridescent stairs made of slick ice led deep within the pool of water. My body shook violently at both the events of the past hours and the weight of my dying friend. Warning signs blared in my mind, but I had to shove them deep. I turned to Aeryn with wild eyes that I knew were consumed with desperation.

Aeryn approached me and scooped Gaia from my arms. He rapidly descended the ice stairs, Idris and myself on his heels. We reached the last stair and stepped onto a cool, slick marble surface. The stairs vanished the moment I lifted my foot from the bottom step. I was nearly panting as my eyes widened out of pure shock from the magical space we stood in. Where were we? Was this... a chamber beneath the pool? I glanced up from where we had come, the pond's surface above acting like a skylight, allowing beautiful twilight to illuminate this chamber below.

"Welcome to my sanctum," a strong female's voice boomed above us.

I looked to the voice, up the nearly transparent crystal steps leading to a throne of ice and diamond. Sitting upon the throne was a delicate female with glittering skin of deep purple. It wasn't an unnatural purple; she had dark skin like Gaia's, but the chocolate was twisted with notes of a musky blackberry wine. Flecks of gold splashed her face in random patterns, like freckles. Her eyes glowed yellow, and short hair flowed around her in ivory and steel blue hues. Everything about the female before us was mystical and wholly royal.

Aeryn lay Gaia on the cold crystal floor near the dais below the Goddess. Idris was at her side in an instant. I looked to Aeryn, who was now bowing deeply on his knees. I stood like a fool, eyes darting between my dying friend, the unmoved Goddess, and Aeryn.

"Save her," I croaked to the Goddess. She only cocked her head at me. "Save. Her," I repeated through gritted teeth. I wanted to—no felt compelled to take in the grandiosity of the room we stood, but I couldn't... not when Gaia lay there bleeding out.

The Goddess snapped and was kneeling before Gaia in an instant. She was smaller up close, around the same height as Idris, but shorter than myself. She placed two sparkling, deep violet hands atop the bleeding hole in Gaia's abdomen. She threw her head back and began chanting in the same unfamiliar language that Aeryn had used. Wisps of gold and cyan enveloped Gaia, forcing Idris to fall back on her haunches in awe. The colors swirled around the pair until the Goddess halted speaking. The colors froze their swirling motion. Everything around us froze. Even the air itself seemed to chill. I held my breath, watching her tend to Gaia in such a mysterious way. The Goddess then slammed a fist against Gaia's chest. Both Idris and I flinched hard but remained where we were. When she removed her fist, a dark gaping hole remained in the center of her chest. Idris lurched forward, screaming. The colorful force around them sent her tumbling back. The Goddess mumbled a few more unfamiliar words before the colors wisped, swirled, and sucked right into the gaping cavity of Gaia's chest. The hole closed in a flash; a second later, Gaia's once limp body regained an ounce of rigidity.

No one breathed.

"Welcome, children." The Goddess spoke in a voice of sweet nectar. She rose from Gaia and stood back so that Idris and I could surround our friend, who still lay on the floor, eyes closed.

There was a new glow about her. She had lengthened fingers and hair an even more vibrant metallic silver. Everything about her was... stronger... more enhanced.

"What did you..." I trailed off as Gaia began stirring, her eyes opening to look at us.

Idris and I gasped. Her eyes, once a deep blue of calm waters, now shone with vibrant ferocity. I knew without a shadow of a doubt that the friend before me was no longer demi-Fae.

"What did you do to her?" Idris growled at the Goddess, who had taken up her throne of diamond and ice. Idris cradled Gaia in her arms as I kept a steady hand on both of their shoulders.

"I only completed her destiny, one that was meant for her months ago," the Goddess spoke to us while examining her hands. I looked to Gaia, my beautiful friend. She was Fae, not demi-Fae. Fae. The Goddess had turned her. How could she—

"Come, child," the Goddess spoke to Idris, extending her hand. Idris hesitated, looking between Gaia and the Goddess. Resisting the Goddess was tricky, but it seemed like Idris would until Gaia lifted her head and nodded slightly. It was all Idris needed before lowering Gaia into my arms and raising her tiny body from the ground. Gaia was entirely unharmed, but I cradled her close to my chest anyway.

Idris strode up the steps to the Goddess, her heels the only sound echoing in the space. Her petite figure grew more distant with every step she took. When she reached the top, the Goddess stood and wrapped her arms around Idris in a tight embrace. I shook my head in both awe and confusion.

The chanting and colors began again, swirling, twisting, and turning around them. I looked over my shoulder at Aeryrn, who remained rocked back on his haunches, watching. With the same motions, the same chants, and halting of colors, the Goddess turned Idris from demi-Fae to Fae right before our eyes. She was distant from me, but I took in her new beauty. Idris was stunning before, in both a simple and complex way. Looking at her now... she roared with intensity. Her stormy eyes raged with a volcanic anger that threatened to consume anyone and everyone.

Hand in hand, the Goddess led Idris down the steps to reunite with us on the slick crystal floor. She was magnificent, the embodiment of smoke and flame.

I shook as the Goddess stretched a hand to me.

"Don't be afraid, child," she cooed, leaning in to grasp my hand. I allowed her to pull me up into a tight embrace. She smelled like she was centuries old, but not in a bad way. She smelled of knowledge and wisdom—of power, strength, and courage. She released from my embrace, cocking her head at me inquisitively. My hands began to tremble slightly beneath her inquisitive gaze.

She leaned forward, her lips nearly brushing mine. I tried not to quiver at the nearness of her. I allowed my eyes to lock onto hers as she brought a hand to my lips and pulled my bottom lip down with her thumb. She didn't break her eyes from me as she spoke an unfamiliar language, her sweet breath warm against my face. I wanted to shiver, to drop to my knees and cry, but I forced myself to stand firm and breathe. She breathed out then, her thumb parting my lips further, and blew a breath of glittering gold into my mouth.

"Breathe in," she whispered.

I obeyed, breathing in the Goddess's breath. A moment later, my body surged with strength and pain. A golden light emitted from every part of me, surrounding me and the Goddess. It died down slowly, seeping and crawling back beneath my skin. I touched all over my body, my face. My fingers felt longer, breasts fuller, face sharper. Why had my turning been so much different?

The Goddess smiled at me and said something that brought me to my knees.

"You were already Fae, child."

Chapter Seventeen

Selene

My world was spinning as I remained on my knees before the Goddess. All I could think of was my mother. My... Goddess. Who was my mother? The woman I had called mother, the woman I had only been allowed to see once a month... she... My breathing picked up, and I clutched at my chest, clawing as if I could open it to help the breath come easier. My knees dug into the hard, freezing floor of the Goddess's sanctum. She continued to speak from above me, but her words sounded like a whisper inside my spinning, screaming head.

"You were disguised as demi-Fae..." Her words brushed off the edge of my mind as I tumbled into an abyss.

"Bloodlines don't tend to cross..."

I was allowing all of the lies I had been told my entire life to entirely consume me. I didn't care about anything. Everything I had known, loved, and hated was a lie. I never loved the right person; I cursed and hated the wrong people. Eighteen years. Eighteen years of deceit.

"Wind and Ice is an unusual pairing, but..." The Goddess's words kept barely scraping the surface of my consciousness. My breathing was ragged, my sight dulling and blurring around the edges.

Eevy A.

"Two high Fae parents."
I blacked out entirely.

* * *

I WOKE to Aeryn pressing a warm rag against my bare chest. I felt around my body; I was stripped down to a tank top that allowed him access to my chest.

"Your chest was like a brick of ice," Aeryn said as he pressed the warm, damp rag against me.

"I'm hot. Get off me," I shoved his hand away, allowing the cold in my chest to pulse through the rest of my body.

"Where are—"

"Gaia and Idris," Aeryrn interrupted. "In their room, they wanted to share. I promised them to be here when you woke... It was the only way I could get Gaia to rest."

I nodded and closed my eyes, picturing the Goddess in my head. How... *real* she was. I had imagined her as a ghost of a being, a spirit. But, no. She walked and talked like one of us.

"She freaked me out too, my first day here," Aeryn shrugged as if sensing my thoughts. I cracked my eyes open to peer at him. He rubbed the back of his neck with a hand. "She isn't all-knowing like people seem to think she is."

I let his words sink in for a moment. "They say the Goddess knows the past..."

"She can see your history if she touches you. That's why she was able to tell you about..."

My parents. Sired by an ice-wielding high Fae, daughter also to a wind-wielding high Fae mother. I looked at Aeryn, realizing now that he had also been turned Fae. I don't know how I didn't notice it before, perhaps because I was so used to the Fae from the Hideaway.

"Did it hurt you, too?" I asked him.

"I was sore for about a week after my transition," he said, frowning. "It gets better."

We sat in silence for a bit before Aeryn rose from the side of the bed. "Is it weird they want to stay together?"

"No." I smiled. "It's not." A prick of jealousy flowed within me but died down quickly.

"The Goddess wanted me to inform you that because you made it here, she removed the curses from the human kingdoms."

I sagged. I had forgotten about the curses. No matter how much it hurt to leave Dayne, it was the right to come here, if only to stop those curses. I had nothing to say to Aeryn, but I felt a weight removed from my chest that I hadn't even realized was there.

"Well, if you're good, I'm going to head to my room for the night," Aeryn walked to the door, hesitating in the doorway.

"Yeah, yeah. I'm good." I was not 'good,' but I flicked my hand in his direction. He was gone a moment later, leaving me alone with my thoughts.

I looked around the room. The entirety of the space was made of things of varying hues of blue. While the walls and floor were made of an opaque crystal, it resembled ice, creating a cool, almost sterile feeling environment. The room had multiple beds, each with blue quilted covers. I wondered if the room was meant to house many.

I scanned the room, eyes catching on a luxurious-looking antique sphere sitting atop a dresser that, too, was painted blue. Everything in the Goddess's sanctum seemed to sparkle. The walls looked like they were sweating, perhaps slick with condensation. The washroom door was slightly ajar, and I could barely see a showerhead around the edge of the door. I thought to the Hideaway, my only option was a bath. My body urged me up, craving to feel some form of warmth to help dissipate the ice from my bones.

Swinging my legs off the edge of the bed, I winced at the deep soreness within every bone of my body. 'You had been disguised,' the Goddess had said. I remember learning of Fae that could lay a fog over things, disguising it how they wanted it to look. I never realized that someone would do that to another *person*. I hauled myself upwards, wincing further at the pain shooting through my body. I shuffled towards the washroom and stood before the mirror with my eyes squeezed shut. I opened them slowly and took in the person before me. My breath caught in my throat. I looked the same, mostly, but enhanced in every way. My long, golden, white hair held more shine. My pouty lips were fuller, pale skin paler but bursting with life in the form of faint freckles and blushed cheeks. My eyes... I blinked. The centers of them, just around the pupil, were pure icy white. The milky centers melted into a shining golden rim. My mother always told me I looked like a beautiful deer scampering through a snowy forest. I had never seen it until today.

I stripped my clothes off, leaving them on the floor. I was thin like I had been but more toned and structured. My breasts were fuller, and my pink nipples peaked at the cold air around me. My waist was small, my stomach flat and slightly toned. I felt my hips; they seemed fuller. I looked from the mirror down at the V between my legs. I was entirely hairless there and... I felt my legs and under my arms. Well, hairless everywhere. I shrugged. Apparently, the Fae don't have much body hair.

I stalked to the bath that doubled as a shower. It was a crystal clear tub with a transparent pipe running up to the head of the shower. I turned the handle, allowing water to flow through the pipe and out the head of the shower. I stepped into the tub and moaned as the warm water spread across my body. I let the water wipe away the filth of the day.

I considered the last time I showered. It was at the inn with Dayne. I shook him from my mind, feeling ill at the thought of him. I was not mentally strong enough to shoulder the pain of missing him or the idea of what his father would soon do to him.

I lowered myself to the tub floor, bringing my knees tight against my body. The water hit the top of my head and trickled down my face. This place was entirely silent. I felt alone and craved crawling into bed with Gaia and Idris. I wished I had asked Aeryn where their room was. There was no way I would venture out alone, not knowing where to go.

I sighed, closing my eyes and tipping my head back, allowing the water to wrap around my throat. My hand shot to my neck, and I sighed as I grasped the opal stone that hung there. I didn't allow my thoughts to go deeper than that. I just held the stone between my fingers and rocked myself back and forth until every part of me pruned beneath the water.

Numb and unhurried, I forced myself from the tub. I climbed into bed soaking wet and naked, allowing my mind to focus on how uncomfortable it was to be atop the wet sheets. It was easier to do that, to focus on something so minor and allow everything else to float away slowly. I focused hard on it, not allowing any ounce of what I had learned today to take up space in my mind. It was only me and the disgustingly wet sheets beneath me.

Chapter Eighteen

Selene

I AWOKE TO A KNOCK AT MY DOOR. MY EYES FLUNG OPEN WHEN I heard the hinges of the door creak. Aeryn's head poked in to tell me I needed to get up. I rubbed my eyes and realized I was still naked after last night's shower. I was thankful I had been thoroughly tangled within the covers at Aeryn's rude awakening. Instead of rifling through the navy-painted dressers in the room, I threw on some clothes that Dayne had packed in my bag. I didn't let my mind think of him but allowed the clothes to bring me a shred of comfort. I opened the door of my room, finding Aeryn resting cooly against the wall ahead of me.

"About time," he said in a tone that was far from joking. I just rolled my eyes. He pushed off the wall and began leading me down the long, unfamiliar hall. It was arched all the way down, with several doors on either side of the hall as we walked. I wondered if one of those rooms was his. I trailed him, watching his auburn waves bounce as he strode ahead of me. At the end of the hall stood a pair of double doors that Aeryn wasted no time in shoving through.

"She provides for us," Aeryn said as we entered an enormous, lengthy room. The long oak table was filled with so much food that some of it spilled over the edges of the table. I wanted to mock him for that statement but bit my tongue instead. There were at least twenty chairs set around the table. It was clearly the main attraction of the room, as the rest of it was mostly bare. Counters bordered the walls but remained empty and seemingly unused. Gaia and Idris were already seated at the table, but they stood and ran to me the moment we entered. The three of us embraced. Power and strength thrummed through and around us. Gaia furiously kissed my cheeks, my forehead, and nose. She then fell to her knees before me, quivering while holding my hands. I didn't understand and couldn't stand the sight, so I knelt to meet her face.

"For bringing us here," Gaia said, "I thank you." I looked up at Idris, who was shrugging. I wrapped my arms around my friend. "I am so happy you're okay."

The four of us sat around the table, waiting for the Goddess to arrive. Idris had already begun eating, landing her a steely glare from Aeryn. I shifted from the enormous chair I sat in, the wooden back of it reaching higher than my head. I wasn't sure what to prepare myself for today, but I knew that it would likely knock the wind from my lungs once more. It seemed everyone else knew so much more about me than even I did.

The Goddess swooped in, wearing a cape of vibrant shimmering cerulean. Everyone's attention fell upon her as she sat at the head of the table and began silently filling her plate of food. Aeryn shifted, my attention turning to him. He reached a fork out and began spearing several sausage links to put on his plate. Gaia and I glanced at each other and did the same.

"I will speak now," the Goddess said with booming authority. I nearly laughed at the proper way she spoke to us, her voice sweet but commanding. "The months before you were all conceived," she gestured to the four of us, "were terrible times for many on the Fae continent." She took a bite of a strawberry, allowing the red juice to slide down her chin dramatically. "As you know, five hundred of my children were slaughtered by the hand of your human kings." Her yellow eyes flickered. "For the role each of your kings played in the downfall of these males, I cursed them with," she paused. "Well, I cursed them with you."

If I was hungry when I woke, I wasn't now. We were apparently not wasting any time for pleasantries.

"Our Fae kings aren't much better off than the humans," her face twitched with disdain. "While the Fae are my children, I vowed as the Goddess to protect human and Fae alike." She took another bite of the juicy strawberry.

"There is much friction between the Fae kings," she continued with a mouth full of strawberries that made her royal aura seem more casual. "Some fighting to conquer more land, some with no care if their kingdom rose or fell." She tapped a spindly finger against the table. Every muscle in my body remained flexed as if preparing for some blow to the gut.

"Over 1,000 years ago, my predecessor ruled as Goddess. The Fae kings of this time had similar qualms. She introduced peacemakers within each kingdom. The peacemaker's role was simple. To aid the kingdom in which they were placed, and keep the peace between the lands."

I remembered learning of the peacemakers during my time in Avalon. The Goddess had to strike them down; for whatever reason, her plan backfired on her. Apparently, they took over their respective kingdoms. They ran them into the ground with little training to rule with strength and compassion.

"The idea was a great one. Keep the peace; the lands will prosper. That's where you come in, my children." Her voice was thick like honey, but her seething face told another story. It made me wonder what her relationship with her predecessor was like.

"To put it plainly, I killed two birds with one stone. I needed new peacemakers for the Fae kings, and I needed to punish the human kings for their deceitful and reckless actions." The Goddess sat, hands intertwined and resting on the table before her.

"Only..." The Goddess leaned forward and grinned. "I created you with the compassion of a human and the strength of a Fae." I still didn't understand where she was going with this. "My children. Now that you are here, our training begins. I will teach you how to rule, to never succumb to the temptation of domination. You will learn through me, the most powerful ruler, and you will become my mirror image. You will lead your kingdom for centuries to come."

I looked to Idris, who was scowling at the Goddess. Then to Gaia, who kept a neutral face. My jaw loosened, and it took every ounce of strength not to let it hang open.

Lead our... kingdom?

"Aeryn's journey has already begun," She gestured to him. "He will tell you the rest." Everyone sat in silence. "I am so happy to finally have you here with me." She smiled and then vanished with a poof of cerulean smoke.

Yep. The sodding female *vanished* after saying all of that. My stomach churned.

The three of us looked at Aeryn, who was eating breakfast, ignoring the rest of the world. I opened my mouth to speak, but he beat me to it. "She left out a tiny part," he said between mouthfuls. "She is to train us to assassinate the current Fae kings and rule in their departure."

My mouth fell open now in utter disbelief. No way. No way was this the plan for me. I was supposed to be dead, yet... I was never meant to die in the first place. I gripped the table to steady myself. I was meant to learn from the Fae Goddess herself, assassinate a Fae king, and take up his throne? Even within the chair, my body wobbled at the grandiosity of it. I couldn't *kill* anyone.

Gaia, Idris, and I exchanged more-than-weary glances. My stomach turned. It turned not from what I was meant to do but from how everything was aligning. Questions about this curse that I have had my whole life suddenly made sense. I was never alone, never meant to die on my eighteenth birthday. I was meticulously crafted to be who the Goddess needed. I wasn't so sure I turned out how she expected. I twisted my hands in my lap.

"Obviously, the King of Wind intercepted you before the Goddess could claim you and bring you here." Aeryn gestured around us. "We've learned he doesn't know much, but him knowing our existence has complicated things."

"What do you mean?" Idris asked, clearly leashing a snarl.

"As far as we know, all he knows is that four demi-Fae forged by the Goddess herself exist." I winced at the word *forged*. "We will train, learn, and grow until the Goddess feels we are ready to be placed in our respective kingdoms as peacemakers." Aeryn paused, still not having answered Idris's question. "However," Aeryn's voice became warning, "The King of Wind has progressed with his less-than-ideal plans beyond what the Goddess anticipated. You'll have to train fast. If we must depart here sooner than planned, you'll need to be as far into training as possible."

"And if we won't?" Idris barked out a laugh, "If we stand up right now and leave—"

"How do you plan on leaving?" Aeryn sat back in his chair, smirking. Idris and Aeryn's gaze latched onto each other in fierce competition. I swallowed hard, realizing that we were quite literally *stuck* down here.

"I understand it is a lot... saving the Fae continent and all that..." Aeryn broke from Idris's glare, "But she *made* us for this." He looked at each one of us with a confident, intense gaze. "You may feel underprepared now, but no one is better equipped for this task than *us*," Aeryn said.

"Is that what she told you," Idris spat back, hardly letting him finish his sentence. "You can't just make someone *exist* and expect them to come in and save everything. The continent seems fine. The bastards in the Hideaway were jolly enough—"

Aeryn shoved from the table into a standing position. "The King of Wind is pushing troops into the Kingdom of Nature as we speak. We'll be lucky to make it through training before he tries to overtake them." He pinned Idris with a deadly glare before turning to me, "The King of Ice sits and wallows in his own disgusting pity party while his kingdom is rotting beneath him." I blinked, realizing why he was addressing me. I must be tasked with killing the King of Ice. Aeryn turned back to Idris, "The Goddess will tell you the rest, but if you even consider trying to get out of this," Aeryn lifted his shirt, exposing a long still-healing scar across his abdomen, "You probably won't be as lucky as me."

All three of our eyes widened as we beheld the scar that ran diagonally across the front of his chest.

"Why would we want to work with a Goddess that would do *that* to us," Idris growled, still fuming about the situation. She was right. I found myself nodding along with Idris, horrified at Aeryn's enormous raised scar.

"Because, Idris..." he sat back in his chair in a chillingly calm fashion, "Because the alternative is far worse," he folded his hands on the table before him, "What is so bad about ruling a kingdom?" He asked Idris genuinely. "You will get notoriety, wealth, purpose—"

"We'll be separated," Idris whispered.

A pang of jealousy rang through me. I knew she was referencing Gaia, not me. We sat in silence, Aeryn clearly being thrown off by Idris.

I cleared my throat. "Who are we tasked to kill?" The words felt like acid in my mouth.

"I am to assassinate Theon, the King of Wind," Aeryn said. "My training will differ slightly from yours, given the complexity of him knowing we exist." Ironically, I was relieved that killing the King of Wind was not part of my task.

"Idris, you'll be placed in Krakata, The Kingdom of Fire with King Jules, Gaia in Belgar, the Kingdom of Nature with King Galen, and Selene in Seldovia, the Kingdom of Ice with King Erix."

A shiver ran down my spine as the name Erix left Aeryn's lips. I didn't know much about the Fae kings or how they ruled. I hoped Erix would be... well, I don't know what I hoped for him to be, but I was sure I would soon learn.

Idris's fists began glowing red, her already heightened anger rising.

Aeryn put his hands up in the air, palms facing Idris. "I understand. I was angry too," he spoke. "You will adapt and overcome," he shrugged. "I did."

Gaia rested a hand on Idris's shoulder, her flames snuffing out in annoyance. What choice did we have? I wanted to mock him. This was my life—our lives. I was used to this whole *never having a choice* shit, but... I... we... none of us had any say in what happened to us. In what we did. In where we went. There was always a consequence if we failed to act. I ground my teeth together.

What lay before us was terrifying. That was somehow an understatement... It was all-consuming. I realized the complexity of *stuff* we would need to learn would take us months... if not years. I thought of Dayne and allowed a singular drop of grief to trickle through me. I wouldn't succumb to it but allow it to be seen and felt. Taking on this task seemed more than impossible... but what was the alternative? Staying here forever while the Goddess sliced piece by piece off of us until we were whittled down to nothing? Why couldn't *she* kill the kings herself?

"What now?" Gaia broke the tense silence. Sweet, sweet, Gaia.

Aeryn spoke. "Take the day. Adjust to the news. When you have more questions, I will be here."

I slumped against my chair. The news... It was devastating, to say the least. I didn't know how to become strong enough to do what the Goddess demanded of me.

177

Chapter Nineteen

Selene

"YOU'RE LOOKING BETTER." THE GODDESS'S VOICE, LIKE A GENTLE caress, unfurled from across the small crystal table. Her presence imbued the sanctum with an aura of regality. Twilight streamed through the small pool above our heads, casting long, silver shafts of light that danced upon the polished floors.

"I'm feeling better," I forced a smile onto my face, yet it pained me to look at her. It pained me to be near her, the person who forced me—us—into a life of misery.

"Today, we will be discussing many things. You will learn from instructors in the future, but today, you will hear from me." She set her hands before her palms facing up. I admired her deep violet skin, like dark chocolate-dipped blackberries. I reached my hands out, allowing my palms to fall upon hers. Her skin was oddly cool, like the sanctum's cool, slick marble floors. She smiled and closed her eyes.

"Do you want to know your history?" she asked, eyes remaining lightly closed.

"Yes," I squeezed her hand in reply. I wasn't so sure I actually did.

"Very well." The Goddess's nose scrunched tightly as she dug through my past.

"I can only see what you have seen and done with your own eyes," the Goddess began, "even if you do not remember." My fingers began trembling, and I considered rising and walking from the room. I wasn't sure I could shoulder anything more than I already was.

"The Queen of Avalon," she meant the woman I had thought to be my mother, "There is not much here," the Goddess's lips twitched, "but it seems she took your creation into her own hands."

My breathing picked up slightly, not understanding what she was getting at.

"Your mother is most definitely a high Fae with an affinity for wind," My breath caught in my throat. If my mother was a high Fae in the Kingdom of Wind... then Dayne and I were... related?

As if sensing my fear, the Goddess followed up, "Your magic is too strong to be that of an ordinary wind magic. I am sensing ancient magic here. It is likely from the previous generation of Olvidare rulers. The Queen of Avalon did not carry you in her womb." I wasn't related to Dayne. My shoulders drooped in relief.

"Why didn't she have a human carry me?" I found myself asking.

"I know nothing of her intentions or reasoning." I swallowed at the harshness of the Goddess's tone. "Well, dear, you know the rest." She pulled her palms out from beneath mine and opened her yellow cat eyes to look at me. Did I know the rest? A panicked feeling overcame me. "We have much to discuss, so ask your questions of your past now or forever hold them to yourself," she said.

My mind raced. Questions... Did I have questions? Oh Goddess, did I? I could think of none, while I could think of a million. I shook my head, unable to regain composure of my thoughts.

"Very well."

"Your task," she spoke with authority. "Kill the high Fae King of Ice; take your rightful position as high Fae Queen of the Ice." Her eyes flickered at the grandiosity of the statement.

"Sounds easy enough," I joked nervously.

"He may beat you to the job, so it very well could be." She was far from joking as her yellow eyes pinned me to my chair. I didn't shift or even breathe as I waited for her to continue.

"King Erix of Seldovia is... well, he's been a problem for about seventy-five years now." She tapped a finger against the crystal table, the soft noise resonating in the empty space around us. "His wife died during childbirth, their child along with her. He is in a state of... he's in a dark place." She finished, her eyes crawling all over my face for a reaction. My stomach churned. I couldn't help the feeling of being studied—manipulated.

"Erix has been king for many hundreds of years, a decent ruler once upon a time. Now, he allows Seldovia to fall and perish along with him. It is a miracle that Theon of Olvidare hasn't waged war for his lands."

Dayne's father. A twinge of relief overcame me that Gaia, Idris, and I had not gone to Olivdare with Dayne. While the alternative was... incomprehensible, at least we weren't headed into King Theon's hands.

"I have my suspicions that Theon has his eye on a much more... fruitful target." Despite my peaked curiosity, she didn't continue.

"Seldovia needs a compassionate leader. They've lost hope in any reform with a king who lacks not only compassion but has no feelings at all. Can this compassionate leader be you?"

I chewed on my lip, shrinking beneath her blazing yellow eyes. I gave her a shallow, rigid nod, if only to relieve that tension she placed upon me.

She blinked then, a slight smile forming on her face. "Good. There will be much to overcome before you are."

How could she have so much faith in us? I was certain I could not make it through any form of rigorous training. I was certain I would resent the Goddess for forcing this upon us. It took everything in me to keep the scowl off of my face.

The Goddess changed tones. "King Erix," she put a finger to her mouth, thinking, "his weakness is his heart. He may be empty now, but your job is to refill him. Give him reason to live, to trust you. It won't be simple, not in any way. Seduce him, Selene, and you will have his throat at your teeth."

Despite all the Goddess said, Dayne was all I could think of. I didn't want to *seduce* anyone. I wanted Dayne. If I was forced to do this... I could use the pain of missing him to my advantage. I could... couldn't I? I would allow it to drive me so that my sword could find its mark. My insides churned.

Sodding hells.

"If he has no feelings, won't seducing him be... a little difficult?" I blurted out, feeling too much weight crashing down on me. The look that crossed the Goddess's face had me wishing I never opened my mouth.

"All of this will be a *little difficult,* Selene. None of this will be easy. I have watched these rulers for centuries. Erix is cunning. More cunning than he will lead you to believe. He must be manipulated by an equally cunning temptress. His heart is the only way in."

I stared at her, unbelieving. "Wouldn't it be easier to just sneak in and—"

"No," the Goddess snapped. I was again cursing myself for speaking. "If you all are to rule, you must spend time in the kingdoms. You will need to learn, understand, and love the land you will serve." Her yellow eyes pinned me so hard that I swore I felt them burning a hole into my face. Perhaps it was just my deeply blushing cheeks.

"However, if you get an opportunity to kill him," her eyes softened, "you must take it."

"What if I can't," I whispered, sadness consuming me at the thought of murdering someone.

"Once you see his people, Selene, the squalor he has driven them to live in... you will be able to."

"I don't know..." I trailed off, not entirely on board with having such an extreme future set out for me. I wanted to go back to Dayne. I didn't care about *any of this.* I wanted no part. I wanted—

"I need you to understand that you are saving hundreds of lives by completing your destiny. I created you," she gestured to me with both hands, "for this very task."

I swallowed, watching her arms move in fluid, graceful movements before falling back on the crystal table before her. I couldn't win. Eighteen years, I had no future in store for me... All I wanted was a life and a purpose. This was almost an ironic joke. This purpose she laid out before me... it was too much.

There once was a girl who had no hope—no light. Was *this* my light? My hope? I shrunk. It didn't feel right.

"You have no choice but to succeed in your training. If you choose not to participate or betray the process in any way, I will shackle you back to your same curse. What sounds like a good age for execution this time? I could do another ten years, so you'd be what... twenty-eight? I'm sure the people of Avalon would be thrilled to see you again—"

"Stop." I ground out, forcing my palms on the crystal table as if I would rise. I remained in this position, staring at a smirking Goddess who I knew would make those words come true. The sad reality was she didn't need to threaten me further. I could not go back to Avalon. I would rather die trying this than find myself a prisoner of death once more. We stayed like this for minutes. Her soft, serene face smiled across the table from me. My heavy, labored breathing beneath the crushing weight of the choices laid out before me. As the minutes passed, I regained an ounce of composure, sliding back into a slouched position in my chair.

"It seems we have come to an agreement, then?" She cooed at me. I flicked my wrist in her direction. I suppose we had because I would do anything to never see Avalon again.

"Why can't you kill them," My voice was deflated, empty of even an ounce of emotion.

She chuckled, the sweet sound of it reverberating in my ears. "My child, the benevolent Goddess, loved by all, could never kill her children." She picked at her nails, "You will come to learn this is for the greater good. Some of my children have to suffer for the masses to flourish."

Goddess sodding damn her.

She was right in some ways if the continent's state was as bad as she claimed. She had crafted us all to have compassion for those lives, and damn it, it was working.

"What do I have to do," I began rubbing my eyes, too exhausted to care that everything she was saying was crushing me from the inside out.

"In the coming months, your instructors will train you in battle, history, and politics. You will grow as a person—a ruler. They will guide you to become a temptress, and you will prevail. Your first lesson," she snapped, and a ghostly image appeared on the table before us. "Trust yourself."

I halted, rubbing circles on my eyes, allowing my hands to fall in my lap. I

182

looked at the opaque image. It was an... obstacle course? It looked to be made up of several harrowing-looking obstacles.

"You won't complete it well; you may not complete it at all. Trust yourself that you won't fail."

I looked from the Goddess back to the display before us. I tried to make out the obstacles, but they vanished before I got a good look.

"The course is designed to test five abilities or traits. Speed, strength, endurance, knowledge, and intuition." I kept my breathing as relaxed as possible as I realized I might be thrown into this course in a matter of minutes. "You will have the course perfected by the time you are ready to leave here. It acts as a measurement of your success. I will leave you with your mentor."

The Goddess was gone in a flash, leaving me to introduce myself to the female who now entered the room. She skipped right up to me and wrapped both arms around me in a tight embrace. Her loose yellow-golden curls tickled my face as he squeezed me tight.

"Hey, I'm Hauna." She finally released me. I took in the rosy-cheeked instructor with an adorable haircut. She ushered me out of the room into the corridor beyond. We walked side by side, her taking striding steps forward to lead us somewhere else.

"It's great to meet you finally; I've been waiting eighteen years for you, ya' know?" Hauna's voice was bouncy and full of life. She spoke to me with such casualness. I took an instant liking to her.

"It's great to meet you," I replied, unsure what else to say.

"We have to put you through the course, but I promise you, the next time, I will have you so much better prepared." Oh great. We walked ahead, taking a few turns, before we stopped in front of a set of French doors. "It's just through these doors, now." I looked up at the tall, intricately carved designs on the doors. Hauna rested a hand on the beautiful spiraling door knob. "Trust your mind and body." She smiled as if that was going to help me.

She twisted the knob, sending me through the doors, and closed it quietly behind me.

I hadn't known what to expect, but a whole sodding *mountain* was not it. The room was enormous, twilight casting an eery yet ethereal glow throughout the space. It was almost as if the air before me shimmered with a soft luminescence. I shifted on my feet, taking an inching step forward. At the far reaches of the chamber, a towering mountain-like wall loomed, its jagged peaks reaching toward that twilight that danced through the air above it. I took a full step forward now, my attention falling to the mulchy ground. I scanned the horizon and the vast expansive floor before me, wholly covered in... wet mulch? I sniffed the air, my gut suddenly clenching as a thought pricked my mind. I bent down and ran a finger over the mulch, bringing it up to my nose. It was a smell I knew all too well, the fluid we use to start and keep fires roaring during the frigid nights in Avalon. I stood straight up, now taking quick steps forward. A slight shifting sound came from above my head, snapping my attention there. A piece of the ceiling shifted, and Hauna appeared far above me. She smiled and waved at me before lighting a match.

Holy sodding Goddess.

I took off running towards the rocky wall, the only place to escape the mulch that was about to roast with flames. After the Goddess lifted the demi-Fae disguise, all of my senses were doubled, if not tripled. I swore I could hear the match falling through the air, plummeting towards the mulch soaked in ignition fluid. I flung myself toward the wall, not making it very high, before the match collided with the ground. The roaring flames were immediate. I didn't look back; I only climbed up and up and up. I was too slow; the flames engulfed the entire room and were licking at my heels.

The rocks were sharp. I shredded my hands, grasping at them, pulling myself up and up. I didn't have time to consider how winded I already was. Shifting noises sounded above me, forcing me to glance up as another round of soaked mulch dropped to feed the glutinous fire. The flames grew taller and hotter as they were provided more and more. I hauled myself upwards, blood leaking from both of my palms. My foot slipped then, threatening to send me plummeting into the flames below. I roiled ice into my veins, allowing slippery ice pedestals to form above my head. They were slick but more accessible hand-holds than the razorlike rocks. I grabbed one after another, lifting myself up. The ice melted quickly as the flames grew closer and closer. I was close. I was so close. I extended my foot, ready to push myself the last of the way up the rocky wall. I planted my foot on the previous ice pedestal before it shattered beneath my foot. My body fell forward, but I had enough upward momentum that I was able to pull myself the rest of the way to the top. I rolled away from the ledge and lay panting on the ground. I was sweating from the flames but was alive and wholly exhausted. If any running was involved in the subsequent trial, I was doomed.

'Trust yourself,' Hauna had said. All I had to do was survive.

I forced myself to roll onto my knees, looking ahead at the next obstacle. Before me lay nothing but a sprawling white floor that led forward to my next task. My eyes narrowed upon a heap of something on the floor several paces ahead. I strode toward it, realizing that it was *someone* huddled on the ground, unmoving. What?

I jogged to them now and rolled their body over. I jumped back as they suddenly began flailing their arms and legs. I was horrified to see it was, in fact, not a person, but a human-esque body with no face or features of any kind, yet it flailed around like an actual injured person. It was a living... not breathing dummy. I tried to soothe the dummy, but it kept clutching its stomach where stuffing poured out as if gravely injured in the abdomen. I looked around, less frantically, now that I realized it was just a dummy. I saw a thin beam before me leading to another sprawling white marble floor.

On the other side of the beam, a red cross was painted on the ground, a stark contrast to the floor. I had to get the dummy across to the other side. If I was lucky, it wouldn't weigh the same as a human. I left the dummy's side and ran to look over the edge at the small gap between the platforms. Flames roared beneath, but the drop alone would kill anyone. I looked at the thin wooden beam I would be crossing. It looked like it could barely support me, let alone both of us. I bit my lip but hurried back to the dummy. It still clutched its stomach, writhing in pain. I bent down and tried to pick it up. It weighed as much, if not more, than an average person of this stature. I was so weak. I tried to cradle the dummy in my arms, but it was impossible between its flailing and weight.

Hells.

"Stop moving, Goddess, damn it," I screamed, and it stopped for a moment. Oh. It can understand.

"I'm going to get on one knee. I need you to climb onto my back so I can lift you across?" The dummy shook its whole body as if it was trembling with fear. "Now," I growled while lowering myself to the floor, keeping one knee under me so I could rise with our weight. The dummy climbed atop me, clutching me around my throat. One knee lowered, the other bent and I attempted to rise. I had to get this knee off the ground. In a jerking motion, I lurched forward and got my foot beneath me. Another lurch and both feet were beneath me. The weight of the dummy was overwhelming. I took a labored step forward, swaying only slightly. The dummy writhed in pain.

I took another step. I don't know why I was so stupid. The dummy climbed atop my back ten steps from where the beam started. Another step, and another. I was going to collapse. There would be no way I could get us both across. I was fully leaning forward now, the dummy's weight shifting awkwardly. I stumbled a step, the dummy falling straight forward off me, tumbling into a heap of its own stuffing. I fell to my knees in frustration. I wasn't going to get us both across. I rubbed my eyes, racking my brain for some sort of clue. If this was strength, then no amount of cunning would get us both across.

Trust your body. Trust yourself. I knew I wasn't capable. I would have to cross alone. Was that what I was supposed to do this whole time? I doubted it, but I rose to my feet anyway. I walked slowly to the beam, wincing at the ambient heat from the roaring flames below. I looked back once at the dummy; it was still clutching its stomach and 'looking' at me with its featureless face. It stretched a hand to me. "I'm sorry," I whispered to it before turning back to the beam and scampering across it quickly. I stood momentarily, waiting for something terrible to happen, like some otherworldly force smiting me from above after leaving the dummy behind... But nothing happened. I wiped the sweat forming on my brow and stalked away from the beam, taking in my next obstacle.

This time, the next task was on the same platform, the same sprawling white floors. I narrowed my eyes at the sound of rushing water as I jogged forward. Flush with the white marble floor stood a pool of water furiously spinning, creating a tremendous vortex in its center. I walked around its edge, trying to figure out what this obstacle was. The spinning water cooled the surrounding air, fueling me with strength and confidence. I glanced around, finding a countdown marker on a wall made of the same white marble as the floor. It was far above my head, reading ten minutes. I walked to the pool and removed my shoes. I dipped a toe in, and the countdown began. I removed my toe, and it reset to ten minutes. Endurance. The center of the vortex would hold even the best swimmer beneath, killing them swiftly.

I focused on the center of the vortex and willed the waters to calm. A moment later, the thrashing waters relaxed into an unmoving sparkling pool. I jumped in, watching the ten-minute countdown once more. The water began spinning again, working to create a violent vortex to pull me under. I eased it into a gentle slumber each time. I simply soaked in the calming waters for ten minutes. Once the time was up, nothing too grand happened; only the water began draining from beneath me. I swiveled my head, scanning all sides of the pool walls as I was lowered deeper with the draining water. The top of a door appeared to my right. The water drained the rest of the way, fully exposing the metal door. I stepped towards it, annoyed that I was now soaking wet. I willed the water out of my clothes with a smirk and straightened my shirt—Dayne's shirt. I winced and began striding for the door. I reached my hand out, turned the knob, and swung the door open before me.

Inside sat a small crystal table in the center of the small room. Atop the table were three goblets, each half full with crystal clear liquid. I approached the table, glancing around the empty space for any clue. As I approached, I noted a small card sitting before the three goblets. It read, 'Drink one.' I took a deep breath and turned to the first goblet, taking in its ornate stem. I picked it up, brought it to my nose, and sniffed. Nothing. I picked the next and smelled the slight floral scent of belladonna. Poisons. I picked up the third, no smell.

I set the middle glass to the back, examining the first and third next to each other. They were both clear and smelled identical. I had no way of knowing. I tapped my foot in frustration. I didn't have anything to help me discern what was poison. I knew many toxins reacted when burned. Idris would've completed this obstacle with ease. I began pacing the room, forcing both of my hands through my hair. It was the only thing I could do to keep myself from biting my nails. What poisons did I know? I squeezed my eyes shut, trying to remember something—*anything* about poisons. Could I freeze them? I stalked back to the table and poured a small amount from the first and third goblets onto the crystal table. I took a deep breath and sent a whirl of frozen air at both small puddles. Nothing happened. I slammed a fist onto the table, the liquid in the goblets sloshing. Were all three poisons? If only I had a way to make... Fire.

I grabbed both goblets and ran out the door behind me, careful not to let any liquid spill. I climbed out of the now-drained whirlpool and jogged back to the edge with a beam connecting the two platforms. I scanned the area on the other side of the beam, finding that the dummy had vanished. I looked over the edge, flames still roaring. I poured a small amount of the first glass into the fire. I waited for a faint smell, but nothing. Sod this entire course. I poured the second glass into the flames and waited. I continued to sniff. I was out of ideas now. I inhaled deeply, and the faintest smell of garlic pricked my senses. I knew that smell. Arsenic. I dropped the glass in the fire, and the smell of garlic consumed my nostrils. I glanced at the other glass in my hand, unsure why it hadn't frozen if it was water. I shrugged and tipped it back into my mouth. A sweet taste coated my tongue, sending a wave of worry through me. I waited for a moment, but nothing happened. I jogged back to the room beneath the pool, unease sliding away. Another door had now appeared at the end of this room. I shrugged. I wasn't sure what the final liquid was, but it seemed safe.

The poisons must have been a test of knowledge. Which meant... the last obstacle was intuition. Trust yourself. I entered the new room, finding it just as bare as the one before it. Instead of three goblets atop a table, I found three strangers sitting behind a small wooden desk. I scanned the three of them, finding the way they sat to be uncanny. My eyes fell on a bearded Fae male seated with his arms crossed in front of him. A blonde female, also Fae, sat with her elbows propped up on the table. The last was a younger-looking brunette female sitting with her hands in her lap. I looked at them nervously before stepping through the door and allowing it to swing shut behind me. The room was almost too bright as I stalked forward, wincing at the harshness of it. The blonde female stood and walked over to greet me. She smiled, extending a hand in hello. I shook her hand, remembering that Fae didn't shake hands. It was a human trait. Yet the three before me looked Fae. I stood quietly for a moment before the male spoke, "You can trust me," he said with a genuine smile.

"What?" I said aloud, scanning the three. The young brunette female stood now and walked towards me. "No," she said, "they lie, it's me. Leave with me."

Leave with her? I looked around the room, the door behind me gone. The

188

room was bare, with no apparent way out. Only the three strangers, three crystal chairs, and a matching table.

The blonde female retook my hands. "I will not hurt you, child." I shook my head and stepped back from her, snatching my hands away. The three surrounded me now, all speaking at the same time. I heard a mish-mosh of "Trust me." "Leave with me."

Sweat pricked my face as I began to be overwhelmed by both the strangers and the weight of completing this obstacle. What was this test? I walked around the room as the three followed close by. There was nothing. I need to think. This was an intuition test. I must have to pick one of them, but how do I pick one? Why do I pick?

I put my back against the wall and slid to the ground. A slight tinging sound was made at the force I plopped against the floor. I reached into my pocket, fingers wrapping around a cool hilt. Oh. I didn't remove the dagger that had appeared in my pocket.

"Sit down," I commanded the three, wondering if they would obey. To my surprise, they did. I stood now and began circling the table they now sat at.

"Male." I spoke to the bearded male, "Why should I leave with you?" I had no idea what I was doing or saying, but I put on a brave face.

He held up his hands. "I have a daughter. And a wife." So, they knew about the dagger?

I pointed to the brunette. Her voice quivered when she said, "I'm only sixteen, a child." I looked closer at her; she looked young.

My eyes fell on the blonde female last, the one who had taken my hand in hers upon greeting. "I don't want to die." She cried out. They definitely knew about the dagger.

I circled them, taking in every detail of their mannerisms and clothing. Was I supposed to know who was human? Or perhaps Fae? Who was lying? Were they... real? None of this made any sense. I stopped circling when I stood behind the blonde woman. I removed the dagger from my pocket and turned it over in my hand.

Goddess, save me. They're fake... They're fake... They have to be

I stepped towards the seated woman, closed my eyes, and slid the dagger across her throat. I blinked. It hadn't *felt* like skin, but I had never sliced skin

189

before. Her body was limp in an instant, falling forward face-first into the crystal table. I kept my eyes squeezed shut, but there was no hiding the trembling in my fingers. My teeth ached at the feeling of slicing that dagger across her throat. I opened one eye and then the other. No blood? I glanced at the other two strangers still seated at the table. They seemed to have no reaction. I grabbed a handful of blonde hair and pulled to inspect the injury I had just given her. I took in the featureless face, stuffing falling out from her throat. I dropped her hair, letting her head fall back to the table with a thud. I let out a sharp breath, relief swirling within me. Dummies. I circled back around, looking at the girl and the seated male. So, two are dummies, and one is... real?

"I won't hurt you," the male had said.

Maybe they're all dummies, but kill the wrong one, and the last one turns on me? I twirled the dagger in my hand as I watched the remaining two.

They put a child here thinking it would trick me. I would spare the child... right? Or they thought I would spare the child? My head began aching. I wanted to be out of this sodding room, out of this trial.

"What's my name?" I pointed the dagger at the girl.

"S... Selene" she said.

"Where am I from?" I asked the man

"Avalon."

I watched the two, noting that the girl displayed no signs of nervousness, only in her voice. I expected wringing of hands or shy glances out of the corner of her eyes. She displayed none of that. I walked behind the two. I waited a moment, hovering behind the young girl's back before lurching out and slicing her throat. Not even a heartbeat later, the bearded male threw his chair back and rushed at me. I stumbled back a step, but he had the element of surprise. He lunged for me, fury burning in his brown eyes. I turned and ran to the opposite side of the room, trying to get the table between us. He seemed to know my moves, what I would do, and the speed at which I would do it. He slowed and began walking toward me. I walked back in mirrored movements. I couldn't just run in circles away from him this whole time. I would have to fight my way out of this. Kill my way out of this. A smile curved on his face.

"You over-thought it," he stated, tormenting me. He continued stalking me as I continued stepping away.

190

"I know, I have such a pretty, trusting face." He touched his face with his hands. Was he a dummy, too? He looked *so* real. They all did.

I didn't waste a moment as he stood there smirking, hands still touching his face dramatically. I lurched forward, the dagger slashing out at his throat for a kill shot. He immediately grabbed my wrist mid-air and twisted it unnaturally. I screamed out in pain as he yanked my body towards him. He held me against him, my back flush to his chest. The dagger was at my throat.

"I want to see the light fade from those pretty golden eyes," he said.

He flipped me around and shoved me to the ground. Bile rose, seeping its burning sensation through my throat. Could I die in here? I began skittering backward, but he was atop me in seconds. He straddled my body, his forearm alone, keeping me pinned to the ground. I continued to fight and kick against him. I flailed my arms and legs, but he was so *so* strong. I tried ushering ice into my veins, but the male sent the dagger deep into my throat before I could command my magic. My eyes widened as I beheld the faceless dummy above me, falling now toward my face. I clutched my throat in pain, only to find nothing. No dagger, no blood, no pain.

I looked around the room, and a door appeared. I scrambled to get away from the horrible dummies and this terrible room. I kept a hand on my throat as I reached for the knob. I had felt it go in, hadn't I? I felt the sodding thing sever my vertebrae. I stumbled through the door to behold Hauna standing with her arms crossed, smiling.

"Congrats, you didn't die until the last round."

* * *

THE ENTIRE REST of the day, I continued touching my throat periodically. Hauna had told me that the dagger was a simulation. I used it to slit the throats of the other two, but it was never intended to harm me.

It was terrible. The whole damned thing. Even swimming nervously around in the whirlpool for ten minutes wasn't great. Hauna had left me with the rest of my day and parted ways with a hug. She was far too cheerful, but I needed it in my life right now. I spent the rest of my day sleeping, so I now wandered the halls when the rest of the sanctum was dreaming away. I had no idea if it was day or night here, as no matter the time, it was only twilight that streamed through the skylights above.

I strode down the looping hall. The corridors of the sanctum were beautiful. I trailed a finger against the slick crystal walls only removing it when a door obstructed me from touching it. I breathed the cool and clean feeling air. The constant state of twilight here was soothing, but it also felt ominous. It was always dark, cool, and wet, the opposite of Avalon. I continued down the corridor further, wishing that my mind would tire enough for bed.

Hushed voices sounded ahead, forcing me to halt suddenly. I cocked my head at the sounds. I was intrigued, given the hour, but felt the need to soften my steps. I wasn't headed anywhere in particular, but now I tiptoed toward the voices. The volume grew as I got closer. Jealousy pricked at my heart the moment I realized who the voices belonged to. Gaia and Idris. What were they doing in the middle of the night without me? I still couldn't make out their words, but I could hear the hushed giggles. I should've turned around—gone back, but my jealousy and anger propelled me forward. They should've checked on me; they should've—

I stopped dead in my tracks as I crested the rounded corner of the hall and beheld the scene before me. Around the bend, Gaia and Idris bathed naked in a small silver-glinting twilight pool. The moon's light reflected radiantly off the skin on Idris's back as she... Oh, Goddess... as she trailed gentle kisses down Gaia's throat. I watched Idris grope at Gaia's breasts and continue her kisses down until she was flicking her tongue around one of them.

My face heated, no doubt turning blood red. I backed away slowly until I could no longer see the intimate moment. Gaia's soft moan echoed in my ears as I slunk in the shadows away from the pool.

What the sod. What. The. Sod.

Once I was far enough away, I found myself running—tripping back to my room. My jealousy vaporized, and everything made sense... The time the two spent together before Dayne brought me, them requesting to share rooms... I felt close to them like sisters but never seemed to have the same intimate connection that the two had together. Goddess, it all made sense. I ran into my room and shut the door quickly behind me, sliding to the ground with my back against the door. I smiled into the dark twilight-lit room. I smiled at their happiness. My cheeks were still burning hot from seeing their intimate moments, but... somehow, I felt I knew them on such a deeper level now. I pulled my knees up to my chest and clutched them. Thoughts of Dayne slipped in, souring my mood. I glanced at the bed and sighed. Another night alone. I shoved off the ground. I was used to being alone. I could 'do' *alone*.

Chapter Twenty

Selene

I WOKE UP AND DRESSED MYSELF IN BLACK LEATHER PANTS WITH A plain white top. I kissed the opal stone I wore around my neck, fighting the urge to cry. I tucked the necklace beneath my shirt and strode to the dining hall from my room.

"Hey," I strode casually through the double doors into the dining hall. I still didn't understand the enormity of the table for such a private, hidden place.

"Hi," Gaia sang, eyes lighting with joy as they met mine. I smiled at her as I swallowed the wince after seeing them in such compromising positions last night. I slipped into a seat near Aeryn and across from Gaia and Idris. I wanted to stare, searching for every tiny sign that they were in love. I tore my eyes from them and leaned against the tall-backed wooden chair.

My gaze fell on Aeryn now, who had not even lifted his head when I entered the room. His brows were set low as he speared some fruit with his fork. His commanding, all-business personality created tension in the air around us. Even when he indulged us in small talk, I could sense the annoyance brewing within him. His lack of jokes and logical persona made me squirm uncomfortably from where I sat. I reached out to grab an apple off the table as I half wondered if he was this way because of his mother. My heart wanted to befriend him, yet... I worried his sour take on life would seep into my very bones. I wasn't sure I could shoulder any more sadness. I glanced away from the stone-faced Aeryn to my lap.

"Who is your mentor?" Gaia sang to me from across the table.

"Hauna," I smiled, remembering the joyful, bouncy blonde female who offered me a faint flickering light.

"Lucky," Idris stuck her tongue out at me, "At least you don't have a dusty old stick in the mud." I raised a brow, waiting for her to continue.

"He's actually a lot like you," Idris's eyes flashed, falling upon Aeryn. I winced at her joke but knew better than to intervene. None of us wanted this life, yet we all had to be here. Idris was still... adjusting. We all were. I glanced at Aeryn, who acted like he hadn't heard anything.

"So then, Hauna and..." I trailed off, realizing I didn't know the other mentor's name.

"Orphic," Aeryn interjected gruffly.

So he was listening.

I nodded, "Hauna and Orphic are our instructors?" I watched Aeryn, knowing only he could answer my question.

"Hauna will instruct in fighting and creatures," he paused, knowing I would have a reaction to this. Surprised, My mouth dropped open as I thought of the sweet, bouncy blonde female wielding a sword.

"Orphic will be for more general topics. History, politics..." Aeryn trailed off as he shoved a small berry around his plate with a fork.

"Aren't you all so very excited?" A stoic voice boomed from the door of the dining hall. I had an unnatural sensation to rise as I beheld the ancient-looking male. I remained seated but took him in. He was old... I considered the aging process of the Fae. Even the first generation of Fae could still be found. They were decrepitly old-looking but hundreds of thousands of years old. Orphic looked in his fifties, meaning he was likely thousands of years old. I shuddered at the slow, unnatural aging process. It meant you got to love and be loved for all of eternity... Or... spend all of eternity alone. I shivered, refocusing on the male. Despite his age, he was still quite handsome in a sort of intellectual way. His grey eyes embodied wisdom, while his slicked-back salt and pepper hair gave him some edge.

Eevy A.

"Each day, you will rotate between my instruction and Hauna's," Orphic scanned the four of us, chin held high. He hadn't even greeted us before jumping straight to business. I studied him further. He wore glasses that fell at the tip of his nose, making him look even older than he was. He kept his greying beard short, which surprised me.

"If you've eaten your fill, I would ask that you come with me now," Orphic turned to walk from the hall.

I bit down on my laughter, glancing to see that Gaia and Idris were doing the same. The way this male talked had us all, not including Aeryn, clutching our guts to keep from bursting.

Orphic led us down the winding marble corridors to a set of large wooden double doors. He shoved through them into a large open room filled with books as he chattered about his lecturing style. Idris was right. He was a stick in the mud. I strode through the doors behind the rest of the group, basking in the room's warmth. The space was eclectic and warm, a significant shift from the rest of the rooms in the sanctum. The walls brimmed with aged books, some undoubtedly older than even Orphic himself. I spun, taking in every inch of the space. A large patterned rug was spread out on the floor, a rectangular oak table in the center of it. Behind the table were a few stone steps leading to a platform where a small, messy desk stood. Orphic strode up to the desk and sat in the chair behind it. "Each of you will come up, have a short discussion with me, then pair up," Orphic said.

Aeryn was already striding for the oak table in the center of the room. Gaia, Idris, and I followed him.

Orphic called up Gaia first. I watched her gracefully saunter up the steps towards his desk.

I turned to Aeryn, "How has the training been so far?"

"Fine," he reached for a book that lay open but face down on the oak table.

"Fine?" I repeated, anger chilling the blood that circulated in my hands. Aeryn glanced up from his book, eyes falling on me. He looked so indifferent. So uncaring.

"You're a real joy," Idris was scowling at him. Aeryn shifted his head, turning to watch Idris now.

196

"This isn't a game. It isn't supposed to be fun." Aeryn snapped, showing more emotion than I'd seen him have yet.

Idris glanced at me, a look I knew all too well written all over her face.

Hells.

"We've all been through shit, *Aeryn*," Idris's mocking tone went wholly unchecked, "Just because your mother was too idiotic to—"

"Hey," I interrupted Idris before she said something she would regret. She was hot-headed and rash, but the female had big feelings. Guilt included. "We're all stuck here," I glanced between a stoic Aeryn, who was trying to ignore us by staring into his book, and an irritated Idris, "Let's just try to meet each other in the middle, yeah?" I chewed on my cheek, relaxing slowly as Idris's lit volcanic eyes became slumbering.

"Selene," Orphic spoke, beckoning for me to rise. I hopped up, happy to be leaving Aeryn and Idris. I scampered to the table and gave Gaia a sympathetic look as I passed her.

I plopped into the chair before the ancient male. "Seductress of Erix." Orphic looked at me over the tops of his glasses.

Goddess, save me. 'Seductress of Erix'.

I nearly scoffed but held it in, forcing my lips into a hard line. "Of the four kings, Erix is the only king we will tempt with love and lust. The Goddess and I planned your sire greatly to compliment your mother's looks." He tapped a bony finger on the table. "It seems she took things into her own hands." He was referring to my birth mother, a Fae with an affinity for wind. "And your father, getting his high Fae title by marrying into Seldovia's bloodline."

I nodded at the information. I hadn't known precisely how I was related to the high-Fae bloodline of Seldovia, but I supposed it was good to know I wouldn't be seducing someone whose blood coursed in my veins.

"Despite the... mishap, the Goddess and I both agree that you turned out perfectly," He said, not as a compliment to me, but rather one for himself in crafting my genetics. I blushed anyway.

Orphic shuffled papers before continuing, "There is much that the King of Ice has been put through," he twisted his lips in thought. "He killed his own father, the previous king, to avenge his mother. He lost both of his parents on the same day." Orphic looked genuinely saddened by his words. "Erix ruled poorly at the start... Until he met Leyola." His eyes darkened. I knew that Leyola, along with their child, had died during birth. "She brought him out of the dark place he was in. After their death..." Orphic shook his head. "I pity the male, but he has responsibilities. He will only drive his people further and further under."

"What does he..." I considered my words, "*Do* all day?"

Orphic scoffed, "He floats through life. He's lucky to have a sister, Ynette, who takes care of what she can. What we can't figure out is why she won't use her magic. She stopped that day the king and queen perished." Orphic pressed a finger to his mouth in thought.

"King Erix has another young fellow, Aven, I believe is his name... Anyway, not even that poor sap can do anything but watch him rot away in his room." Orphic shoved his glasses higher on his nose, "A shame. He was a good king for a while."

While Leyola was with him. I shuddered at the pain the male must feel. I knew that suicide was possible for the Fae, but it took a lot for it to succeed. I wondered how many times he had tried.

"You mustn't feel sorry for him, Selene," Orphic pinned me with harsh grey-blue eyes, "If he couldn't handle being king, then he should not have put himself in that position."

I kept my face neutral while every part of my insides tightened. He had avenged his mother. He hadn't *chosen* to be king... I bit my tongue, knowing that I would still have to complete the task no matter what I felt, whether I thought he deserved it or not.

"Three houses have collapsed this year alone, killing the families inside," Orphic spoke in a stern voice.

Oh, Goddess. The tightening loosened. If he was allowing his people to perish...

"Once you see the city, my dear, it will be a miracle if you don't waltz into his castle and kill him on the spot." Orphic gave me a sad smile. "He may not look it or have the age of the other kings, but... I have my suspicions he is the wisest. Wise beyond his years. Forced into knowledge and manipulation. We will prepare you for any maneuvers we think he may try."

I nodded, unsure of what else to say. "His unpredictable nature makes it

198

difficult to train you, so you will learn to think on your feet. To adapt to any situation." I nodded again. "If you are successful, you will notice the lessening of females going to and from his bed chambers."

Sodding Goddess.

So he had time to screw a bunch of females? Maybe he did deserve this.

"Everything is about timing, my dear. You may have the easiest king to take out or perhaps the most difficult. Understand this," Orphic leaned forward, "As soon as kings begin falling like peglins during the culling season, there will be warning bells. At the successful completion of your training here in the sanctum, you will each receive a small tattoo on your ankle." I cocked my head, curious at that. "Three small lines. One connected to the life source of each king. When the first line disappears, a king has been taken out by one of your classmates." I shuddered at the word classmate. It felt far too casual for what we were discussing. "Once the first line is gone, you will have one week to kill your respective king, but I wouldn't wait that long if you can help it." Orphic pinned me with his smoky eyes. Despite what we discussed, I couldn't help but wonder what his affinity was... Perhaps fire.

"However, it is imperative you give your classmates ample time." Orphic leaned forward further, snapping my attention back to his words. "No one must touch their king for a minimum of six weeks." He again waited until I nodded. "If you get an opportunity to kill Erix after six weeks is up, whether he desires you or not, *take it.*" Orphic's eyes were wild.

I let out a slow breath, not fully believing where I found myself. Maybe I did die that day on my execution. Perhaps this was some sort of hell I was living. Hearing all of this— all of these *rules* for killing someone... killing the Fae King of Ice... it was ludicrous. It was not *me.*

"Six weeks to set your trap is plenty of time if you work efficiently like we will train you to do. He will be tough to crack, but the Goddess and I are confident that Erix will be the easiest to take down."

I wasn't sure that was all that relieving.

"You must remember to check your tattoo. Each morning. Each night. One week may be too long for your classmates to maintain a ruse. Once word gets out of the deaths, everyone will look to the kingdom's new peacemakers.

Word will get out to the other living kings. They will make plans," Orphic sat back in his chair casually, "or they will kill you first."

I swallowed, "Okay. Check the tattoo twice a day." I repeated, if only to make Orphic feel better. I was still barely processing any of this. I wasn't sure how I managed to sit upright.

"Will the other two be a problem? I forget their names..." I trailed off.

"Ynette and Aven? Not after your training," Orphic smirked, "I hope you are prepared to fully understand what it means to descend from high Fae, Selene."

I wasn't so sure I wanted to find out. But here I was.

"We start your training today with something simple. Pair with my other mentee, Aeryn, and explain how you believe you will successfully fulfill your task."

I blinked, unsure what to expect, but it seemed easy enough.

"Well, go on." Orphic shook his hands in dismissal. I jumped up from the table and returned to the rest of the group. Gaia and Idris were already discussing.

Aeryn had his nose in the same book from earlier. I stood in front of him on the other side of the table. "I guess I'm supposed to talk you through my ideas?"

Aeryn glanced up at me briefly before slowly lowering the book to the table. "I'm all ears," he said, standing from his chair. He walked a few paces from Gaia and Idris. I followed behind. He stood before me, arms crossed and stone-faced.

"Well, uh." I began.

"Great start," Aeryn said. I flinched at the brashness of his tone. A flare of annoyance flashed in me. I had defended him earlier.

"I'm to seduce the high Fae, King of Ice. I will be placed with him as a..." I fumbled for the word.

"Peacemaker," Aeryn said to me in an acidic tone.

"Right. Right. I'll be placed with Erix as a peacemaker." I tapped my finger against my chin in thought. "I suppose I would have to start small, a brush of my hand or some gentle flirting." My face grew red; this was terrible. "Then... I guess progress until he seems to reciprocate the feelings."

"Real specific," Aeryn said in a flat tone.

"Well, what am I supposed to say? Aren't they going to tell us what to do?" I asked, exasperated.

Aeryn's eyes bore into me. "You have to have a mind of your own, too, Selene."

I shrunk into myself. "Right. Well. I would flirt with him, get him to trust me."

"How?" Aeryn raised an eyebrow.

I glanced around the room as if it would give me the answers. "I don't know, I'd share something that hurts me, make him feel like I've been vulnerable." I paused for Aeryn's response, but none came.

"I'd be vulnerable with him, so he will be with me, too. Then I'll have a foot in the door."

"Mhhmm," Aeryn prompted me to continue.

"Then... I'll work up to an intimate moment. A kiss, maybe? Set a time when he would feel inclined to kiss me first so it doesn't feel too pushy. I think... I think after the first kiss, it'll become easier."

"Hmm," Aeryn said. I tapped my foot. "And what about the *killing* part?" Aeryn emphasized the word killing.

"He'd have to be in a compromising position. Perhaps when... When we're kissing, I can—"

"You do realize you will have to do more than *kiss* the poor sod?" Aeryn interrupted, now scowling at me.

My face warmed. Both at what I would have to do and at the building annoyance. Why was he so rude? "I know that," I snapped in embarrassment.

Aeryn and I stood facing each other with our arms crossed at our chests.

"So that's it then? You'll flirt with the guy, tell a little sad story, and kiss him?"

"You're annoying," I snapped.

"You're naive," he snapped back.

I stepped back from him, hurt by the truth in his words. I was naive. I was the most naive for this task. I just had my *first kiss* weeks ago. I was doomed to fail. I would not be the leader the Goddess needed me to be.

"You're spiraling; I can see it on your face." Aeryn's tone remained harsh, but he stepped towards me.

"I am not," I ground my teeth together now.

"I spiraled, too. The first two weeks, I didn't think I'd ever be good enough. In the third week, I hated all of you for escaping this same destiny. The fourth week I thought I was hot shit, and the fifth, I wanted to kill myself."

I flinched hard. "What are you now?" I managed to whisper.

"I've accepted it." He shrugged. "Embraced the reality of what I need to do. I'm stronger, more intuitive, and very much capable of what I was born to do."

I frowned at him. "It won't be any easier for you." He stepped a pace away from me. "At least you have someone at the other side pulling you through all the sodding nonsense." He smiled. I narrowed my eyes, trying to decide whether he was genuine. "Repeat it." He straightened.

I straightened, too. "I'll be placed in the Kingdom of Ice at the side of the King of Ice as his peacemaker. I will fulfill my political duties by day and wreak havoc by night." I chewed on my lip but continued, "I'll slowly worm my way behind the king's defenses, making him more and more vulnerable to me every day. I will seduce him into my bed and cut his head off before he can penetrate me." I regretted using the word penetrate before it even left my lips.

Aeryn was smiling, though, huge and proud. "You're going to conquer a high Fae king and never even screw the guy in the process," He was full-on laughing now.

I blinked, completely shocked that Aeryn could smile, let alone laugh. My face burned red again, and I shoved him. He rolled his eyes at me in reply. I blew out a breath, trying to calm the burning sensation in my cheeks.

"Regroup," Orphic announced over us. We clambered to the center of the room and stood before the instructor.

"Partners. How did the other do?" Orphic gestured to Idris first.

"Perfect," her eyes were shining proudly. "She will penetrate the king's weakness of trusting too easily by building perfect rapport."

Aeryn elbowed me at the word penetrate. Neither of us could stifle our laughter as our eyes met.

Goddess, I would never live this down.

Orphic nodded to Idris but scowled in our direction. "Gaia?"

"Idris will gain trust through doing the king's evil biddings, allowing her access to him in times he wouldn't allow any others."

"Aeryn?" Orphic turned to us then.

"Selene will break down the emotional walls King Erix has constructed around himself. She will slowly seduce him until he finds himself in a compromising position."

Orphic nodded.

"Aeryn, you're farther along. Would you like to share how we will bring down the King of Olvidare?"

Aeryn stepped forward and cleared his throat. My chest tightened; it was Dayne's father they were talking about.

"Theon of Olvidare is suspecting strange goings on with the Goddess already. He is unaware of our reason for being created but knows we exist. His weakness is also his strength—his hunger for more. I will serve Theon everything he wishes on a golden platter. Like Idris, I will do unspeakable tasks granting me access to the king during vulnerable times. I will use my strength in fighting to take him at the first opportunity."

I shuddered at the emotionless way that Aeryn spoke. He was like a soldier. He had entirely accepted the terrible things he would soon be asked to do. I swallowed, remembering that it was still the lesser evil. Right?

"Good," Orphic began, "Now I want each of you to grab a book," he gestured to a pile of assorted books that read things like *The Downfall of Goddess Lyzira* and *The Lessons of Fae*. "I will meet with you again one at a time to discuss our plans for you in much, *much* more detail."

Chapter Twenty-One

Selene

THE FOUR OF US STOOD IN A LARGE CIRCULAR ROOM OF STONE. IT was dark, only the faintest twilight beaming into the room from the grove above. I scanned around the wild-haired and rosy-cheeked Hauna, eyes falling on the arched doors that lined the room's circumference.

"Don't worry about the doors," Hauna said as she watched Gaia, Idris, and I glance around nervously. Gaia and Idris stood close, pinky fingers latched. I'd been considering telling them what I knew—what I saw. It was difficult to, given what exactly I had witnessed. I half hoped I could catch them kissing to make it easier on me, assuming they were a little more... clothed at the time.

"I understand that you have already encountered a few beasts," Hanna beamed at us. Gaia's hand instinctively rose to her gut, where the iron creature had stabbed through her. "Mansche," Hauna was looking at Gaia's hand, placed protectively over her abdomen.

"A man-she?" I asked, cocking my head at the beaming blonde female.

"Named because they take on the form of a male or female, man or woman made of iron. Real great name, isn't it?" I swear Hauna never stopped smiling, no matter the subject. I held in a giggle at the ridiculous name.

"And a howler," Hauna looked at me now. I winced as I remembered those slimy, greasy fingers rubbing along the inside of my skull. "Lovely invisible beings. Can't see em', but if you walk through their den, they will make themselves known."

I wasn't sure *lovely* was the proper term for them, but...

"If you obey their beckoning, they latch onto your mind and break pieces off until you are nothing but a mindless shell of a being. One step towards it's beckoning, and it snaps your mind like a twig."

Hells. I hadn't realized how close I was to being the howler's victim.

"You didn't die, though." Hauna smiled at me.

I glanced at all those locked doors again and prayed one did not exist behind them.

"It is unfortunate your training is at different spots." Hauna gestured to Aeryn, who was likely already slaying beasts daily. I rolled my eyes, annoyed that he was further ahead than us. "I will allow Aeryn to bring you up to speed the first few weeks at a faster pace than he learned." I found myself rolling my eyes even harder.

"I'll leave you to it then," Hauna waved to us and skipped through a door, disappearing behind it.

The four of us took up a small round table with scattered books and papers. Aeryn grabbed a sheet and a pen. "So, what creatures do you know or have encountered up to this point?" He poised the pen above the paper in waiting. My lip curled as I took him in. I was disgusted with myself, but I found it hard to stomach how different he was from us—from Gaia, Idris, and I.

"Mansche," Gaia whispered, cutting off my thoughts. Aeryn scribbled down the word Manshe in terrible handwriting.

"Absolutely not," Idris grabbed the paper from Aeryn, rewriting mansche in delicate, beautiful calligraphy. Aeryn only looked at Idris but shrugged and leaned back in his chair.

"Is that it?"

Gaia and Idris both looked at me. "Howler," I croaked. Idris wrote down the name in that beautiful writing.

"Peglin. That's what they were hunting at the Hideaway," Gaia said.

"Fury and scuttler." I chimed in. Aeryn's head shot up, eyes locking onto mine.

"What?" I crossed my arms.

Eevy A.

"You've seen a fury?"

"I've run for my life from one after it almost liquified me into disgusting goo."

"They're scarce but more commonly found this time of year," he shrugged, unbothered now.

"So that's it then?" Aeryn eyed the three of us. No one spoke.

"More than I expected." He smiled at us, but only slightly. Idris blew hot air toward Aeryn. He swatted it away. "Hey." Idris smiled at him, her ashen eyes smoldering. Gaia and I laughed but were quickly rewarded with a deathly glare from Aeryn.

"I don't suppose we will ever hear you laugh again?" I cooed at Aeryn. He only rolled his eyes in response. He took everything *so* seriously.

"Throughout the next couple of months, the length determined by how well we do, we will come into contact with four creatures. You will learn about every creature that roams the Fae lands, but get practice with the four most common."

"So what are they?" Idris asked.

"You've named two."

"Peglin," I said, and Aeryn nodded.

I let out a breath of relief. I think I can handle a peglin... Gaia, Idris, and I squinted down at the sheet of paper. It wasn't a fury, and I doubted a howler would be all too common.

"Scuttler?" I asked, hoping with my whole being that Gaia wouldn't have to see a mansche ever again.

"You got it. The last two are draves and silkies, neither living within the Twilight Grove."

I'd heard of silkies, I realized. Even in the human lands, we knew of a few creatures... I racked my brain for more but came up with nothing.

"Draves are quiet furry beasts that live in large groups. They are easily spooked and only attack if they feel threatened or they are desperate for... a meal." I shuddered at Aeryn's words. "They're small, about one-third of the height of Idris."

Oh, Idris was not going to like that. She scowled at Aeryn, but he smiled.

206

"Was that... a joke? I am so proud of you, Aeryn." I clapped for him dramatically.

He rolled his eyes at me. "Anyway, one drave can be taken out easily. But one hundred... your bones will be picked clean before your next breath."

Undoubtedly, we would be taking on hundreds of draves whenever Hauna deemed us ready to do so.

"And what of the silkies?" Gaia asked this time.

"Many Fae have tamed a silkie, but it takes years. They're very untrusting creatures; you'll likely lose an arm or a leg trying to tame one for yourself."

"What are they?" I asked.

"They're like tigers of snow. An oversized cat of pure white fur and onyx black stripes. Once tamed, they are incredibly docile and loyal. If you have a year to spare and maybe an arm, then by all means, you can try for yourself."

"Do they live in groups?" I asked.

"Not large ones. Some will live in solitary, some in small even groups of two to four, always with a mate. They prowl the snow-capped mountains of Seldovia." He looked at me.

I crinkled my nose at him. I doubted I would spend much time in the mountains.

Aeryn took the list from Idris now that she had added the new creatures. "Those are the four you will find yourself in combat with within your time here in the sanctum. You still must familiarize yourself with every beast, its abilities, and weaknesses," Aeryn tapped on a book that looked like it weighed more than Idris. I kept the joke to myself.

"Chapter one through twenty," Aeryn said while rising. "You go twice as fast as I did to catch up."

Gaia, Idris, and I looked at each other, then at Aeryn, who was already walking in the direction Hauna had disappeared.

I held a vulgar gesture towards his back as Idris stuck her tongue out at him. We both covered our mouths to keep in our laughter.

"I can read," Gaia said, reaching for the book and clearly interrupting to keep the peace.

Gaia read the chapters aloud, not allowing us to take over even when her voice became hoarse. Listening to her was a mixture of lovely because of her voice and horrible because of the terrifying creatures that walked the lands above us. I was thankful for the four beasts we would encounter. They seemed much more manageable compared to some of what was in these chapters. Once we finished, Aeryn returned with a word from Hauna. She wanted us to begin our general combat for the remaining time before our dismissal for dinner.

"We begin with defense. Even if you're the finest warrior, you die if you can't keep yourself safe." Aeryn ushered us to the center of the room again, away from the table of books.

I rolled my neck as I stood near the center of the room, happy to be standing.

"Idris," he gestured to her to stand before him. "Don't let me touch you," he yelled before lunging at her. She jumped back quickly, but Aeryn still rammed right into her, knocking her to the ground. She clambered backward, but he was atop her in moments. He smiled down at her before she sent a blast of heat at him, knocking him not only off of her but flying back fifteen feet through the air.

Aeryn landed hard on his back, scrambling to his feet. "No magic," He growled, looking at his shirt to see the destruction.

The front of his shirt was on fire, literally. She had singed the loose white tee he wore, and it now bore a large hole, still smoldering at the hit. His entire chest and muscled abdomen were visible through the gaping hole. I touched my own stomach, flat but soft. I wondered if we would all have rippling abdominals by the time we made it through this training.

Idris stood and began dusting herself off. "Well, you didn't tell me the rules," she shrugged with a sly half-smile. Aeryn beckoned her forward again and stood in an offensive stance. He lunged, and Idris hopped easily to the side. He flipped to her, thrusting again, almost grabbing her, but he wasn't fast enough. He took a half lunge towards her but turned a heel at the last second, anticipating her sidestep. He grabbed her short brunette hair and put her into a headlock within seconds. Idris squirmed at his grip, but he was far too strong. He released her, and she fell to the ground coughing.

"Who's next?" He walked from Idris, stalking back to the center of the room. I couldn't bear watching sweet Gaia take on Aeryn, so I raised my hand and stalked to meet Aeryn in the center of the room. I calmed my shaking with a flux of ice through my veins, wondering if that was cheating. I let out a deep breath and straightened my spine as I beheld my opponent.

Twilight bounced off his now-exposed abdomen, yet he still wore the ruined shirt. His face was neutral, yet I could sense he was enjoying this. It was as if this moment was finally worth all the time he spent rolling his eyes at us.

Aeryn didn't lunge at me; he only walked toward me predatorily. I walked back in sync with his steps, instantly reminded of the male from the last obstacle of the course. Our heels clicked against the stone in sync, eliciting that too-vivid memory. I had lost the intuition test because I didn't act first. I couldn't get into a position where I was being chased again. I stopped backing away and instead stepped forward. Aeryn smiled, his eyes zeroing in on me. We walked towards each other slowly, now only six paces away. I forced my ice to sputter and die out. I had to get through this without magic.

When we were two paces away, Aeryn swung at my head hard. I ducked, avoiding the blow, but his other hand swung in anticipation of my duck. His fist collided with the side of my face, sending me rolling sideways. I fell to the ground, hands already at my aching jaw. It was on fire, pain singing through my jaw, down my neck and vertebrae. I began seeing bubbles of light flash and burst in my vision as my head exploded into a blinding headache. I blinked and shook my head gently. It felt like my jaw had been jostled loose. I cradled my cheek, feeling the sensation of blood. Aeryn stood above me, only looking down at me for a moment before striding back to the center of the room.

Sodding pile of peglin shit.

I spit out blood in the direction he walked. If he knew I had done so, he didn't react.

Idris turned her back now, knowing he would beckon Gaia forward. I wanted to turn away, but I couldn't. I kept pressure on the side of my face, still crumpled on the floor, as Gaia walked up to meet her opponent. She bowed slightly to Aeryn before he started walking in circles around her. He was light on his feet, given his size. While slender, he was still quite tall and toned. Gaia twisted on a heel, tracking him as he circled around her. He switched the direction of his circling a few times before lunging forward at Gaia. I held my breath. Gaia dropped to the floor, kicking a swinging foot out, that knocked Aeryn's feet out from beneath him.

209

I slapped a hand over my mouth in complete awe at the sight of Aeryn toppling face-first to the cobbled floor. A moment later, Gaia was on top of him, working to get her legs around his middle. He flipped violently to the side, but Gaia's grip was tight. His left hand was trapped beneath Gaia's legs, the right furiously ripping at her to remove them from around him. Suddenly, Gaia lurched forward, freeing Aeryn's hands. No. What was she doing?

She wrapped her hands around Aeryn's throat for a moment before leapfrogging over him, sliding her legs tightly around his neck. She remained in a sitting position, Aeryn's head nearly in her lap, her legs keeping his head tightly restrained. He flailed at her grip, trying to toss and turn, but Gaia held strong. She released him a breath later but remained sitting, his head entirely in her lap, staring up at her.

Idris had turned now. She was gaping like I was. I didn't doubt for a moment that Gaia would excel at everything we would do over the next few weeks, but fighting was not something I expected her to already know. She patted his shoulder before heaving upwards, shaking him off.

"You can fight," Aeryn said, his cheeks either blushing hot at the defeat or glowing from the lack of air from Gaia's tight grip on him.

"Better than you," Idris barked out a laugh and was jogging up to Gaia.

I pushed off the ground, blood caked onto my cheek from where Aeryn had punched me. My head was throbbing, but what hurt worse was how atrociously terrible I was at fighting. Even Idris held her ground for a minute. My fight was over in seconds.

"When were you going to tell me you could kick ass like that?" I jogged over to Gaia and Idris. Gaia touched my cheek gingerly, allowing the cut to seal itself up in moments. Many Fae with an affinity to nature had strong healing abilities. Fae already healed quickly, but healers were necessary for grave injuries or aiding the process.

"It is a skill I was taught at a young age in Munique." She smiled at the thought of the home where she had spent eighteen years of her life.

Aeryn was sulking but walked over to us, slipping off his burnt and useless shirt and throwing it to the ground.

"Why do all of you males have to be shirtless all the time?" Idris barked at Aeryn.

"You ruined it," he gestured to the pile of burnt tee, "and by all means, you can go shirtless too."

"Two jokes in one hour?" I nudged Aeryn with an elbow. "Look at you." I beamed up at him, feeling genuinely proud.

"Yeah. Yeah." He waved us off.

"Well, *apparently*, Gaia can help me teach you two to hold your ground." He looked between Idris and me.

"I was locked in a box for eighteen years. What do you expect?" Idris spat.

Aeryn held his hands up and looked at me. "What's your excuse then?" He looked at the blood that still caked my cheek. "Sorry." He looked to the floor.

"I have to learn eventually, don't I?" I meant it; I wasn't just trying to make him feel better. I was ashamed of how terrible I was. I remembered watching the males brawling at the Hideaway, and my mood was instantly soured. Dayne. My insides flushed with icy rage at how much I sodding missed him. I wanted to think of him and remember our short time together, but I couldn't bring myself to. It was too painful. I refocused my attention on Aeryn.

"I'm going to teach you the basics," Aeryn spoke to only myself and Idris. "Starting with how to make a fist."

"I can make a fist just fine, you feywit." Idris leaped forward, punching Aeryn in the center of his bare abdomen. He doubled over at the shock, but all four of us burst into laughter.

No one mentioned that Aeryn finally bantered back with us. We were healing him, and in many ways, he was healing us, too.

Over the next couple of hours, Gaia and Aeryn taught us fundamental defensive tactics. We learned how to hold our core tight and stand with sturdy balance. They showed us how to shuffle and parry basic lunges with our forearms. I found myself on the floor more than I'd care to admit. By the end of our lesson, Idris and I were drenched in sweat and exhausted from all the bouncing back and forth we had to do.

Hauna returned to dismiss us for dinner, and we all walked the corridors together, poking fun at how terrible Idris and I were at fighting.

"If you'd just keep your head straight instead of dipping it down constantly, you'd see my fist coming, you know." Aeryn poked me in the side while we all took a seat in the dining hall.

"If your fist didn't fly at my face so fast, I wouldn't need to." I countered.

"You truly are terrible at fighting," Idris said to me with a smirk.

"Says you," I shot back, now offended that I was deemed the worst of the group.

"Oh, don't let her talk to you like that," Gaia chimed in. "You're both so terrible in your own special ways."

We burst into laughter, surprised by Gaia's playful words. Idris shoved Gaia, but it was lovingly. I watched the two closely for the rest of the meal. I smiled at how they would brush the other's arm or give the other a sideways glance. I would tell them I knew tomorrow. Maybe.

We stuffed our bellies full of roast lamb, potatoes, and peas. Idris ate about twenty dinner rolls; I had yet to learn where all her food went. Her attitude must take a lot of energy to support.

Gaia pushed from the table first, Idris following at her heels.

"We will see you all in the morning." Gaia bid us goodnight. The two bumped shoulders as they strode from the hall.

"Thank you for," I paused, thinking. "For all the help today."

"Don't mention it." Aeryn shoved back from his spot, preparing to leave me at the table alone.

"Is there anything to do around here that isn't just train, eat or sleep?" I asked before he managed to leave the room.

He shrugged. "The pools... or I'm sure some games are lying around here somewhere." He started for the door again.

"I'll see you tomorrow then," I called after him. A nod, and he was out the door. I slumped in my chair, taking in the leftovers and scraps. I was exhausted, but I craved nonsense. I craved something so basic, so... unimportant. Anything but walking back to my room and staring at the ceiling until I fell asleep.

I sat for an hour alone at the table, picking at an assortment of food even though I was full. It at least stimulated my mind—distracted from Dayne and the aching in my chest. I pushed from the table and wandered out into the corridors ahead. I walked around for a while, strolling down halls I hadn't been down yet. Wandering the halls in the evening had become somewhat of a ritual for me. While the sanctum was like a maze, every corridor looked, smelled, and felt the same. It lulled me into a sort of twilight state. It at least kept my mind off Dayne... Off how awfully I missed him... his arms around me... his lips.

My ears perked up at an odd sound. I shuddered, remembering what had happened the last time I had heard sounds from down the hall, but decided to creep toward it anyway. As I grew closer, I could make out the sound. It was someone... grunting? I turned a corner and saw an arched opening to a doorless room. I tiptoed toward it and peeked around the wall to find Aeryn, bloody-knuckled, punching a massive hanging sack made from burlap. The room was small, an assortment of tools and training items tossed haphazardly in the corners. A slight layer of dust lay atop the entire space. I hesitated but decided to step into the clearing beneath the arched entrance. Aeryn looked up, sweat gleaming and dripping off his face and shirtless body. I put my hands on my hips dramatically. He swiped sweat from his brow with his forearm, careful not to smear blood on his face.

"It's how I get stronger." He shrugged.

"I'd like to get stronger." I mimicked his shrug.

"I don't think—"

I interrupted him and strode into the room. "You don't think what? That you should be the only one who comes down here and punches a bag all night?" I poked the burlap sack, surprised by its weight.

"No." He started wiping the blood from his knuckles onto his pants. "I think," his tone was edgy, "that if you want to spend extra time with anything, it should be something more useful to a *seductress*." He nearly spat the word as if it was poison.

I crossed my arms, the burlap bag swinging between us on a squeaky hinge. I focused on it for a long moment, allowing Aeryn's figure to blur in my peripherals.

"What?" Aeryn huffed.

I flung a fist as hard as possible towards the burlap sack between us. It connected with the bag, my fingers crunching in dissatisfaction. I screamed, doubling over and clutching my hand in pain. It took everything in me not to fall to the floor.

"What is that filled with?" I exclaimed.

"Sand," He stated coolly. He didn't look too concerned with my injury but raised a brow in my direction.

I shook my hand, trying to shake the pain out of my fingers.

"You're going to want to start smaller," Aeryn gestured to a pile of assorted sacks and training items behind him.

"But I do have a question."

I narrowed my eyes on him.

"Are you here to train, or are you here to keep busy–to take your mind off something?"

Someone. I thought.

"Train," I lied a little too slowly.

Aeryn's eyes narrowed on me. "The male from your memory, then?" He asked, taking me utterly by surprise.

"I... I didn't realize you three could see that too..." I trailed off, looking toward the ground, recalling the howler from the Twilight Grove. The way it morphed Dayne's soft, caring face into something of my nightmares.

Aeryn's stern face softened. "I'm sorry I had to take you from him."

"Don't be. I needed to be here." I snapped a little too quickly.

"If it makes you feel any better, I left someone behind too." Sorrow filled Aeryn's eyes.

"Why would that make me feel better?" I whispered, hardly able to speak.

"Strength in numbers," Aeryn shrugged and straightened, snapping out of his moment of grief.

I stood, twisting my foot into the dirt-covered marble.

"I'll set you up a water bag." He inclined his head to the empty chain hanging from the ceiling on the other side of the room.

"Oh no, you don't need to. I'll leave you to it." I turned to leave the room, suddenly regretting even coming in.

"It's non-negotiable," his voice was commanding. He was already shuffling through the pile of items by the wall.

I turned back, thankful he was forcing me to stay. The alternative was more aimless wandering. Aeryn heaved a flexible blue bag over his shoulder. He hefted it above his head, holding the heavy bag with one arm, reaching out to clip it to the chain with the other. He turned to me with a neutral face.

"Talking isn't always an option," he started, "but this," he slapped the jiggly water sack, "will always be here for you."

"How romantic," I rolled my eyes at him. I'd only known him briefly, but I could tell he would make a good friend despite how hard he tried not to.

"And if you do need to talk," he continued, face wholly serious, "I can do that too."

I nodded and walked over to the blue sack, and poked it. It had much more give than the sandbag.

"You're going to have to hit it a little harder than that." I shot a glare in his direction. I hovered before the bag, unsure of how to start.

"So, you could freeze that if you wanted to?" Aeryn shifted before me, watching me curiously.

I blinked, and the sack became as rigid as a stone. "Cool." Aeryn breathed, walking over to poke the sack of ice that now swung around from its chain.

"I always thought wind affinity was lame," he huffed as he used his magic to calm the swinging block of ice.

"It is kind of lame," I agreed.

"You're not supposed to agree." He kicked his foot out at me playfully. "You're supposed to feed my ego, 'Oh Aeryn, no, your wind magic is sooooo attractive,' and then fan yourself dramatically." I flung the back of my hand to my forehead as if I was about to faint. "Thanks." He smiled.

I blinked, and the blue sack returned to its jiggling, flexible shape. I waited momentarily for Aeryn to calm the swinging of the sack, then punched. I punched again and again and again. I couldn't stop. I furiously hit the sack until I was doubled over, panting from all the movement. My mind was serene; a once violent ocean calmed into one of the sparkling twilight ponds of the sanctum. I looked at Aeryn, a smile creeping across my face.

Aeryn nodded as if he understood the feeling completely. I knew he did. It was why he was down here in the first place.

We both returned to our respective punching sacks and got lost in them.

Chapter Twenty-Two

Selene

We were back in the study room with Orphic the next day. It was a horribly dry lesson on the complete history of Fae politics. It began long before the continent had been split into kingdoms. Orphic explained their worry that the kings desired to unite the regions into one again. We learned of a third continent that was hidden from all: An island with a magical cloak over it. No one could find it, and no one could leave. That was if anyone was even *on it*. I knew a tale of such an island. Humans called it the 'hidden isle'. I was surprised to find out that it was very real and very mysterious, even to Orphic, it seemed.

"Our Goddess's predecessor created the isle," Orphic spoke in his monotone teaching voice that threatened to put me to sleep, "we have an entire team dedicated to finding it," he frowned deeply. Still, it was all he said on the matter.

I twisted my hair around my finger, wondering if what the old male taught me truly mattered much. How much of this all *mattered*?

"Gaia and Idris, please seek your mentor... Aeryn," Orphic beckoned Aeryn over to him. I supposed I was meant to stay and wait for my turn. I sat at the oak table as Gaia and Idris filtered out of the room to find Hauna. I flipped through a book about plants found only on the Fae continent. Orphic was calling me to meet him after only a handful of minutes.

Aeryn gave me a half smile before leaving me in the eclectic library alone with our mentor. I sat across from him, eyes focusing on the flickering firelight that lit this room. He kept it dim and cozy in here. It was such a refreshing space from the harsh, clean coldness that was the rest of the sanctum.

"I want to congratulate you on how well you have been doing thus far," Orphic smiled and removed his glasses from his face, setting them on the table between us. He looked different without those outdated spectacles—younger.

I shifted in my chair, "Oh, I haven't done much..." I trailed off. "I'm not the best at fighting." I finished.

Orphic leaned back in his chair, the flickering light casting shadows on his face. "Fighting is useful, yes, but your beauty will help you succeed," the older male smiled sweetly at me in a way that made my stomach clench.

I took in a breath, unsure of what to say back.

"No doubt those golden eyes are from crossing wind with water," Orphic leaned forward, examining my face. I forced my body to remain stationary, even though every ounce of me wanted to shift back. "Radiant," his eyes locked onto mine. Goddess, why was he complimenting me so much?

"Do you mind standing, my dear?"

"Um," I bit my lip, "Sure." I hesitated but for only a moment before shoving back from my chair and standing before him.

"Over here, please," he beckoned me to his side. I walked over to the other side of the desk to stand before the male. I clasped my hands in front of me. My success in moving forward was solely based on his word. I shifted, waiting. Orphic's eyes trailed up and down my body. "Truly, a work of art," he mused, clapping his hands together.

"Thanks," I mumbled.

"Have you ever been with an older male?" Orphic stood now.

My body involuntarily stepped away. Confusion and fear spiked within me at my approaching mentor.

"You don't need to be afraid," he whispered, taking another step toward me.

"I..." I stammered. I had nothing to say. I wanted to leave this room. I tried to squeeze my eyes shut and appear anywhere but here.

Orphic's face was serene, a soft smile on his lips. Goddess, what the sod was he doing? Were my looks *that* powerful? I didn't think that—

Orphic brought his hands to the top of his shirt and unbuttoned, cutting off my thoughts. My brain turned to solid ice as he continued unbuttoning his shirt. I couldn't move, not even my head tilted down as I tracked his hands. A sliver of muscled abdomen appeared in the space he had just opened on his shirt. I was shocked that the male had such a nice body for his age. It was, no doubt, attributed to his Fae heritage.

"Orphic," I warned now, watching him close the last few feet of distance between us. He ignored the slight warning tone in my voice and brought his hand out to graze my cheek gently. My legs were frozen. My mind was frozen. All I could think was, 'What the sodding Goddess is going on right now?' I couldn't form words. Couldn't swat his hand away.

"Just a kiss," Orphic whispered, leaning closer to me but keeping his body a few inches from mine.

"I don't think this is appropriate," I spoke flatly, my head straight, eyes staring ahead. I couldn't even look at him right now. My stomach bubbled with acid that refluxed, burning into my throat.

"The Goddess doesn't need to know," I could sense the smirk in his voice. He ran a finger down my cheek and leaned his face before mine. His lips hovered there for a moment. His eyes were locked onto mine, but I kept staring straight ahead. I could not—would not look at him. I wanted to cry. I wanted to scream. I didn't understand why he was doing this, yet... I needed to pass this training. I needed *him* to pass me.

"Selene," he whispered, forcing my eyes to flick to his. They were sickeningly full of lust. "All I want is one kiss, and then I will leave you be." He was so close I could feel his breath on my lips.

I blinked long and hard before digging into my well of magic. I didn't want him to kiss me. I didn't want him to touch me. I swirled the ice within my blood, forcing it to my fingertips. "No," I said, staring straight into his ashen blue eyes.

"You are irresistible," he cooed at me, trailing the finger at my cheek down to my throat. His words were like fuel to my icy rage.

"Get ahold of yourself," I said through a clenched jaw but remained standing strong. Backing away felt like a retreat. He would step away from me. He would apologize.

"Let me taste you, just this once," he leaned in even further.

I stumbled backward, bumping into something behind me, a crash sounding against the stone floor. I didn't dare remove my eyes from him to see what I knocked over.

"Step back," I snarled at my mentor.

He was on me before I could blink. He shoved me with force against one of the bookshelves, the wood digging into my back. He barred his teeth in my face, hand wrapping around my throat. I twisted my neck, but his grip was too firm.

"Get off me," I wasn't sure how, but I managed to keep my voice low and steady.

"You're a fool," Orphic flashed his teeth at me once more before shoving me hard against the bookshelf, forcing several books to fall down around me. He released his grip on my throat and stalked back to his desk, casually plopping himself into the chair.

What the—

"You failed your first test," Orphic kept his eyes trained on the desk as he fumbled for his glasses.

"I... what?" I furrowed my brow, hand finding the spot on my throat where he had gripped me. He began scribbling on a sheet of paper. His shirt remained hanging open, the sliver of skin down his front still exposed.

"Wait, stop." I hurried over to the other side of the desk, finding the chair. My brain was an icy mesh of confusion and anger.

"I told you that Erix will manipulate you. He may reverse the roles," Orphic finally looked up from the paper he was scribbling on. "Tell me, Selene, did you think that act was true?"

I didn't have to answer. We both knew I thought it was real—That I thought I had somehow wooed my instructor with my looks or charm by not even trying. I was so sodding stupid. I frowned at him. He frowned back.

Eevy A.

"Have a good evening, Selene," my name was like gravel in his mouth. His disappointment burned into me. It burned through my cheeks, my blood, and my bones. I shoved from the table, and half walked, half jogged away from his desk. I hovered by the door momentarily, "Sorry," I said, but I didn't have it in me to meet his eyes. I didn't wait for his response before scampering out into the hall. My brain misfired and glitched as I strode the icy corridors. My legs had a mind of their own, but I knew exactly where they took me. To clear my head.

I found Aeryn in the storage room, already gleaming with sweat. We greeted each other with only a nod before turning toward our respective punching sacks and breaking open our knuckles. I oriented myself before the swinging blue bag and punched. Once. Twice. The water sack didn't make my knuckles bleed, but they quickly became very sore. It didn't compare to the pains that still ached in my bones from shifting to full Fae. I punched again, feeling the new strength behind each punch. I was stronger; there was no question about that. I pushed through the pain, which fueled me to punch harder. I may be stronger, but I was still weak compared to Aeryn; it shouldn't hurt this badly. Tomorrow, I will be stronger. Tomorrow, it would hurt less. I began punching hard and fast; it felt like my fists were a blur before me. Orphic flashed in my mind, the thin slice of abdomen he had exposed to me. I swung my fists into the bag even harder at the thought.

How had I been so idiotic? I kept punching until nothing but a peaceful hum was in my mind. Until Dayne, Orphic, and my destiny were far away worries. The longer I stood here, sinking my fists into the water sack, the more peaceful my mind grew. I indulged myself in the serenity of it. I punched harder, the pain ripping beyond my fists into my forearms. I didn't care; I was weak. If there was pain from this, I deserved it. The only way to get stronger was to work through the pain. I squeezed my eyes shut, no longer seeing the blur that was my fists before me. I felt everything down to my bones. My mind was in a slumbering sort of state while the bones in my forearms screamed. I ground my teeth together at the pain but continued anyway. Over and over, I shoved my arms forward, connecting with the bag. I brought my right arm back, farther this time, ready to connect hard with the bag. I sent it flying forward. My eyes flew open when my fist did not collide with the water sack. I found Aeryn gripping my fist only inches from the blood-stained punching bag.

I blinked up at him. Tears were streaming down my face that I hadn't noticed before. I looked at my knuckles, busted open entirely, blood dripping from them onto Aeryn's hands.

"You froze it," Aeryn spoke in a gruff, monotone voice. His eyes widened with concern. I turned back to the frozen sack, my blood dripping down it, cooling into frosty streaks. He held my wrists firm as I began to shake. My mind had been serene. Quiet. I had no idea that... "I'm going to let go now," he said and released his grip on my bloody fist. I pulled both hands to my chest, cradling them into myself. Aeryn turned to the ice bag, reaching up to unclip it.

"What are you doing?" I demanded.

"No more water."

"No." I shoved him.

"Take it easy." He pushed me away as he hauled the still-frozen bag from the above chain. "You can use the other side of the sand one," he said, tilting his head towards the burlap sack.

I was still shaking when I allowed the ice to return to its water form as Aeryn hauled it back to the pile in the corner. It flopped against him in an instant. He tossed it down, not caring where or how it landed. I shifted from where I stood, annoyed at myself for causing this. My knuckles were pulsating with pain. Aeryn walked back over to me, eyes set on the blood still dripping from my hands. It was already beginning to heal, but I had ripped deep into the skin of my knuckles.

"Sorry," I mumbled, unsure why I felt the need to apologize.

"Sit." He pointed to a small stool tossed near the wall of the room. I felt like a dog with its tail between its legs as I slunk over to turn the stool upright and plop onto it. Aeryn bent down, face to face with me. "Gaia and Idris have each other," he started. "And while I can tell how much they love you, they're still closer. That means we're stuck together whether we like it or not. So, you can either sit here and cry." Sod, I was still crying. "Or you can talk to me and get whatever it is off your chest. Your choice." He remained before me, knees bent in a squatting position.

"I don't think I'll be able to do it," I said, cringing at the meekness in my voice. "What the Goddess is asking us to do... I won't be able to do it." I wasn't sure how, but I kept my eyes locked on his.

Aeryn rocked back from his squat and plopped into a sitting position on the floor before me.

"So, tough love doesn't work on you, then?" he asked because we had already had this conversation a few days ago. He had told me to toughen up; we were born for this.

"I didn't realize that was love."

He shrugged. "Look. Whatever it is, if its the guy, or the stress or—"

"Stop." I interrupted him. "I... I went my entire life thinking I was going to die at eighteen. When I didn't die, I was shoved into life—into this world I hated for eighteen years. I stand before the very Goddess that put a target on my head before I even existed. One that is now threatening to send me back to that life if I don't comply." My hands shook. "I'm just... adjusting."

Aeryn ran a hand through his auburn hair, tousling it. "I understand."

After a few minutes of silence, Aeryn spoke again, "You're stronger than you think." I laughed, gesturing to my now healed but still bloodied knuckles. "Strength isn't the same for everyone." He paused. "I hear the questions you ask Orphic," I winced at the name—the recent memory all too real. "You ask things I would never think to ask. The way you catch on to every lesson faster than the others. The way you blink and that," he pointed to the water sack, "and it turns to ice." I blinked at him. "You're stronger than all of us."

I huffed a noise that resembled a laugh.

"I mean it," he countered. "Both of your parents are high Fae; we may be turned Fae, but none of us have the same type of raw strength coursing through our blood that you do." His eyes shone as he spoke. I couldn't tell if it was pride, or awe, or what exactly it was that shone there. I didn't think I deserved it either. "Whenever you're ready to hear that again, I'll be ready to tell you." Aeryn pushed off the ground to stand and extended a hand to me. "You're the strongest. You just don't believe it yet."

I took his hand and allowed him to lift me to my feet. I lunged at him, wrapping my arms around his center. "Thank you," I said into his chest. He seemed taken aback but eventually wrapped his arms around me for only a moment. I stepped back from our quick embrace, "You're a good friend."

"When the time is right, I'm sure you'll reciprocate," he half smiled. "I'm going to finish, but you should probably clean up." He made a disgusted face at the crusty blood all over my hands. My blood remained on his own hands still, too.

"Yeah, yeah, whatever," I waved a bloody hand at him before stalking from the room. I walked back to my room, clutching my hands to my chest. I felt good, somehow, a weight lifted from my chest. I thought about Aeryn's words, the genuineness with which he spoke them.

You are the strongest.

I smiled. Maybe I was.

Chapter Twenty-Three

Selene

EACH NIGHT AFTER DINNER, I MET AERYN IN THE STORAGE ROOM. Some nights, we only spoke hello and goodbye as we wordlessly remained on opposite sides of the burlap bag, punching ourselves into silent oblivion. It became more and more therapeutic as I felt my hands–my body become stronger. Some nights, we would wander the halls afterward, talking. Tonight, we did just that.

"Can you believe Idris called Orphic a 'diddling sorry old sack'?" I covered my mouth to keep the laughter in as we strode down the never-ending circle of the outer corridor. I had seen Orphic again for training. While the first few minutes were uncomfortable, he seemed to be the same old Orphic. I still cringed when I thought of that night, but at least I can rest easy that it was, in fact, all a ruse.

"The way he just pretended not to hear," Aeryn huffed a laugh. I smiled as we walked. It was good to have a friend. I needed it. I could tell Aeryn needed it, too.

"Do you think we will all succeed?" I asked Aeryn as I trailed a finger down the marble corridor wall.

He thought for a moment. "I think we all have the ability to," he started.

"But?" I nudged him with an elbow. I knew there was a but.

He sighed, "But separating from one another may prove more difficult for some." Gaia and Idris's faces flashed in my mind. I knew it would be an issue but hadn't truly allowed myself to think about it yet. I would be devastated to separate from them. From all of them. But those two? They would be heartbroken.

"Gaia is strong—" I started.

"It isn't Gaia I'm talking about," Aeryn interrupted. I considered his words. "Idris will be—"

"A mess," I finished for him. I frowned as we walked. If I could stop her—them both from that pain of separating, I would. It crushed me to imagine them both alone, missing the other. Somehow, it destroyed me more than the thought of myself being alone. But what hurt the most was the thought of Idris being sent back to Hiareth, forced again into that iron box of death. I sighed, glancing at Aeryn out of the corner of my eye. He was nothing like Dayne, but he was becoming just as important in many ways. As if he had read my mind, Aeryn asked, "So tell me about the King of Wind's son."

I winced. Aeryn was tasked with killing his father. In the same way, I felt like I was betraying Dayne by not getting word to him. Not that I even had a way to do that. In many ways, I would be crossing Aeryn if I told Dayne. I bit my lip, forcing the entire thought deep within. "Only if you tell me about the one you left behind in Florence."

Aeryn stiffened from beside me, "I suppose neither of us will ever know, then," he shrugged. I rolled my eyes at him, even though he kept his head facing toward where we walked. I didn't push it and allowed silence to fall between us. It was a comfortable silence. So much understanding flowed between the two of us. So many of the same traumas flowed in our blood. We walked like this until we were both too tired to continue and retired to our bedrooms.

* * *

THE FOUR OF us sat in the dimly lit library, waiting for more instruction from Orphic. He had tasked us with reading a terribly dry book called *The Downfall of Fae Rulers*. It was exactly what it sounded like, too.

"Selene," Orphic called me up. Idris stuck her tongue out at me as I rose from my chair to head toward Orphic's desk. I shot a small amount of ice at her, bouncing it off her outstretched tongue. I sat before the old male and crossed my hands atop the table.

"I know we have not spoken about your failed lesson," Orphic looked at me over the tops of his glasses, "But I hope you do not feel uncomfortable by me." He waited. I did feel uncomfortable, but I simply waved a nonchalant hand at him, hoping he would drop the subject. Thankfully, he did.

"Today, I have a list of prompts for you to run through with your class-mates," he slid a paper across the table to me. "Have them role-play the prompts. I will observe your reactions to each." I swallowed, wishing I had been tasked to kill any other king. Of course, I was tasked with the one requiring seduction. I nodded and grabbed the paper from him before trotting to meet Gaia, Idris, and Aeryn. Only Gaia raised her eyes to meet mine. "I need someone to read these," I extended the paper, not caring who took it. Gaia took the sheet from my hands in a graceful swoop.

I glanced up at Orphic, who was watching us from his desk. "If you'd both stand," he looked at Gaia. She rose with the same grace she always had. We oriented ourselves between the table where Idris and Aeryn sat, who looked thoroughly entertained by what was happening, and Orphic's desk.

Gaia cleared her throat. I glanced at Idris and Aeryn. They both had smirks on their faces, their full attention trained on us. Goddess, this was about to be embarrassing.

"I'm feeling quite tired," Gaia yawned, getting into character as she read off the sheet, "mind if we call it a night?"

I blinked at her, letting the words soak into my mind. Orphic had told me over and over. Leverage every word to my advantage.

"Oh, you wouldn't mind staying up just a bit longer for me?" I cocked my head at Gaia but shot a sideways glance at Orphic.

Gaia held my gaze, taking on her new role in its entirety, "I have such a busy day tomorrow," she sang. I pressed my lips together, imagining Erix was saying these things. I let everything I knew about the male swirl in my head. "I don't think you do," I allowed my voice to drop into a deep sultry tone. Gaia smirked at me, a look I had never seen on her face before. "Haven't you seen my sched-ule, peacemaker?" I could hear Idris snickering, but I remained focused on

Gaia. Leverage the words, I reminded myself. "I'd love to take some things off your plate," I was building my leverage slowly.

"Stop," Orphic spoke over Gaia as she began formulating her response. We both looked at him, waiting. "You walked him away from the path of going to his bed. Selene, is your task not to get into the male's bed?"

"I..." I stammered, "I was getting there," I scowled at Orphic. He knew things took time. He was the one who told me that this would be a tedious process. "Next," Orphic yawned, turning to the papers on his desk. I kept my eyes on him even as Gaia began reading the following prompt.

"A glass of wine for the lady?" Gaia's voice was like honey. I ripped my gaze from Orphic to stare into Gaia's calming ocean eyes. I held in the laugh that bubbled in my throat. I could sense that she was, too.

"Of course."

Gaia mimicked the action of pouring a glass of wine and handing it to me. I took the invisible glass and sipped.

"No wine," Orphic growled from where he sat. I threw back the rest of the invisible glass, wholly ignoring Orphic now.

"That was lovely. Would you mind if we moved this party to your room?" I winked at Gaia.

"I would simply love that," Gaia cooed at me, reaching out to take the now-empty invisible wine glass from me.

Orphic was standing at his desk now. I turned to him, a smile plastered on my face. "Next prompt," I said to Gaia. Orphic's eyes bore into mine, his aura thick with anger. I didn't care.

"I don't want to talk about it," Gaia suddenly snapped angrily from before me. I whipped my head back to her. Her devious, smiling face did not match that of her tone.

"Then let's not talk," I narrowed my eyes on her.

Gaia snorted air out of her nose at my response. I took a step forward as if I would kiss her. She mimicked the motions, reaching out for me.

"Enough," Orphic now strode down the stairs, stepping between us.

"What?" I barked at him. But I knew what. None of what I would do in the Kingdom of Ice would be that easy. It wouldn't be anywhere near that easy.

"You know what," he snarled in my face. He snatched the paper from Gaia and motioned for her to sit. I stood tall as he oriented himself before me, looking at the following prompt. "Haven't you got better things to do?" Orphic barked at me, shaking a finger in my face.

I blinked at him. Thinking. Leveraging.

"Haven't you?" I spoke in a calm tone.

"I wish they'd take you back," Orphic replied.

"I wish they would, too. I wouldn't have to be stuck here with such a sorry sod," my voice was hauntingly collected.

Orphic eyed me before saying, "You know nothing about—"

"About what?" I interrupted him, Erix's history flashing in my mind, "Your poor, sorry life? Everyone has their shit, Erix."

A flash of surprise shone in Orphic's eyes. "Get out."

"You need me," I countered, stepping toward Orphic.

"I don't *need* anything."

I allowed the words to hang in the air for a moment. "Let me help you," I whispered, reaching out to place a hand on Orphic's shoulder.

"Good." Orphic broke character and stepped out of my touch. He strode back to his desk, leaving me standing before my friends. I turned to them, a wince already forming on my face. I looked at each one of them. Idris's eyebrows were high in shock, and Gaia had a soft, placid smile on her face. And Aeryn. That was pride that shone there. This time, I was sure of it.

Orphic forced the four of us to read for another hour before dismissing us for the evening. "Selene," he called before we exited the room. I looked at Aeryn, who was cocking his head at me in question, but I just shrugged. My friends shuffled out of the room, confused but obeying the dismissal.

Orphic shuffled papers until he found what he was looking for and pulled on it. "We've discussed the basics of your plan." He licked a finger and flipped a couple of pages. "The Goddess requested we discuss a potentially," he winced, "uncomfortable topic." I swallowed. There wasn't much more that Orphic could do that would make me more uncomfortable than that night. "As you know, we can do only so much planning together. Your job will require you to be very attuned to the king, changing tactics as you go."

"Right," I said, hoping he would get to the point so I could join the others for dinner.

"The Goddess would like you to complete a successful trial run before leaving the sanctum." He folded his hands on the table before him.

I laughed. "What do you mean?"

"With Aeryn."

I couldn't help it. My hands shot to my face in shock, covering my gaping mouth. "I won't do it." I shoved back from the table, starting to rise from the chair. Inside me, I knew that the Goddess would make me no matter what I had to say.

"Sit. Down," The male yelled. I immediately plopped back down at his tone. He usually spoke in a near whisper, so for him to yell...

"You do not have a choice. The task is too important; you need to be able to practice with a timeline."

"We're friends. He... he won't trust me after," I muttered.

"I'm sorry, Selene. There is no other way. You need practice."

Ice filled my veins. The shock turned to anger quickly. "What if I don't."

He smiled. "The Goddess made you; you surely don't think she can't unmake you?"

Wench. Bastard. Both of them.

"She needs me. I have the leverage." My voice was quivering with anger.

"Obey the Goddess, Selene. There is no other way." He was right. I had leverage, but it wouldn't mean anything. She had the power to send me back to Avalon. I swallowed the large lump in my throat. I stood from my chair. "Do we have an understanding?" I began walking to the door, and he repeated himself to me, slightly louder this time. "Do we have an understanding, Selene?"

"Yes," I spoke with venom. "We have an understanding."

I walked back to my room, skipping dinner entirely that night.

Chapter Twenty-Four

Selene

I WENT THROUGH THE MOTIONS OF THE COMING DAYS BUT FELT numb inside. Aeryn questioned why I wasn't seeking him and the punching bags after dinner. I told him I just wasn't feeling well. I avoided all of them, sitting farther during lessons and asking if I could partner with Gaia during Hauna's exercises. I allowed the skills I was learning to take all of my attention. I honed my skills and crafted myself into someone capable. Aeryn watched me with concern but never asked.

During our general lessons, Orphic would send dagger-sharp glares through me, but I didn't care. Every time something good happened, it was ripped from me immediately. I knew it was only a matter of time before Orphic pestered me or the Goddess came to speak to me herself. He hadn't given me a timeline, but I wasn't sure he expected me to obey the command in the first place. He was right. I wouldn't, not until I had to.

After a few more days passed, and we'd already fought the peglins and scut-tlers in creatures, Orphic approached me in my room.

He slipped in without even a knock. "You will start tomorrow," he growled, towering above my bed. I kept my eyes squeezed shut. "You have three weeks." I didn't speak or acknowledge hearing him before he slipped out of my room. I didn't sleep that night. I only lay with my eyes squeezed shut so tightly I hoped they would pop.

* * *

I WOKE THE FOLLOWING DAY, bathed, and dressed before stalking to the mirror in my washroom. It was enormous compared to me. I shrunk back, finding the sight of myself nauseating. Everything I had to do... everything I was forced to agree to do was utterly repulsive. I reached for the stone around my neck, seeking comfort in something familiar. These tasks were going to hurt everyone I knew. This would crush Aeryn, forcing him to never trust me again. It would fracture Dayne once he learned. I would be soiled—dirty.

I forced myself to meet my own eyes. I straightened my shoulders, pressing my pink blushed lips into a firm line. I cleared my throat and stood taller.

"You are strong." My golden eyes flickered, the icy core around my pupils roaring. It was time to seduce my friend. I needed to begin today. My insides churned, the image before me becoming a ghost of myself. I looked strong—looked brave, but I didn't look like me. It felt good to become stronger, but when I remembered *why* I had to strengthen both my mind and body, I winced.

"*You* are strong," I tried convincing myself that no matter my tasks, no matter why I became stronger, it was still me inside. Whether I believed it or not, I said it three more times before taking a shuddering breath and leaving my room.

Aeryn watched me closely as I entered the dining hall for breakfast. I gave him a huge smile, greeting all of them. I hoped it didn't look too forced.

"Good morning," I chirped.

Aeryn cocked his head at my hello, while Idris mumbled a greeting, and Gaia beamed up at me.

Aeryn and I stumbled into conversation at first but regained a sense of normalcy once Gaia and Idris joined in. I was thankful for them and their quick analysis that something was off. I had considered filling them in this past week but thought it better to keep it to myself.

"We get to see draves today," Aeryn said. We were nearly caught up to where Aeryn was, plowing through lessons and training over twice as fast as he had.

"Those are the hairy ones?" I asked through a bite of sausage.

"They are," he replied.

I was thankful the concern was wiped from his face, but I caught him glancing sideways at me too often. He knew something was up. I couldn't blame him; I'd been distant and strange, avoiding them all. Even more telling, I no longer joined him in the evening to punch myself into serene oblivion.

* * *

"Hey," Aeryn stepped beside me as we strode down the several corridors toward the room where Hauna held her lessons. I learned Hauna called it her Pet Room. Fitting, I thought as I imagined those iron doors that Hauna kept her 'pets' behind.

"Hey," I kept my eyes on the cool crystal floors, suddenly feeling sick about the interaction I was about to have.

Only deafening silence hummed through the space other than the clicks of our heels against the crisp white floor. My mind was flattening beneath the weight of Orphic's threats. It was too much.

"That, uh, shirt looks nice on you." I glanced at Aeryn, suddenly blushing at the half-assed compliment.

What the sod did I just say?

He crinkled his nose as he glanced down at his plain white tee.

"This?" He pulled at the center of his shirt and released, allowing the stretch of it to spring back and create ripples in the fabric.

I shrugged, cheeks burning beneath his inquisitive gaze. This wasn't right. There was nothing I could say or do to make this feel better.

"Yeah. I mean, the shirt is fine," I stumbled over my words, "You make it look good."

Hells. I can not do this.

He snorted a breath out of his nose in a clipped laugh before shoving me into the corridor wall.

"What," I snapped, "Can't I compliment you?" I glared at him, finding only curiosity shining in his face.

"Thank you, Selene." He smiled, but then it deepened, becoming more playful. "You make all of your shirts look good, too." He winked at me.

"Piss off," I rolled my eyes, sprinting to that sense of normalcy his joke offered. "And I didn't say you looked good in all your shirts, just that one." I countered.

"My bad," Aeryn held his hands defensively, an amused grin still plastered on his face.

I chewed the inside of my cheek, deciding I could no longer will more compliments or shitty flirting out of myself.

We made it to the Pet Room only a few minutes later, finding Hauna standing in the center of it.

"Draves," Hauna chirped to us, "are cute and cuddly little bastards." She beckoned us to the center of the Pet Room. "Behind each door, you will find twenty draves."

All four of us started doing mental math, counting the doors around the room. Fifteen doors. So that's... three hundred draves.

Goddess.

"Do we remember their weakness?" Hauna asked the group.

"Everything," Aeryn answered with a laugh.

Hauna chuckled in reply. "And their strength?"

Gaia replied this time, "Overwhelming us with sheer numbers."

Hauna nodded and pointed to the rack of weapons. Over the past few weeks, I had become very handy with one of the shorter copper swords. I had excelled in killing the peglins, but the scuttler was another story. Aeryn was ultimately the one to slice its disgusting scorpion-like head from its body. I spent half the time willing myself not to cry as the creepy beast reminded me too much of Dayne and the time we came across a scuttler in the wild.

After my less-than-stellar performance with the scuttler, Hauna told me that she observed my weakness: I run rather than hold my defensive when I am chased. I would not run today. I walked to the rack, and Aeryn tossed me the copper sword. I nodded to him in thanks. I was still clumsy, don't get me wrong, but I was getting more comfortable.

233

Eevy A.

"Center," Hauna yelled.

We all approached the center of the Pet Room, forming a circle with our backs to each other, facing the doors surrounding us. Aeryn was to my left, Idris to my right.

"I'm sorry to tell y'all that I've been keeping these bastards hungry for weeks now," How Hauna sounded so happy when saying that was beyond me. She jogged out of sight, releasing the draves upon us. I shifted my weight, finding no calm in the dark lighting the Pet Room offered. I rotated, taking in the stone room and intricate iron doors. I knew in a matter of seconds, each one would swing open.

A loud tink sounded before all fifteen locks broke free from their doors. The four of us remained frozen in our defensive stances. I would not run away today. I would show Hauna I could improve on my weaknesses.

It took a moment for the draves to feel comfortable venturing out of the small rooms they were locked behind. A few waddled out on two stubby legs. I squinted at them. They were about knee-high, with shaggy brown fur and beady red eyes. They had sharp-looking claws on their stubby arms. They didn't hold much shape as their coat hid most of what was beneath it. It took a while for the first few draves to adjust to the large room and the meal standing before them. One courageous drave locked eyes with me, made a squeaking sound like a mouse, and took off running for us. Moments later, the room erupted in horrible squeaks as draves spilled around us. They shifted clumsily forward, some of them tripping but most of them waddling quickly. I would not run. I ground my teeth together, assessing the approaching beasts.

My eyes landed on a smaller group of hairy creatures. I broke out of the defensive circle, lunging forward in a dead sprint towards them. "What are you doing?" I heard Aeryn yell behind me.

I ignored him, sprinting straight for that group of draves my eyes were set upon. My senses zeroed in on them as I lunged forward. The room around me silenced, only this smaller group's squeaking sounding in my ears. I was only a few paces from bloodshed. I began swinging at them, their heads flying from their bodies. My sword cut through their necks with much more ease than I thought it would. One after another fell before me, their pale red blood leaking all over the floor. The scent of iron clung to the

234

air. It became thicker and thicker the more blood that I spilled onto the dirty ground around me. After I cut down the last drave from the group, I twisted, finding the next herd already sprinting for me. I dug within my magic this time, roiling it to every vein in my body. I formed a long spear of ice in my hands, gripping the icy girth of it before propelling it forward. The icy spear whistled through the air, piecing three draves with one throw. Many of the surrounding draves toppled over by the force of my throw. I wasted no time and was upon the squirming hairy beasts a heartbeat later. I hovered over the creatures, watching the furry things try to scramble onto their stubby feet. I began sinking my sword in one after the other, the copper blade sliding in easily. Once I had cleared the second group, my ears perked up, listening for the others fighting behind me. I glanced over my shoulder at them. All three fought in the center of the room still. I turned back to the side of the room I had been clearing. The metallic scent of blood was nearly unbearable.

I twisted around to head back toward the group, cutting down a few draves with either copper or ice. The draves were overwhelming the other three. They had waited for them to fully approach the center. I scanned all three of them, taking in the scene and deciding who may need help. Aeryn swung his sword in a complete 360-degree turn, injuring or killing at least six beasts in one move-ment. I twisted to Gaia and Idris, who were far less graceful in their attacks. I stepped toward them as drave lurched out and clawed Idris in the leg. She let out a howl that pierced through all the echoing squeaks.

"Sod," I whispered to no one. More draves were already approaching me, but Idris needed help. She needed it now. I ducked out of the way of several approaching beasts, allowing their bloodlust to send them in blind pursuit of me. I was faster. I sprinted for the other side of the room, where the furry-eyed creatures were clawing their way forward.

Idris was backing away fast, allowing the draves to now chase her. I pummeled into the group, taking three heads in one swing. Idris shot a fireball in their direction, burning only a few at once but slowing many of them. The metallic scent of blood and ash created an even more unbearable stench.

Idris and I worked together, standing side by side as draves pummeled into us. We sliced or plowed into them, learning that clumsiness was a considerable disadvantage of theirs. If we didn't have the energy to swing the sword, we could knock them over to give ourselves a moment to recuperate.

Idris and I cleared the draves around us, and began looking around to assess what was left to do. There was at least half a room of draves left to fight. They were disproportionally spread throughout the room, most cutting their way toward Aeryn. I blew out a breath and found that it was shaky with nerves. I forced ice to pump within me. I glanced back to Idris, but she was already off, sprinting to Gaia's side. I whipped my head back to Aeryn, finding an easy route to the back of the herd of draves upon him. In a flurry of shaggy hair, copper, and blood, I cut down several draves from behind. I almost felt bad for them. Almost. It only took the back half of the herd several moments to realize there was a closer meal to them. And it was me. I blinked, watching the pack shift their direction from approaching Aeryn to tumbling over one another toward me. My heart began beating faster as I took in their beady red eyes, filled with an unmistakable hunger. A scream ripped through the air the same moment I brought my sword up, ready to swing.

Gaia.

My head snapped in her direction before I could finish my swing at the approaching group of starving beasts. A fatal error. The moment I had spent looking away was all those famished draves needed to fully advance on me. I took a wobbly step backward as the draves tumbled over one another.

Do. Not. Run.

I shoved off from the foot that had retreated, flinging it out in front of me. My heel collided with the front row of draves, sending the first few rows tumbling backward. They really were clumsy. A smile crept across my lips despite the grave situation I was in.

I could do this. I would sodding do this.

I felt Aeryn's eyes boring into me, but I refused to look up. I refused to do anything but hold my ground. Drave after drave clambered over their fallen and squirming den mates. Their beady eyes were set on one thing. Me. I lunged out with my sword, watching the copper glint with blood as it connected with neck after neck. I zeroed in on the group that tumbled forward. Almost the entire herd that was on Aeryn had shifted direction. They were all upon me now. Sod. I had hoped to split up the group.

My swings became more and more panicked as the realization set in. I didn't have a moment to spare to glance at Aeryn—to plead for help. My voice caught in my throat as I opened my mouth to yell for him. I swung and swung. The moment I cleared two, three appeared in their place. I took a few stumbling steps backward, cringing at the retreat. I ground my teeth together, forcing everything from my mind. The smell of the blood-stained floors. The singed, burning hair. The hurried squeaks that still pierced the air. I switched all of it off. I pulled my sword back to strike hard and true.

Before I could connect, the beasts started toppling over one another. I glanced to the back of the approaching herd to see Aeryn pumping an enormous wind. The creatures fell like dominoes. I pulled my sword back to my side, eyes widening in late realization. The top line of draves toppled forward, the wind hitting us hard and fast. I fell backward, then. I watched in horror as the draves began crawling and hobbling towards me. Most didn't care to get back on their feet; they simply dragged their stubby arms forward to sink their claws into my ankles. I began kicking them in the face, one after another. I was screaming now. I knew I was calling his name, yet I could not hear it. Icy waves crashed in my mind, trying to soothe my panic. Yet I screamed and screamed. All I could do was kick forward, hoping I could keep the draves off of me for long enough.

A claw suddenly latched into my ankle. I was being yanked into the air before I could even howl in pain. Aeryn wrapped an arm beneath me, forcing me to stand. A drave sliced through his calf just as he released me. My senses came back to me sharp and fast. I heard Aeryn's bellow in pain. I listened to the squeaks of the draves and their little patters as they crawled towards us. I formed several thin shards of ice with a tip so sharp I needed to cradle them carefully. I sent each bit of ice through the faces of six draves, watching them fall instantly.

Aeryn forced me to retreat by dragging me to the center to regroup. "What are you thinking?"

I shoved him. "Why did you pull me back here?"

I was mad. I didn't want to run—didn't want to retreat. I spun around, taking in the rest of the room. By this point, Gaia and Idris had cleared the last large herd that had nearly taken Gaia out. They were both bloodied, their deep red blood mixing with that distinctive pale pink of the draves.

The last fifty or so draves should have been easy for the four of us, but we were exhausted and injured. I lunged first, fueled by the rage from my retreat. I didn't care if we were told to limit our magic in these battles. I formed more sharp shards, sending them whistling through the air at a group of charging draves. I was panting now, utterly exhausted. Aeryn ran ahead of me, taking out another group of hairy beasts. Idris sent a fireball on the final group, scorching them to dust.

The four of us all doubled over, panting as Hauna walked into the room, clapping. "Well done, group, very well done."

"One of you," she began. "Used their strength against them." Hauna sounded proud.

"Selene," Aeryn answered. I shot him a look, then back to Hauna.

"Correct," Hauna smiled at me. "Come, child. Tell us all what you did differently than the others." She beckoned me, but I couldn't move. If I took a step right now, I wasn't sure my knees would support me.

Aeryn stood up straight to answer for me. "She broke out of the defensive. She got to them before they got to us." He sounded in awe, even though he yelled at me moments ago.

Hauna clapped. "You all did just wonderful, though."

None of us had the energy to reciprocate any form of excitement.

"You're dismissed once you burn them," Hauna said with a smile, leaving us with a room of three hundred scorched and bloodied drave bodies to drag to one spot and burn.

Idris cursed in Hauna's direction.

"I heard that," Hauna sang.

We gathered our strength for a few minutes before starting the clean-up process.

"We'll take this side, and you two take the other?" Idris asked us.

"Sure," Aeryn answered for us.

Aeryn and I began grabbing drave bodies and heads, piling them up so Aeryn could lift each pile to the center of the room with his wind. We worked our way to the edge of the room. The stench of charred hair and blood burned my nostrils. My legs and arms ached after the lesson, but thankfully, most of the death and destruction occurred near the center, where we were piling the bodies to be burnt.

"That was pretty amazing," Aeryn told me while flicking his wrists, forcing a pile of drave bodies to ride his wind to the center of the Pet Room. "You became this... I don't even know; it was like you were dancing."

I choked on a laugh. "Dancing?"

"Really, the way you skipped around the room, you knew exactly where to go... It was just... it was really impressive, that's all."

"Thanks." I shrugged. My screaming echoed in my mind as a symbol of failure. But I hadn't failed.

"Am I allowed to ask why you haven't come to the storage room after dinner?"

I kept my eyes on the draves before me and shrugged again. I reached down, grabbing a handful of shaggy brown hair, "I've drained lately."

"So I've noticed." Aeryn's eyes narrowed but remained on the task before us.

Aeryn had remained task-oriented in the time we've spent together, becoming friends. For him to be asking this felt strange. "I'm feeling better," I forced a smile, looking him in the eye. "I'll be there tonight."

"Only if you need it." His eyes narrowed.

"Oh, I need it after today." I forced a laugh, and he seemed to force a chuckle along with me.

"If you say so."

I hated this. Every bit of it. The deceit, the loss of how our friendship had felt a mere week ago. Everything was forced now. If I was going to appease the Goddess, I needed to take a tremendous step in the next couple of days. I glanced at Aeryn. Concern bloomed on his face. It could wait, though, at least for now. We dragged the remaining draves to the center in complete silence. Idris sent them up in flames with a flick of her wrist. Aeryn and I sat to watch the fire as Gaia and Idris got us some food. It would take the fire some time to burn down to nothing, no matter how much heat Idris pumped into it.

The two brought us full plates of creamed chicken over potatoes. It was one of my least favorite meals since we had arrived at the sanctum. Aeryn and I both set down half-eaten plates.

"Not a fan of it either?" I nudged Aeryn with my foot. We were sitting, leaning our backs against the wall of the Pet Room, legs sprawled before us. The fire was crackling loud, the smell of smoke almost nauseating. Aeryn shook his head. He seemed sad.

"Hey, do you want to do something different tonight?" I asked, feeling guilty because of the reason I was asking.

"What's that?"

I watched the fire for a moment; it was nearly all burnt to ashes.

"I haven't been to the large pool yet," I said.

"Ah." He sounded like he was considering the offer. "Don't feel like beating your fists to a pulp after all?"

"It can wait a day." I smiled at him, forcing myself to lock eyes with him. He looked inquisitive as if trying to read me.

"Alright," he said, heaving himself up. The flames were gone; only embers and glowing briquettes remained. He extended a hand to me, and I took it.

We walked and chatted before parting ways to change for the pool. I was frantic about finding something to wear. What screams, 'Hey, please let me seduce you, but don't be mad when you learn I don't actually want you like that.'

A knock at my door. Goddess, that was quick. "One second," I called out. He clearly didn't put much thought into his outfit.

For the first time since coming here, I began digging through the closets of my room. I found a stringy white two-piece swimsuit and threw it on. Another knock. "Almost ready." I looked at myself in the mirror. The top consisted of two small triangles covering... well, not covering much. The bottom was high cut, the back was exceptionally cheeky, and the front gave me little coverage.

Absolutely not. I ran back to the closet.

A third knock.

Sod him for being so fast. I huffed a breath. What I had on would have to do. I grabbed a towel, tied it around me, and opened the door. Aeryn had black bottoms on and a white towel draped over his shoulder. He only glanced at me for a moment before walking toward the pool. I skipped up to follow him.

"It's not all that different from the others," He said about the large pool we were going to.

"I know, but it's the biggest one."

He laughed.

As we approached the pool, I sucked in a breath. It extended down the entire length of the cool crystal room. It looked almost endless from where we were standing. Twilight streamed in from the ceiling pool above, casting beautiful moonbeams on the water's surface. The entire room echoed our footsteps as we entered.

"In all her glory," Aeryn gestured to the pool.

"I love it." I smiled. I meant it, too. I could spend the entire day swimming laps around the beautiful twilight-lit waters. In a lot of ways, this space was romantic. I glanced at Aeryn. Maybe it would work to my advantage tonight.

Aeryn tossed his towel near the pool's slick crystal edge and dove in, splashing me a little. I stood by, wishing I was not here. I wished I had not *lured* my friend here.

"You coming in?" he asked while paddling around on his back.

"No, I'm just going to look at it," I replied. I untied the towel from around me and tossed it to the side of the pool. Aeryn looked away. "Is it warm like the others?" I asked, and he looked back at me.

"Come feel for yourself." His eyes never left my face. Not as I strode to the edge and lowered myself into the pool. He was going to make this challenging, wasn't he?

"It's nice," I purred, dunking my head back into the warm water.

We both waded around in silence for a bit.

"I'm glad you're done being weird." Aeryn broke the silence.

"What? I'm not weird."

"Well, *you* are weird. But you were also being weird."

I gulped and lied through my teeth. "I was taking some time to battle the fact that I would never see Dayne again." Sod. It hurt to say. Not because I was lying to him but because there could be truth behind that statement.

"I can't imagine that was easy to work through." Aeryn looked away, a deep sense of sorrow consuming him.

"It wasn't," I lied again about the reason for being 'weird.'

"Are you... feeling better now?"

"I am... I've... moved on." Another lie.

"Okay... Good," He said hesitantly.

I swam up close to him. "I'm sorry I didn't talk to you about it. It was just... something I needed to work through on my own."

He looked at me then. "Don't apologize for that. As long as you know, you can come to me."

I nodded. "You can too, you know?"

"Okay."

I lurched forward and attempted to shove his head underwater. My plan backfired as he grabbed my waist and threw me into the water.

I crashed into the water and swam up quickly. Bursting through the surface, I gasped for air dramatically as if I didn't have an affinity for water. "Different strengths, remember," he winked at me.

I swam back over to him. "Want to have a breath-holding contest?"

"With the Ice Queen? Absolutely not. I don't like to lose."

I shoved him, and he fell back into the water, clutching where I had pushed. "You're dramatic," I said as he continued falling until his whole head dipped below the water. I swam to the edge and propped my elbows on the side of the pool. Aeryn joined me once he was done fake dying.

"So, you're doing okay then?" he asked me.

I smiled at him, then brought a hand to his cheek. I hesitated for a moment, nervous to continue down this path. I touched his cheek briefly before dropping my hand from his face. "I'm doing okay, Thank you." He blushed at the contact. I hated every fiber of my being right now. Every single part of me. I felt disgusting.

I allowed normal conversation to take over, avoiding any more physical touch. I didn't want to be too obvious, plus I was having a hard time stomaching what I was doing to him.

I yawned. "I'm getting tired."

"Ready to head back?" he asked, lifting himself from the pool.

"Sure."

Aeryn grabbed his towel and dried off as I hoisted myself out of the pool. His eyes dropped for a fleeting moment from my face to my chest and then away. I felt like a horrible, terrible person as I walked up to my towel on the ground before him and bent over at the waist to grab it. I dried my legs in the same compromising position, allowing as many seconds as I could stomach to pass by bent before him. He shifted but didn't turn away. I continued drying my body and draped the towel over my shoulder instead of tying it around my body. This was horrible.

"Ready?" Aeryn asked with a blush covering his face.

"I am." I forced my smile to appear as naturally as possible.

Aeryn walked me back to my room. We parted with a simple goodnight and see you tomorrow.

I stripped off my swimsuit, climbed into bed naked, and cried myself to sleep.

Chapter Twenty-Five

Selene

OUR LESSONS AND TRAINING BECAME FAR MORE VIGOROUS OVER the next few weeks.

After being praised by Orphic for my extraordinary knack for argument, Aeryn teased me that I would make quite a persuasive leader one day.

One day.

That was one thing that had been hard for me to digest over the last few weeks. I had to infiltrate Seldovia and lead them for centuries to come. While it still shook me to my core, I welcomed the challenge with less and less apprehension each day.

I sat and ate my breakfast listening to the other three chatter around me.

"Okay, I did *not* faceplant." Idris threw a grape at Aeryn's head. We all laughed. Idris was small and nimble, but she had her clumsy moments, and they were hilarious.

"Nothing will ever top watching the giant silkie pin Aeryn to the floor." I chimed in. The feline beast was enormous. The moment it stalked out of the caged door, I thought we were all about to become ribbons.

"The way it pounced on you, then licked your face raw." Gaia was joining in with the fun now.

Of course, Hauna had tamed a Silkie, yet she still released her upon us as if it were a wild beast.

It was Aeryn who chucked a grape now at Gaia. Unsurprisingly, she swatted it away with ease and grace.

"You are all children," I laughed before throwing a grape at each one of them.

I found breakfast together to be the best part of my day. It felt the most natural. We would spend the day learning and training, followed by dinner, where I would then have to force myself to turn my attention to Aeryn for the remainder of the night. We had spent every evening together doing various things. Still, we often found ourselves in the storage room, taking turns punching the sand-filled burlap sack.

He was impossible to win over romantically, that is. We were easy, natural friends. The bastard was too damned polite. Every advance I made was brushed off or entirely missed, no matter how subtle. If we went to the pools, I would be lucky if he glanced below my face even once. Considering I was over two weeks in, I was going to fail. Aeryn was still high-fiving me like one of his male friends. I would give anything for it to stay that way.

We had history and politics today, the worst day but arguably the most important, or so says Orphic. He was likely correct; we might find ourselves dealing with creatures or fighting, but we would most definitely be submerged in politics.

I paired up with Idris today for the lesson. We had gone through much of the history by this point, but understanding the complexity of how a kingdom should be properly led was difficult. Orphic had explained the Fae continent was founded on compassion and strength and should be run as such. He said both had been lost, and we would be the four to restore it. Idris and I spent hours reading about acceptable and unacceptable methods of taxing your people. We swallowed our laughter from time to time as we watched Orphic nod off to sleep and begin snoring. I wished to like the old male, but after his act of flirting with me on top of what he forced me to do to Aeryn... it was impossible to.

"Thou shalt not take human or Fae lives as tax payment," Idris read aloud and elbowed me.

"Darn, I hoped to repay the Goddess for her hospitality by giving her you." I gave Idris a devilish smile.

Idris pressed her fingers to her lips as if she would send me a kiss. Of course, she exhaled, breathing a crimson ball of flickering fire my way. I snuffed it out mid-flight, only the smell of ash remained.

"Show off," Idris growled. She glanced at Gaia, as she had done every other second while we were partnered. I was overwhelmed with guilt for not telling them I had seen them, yet somehow, I felt like I was giving them peace by not sharing. It was their secret... Their world. It would all come crashing down once we were placed in our respective kingdoms. To add any more pain to that already agonizing truth would be cruel. So I kept my mouth shut.

"Selene," Orphic cleared his throat, interrupting us from our reading lesson.

I looked up from the dusty old book Idris, and I had in front of us to find Orphic's smoky eyes set on me.

"A new lesson has been added to your curriculum." Orphic's voice was quiet but direct. He waved me to his desk, leaving the others to continue their reading.

"It's not my day—"

He interrupted me with a wave of his hand. Typically, each of us had individual lessons with our mentors focused more on our specific tasks. I hadn't expected another one for at least a few days. The look on my mentor's face had my stomach twisting.

"I've stocked it for you," Orphic gestured toward a tall armoire with ornate carvings on both front double doors. It sat on the same platform level as Orphic's desk. I had noticed the armoire before but had never considered it unusual for the room. Now that I took it in, it felt odd that it was here... as if it was planted from the very start for whatever *this* was.

"And?" I leashed my tongue, careful not to let too much venom out in my words.

"And," he smiled faintly, "You must show us how you would decide to clothe yourself for King Erix." Orphic's eyes smoldered with intensity as he watched me.

I narrowed my eyes upon him before glancing back to the armoire.

Before I could speak, he followed up, "Take your time going through it. Once you have made your selections, please try it on."

We stared at each other for a long moment. I could feel the heat of Aeryn's gaze on my back, but I didn't dare turn around.

"Feel free to change behind the armoire."

I nearly scoffed at that. I had to try it on *for* everyone. Orphic's eyes danced as they fell upon the table behind me... On Aeryn sitting at the table behind me. I knew then what this was. In a strange roundabout way, Orphic was forcing this seduction of Aeryn to happen. He was *helping* me get started on it. He was putting me on display for him.

I grumbled a curse under my breath before leaving his desk and stalking to the old dusty armoire. I wrapped my fingers around the wooden knobs and tugged both doors open. They creaked as I pulled, and the sound had me checking over my shoulder. Aeryn's eyes were set on me, confusion blooming on his face. I shrugged at him before turning back to the stacks and stacks of clothes before me.

Goddess.

The armoire contained every textile and shade you could imagine. There was cotton, and corduroy, satin, and lace. Lace. My heart skipped a beat as Dayne's devilish eyes filled my mind. I reached out a hand, brushing my finger against the lacy scalloped edge of a blue satin shirt. I rolled my neck, forcing thoughts of Dayne to flutter away. I began filtering through the clothes, suddenly aware of how much I could leverage this moment to work in my favor with Aeryn. I wouldn't leave this place if I wasn't successful with him. My entire body clenched in disapproval, but I knew what must be done.

After several minutes of looking, I decided on a set that would impress Orphic for the lesson and hopefully tempt Aeryn's eyes to linger.

I shoved the clothes under my arm before swinging the wooden doors shut and slipping behind the armoire. I rolled my eyes, finding a full-length mirror hanging on the back of the armoire. I slipped my pants down, ignoring the nerves flushing through me at the nearness of the others. Thankfully, the tall armoire offered full coverage, and I could change out of view.

I slipped into the articles of clothing clumsily, continuously bumping into the bookshelf behind me. I cursed each time beneath my breath, blowing strands of hair from my face as I yanked up the bottoms. I turned to the mirror and took myself in. My cheeks instantly blushed.

I wore a three-piece set of fully sheer shorts and accompanying lace panties that offered coverage to my front but not my backside. The top was cropped to my belly button, made of the same sheer navy material as the shorts. The tank was cut in a conservative V shape at my neckline. While the front wasn't a plunging V, the sheer fabric left little to the imagination. My eyes fell on my breasts, which were fully visible through the shirt. I cringed at the thought of walking around the armoire dressed in *this*. I let out a long breath, relieved by the fact that I could use my hair to shield my very perked, very visible pink nipples. I glanced at the pile of clothing I left on the ground, nearly ripping off the set to put those back on.

You are strong.

I reminded myself of it. I could do this. I needed to do this. It would offer something to aid me with Aeryn. I knew it would. As much as I hated Orphic for this, I knew it would help in my task.

I oriented my hair in front of my breasts before stepping out from behind the armoire.

My eyes were on Orphic first. The corner of his mouth twitched up, but the rest of his face began blushing.

Sod's sake.

"Class," Orphic spoke. I strode to stand by Orphic but risked a glance at my friends. Aeryn met my eyes at the same time as I looked at him. His eyes dropped to my chest, taking in my sheer clothing. My breathing lurched as his surprised eyes met mine again. He winced and looked back down at the table. I couldn't tear my eyes from him, not even to take in Gaia and Idris, who I could tell were gawking.

"Selene has chosen this," Orphic gestured to my clothing choice, "as an outfit for King Erix." He let silence fill the air. I shifted awkwardly as Aeryn kept his eyes on the book before him. I knew he wasn't reading and would need to be forced before he would look at me again in these clothes.

"How do we feel about it?" Orphic settled deeply into his chair, no doubt taking in the clothes or, rather, me within them. I ripped my eyes from Aeryn to find Orphic grinning, staring nowhere but my face. That grin made me regret choosing this outfit. I should have picked something else... anything else.

"Aeryn," Orphic spoke, eyes still on me.

Sod. Oh, sodding hells.

"I apologize, but given you're the only male, I have to ask you to participate in today's lesson with Selene," Orphic spoke coolly.

I ripped my eyes from my mentor to find Aeryn still staring blankly at the table before him. His jaw was clenched so tight that I didn't know how his teeth didn't shatter to bits.

"Lesson?" I barked at Orphic, not understanding.

"Surely we must measure the excitement this outfit induces?" Orphic asked, but I knew it wasn't a question.

My lip curled in a half-snarl as Aeryn winced further at our mentor's words.

"If you would please meet us up here," Orphic gestured for Aeryn to approach us. Aeryn sat frozen for a moment, jaw still clenched. Then, suddenly, as if realizing he must do what our mentor asks of him, he shoved back from the table and stalked up the three steps to Orphic's desk. He didn't look my way even once.

I wished he would. I wished I could apologize, even if only with my eyes.

"Good," Orphic folded his hands before him. "I'd like you to turn to Selene and allow your body and mind to react naturally. Explain how you're feeling. What responses are elicited from seeing her." The edge in his voice made me think he was enjoying this. I furrowed my brows together.

Aeryn hesitated before robotically turning toward me. Every movement seemed painful. His eyes met mine but were far away and dull as if he was attempting to distance himself from this moment. I didn't blame him.

"Go ahead," Orphic whispered.

Aeryn's auburn eyes flashed darker before he tore them from my face to my collarbone. My eyes were locked on him, but I could see Orphic rise from his chair in my peripherals. I allowed my arms to hang loosely at my sides as Aeryn's gaze dipped to my chest, which was still covered on both sides by my hair.

Orphic stalked to my side, but I paid him no attention. All of it was on Aeryn, whose face was set in stone as it roamed my chest.

"Now, now," Orphic spoke, breaking the silence, "How are you feeling?"

Aeryn's left eye twitched at the question as his eyes dipped to the exposed skin of my stomach.

"It's nice," he mumbled, eyes now unable to go lower. They hesitated on my waistband before he ripped them from me, falling onto Orphic. I mimicked his gaze, watching as Orphic extended his hand toward me. I took a half step back as I realized what he was doing.

"Your hair," He clucked at me.

I ground my teeth together but stepped back forward, allowing him to swat both sides of my hair back. The crisp air bit at my exposed nipples, perking them further. I knew Aeryn was not looking even before my eyes found him again.

Anger warmed in his face as he beheld Orphic.

"Go ahead," Orphic instructed Aeryn, gesturing to me.

I exhaled, suddenly self-conscious at the loud breath I let out. The silence in the room was far too loud.

"The clothing she picked should satisfy any primal male urges," Aeryn hesitated. He never looked back at me or my now exposed breasts before turning from us both and stalking out of the room without a dismissal.

Once Aeryn was out of sight, my gaze found Gaia and Idris, who remained seated at the work table. They looked at me with sympathetic smiles.

"I'm changing," I barked at no one in particular before stomping back behind the armoire. I felt bad. So sodding bad. Not only for Orphic's actions but my own. I figured it out before I even picked the clothes. I was just as at fault for Aeryn's reaction as Orphic. I ripped the clothing off my body and shoved on my old clothes. I heard Orphic dismiss Gaia and Idris while I was changing, so I knew we would most definitely be exchanging words. I took three deep breaths before stepping out to meet my mentor.

"I'm working on it." I snarled before Orphic could even speak.

"You have four days; he looks at you less than those girls look at each other."

I cringed at him, referencing Gaia and Idris in that way. "You will hold them all back, you know." He cleared his throat, "if you can't complete this part of your training—if Theon of Olvidare advances on the other kingdoms, and you haven't—"

"I have it handled," I barked as I strode out of the room, not addressing what he had forced Aeryn to do.

"Do you?" he said from behind me as I took shaky steps into the icy corridors beyond Orphic's office.

I didn't have it handled. Not in the slightest. My chest became tight. I would have to make a drastic move to get anywhere with him, which was risky since he had not been warming up to my subtle advances. It didn't matter, though; I had four days and had gotten nowhere. I shivered, recalling Orphic's words. 'You will hold them all back.' I didn't need more context to know that the Goddess would use what was important to me against me. She'd force us all to stay here. Prolong our training. Make the split up even worse on us all. I jogged past Gaia and Idris toward the storage room where Aeryn would be headed.

After nearly slipping on the slick crystal floor, I decided it best to walk the rest of the way. I took the last turn and strode through the arched doorway to find Aeryn sitting atop the blue water-filled sack as if it were a cushion.

He didn't look up or even acknowledge my presence.

"I'm sorry," I breathed, "I didn't know he was going to do that."

Aeryn's face hardened, but he didn't look up at me.

I stalked forward, positioning myself above him from where he sat, sinking into the flexible sack. "It's not a big deal," I shrugged. He stared at my feet for a moment before looking up at me.

"Why have you been so weird lately?"

"I haven't." I wrung my hands, unsure of where this was coming from. He completely disregarded what had *just* happened in Orphic's office.

"You have." He eyed me now, his cheeks still flushed from earlier."I didn't mention it before, but..." he trailed off, waiting for my response.

You have four days. Four days. Four days. Orphic's warning rang in my head. An idea sparked... a risky one. I plopped down on the blue sack beside him, bouncing him up and down. The nature of the flexible, fluid-filled punching bag forced our bodies to slide into the center, our thighs resting on each other.

"Easy now." He scooted away from me slightly to make sure we were not touching. Of course.

"I..." I started, "I don't know how to say this." Aeryn straightened at both my tone and my words. Well, here goes nothing. "I've been feeling really lonely,"

Aeryn's flushed face pinched together in confusion.

"Your time is spent either sleeping or with one of us," He raised a brow, keeping his auburn eyes on mine.

"Will you let me talk?"

He held up his hands. "Sorry."

I scooted towards him so our knees were touching. "I mean," I swallowed. Here we go. "A certain kind of lonely."

I managed a sultry tone, somehow. I was proud that my voice hadn't cracked or that there weren't already endless tears. Maybe I could do this. I took a breath in, watching his face twist in confusion. I don't know why I hadn't thought of this before. It didn't have to be feelings related; I could seduce him in a different kind of way. It still counted, didn't it?

I brought my hand to his knee, forcing it not to tremble. Aeryn stiffened immediately but did not shift his knee from beneath my touch. I trailed my hand from his knee up his thigh, skirting dangerously close to where I knew would be a dead giveaway on whether or not he enjoyed the touch. I couldn't bring myself to look there. Not just yet. I continued trailing my hand up his abdomen to his face, my eyes following my hand. We met eyes. He opened his mouth as if he would speak but then closed it. Everything about him was stiffened, yet he wasn't stopping me—he wasn't pulling away.

"Have you been lonely too?" I asked in a devilishly seductive voice, surprising myself at the sickeningly sweet tone I had manifested.

His eyes flickered at the question, but he didn't answer. He closed his mouth finally, clenching his jaw to mirror his rigid body. I brought my thumb to his lips and pulled down his bottom lip. He trembled ever so slightly beneath my touch. I couldn't yet tell what that trembling meant. I scooted closer to him, trailing my hand to his chest. If it weren't for the ice I kept coursing through me, my entire body would be trembling, too. I allowed my hands to trace down his arm to his palm that faced the ceiling. I drew a circle there, in the center of his palm.

"Aren't you tired of using this," I flicked his hand, watching the breath catch in his throat.

"Just for fun," I leaned to whisper in his ear. "Friends."

He swallowed hard but remained still and unanswering. A flash of annoyance flared in me. There was no way I was getting out of this without being embarrassed to my core. I refocused, shoving the annoyance deep within. My mind was too aware of how much it hurt me to betray him like this. Even though it kept me from trembling, I didn't want any ice to swirl in my veins. If I could cloud my mind—block my own words out... I could detach.

"Tell me to stop," I said, taking an alternative route, hoping I could get a word out of him. I brought my hand back to his thigh, now glancing at the part of him that gave him away. I traced around the bugling in his pants, watching it grow. There was no denying that he wasn't at least interested now.

"I think that's answer enough." I continued tracing lines and swirls near, but never on that part of him.

His eyes narrowed on me, assessing me. Finally, he showed a flicker of emotion. If he would just give in, this could all be over. I blinked for a moment, forcing a neutral face at the realization. What makes it over, though? Is a kiss enough? It most definitely wasn't. What would satisfy the Goddess as a successful seduction? Had I sold my virginity to the Goddess on this stupid trial run she forced me to do? I felt ice prick at the edges of my mind, regretting not having let Dayne be the one to take it. I was a feywit. I suddenly felt self-conscious; I wanted to shrink in on myself. Become small. I couldn't do this, not to myself, not to Aeryn. Not to Dayne. I pulled my hand from him in retreat, but he caught it mid-air. I blinked, taken aback by his firm grip. We locked eyes, breath catching in both of our throats before he cocked his head at me curiously.

"Just fun?" he asked.

His sudden change of heart had me reeling. I could do this. Couldn't I? It could be just for fun; he wouldn't have to know it was all orchestrated anyway. I cringed at the thought. Aeryn was such a great friend, but my feelings for him differed so much from those I felt for Dayne. One time. It was one time. I could do it. I could lie to him this one time.

"Just fun," I assured, returning my hand to his chest.

He stood, picking me up from the water bag. It sloshed around and flattened at the loss of our weight upon it.

"Not in here," he said while leading me by hand back to Goddess knows where. Probably his room. He led, steps ahead, his arm extended backward, hand latched to mine. The walk was... awkward, to say the least. It seemed he had overcome whatever internal battle he was fighting against earlier because once we were in his room, his shirt was off in an instant. The pale scar that ran diagonally across his chest and abdomen shone in the moody twilight of his room. I shifted, darting my eyes up from his center to his face. He took a deep breath before striding forward to me. He slipped my shirt off over my head with ease. He took a step back and wordlessly removed his pants. I fiddled with the button on mine, in sync with him. My heart was racing. I was sure he could hear it pounding like thunder in my chest. Aeryn kicked his pants away from him. I mimicked him, kicking mine away in the same direction. The mimicry found its intended mark as he huffed a laugh at me. This was... so much different than with Dayne. Much less... touching.

Aeryn only looked at my face as I fiddled behind my back to unclasp my brassiere. After a moment of toying with the back, I released the hook and allowed it to fall to the ground, breasts fully exposed before him. His eyes did not dip below my chin. I snorted air through my nose. "You can look, Aeryn."

"Are you sure? Because there's no going back..." he trailed off as I bent over to remove the plain cotton panties I had on. He looked.

"Holy... Selene." He ran both hands through his hair, looking everywhere *but* my face. I was on display before him, showing him more than even Dayne had seen. I had to take a deep breath to steady my nerves. Aeryn stepped forward, still clad in navy undershorts that fell just above his knee. He extended both arms, hovering them around my waist. "Just fun," he repeated in my ear. I gave him a clipped nod before he finally rested his hands on my hips. I shivered at the touch, suddenly aware of how cold it was here. He pulled my hips forward so that our bodies could lay flush against each other. So much exploded in my mind at the feeling of his bareness against mine. My heart pounded even harder against my chest. My thoughts became swarming, clouded by the annoying heat fluttering between my legs. Aeryn meant so much to me. Feeling him bare and flush against me was... odd, but held a strange form of intimacy that I didn't balk at. Images of Dayne flashed in my mind, mixing with the thought of Aeryn finding out I had tricked him and hating me forever. It took all of my strength not to frown.

Aeryn's hand shifted to my back, allowing his palms to rub slowly around. I knew I was rigid now. I wanted to keep my mind clouded and detached from this moment. I couldn't take the hectic threads of thoughts crossing paths in my mind. I couldn't think about the present. I could only stand here, rigid. I allowed just a pinch of icy relief to flutter into my mind, soothing my thoughts almost immediately.

Aeryn's roaming hands moved up to the back of my neck. I allowed my body to relax against him, bringing my hands to his back. He grasped a handful of my hair and gently pulled until my head shifted back, face tilted up at him. "Is... kissing allowed?" His eyes were aflame. A once auburn red was now a swirling melting pot of topaz. I parted my lips, giving him a shallow now. A smirk flashed on his face as he leaned in. He did not hover his lips before mine as Dayne had. He immediately pressed them against mine with intent. It was rougher than Dayne, more matter-of-fact. His other hand trailed from my backside to the front of my thighs.

I took a half step out with my right leg, offering him the part of me that was embarrassingly aching. He shifted his hand between my legs a moment later. I jumped slightly, flinching at the intense feeling of his fingers against me. It felt annoyingly good. It was so good I could feel the moisture building up between my legs. I knew he could, too. I bit down on the unnatural feeling of it all. It shouldn't be with *him*. But it was. And at this moment, as sparks of heat exploded in my core, I was okay with it. Aeryn broke his lips from mine and began kissing down my neck. He removed his hand from my hair to grope at my breasts. I fiddled with the top of his undershorts for a moment before he stepped back from me and dropped them to the floor.

255

"Oh," I said out loud, biting the urge to slap a hand over my mouth. Did I say that out loud? My eyes roamed over his length.

It was... big.

Aeryn snorted a laugh and stepped forward again. He locked his mouth on my lips, tongue swirling into mine. I swirled back, hands still roaming his hardened, muscled back. He rotated his hips forward against me. I could feel its stiffness as he rocked into me.

I let out a quivering breath as every sense tingled. His tongue on mine, his body flush against my bare breasts. I needed a clear mind. I couldn't let how good this felt drive me. I forced another ounce of ice into me, cooling my core, but only slightly. Aeryn released his lips from mine. He locked eyes with me for only a fleeting moment before leading me to his bed. He laid me down slowly, positioning my back against the bed and tugging my hips to the very edge of it. He leaned over me, propping himself up with one hand and grasping his own length with the other.

My eyes widened as he grasped it, his other hand flicking over my aching center. Sparks exploded throughout my body once more.

"You're wet." He leaned forward to breathe in my ear. I swallowed hard, finding my throat pinched tight.

Aeryn removed his hand from between my legs and propped it against the bed near my face. With his other hand, he guided the tip of him to my entrance. The moment I felt him there, I let out a soft whimper, ashamed at the sound the moment it left my lips. His eyes burned bright at the sound, as Dayne's did.

Aeryn nudged himself forward ever so slightly as he nipped at my bottom lip. He let out a soft grunt as he shifted forward so slowly and gently. The very tip of his length sunk into my wetness. My breath caught in my throat as he paused there, not sinking himself any further. My mind was reeling, yet warning bells sang at the newness of these sensations. I had never done this before... I had never—

"Does it hurt?" I found myself whispering. I hadn't expected to feel nervous about the pain. Then suddenly, Aeryn was off me in an instant.

"What the hells?" I yelled at him, eyes searching him with confusion.

"Put your clothes on." His voice was flat. Soulless. He bent down to slip on his navy undershorts and stood facing away from me.

"What... I—"

How did I mess this up? I didn't understand... I was so close... I—

"You're a virgin?" he asked, still facing away.

Shit.

"I—"

"You what? You weren't going to tell me that it was your first time having sex, *ever?*" If it weren't for the situation, I would have found it funny how he spoke with his back facing me. I took in a shaky breath. I knew it. I knew I would screw this up, and now he was going to hate me forever. And forever was a long sodding time when you were Fae. He was angry... angrier than I had ever seen him. I bowed my head in shame. I was ashamed of so many things.

"You know, at first, I thought Orphic had put you up to this." My head snapped up at that. As if sensing the motion, Aeryn choked on a laugh. "You've got to be kidding me," he said, rubbing his eyes.

I lay there, stunned and ashamed, until I realized how he must be feeling. I was out of bed and to him in a moment. I pressed my hands to his bare back, "Aeryn."

"Will you put some damn clothes on so I can look at you?" he yelled at me, still rubbing his eyes and temples.

I tripped over to my pile of clothes and started dressing in a hurry. I was back over to him in a second. "Okay."

He turned to look at me. His eyes were red from all the rubbing. "I know they probably didn't give you a choice—"

"They didn't. I said I wouldn't do it, but—"

"Stop. Let me finish." I bowed my head in shame. "I know they *didn't* give you a choice, so I won't hold that against you. I hope you know how humiliated I am by falling for it and crossing that line with my friend."

"Please, I—"

"I'm not done," he cut me off. "But what fills me with rage, Selene, is that you were going to just let me take that... that sacred *thing* from you."

"Aeryn, I'm so sorry I... it was the last thing I wanted to do. I didn't want it to

257

Eevy A.

ruin our friendship, although it probably already did. I didn't have a choice whether I had my virginity or not, so what was I supposed to do? If it wasn't you, it would have been... Erix." I choked, realizing and suddenly wishing we had gone through with it just so I didn't have to lose that sacred thing to such a terrible person.

Silence hung in the air. I kept my head hanging low, eyes set on the ground. I knew he kept his eye on me. I couldn't bear to look at him as I spoke, "Please don't hate me,"

Aeryn sighed. "Honestly, Selene, you're a beautiful female. You were crafted by the Goddess *to be* beautiful. I wouldn't blame any male for wanting you, even if just for a fun, fleeting moment, so I won't blame myself for that. Do I feel like a feywit for not realizing I was a part of your training? Yes. But I need you to know that nothing, not even this, would make me stop being your friend."

I wanted to fall to my knees. He was too good. Too good for this world, too good for this forced destiny. I suddenly found myself enraged for him. He should be back in Florence with his mother and the girl he left behind.

"I'm sorry," I said, now lifting my chin to look at him. He stepped forward and wrapped his arms around my shoulders. I didn't waste a single moment before flinging my arms around his center. I hugged him back fiercer than I had hugged anyone in my life. "I am so so sorry," I repeated into his chest over and over again. "I am sorry, Aeryn. I am so sodding sorry." He stroked my hair softly in reassurance but let me repeat myself. He knew I needed to say it, whether he needed to hear it or not.

"Let me walk you back to your room," he pulled away from me only after I stopped trembling. I nodded, allowing him to walk me back to my room by hand. My whole body felt uneasy. How close I had been to losing my friend. I shook my head, unbelieving how forgiving he was.

"It's going to be okay." He squeezed my hand. All I wanted to do was apologize, but I bit my tongue.

When we reached my door, I looked up at him, frowning. He smiled weakly at me.

"Is it inappropriate for me to ask you to stay on one of the other beds in my room tonight?" It felt inappropriate to ask... but I couldn't be alone. I held my breath, waiting for him to reply.

He chuckled and released my hand. "I thought you'd never ask."

We took turns getting ready for bed in the washroom, each curling up in our beds for the night. We lay in silence for many minutes.

"Friends?" I asked into the darkness, hoping he was still awake.

"Friends." He echoed back to me.

Chapter Twenty-Six

Selene

I COULD HEAR AERYN SHOWERING WHEN I WOKE FROM A surprisingly restful sleep. I sighed and sat up. I felt an insurmountable amount of weight missing from my chest this morning. There would be no more evenings spent batting my eyelashes at Aeryn. No more moments praying that he would forgive me. I was free from the terrible thing Orphic and the Goddess had forced upon me. Well, free from at least one of those things.

The shower shut off, and I shot out of bed, taking the time to change before Aeryn came out. I couldn't help but replay the mental image of Aeryn standing naked before me. My cheeks blushed. Goddess, I hoped we could laugh about this someday. My blush deepened as I remembered how much of me he saw. Where his mouth had roamed. I prayed he meant what he said, that nothing would stop him from being my friend. I needed his friendship more than I felt I needed air.

"Hey," Aeryn shoved through the washroom door, thank the Goddess, he was fully clothed.

"Hey," I said, waiting for awkwardness to cling between us. It never did.

"I did some thinking," Aeryn started while drying his hair with a small white towel, "I'll talk to Orphic about last night. They'll be concerned with your... level of success." I nodded. "I'll tell them the truth. Since you were...

successful…" he winced, but only slightly, "They should reward you anyway." He shrugged.

"At least not punish me," I shrugged. I didn't expect a reward.

He smiled at me. We held eye contact for a long moment. I was in utter shock at the outcome of all of this, so much so that I felt like I owed him. I needed him, but I did not think I deserved him.

* * *

I WALKED beside Gaia towards our lessons for the day. Idris hung back in stride with Aeryn, who wanted to talk to her about her shield work. She now fell behind me in fighting. I wasn't great by any means, but as Aeryn lovingly puts it, 'most improved.'

"My dear, Selene, how are you today?" Gaia slumped an arm around my shoulders as we walked. She exuded comfort, and I allowed myself to wholly lean into her.

"I'm feeling rested." I smiled and meant it. Today, I felt like I could breathe. Gaia squeezed my shoulder with an arm draped over me.

"You are getting strong," she said.

I thought about the first day Gaia showed how well she could fight. It was a miracle that I managed to best her in a few paired lessons. Hauna is open about our strengths and weaknesses, allowing us to speak freely. Gaia's magic will always be her downfall when it comes to fighting. While her magic was extraordinary and beautiful, it didn't hold up the same in battle. She could make an ancient butterfly appear in mid-air, where it flapped its wings thousands of years ago. Still, I could send a spear of ice toward her, pinning her shirt and herself to the wall before me. Both magics were equally impressive, but it didn't change that mine was better suited to fight.

"Hauna is letting us use our magic freely now," I started, "It's the only reason I can even sort of keep up with you." I looked at Gaia in complete awe. It wouldn't matter if I became stronger than her; she and her abilities would always be inspiring. She was a captivating Goddess-like being. I leaned my head on her shoulder for a moment, taking in her sweet scent of mandarins. I didn't want to leave any of them.

Eevy A.

She squeezed my shoulder. "You do not need to say this," she smiled, "I look forward to seeing your growth every day; it is extraordinary."

I smiled and tossed my arm around her as we walked. I avoided thinking of it, but each day, with each new skill I learned, I could feel the well of me, the pit inside growing deeper and deeper. It was as if my knowledge and practice directly impacted the strength of my magic. I learned not only how to harness it but how to understand it—nurture it. I didn't avoid the thought because it scared me. Instead, it overwhelmed me, thinking of what immense power lurked beneath my skin. Two high Fae parents. I shivered.

The four of us entered the Pet Room, where Hauna sat on a small round stool in the center. It was low to the ground, so her knees were bent as she sat. I took in the odd scene around her. Boxes and boxes of... armor? No. A linked metal chain spilled from the box near Hauna's left leg. It wasn't just armor, but metal. Scraps of it, matching sets, mismatching sets. It was strewn in a way that felt like organized chaos. Hauna heaved herself up with a slight humph sound. "Welcome, my dears." She strode toward us, yellow-blonde hair bouncing around her rosy round cheeks. "Orphic informed me you got past the history of Fae and iron lessons this past week?"

It clicked. The piles before us, the chains and cuffs, the bars and boxes of metal... of iron. Orphic went through the history of how humans and Fae have used iron to suppress magic. The lessons were brutal, not because they were boring this time, but because of the atrocities committed on both Fae and humans alike.

Hauna continued in her bright, shining voice, "Who wants to be first?" She smiled at us. First, at what? I knew we were all thinking. Yet somehow, I knew we all knew. What else would the iron be for than to learn what it can do to our magic? To feel our strength snuffed out.

I stepped forward, prepared to go first. Over the past few weeks, I'd gone from being an observant, hesitant student to being the first to do or to fight. It wasn't that I *wanted* to be that person. It was that I needed to be. I would never grow if I succumbed to that shrinking feeling I always felt. I would never succeed in the Goddess's task, and I was not going back to Avalon. So, yes, I was the first to take casual strides up to Hauna. She gestured for me to take a seat on the short stool at the center of the room.

I took a step forward and then another, the iron's hum already affecting me. My magic leaped and scraped around inside of me. I stepped forward again and again until I stood before the stool, the iron strewn around me. The pieces were hauntingly beautiful: A picture of death and salvation, depending on who was using it. I swallowed and sat on the stool facing the rest of them. My magic felt as if it couldn't escape the presence of the iron that surrounded me. It felt like it was trying to burrow deep within me, away from the threat.

"We start slow with each of you," Hauna smiled; she was never unhappy. I sat atop the stool as she picked out a set of iron cuffs from the pile. She took a step toward me. Her approach made my heart pound against my chest. She walked to me and hovered above, fiddling with the cuffs. The nearness of the iron swinging near my face made me want to recoil from her. I gritted my teeth at the pure uneasiness of my entire being. It was like never-ending nails scraping against a chalkboard. You can't escape the terribleness of it.

Once Hauna opened the cuffs, she didn't hesitate before clasping them around my wrists and stepping back. I thrashed my head backward, fighting against my recoiling magic. It wasn't pain I was feeling; instead, it was an intense sense of losing myself. My insides turned as if I was about to be sick. My magic bucked and thrashed against the iron touching my skin. I clenched my teeth and flung my eyes back open.

"More," I croaked to Hauna.

She gave me a surprised look but shrugged and began searching the piles of iron. She plucked out two iron gauntlets. I narrowed my eyes as she strode toward me, opening one and clasping it immediately around my left forearm. I couldn't control it when my legs straightened forcefully in front of me. My magic thrashed like the violent waves of the Onyx Sea. It was burrowing into me. Digging its icy claws deeper and deeper until I lost sight of it. I bit down hard at the unnatural feeling—the pain that wasn't quite pain, but something else entirely. Hauna waited for my slight nod before clasping the second gauntlet around my other arm.

The second she released her hands from the other gauntlet, I kicked from the stool and fell to the floor. I was on my hands and knees, saliva dripping from my opened mouth. It wasn't the thrashing of my magic that knocked the breath from my lungs; It was the feeling of it diminishing. It was being snuffed out. Just like Orphic had described. A Fae without magic was... well, no different from a human. It was our nature to despise the feeling of that being ripped from us. With time and the addition of the second gauntlet, I could feel my magic slipping away. Once, it was an icy, roaring sea; now, it felt like the iron was the sea, swallowing my magic, never to be touched again. My head spun, the dwindling of the magic within me overwhelming me to my core. The magic was being yanked from my body, leaving a gaping black hole of nothing in its wake. I brushed invisible fingers against that hole, wincing at the pain it evoked.

I panted on the ground for a moment, allowing the intense feeling to settle. It did, only slightly.

"I'm going to remove the last gauntlet that pushed you too far," Hauna spoke slowly. "Then I want you to use your magic."

I hardly heard her last words. My head was ringing from the imbalance within my body. Hauna unclasped the gauntlet she had just put on me and allowed it to thud to the floor beneath me. I breathed at the near-euphoric feeling of the endless black hole shrinking slightly. A wisp of ice licked up at me. A precious hint of who I was. It was fleeting... but it was all I needed. My eyes rolled back in my head as I reached for it, brushing against its sweet serenity.

"Go ahead and try," Hauna told me, coaxing me to test out magic.

I didn't know how to use it. It felt too far from my reach. I cringed at the thought of touching the black hole that formed within me, but to dig into it? I brushed against the edge of the hole, the remnants of what I could feel of my fading magic. It recoiled away from me with a hiss. I bit down hard against my cheek, feeling and tasting the hot tang of blood coating my mouth. I panted again, letting the blood drip from my mouth onto the floor.

I heard Idris. "Get it off her."

I panted more; my body was nearly convulsing as I remained on my hands and knees, blood spraying on the floor beneath me with each labored breath.

"Hauna," Idris shrieked.

But it was Idris's fear, concern, and love that fueled me. Then I laughed, stopping Idris mid-sentence. A prolonged, deep, and menacing laugh shook from my core. The entire room went silent. I looked up from my position on the floor and smiled, blood dripping from my teeth onto my chin and the floor below me. My friends looked at me wide-eyed. I shoved myself off the ground and wiped the blood from my chin with my shoulder. I balled my hand into a fist, imagining that my fist was within me. I plunged it into the black hole within, punching directly into the center. It was painful then. Blinding, raging, red-hot pain. I dropped to my knees but let out a deep, somewhat demonic laugh that was twisted with a scream of pain. My insides were hot. The iron pulsed red hot heat within me, tempering my ice.

Fighting against it. I thrashed at it, snarling. I bit through the pain that coursed through every fiber of me. I pounded my cuffed fists to the floor beneath me. I punched again and again and again. I could hear myself screaming. I could feel blood fill my mouth once more. I ran my tongue across my teeth, feeling the slick metallic coating. I stopped punching the ground. The sudden sensation of my being free-falling into the darkness within me overwhelmed me. If I couldn't find my magic, I was nothing. I wasn't human. I wasn't demi-Fae. I was Fae, and I loved my sodding magic. A crack sang out, but it wasn't my bones breaking.

The iron cuffs lay in a broken pile beneath me. They were pulsating cold, frost forming on the iron surface. I kept the momentum and grabbed the gauntlet on my left arm. Without warning, I plunged into the black hole inside of me that had dwindled in size since removing the cuffs. It felt as if I peeled the gauntlet from my arm as my magic ripped through me, fighting against me angrily. I snapped the gauntlet from my arm with ease. I grasped it in my right hand so tight my knuckles turned white. Instead of letting it clatter to the floor and allowing the black hole within me to vanish, I held the gauntlet triumphantly above my head. Blood was still leaking from my mouth, but I didn't care. A smile crept across my face, gauntlet still raised in triumph. It didn't break me. I beheld my friends, still wide-eyed, watching me. It wasn't fear or shock on their faces. It was pure amazement that they wore as they beheld me. I dropped the gauntlet from above my head, and it clattered to the cobbled stones at my feet. The black hole disappeared, and my magic swirled once more. It tugged at me. It was begging me to use it. I had felt this feeling before... when I got wrapped up in a lesson, that same need rising. This time, it was strong. Too strong. I succumbed to the desperate cries of my ice, closing

Eevy A.

my eyes and free-falling into an icy abyss. Launching myself forward, not my physical self, but the self within me, I latched onto my magic and roared.

* * *

I OPENED MY EYES. Now shock shone on everyone's faces, Hauna's included. I was trembling, not from fear, for the first time ever. Power thrummed through me as I turned and beheld the shattered, frozen bits of iron that were now scattered around us.

I looked at what I had done and smiled.

Idris was to me first, followed by the rest of the group. My body still trembled from what I had done. She grabbed my shoulders and started feeling my body as if checking for injuries.

"I'm fine," I pushed away from her, still feeling high from the return of my magic. My head was clear, but I reveled in the semi-euphoric feeling for a moment longer. I looked around at all of the destroyed boxes—all of the shattered iron, and I knew. I could kill the Kind of Ice.

"Lesson is over," Hauna said in a graver voice than I have ever heard her use. She gestured to the remaining bits of iron around us. "Selene can clean up; I'll source more iron so you three can participate next time." She walked past me to leave the room but hovered nearby momentarily. "I'm not upset, Selene, but displays like that can only happen here," she said before leaving the room. I watched her go, but her words barely scraped the surface of my mind. My magic was too loud.

Aeryn trotted in front of me and used his thumb to wipe the blood from my face.

"You can not be contained," Aeryn whispered to me, a smile on his face. He dropped his hand from my chin. I smiled at him triumphantly. Months ago, I might've been shy or even ashamed of the display. Not anymore.

"In the nicest way possible, you looked like an absolutely crazy person... that gauntlet raised above your head—all that blood dripping from your teeth," Aeryn said while Gaia and Idris hovered closely behind.

"No, she looked like the Queen of Ice," Idris hissed proudly, stepping forward and taking my face in her hands. We locked eyes for a long moment

266

before Idris dropped her hands from my face and hugged me. I was so stunned I almost couldn't react in time. She was pulling away before I threw my arms around my little fireball and squeezed her back. We hugged for a long moment while I thought of some of her first words to me. "I don't hug."

I allowed her to release from the embrace. Gaia stepped forward next and took my hands into hers.

"You child," Gaia shook her head. It was my first time seeing her at a loss for words. "I think if the Goddess was smart, she would make much bigger plans for you."

My hands would have trembled if it weren't for Gaia's firm grip on them. She released them and stepped back from me. The three of my friends remained in front of me, still just taking me in, and the wreckage of iron around us. We had barely started today's lesson before I destroyed all the iron.

"Well," Aeryn broke the silence. "We should probably get to cleaning."

"I've got it," I told the three, but they ignored me and dragged the strewn pieces of defrosting iron to the center of the Pet Room. We all cleaned in peaceful silence, happy to be together and doing somewhat of a mindless task.

Before we were finished entirely, Orphic strode into the Pet Room, purposeful heel clicks filling the air around us. His eyes roamed around us and the pile of destroyed iron, but he only raised a brow at the mess.

"I need you in the study in ten minutes." Orphic's voice boomed in the echoey room toward us. He was referring to all four of us. Before anyone could ask, he had turned on a heel and was walking back where he had entered.

The four of us looked at each other, but only Aeryn looked worried. I raised a brow at him.

"Something is off," Aeryn stated rather than considered. No one replied; we began cleaning faster to satisfy our curiosity sooner rather than later.

* * *

THE FOUR OF us found Orphic standing in front of his desk in the study. He looked solemn as he stood, rubbing the bridge of his nose in the soft ambient glow. The dim room and faint flickering firelight didn't help the ominous tone.

267

He gestured for us to enter and stand before him. We shuffled in and stood in a line at the base of the steps that led to his desk above.

"There've been developments in Olvidare," Orphic's tone was grave. "Aeryn, you know some of what has been going on, but we have reason to believe that the king is making movements to send troops into the Kingdom of Nature. We worry he will try to push into the city if we don't place our peacemakers soon."

The four of us looked at each other, unsure what Orphic was getting at. How soon? I chewed on my lip, hoping he would get to the point.

"You complete the course tomorrow; you have no option but to pass all levels. You will repeat it all day until you do so. The Goddess has already called for a meeting of kings the day after tomorrow."

I felt a twinge of nerves bite at me. Our time was being cut short, likely by weeks or even months. I didn't think they would let us leave if they didn't deem us ready... but perhaps they felt we were. I swallowed the lump forming in my throat.

"You will each meet with The Goddess separately at the end of the successful completion of the course. She will prepare you for the meeting of kings and your last nights at the sanctum."

The room was silent. I suddenly felt extreme sorrow wash over me. I reached out next to me and gripped Aeryn and Idris's hand, Idris reaching to grasp Gaia's. The four of us stood hand in hand before Orphic. The old male walked to us, now standing close before us.

"You know more than enough to complete your tasks," he spoke. "May you lead benevolently and with compassion and strength."

The tone of the room shifted from ominous to gutting. This was a goodbye.

Orphic stepped before Aeryn, offering him a token in the form of a small iron bead. "Let your strength of endurance and kindness lead you far." He bowed before Aeryn and stepped in front of me. Orphic fiddled around in his pocket and offered me a small white rose encased in glass. I released Aeryn and Idris's hands, cupping them together to accept the token. "May your ferocity for betterment lead you to conquer far more than just the task that lay before you." He placed the fragile glass rose in my cupped hands. I wrapped my fingers around it. I locked eyes with the male for a moment. He hesitated before me, understanding floating between us. I could nearly feel the apology on the tip of his tongue. I hoped he could feel the acceptance in mine. He nodded and began stepping away. I lurched forward and wrapped my arms around my mentor. He let out an 'unff' sound but embraced me back. I fell back into line so he could continue with his gifts.

Orphic stepped before Idris, holding an orb of what looked like a never-ending firelight. "May your light never dim, an eternal flame for reminder." He handed Idris the glowing orb. He side-stepped in front of Gaia. "Let your strength of compassion and wisdom carry you into the highest form of yourself." He dropped a tiny necklace into her palm. A small glass vial attached to it with what looked like the world's tiniest flower.

"A rubiscous," Gaia gasped, "eternal flower."

Orphic bowed to Gaia, like he had the rest of us, and stepped back to take us in. We all held his tokens in our hands.

"You won't be seeing me again for a long while, but it was a pleasure to watch you all become the image of how we had you crafted in our minds before you even existed." He bowed, his hands clasped together before him. Pride shone in his eyes. Pure and undiluted pride. I felt the tears welling in my eyes. I was thankful he dismissed us right after. I had half a thought of embracing the male again but decided against it. Aeryn approached Orphic and tossed an arm around him in a half embrace. They fell into conversation. Gaia, Idris, and I decided to leave the study, a silence roaming over us as we walked the corridors. I watched as Gaia and Idris clutched their hands so tightly that their knuckles paled. They—we had two days left together before we would be separating. It would be impossible to know when we would see each other again. If we were meant to rule our kingdoms... it meant a life apart. It meant their lives, their forever... wouldn't be spent together. I hesitated a step. I wanted to spend every moment with them. I wanted to breathe in their familiar scents and hear their abundant laughter and witty remarks. I glanced back at the manic way they gripped each other hands. Guilt roiled within me.

"Hey," I said, the two looking at me, pain consuming their faces. "I... There's no better way to say this than that I know about you two." I hesitated, making sure they understood. "So, I want to give you your privacy tonight, but just know I love you both. I—" my voice cracked. Goddess, it was going to rip my heart out to leave them.

We had stopped at this point, the two still grasping hands tightly, watching me closely. "Once we are done with... all of this... We meet... as rulers, we will meet." I didn't know what else to say. I needed some tether back to them.

"How did... you know?" Idris asked me.

Heat burned in my cheeks at the memory. "I saw you in the hall one night..." I trailed off. It was enough to explain. They both began apologizing to me at the same time, but I cut them off, "Don't. I understand perfectly. Don't be sorry." I hugged each of them. "All of us deserve to write our own story. I could never be mad at you for doing just that."

We exchanged hugs and sorrowful glances, but no more words were necessary. I sent them on their way to grieve in private. I knew they needed that time together.

I stood in the hall momentarily before Aeryn came around the corner. I had known he was lingering for the conversation, but it didn't matter.

"Pool?" he asked me, and I agreed.

We walked to the nearest pool, not even stopping to put on proper swimsuits. We had seen each other naked at this point, so it didn't matter. I stripped down to my undergarments, which consisted of plain black cloth top and bottom. Aeryn stripped off his shirt as I took off for the pool, jumping in headfirst. The cool water wrapped around my body, clearing my head instantaneously. I allowed my body to slowly float to the bottom of the pool. I let my mind grow deathly quiet. I stayed underwater for quite some time before forcing myself back up to the top.

"Finally," Aeryn said from the side of the pool. He hadn't jumped in and dangled his legs off the edge.

I pushed my hair out of my face and swam over to where he was sitting. I grabbed his leg and pulled him into the pool with me. Aeryn splashed around violently and dramatically as if I had drowned him. He lunged and dunked my head under the water, but I froze him in place, suspended in the pool.

"Not fair," he thrashed against the ice trap I froze around him. With a blink, I shattered the ice, freeing his body.

We swam over to the pool's edge and leaned against it, enjoying each other's company. We would only have two more days together before leaving the sanctum.

"How are you feeling?" Aeryn asked me.

"I'm scared," I was honest. Not for the course tomorrow or even the task that lay ahead. Rather, being alone again, in a strange, unfamiliar place. Leaving my friends as they took on their own set of dangerous duties. If any of them found themselves in trouble, I wanted to know. But I knew it didn't work that way. They were strong, though. I believed in each one of them.

"Me too."

Silence clung in the air.

"I'm going to miss you," I told him, a lump catching in my throat. "So much, it hurts to think about."

He swam closer to me, wrapping an arm around my shoulder. "When I heard of my mother's death, it felt like my heart stopped beating."

My breath became silent at the vulnerable words he spoke to me. I nestled into his side as he spoke.

"The weight of it was crushing. My lessons with Orphic and Hauna were a good distraction."

I wrapped my arm around his waist in comfort. He squeezed me against him tightly in reply.

"It wasn't until you three came that I started feeling alive again." I blinked up at him, wanting to see his face now. "You three, but... especially you, Selene, you pulled me out of a darkness I didn't think I would return from." My heart began to ache for him and the pain he had endured without us. "I felt that crushing weight again today." He tensed, "I feel it right now." I looked up at him in confusion. "The moment Orphic said we would be departing here in two days... I... the thought of anything bad happening to any of you..." He trailed off. "Please be careful."

"We will—I will," I assured him, but his eyes remained sad.

He leaned to kiss the top of my head. "I will do anything for you, Selene." His voice dropped to a deadly serious whisper against my ear. "Say the word, I will leave Olvidare and be to you in two days." It was more of a growl than anything.

I nodded coolly, but my heart lurched. This was the male who wanted nothing but to complete his task when I first arrived here. He now risked everything in telling me that. That brief statement spoke many more words than what came out of his mouth. He was willing to leave behind his fated destiny for *me*. My throat tightened.

"A messenger dressed head to toe in white," he said, and I understood exactly what he meant. If either of us needed the other, we'd send a messenger clad in white, with one goal: Make sure they're seen by either him or me.

We remained clinging to each other in the pool. We simply appreciated the other and grieved the time that was stolen from us. It was never our time to begin with. But we still grieved it.

After all this time in the sanctum, I realized then that the Goddess was a crafty wench. Not only did she handcraft each of us, but she made it so that we'd become close during our time here. When we took our crown, we would be four rulers who all loved each other deeply and fiercely. We would not wage wars on other lands. We would not send out assassins or keep troops at our borders. I shook my head in awe at the Goddess and her deliberate plans for us and this continent.

After thirty minutes of embracing, I broke free from Aeryn.

"Spend the last two nights with me?" I asked him.

"I wouldn't miss it."

Chapter Twenty-Seven

Selene

THE NEXT DAY WAS A WHIRLWIND. ONCE COOL AND QUIET, THE sanctum exploded with activity. The sound of chatter woke Aeryn and me this morning. We poked our heads out of my bedroom door to find at least eight females dressed in gowns of navy, bustling down the corridor. They had kept neutral to smiling faces as they passed us, nodding but sorely underestimating our hearing. The shortest one had snickered, 'he stayed in her room?'

The four of us were already at breakfast, watching the people dressed in blue bustle into and out of the dining hall. Many of them carried something, a pile of clothes, an armful of ingredients... While what they carried was always different, they all acted the same. They'd hurry into the room and glance nervously at us before rushing away. I awkwardly shifted in my seat as a short, plump female tripped over her too-long navy skirt. I shifted further when I turned to take in the red-rimmed eyes of both Gaia and Idris. Idris was furious this morning, I noticed, after she growled some foul words at a nervous-looking male who accidentally bumped into the back of her chair while he was rushing by.

"Aids for the meeting of kings?" I raised a brow, looking at Aeryn. He shrugged, "I guess."

"Is everyone ready for the course today?" I looked around at my friends. I wasn't concerned for them... but hoped they would–that we all would complete the course on the first try. We'd have much more time together if that was the case. Tomorrow was the meeting of kings and the peacemaker placement ceremony, whatever that entailed.

Aeryn shoved a hotcake into his mouth. Not a chatty group this morning.

We were already appropriately dressed in clothes that allowed us to move and fight easily. Gaia had braided my hair into a long, tight braid that trailed down my back. I wore black from head to toe. The color drew out every ounce of life from my skin, leaving me even more pale. While I didn't *look* great in black, it made me feel powerful.

"Gaia," Hauna came into the room with a skip. Gaia rose, dropping Idris's hand. Hauna extended a hand to Gaia, "Ready?"

"Of course," Gaia sang back to Hauna. The three of us watched as the two left the room together.

I allowed my eyes to sweep over Idris, who gripped the table's edge so hard it began to smoke.

"She will be just fine," I assured Idris, who didn't relax even a little bit. She stared straight ahead, her eyes a brewing storm of volcanic ash.

"She's strong," Aeryn cut in now. "I would know; she had her legs wrapped around my throat, choking me to death."

Idris's grip released ever so slightly.

I piped in next, "You've seen what she can do. She will pass on her first try, and you will, too. We all will. You'll get the whole day together."

Idris gave us a curt nod that likely meant she wanted us to shut up but was thankful we were trying. I sighed at her, my attention snapping to Hauna, who was already bounding back into the dining hall. "Aeryn," she called out, extending her hands again. Aeryn rose. Gaia hadn't finished; they must have had multiple courses this time. Aeryn rose and walked toward Hauna without even a glance in my direction. They left Idris and me sitting alone at a table comically too large for only two.

I stood and moved to take the seat Gaia had been in beside Idris. She remained steely-eyed, gripping the table before her. I reached out to touch her hand but recoiled as I felt the heat radiating from them.

"It will take tremendous strength to separate," I started, knowing that she was likely more concerned with what was to come than Gaia passing the course. "But you both are so strong."

"You don't understand," Idris barked at me hotly.

"I do."

"You don't." Idris looked at me. Her ashen eyes looked like an eruption of metallic grey. They were glossy and red-rimmed. I could tell that no tears would fall. She had nothing left to cry. "You both are my only source of light, of happiness. I'm terrified, Selene."

The way she was speaking... It filled me with dread. A dread I could not shoulder as I walked into this task, this fate. I needed hope. Hope that I could do it—that they could all do it. She sounded entirely defeated, and our task hadn't even begun. She had an eternity apart from Gaia, leading Krakata and the Kingdom of Fire with strength and compassion. I waited for her to continue, her smoldering eyes searching mine.

"I spent my whole life in a *box*." She sighed. "Leaving you–leaving *her*." She shook her head. "It is going to destroy me."

I frowned at my friend.

"She is so beautiful, so strong. Everything she touches... it..." Idris stammered. "She will be fine without me, and that is what hurts the most."

I shook my head. "She is resilient, but so are you." I rubbed Idris's back, biting my cheek against the pain that seeped into my hand, her back like hot coals. She would need this fire to get through the course, so I did not dare try to cool her.

"Selene," Hauna chimed standing in the doorway.

"I love you," I whispered to Idris. Planting a kiss atop her brunette head, wincing at the heat that met my lips. I walked to Hauna, taking her outstretched hand in mine, and heard, "I love you too," as we walked out of the dining hall and towards the course.

I had hoped the course would be identical to the first one we completed. I knew I was mistaken about those hopes as I scanned the giant vat of water before me instead of the wet, mulchy ground. I stood on a small ledge just on the other side of the double doors. A step forward, and I would be in the deep pool of water. It wasn't the depth that made me quiver but rather the sprawling length. I cocked my head, looking on the horizon for an end. Even my Fae eyesight could not spot one.

I considered the Goddess's words and the areas we were tested in: speed, strength, endurance, knowledge, and intuition. I shook my head, wondering whether this task would be speed or endurance given the expanse of the water. I would no doubt be swimming. It was essential to know, of course. If I was too slow, I might be gobbled up by whatever sea monster the Goddess sicks after me; too fast, and I will tire by the end. Thankfully, I had a water affinity, so neither outcome frightened me.

I took a long, deep breath and beckoned my ice to my fingertips, just in case I needed it. I looked down at the water for only another moment before launching into it, its icy caress taking me in. My body stiffened at the cold, but my mind was reborn. The ice—the cold, it fueled me and my magic. I threw my arms out before me in a strong breaststroke. I didn't look back, afraid of what I might see chasing me, or rather, what may lurk behind me, beckoning me to stop swimming.

I picked up momentum and kicked with my back legs, propelling me forward. Every moment I was in the frigid water, my body grew more and more awake. I kept a steady speed, not too fast. I may burn out if the test was endurance, but not too slow that a water monster may eat me alive. I allowed a single glance over my shoulder behind me. Nothing. What? I didn't let the confusion slow me; I kept pushing forward. I used my water affinity to propel me even faster as a sense of dread overcame me. It was one thing to understand what you were escaping... but to figure it out while exhausting your body...I forced a giant wave to crash behind me, not near enough to hit me but distant enough to double my speed with its forceful momentum. I glanced over my shoulder once again. Nothing. I had no idea how this obstacle was testing speed or endurance. I paddled faster, feeling panic overcome me. Water splashed in my face and eyes, down my throat, choking me. Then I saw it, the other side of the water.

It was a sliver of marble up ahead, like a platform. Every second that ticked by, more and more of that icy white marble appeared above the water. There was nothing behind me chasing me. No. I was racing to the other side as... as... the wall grew taller? I narrowed my eyes. No. As the water drained slowly from the vat. I needed to get to the other side before the water got too low. I crashed another wave from behind me, doubling, then tripling my speed forward. I swam and swam, watching more and more of that glistening white marble peek up from the freezing water. Strangely, the wall looked like it was growing into a daunting beast before me. I knew all too well that I was just descending rapidly with the surface of the water I paddled on. The closer I got to it, the more I began frantically looking for a way up. I was only a few paddles away now, the marble wall many feet over my head. I sent a wave from beneath me to help lurch me up and out of the water toward the edge of that marble wall. I extended my hand out, connecting with the slick surface of it. I slid down the marble back into the still-draining vat of water. I slammed my fist against the wall, annoyed.

I pulled my fist back, noting a small, near-invisible divot in the marble. I let out a laugh as a different idea floated into my mind. I wouldn't need the divots anyway. I ripped into my magic, allowing ice to flow freely throughout me. I hovered before the wall, steadying myself with a hand. I reached above my head as far as I could with my other hand and froze it. My hand became one with the marble. I did the same with my left hand, heaving my legs against the slick wall, freezing my feet in place. There was about eight feet of slippery marble above my head. I snapped my hands free from their position, moving them up and freezing them in place again. I did the same with my feet and went up the eight feet to the top of the wall. I heaved myself over the edge and rolled onto my back, breathing heavily.

A smile broke across my face. Easy. This would be easy. It was a test of speed, then. I rolled over to my front. Strength would be next, no doubt. The Goddess would want to ensure we were not at peak performance. I shoved from the ground and took in the platform where I now stood. It was a considerable empty space, the floor of the same white marble I had just scaled. The room was bright, almost unnaturally so. It wasn't firelight but some sort of blinding light created from magic. It gave me a headache as I continued scanning the space. My eyes fell on a heavy iron door at the back of the platform. The room was enormous... so much so that I had no idea how it fit in the sanctum below the grove. I shuddered at the thought... unsure if what I saw was real or if a cloak was laid over it. My mind danced to the lesson of the hidden isle... the magic it would take to lay such a cloak over an entire *island*... I shook my head. There were extremely dark parts of this Fae gift that I hoped I never got to know.

I shrugged off the feeling and strode toward the door. The nearness of the iron pulled at my magic, but I bit through the feeling. As I approached the door, I noticed a strange-looking raised button. It was tall, the top of it coming up past my knees. I climbed atop it and jumped. It didn't budge. I looked around, trying to figure out how to get this button pressed. I saw a pile of three huge canvas sacks lying in the distance, about thirty feet from me. I jumped down from the control and stalked over to the pile, poking one with my foot. Sand. I would need to carry them over to the button. I heaved one up; it was heavy but not overwhelming. I cradled the bag and began walking to the door.

After three steps, the room went dark. My body felt weightless for a moment before the unnatural, too-bright lights flashed back on. What? I turned behind me to where I had grabbed the sandbag only moments ago to find three piled neatly. I scowled at them and skipped back over. I picked up a bag again and walked toward the door. Three steps away, the same thing happened. I turned and looked at the neatly piled bags. This time, I picked up a sandbag and heaved it up on one shoulder; I carefully heaved a second on my other shoulder. I felt wobbly from the weight of the two. There was no way I could get the third. I slowly began walking to the door. Nothing. I kept walking, but nothing happened. I got to the door and placed the two bags atop the button. It groaned slightly, and the door cracked up. It needed the third sandbag. I returned to the last sandbag and threw it over my shoulder. Three steps away, and the room went dark.

"Are you kidding me," I screamed to no one in particular.

Thankfully, the other two sandbags remained atop the button, the door still cracked slightly. I kicked the third bag but had an idea. I ran back to the button and climbed atop the sandbags. The button began dropping with the addition of my weight. It lowered slowly until it was flush with the ground. There was a click. The iron door groaned again but slowly started ascending. I waited, nervous that the moment I removed myself, it would fall back closed. Once the door reached the top, I launched from the button, rolling through the iron door as it slammed down behind me.

I got up from the floor, and I wiped a bead of sweat that had formed on my forehead. I looked around this new room, finding relief at the familiar scene. The same whirlpool from the first course stood before me, a countdown on the wall. The whirlpool again? I approached the pool that was again flush with the marble floor and looked into the vortex of water. I dipped a finger in, and the water vanished. A small piece of vibrant cobalt paper appeared in my hand.

"For a perfect score in round one of the course, the Goddess blesses you with a pardon on obstacle three."

I snorted and dropped the small paper to the floor. I swung my legs into the now empty pool, heading for the door that had appeared beneath the water, like the first time.

I twisted the doorknob and walked into the room. It was dimmer than the other spaces I had been in, offering me a pinch of relief. The room was small, like it had been in the first round. But that time, the room displayed three goblets, two with poison. Today, three small white ceramic plates lay atop a crystal pedestal at the center of the room of white marble. I stepped towards the center of the room containing the plates. I examined the contents of each carefully. The first was a simple blackberry, the second a pointed leaf with tiny yellow veins running through it, and the third a gooey foaming, looking liquid with an opaque yellow tinge. I sniffed at it and recoiled. I looked around the room for a hint at what I needed to do. My heart sank as I took in the gas that was now leaking into the space surrounding me. I dropped to the floor, breathing through my nose, hoping for a slight scent.

I hadn't noticed the vents in the room until the vapor began leaking out of them. I peered up at it, swirling through the air, wafting lower and lower as time passed. It was tinged yellow in color and had no scent. I sniffed again to be sure. I squeezed my eyes shut, trying to remember my lessons with Orphic. I was already feeling lightheaded from the gas but pushed through the feeling. Yellow gas. What unscented yellow gas did we learn about? There was hycide, but that killed you almost instantly. No antidote existed. I thought about the contents of the plates above.

The berry, I believed to be poisonous, I would likely just double poison myself by eating that. I reopened my eyes to watch the gas fall in beautiful yellow pillows around me. I covered my mouth and nose in horror. The lightheadedness turned to a pounding headache and a slight high feeling. It was like the Faerie wine but ten times more potent. Instead of floating in the clouds, uncaring, my head was way beyond the clouds, being squeezed so hard by the pressure it may just pop. What was this? My eyes began burning and filling with tears. My body was attempting to shield my eyes—save my sight. Trigoxide was yellow and made your eyes burn, didn't it? We learned something about a plant that could blind you... I squeezed my eyes shut, pinching my nose and mouth shut. I couldn't stay like this for long. I began furiously plucking at memories about trigoxide. It was both naturally occurring and could be made if you could get your hands on the sap of a Trigox Tree. I peeked out at the gas again; it was to the floor now. My eyesight blurred. Shit.

Think. Think.

Trigoxide will naturally occur if you burn a Trigox Tree. It releases an odorless yellow gas... But what... what was the antidote? I felt a wave of sleepiness overcome me, the muscles of my body relaxing. I willed and willed them to stiffen, but they wouldn't listen. I slumped against the floor. The leaf, what was that leaf? The yellow veins of the leaf made me think it was a Trigox Tree leaf, but Orphic had never shown us a picture, had he? Wouldn't the leaf be just as toxic? It would, I thought, it had to be. If it wasn't the berry, and it wasn't the leaf...

My stomach turned, remembering the smell of the foaming glob on the third plate. I forced my muscles to listen, shoving ice through my blood. One after the other, I got my feet beneath me. With my mouth and eyes squeezed shut, I felt around the crystal pedestal for that wet, gooey substance. My legs wobbled so violently that I thought I would fall back to the ground. I had no idea what the foam was, but—

One of my knees gave out without warning, sending me crashing forward into the crystal table. My hand flopped into a sticky, foaming liquid. I wasted no time shoving an enormous mouthful of it into my mouth. I swallowed, and then both of my knees buckled beneath me. I crashed to the floor next to the crystal table, cradling my body in a fetal position. If they let me die during this sodding test... My head cleared slightly. I blinked my eyes open. They still burned as I took in the dissipating yellow gas and a bright red door that appeared before me. I shoved off the ground and ran to it. I swung open the door and crashed through it with so much momentum that I tumbled to the ground on the other side.

I choked and coughed on the ground. My elbows and knees ached against the pressure of the hard, cool floor, but it was nothing compared to the burning in my eyes and lungs. I panted for many minutes, allowing the fresh, clean air to fill my lungs. I sat on the floor until the burning in my eyes subsided, and I didn't think I would vomit everywhere.

My knees shook slightly as I rose to my feet. I looked around the new room, which was entirely white and empty. A simple red door remained on the other side of the room. I supposed I used this room for what it was intended for, panting on the floor while the last of the poison seeped from my body. I bit down on the urge to curse the Goddess.

I trudged toward the door. The final obstacle. I swallowed hard and grasped the handle. Everything inside of me told me that this test would be the same as the first. There would be three strangers sitting, staring, waiting. A smile spread across my lips as I made a decision. Figuring out who to trust wouldn't matter. They were all dummies. I was strong now. I would kill all three upon entering the room and end this now.

I turned the knob and stepped in. My knees instantly buckled as I took in Gaia, Idris, and Aeryn sitting before me. I didn't need to look behind me to know that the door I had just walked through vanished. My hands shook as I pushed myself back up into a standing position. They looked identical to my friends. The way they watched me, Gaia sweetly, Idris without a care in the world, and Aeryn... Aeryn looked toward me proudly.

I swallowed hard and approached the table. They were fake. They were fake. All three of them were dummies. They watched me silently as I patted around my body for the dagger. I slipped my hand into my pocket, and cold metal brushed against my fingers. I wrapped my hand around it and laughed. I don't know what the Goddess thought this would do to me, but I was smarter, stronger than to allow this to break me. I stepped toward the table, and Aeryn rose, extending a hand.

I twisted the dagger out of my pocket and lunged at him, slicing a clean line across his throat. I winced at the momentary look of horror on his face before all of his features disappeared. He fell to the ground with a thud. I didn't need to look further to know that only white stuffing spilled out of the straight slash on his throat.

I turned to Gaia and Idris and asked a simple question.

"What kind of tree did Gaia regrow in the Olvidare Hideaway?"

Idris stood then. The moment her eyes softened, I plunged the dagger into her throat. It was not logic that told me she was the one I needed to kill, but intuition. The softening in her eyes it was not Idris. Gaia fell face-first from her chair a moment later. Had I killed Gaia's dummy, Idris and I would be brawling on the floor like I had with the male from the first course. I turned back to Idris, a now faceless dummy attached to the end of my weapon. Stuffing spilled from her throat, pooling around the blade. I released the cool handle of the dagger, sending her falling backward into a heap of haphazard limbs.

Another door appeared before me. I slumped and walked toward it. I turned the knob and entered the next room.

It was small and entirely illuminated by twilight. I rolled my neck, soothed by the calming lighting. The course had been well-lit and uncannily bright. The Goddess sat behind a table atop a grand-looking ornate chair made of clear crystal.

"Come, child," she cooed at me, beckoning me to take a seat before her. I allowed the ice to sputter within me at the sight of her. All she had done. All the threats she had made. I ground my teeth as I strode forward.

I flopped into the chair across from her. If I was expected to bow, I didn't.

"Well done," the Goddess spoke, her yellow eyes twirling like two pots of glowing golden ore.

"Orphic and Hauna have prepared you up to my standards." I watched her beautiful lips pucker in thought. "It is a shame the King of Olvidare forces you from the sanctum early, but your readiness is of no concern to me." I nodded, wondering if Hauna had told her about the incident with the iron. "The meeting of kings will be tomorrow," she paused. "Come, child; I need your ankle."

I shifted sideways in my chair and stripped off my left boot and sock. I walked to the Goddess and rested my foot upon the throne. This was the closest I had been to her since she held my palms, telling me of my history. Her power radiated around us. She extended her hands and wrapped her beautiful silken fingers around my foot. She traced a line on my ankle. A deep cobalt blue tattoo appeared. She traced two more. She held my foot and looked at me as she spoke.

"Remember, when the first line disappears, it means a king has fallen." She smiled at me, gripping my foot tighter now. "I don't expect you to be the first to fulfill your task," her eyes bounced all over my face, "You have one week after the first line disappears to complete your duties. Wait too long, and people will become suspicious of their missing king. They will point to the peacemakers. Understand?"

I nodded. Orphic had already drilled this into us over and over. I would have to check the tattoo daily. Maybe more than daily. She released my foot, and I returned to my original seat and began putting my sock and shoe back on.

"No luck is needed," The Goddess spoke with power, "We will speak again when you are Queen."

With a puff of glittering cerulean smoke, she was gone.

Chapter Twenty-Eight

Selene

ALL FOUR OF US PASSED THE COURSE ON OUR FIRST TRY AND SPENT the rest of the day laughing, crying, and embracing one another. I tried my best to ignore the red-rimmed eyes of Gaia and Idris, but it was impossible to stand by while they were in so much pain.

"You remember something you told me?" I clasped my little fireball's hands, staring into her dulling ashen eyes. Gaia and Aeryn rested idly by, lounging on the wooden floor of Orphic's office. We found ourselves here often, as the stark contrast to the sterile feeling of the sanctum was refreshing.

Idris shook her head, tugging her hands back into her lap. I frowned at her and stood from where I sat on the three steps leading up to Orphic's empty desk.

I extended my hand before her, waiting for her to grasp it. To my surprise, she did, and I lifted her to her feet.

"Do not weep, girl," I lowered the pitch of my voice to match Idris's sultry tone. The memory sparked in Idris's eyes before I finished.

"This is the skin of a warrior," I said and waited.

"And I am proud to wear it." Idris finished for me, staring at me... into me.

I turned from her then to take in Gaia and Aeryn. They sat up now, no longer sprawled haphazardly on the wooden floor. Tears formed in my eyes as I beheld them. Aeryn rose first, followed by Gaia. They stepped before me, eyes bouncing from person to person, yet no one speaking.

Gaia cleared her throat, calming ocean eyes resting upon me, "Once upon a time, there was a girl who watered her kingdom with her tears." The waves in her once calming irises became violent. "No more. That girl is no more." Gaia stepped forward, wrapping both her arms around me in a tight embrace.

"I love you," I whispered into her onyx and silver hair. "All of you," I stepped from her embrace to grasp Aeryn and Idris's hand.

We stood for many long minutes, understanding that these were our last private moments together before retiring to bed. Tomorrow was the meeting of kings.

* * *

I STARED up at the ceiling of my room, tracking the ornate swirls of navy and silver with my eyes. As promised, Aeryn lay on another bed in my room, only a few feet from mine.

"You look ridiculous," Aeryn stretched his arms above his head and yawned from the bed across the room. Having him here these past few nights had kept me sane. My eyes trailed down the patterned swirls of the ceiling that I had long since memorized. I brought a finger to my face, pressing it against the tacky liquid that was smeared all over it.

A short, bossy female named Mariette had forced me into wearing some gooey facial oil before bed. She told me she was tasked with 'making me beautiful' tomorrow and needed the perfect blank canvas. I was only offended for a moment. The dark-haired female was far too sweet to stay mad at.

"Leave me alone," I rolled my eyes, wincing at the tacky state of my face.

Silence fell over the chilly sanctum room. I knew where both our minds wandered. Our tasks... tomorrow... the meeting of kings.

"We're going to be okay." Aeryn sliced through my thoughts.

He was reassuring me, I think, but I somehow felt I didn't need it. "I'm sure of it."

Eevy A.

We both nodded off to sleep before saying another word.

* * *

MARIETTE WAS in our room before it was even five in the morning. She bustled around me, clicking her tongue to shoo me out of bed. Aeryn groaned from his bed, covering his head with a pillow. Mariette tutted at him before ushering me to the washroom. Despite my groaning, she had no qualms, forcing me to do what she needed me to do to 'make me beautiful.'

I was given absolutely no privacy as she stripped me down naked and shoved me into the crystal tub. She uncorked several glorious-smelling scents and oils before turning and dumping each one into the filling tub around me. The smell of rosemary and orange wafted around me as I sank below the water's surface. To my dismay, Mariette scrubbed my body for me. She had set up a small table cluttered with various tools, lotions, and makeup. I could hear Aeryn groaning from his bed in the other room, and I rolled my eyes at the sound of him.

Mariette worked on scraping any dirt or grime from beneath every finger and toenail as I submerged my head below the water. She tugged me above water by my cheeks to drown my hair in a thick, minty, citrus-smelling soap. She scrubbed my hair, being careful not to break off any of its length. She dunked me under, once and then twice, before gently ringing my hair dry. She made me sit against the tub's edge so my hair could hang out of the water. When she stopped fussing over my hair, I found the lack of stimulation to jog my mind. I winced as thoughts of King Erix floated in. I would see him today. I wondered what he was like. If he was anything like what Orphic described. If he was an empty shell of a being. I hoped he would make me hate him. I hoped he would make this task easy by being terrible.

My attention snapped back to Mariette as she began scrubbing with vigor down my body. I grimaced at the female's strength as she washed me all over, making sure no speck of dirt or hair was out of place. She scooted a stool beside where I lay my head, with my hair dangling from the tub's edge. She closed my eyes with her fingers and began applying various liquids and oils to my face. Some burned, and some smelled so sickeningly sweet I could vomit.

"Beauty is pain," Mariette clucked at me while fussing over my eyebrows. I winced as she plucked at a few hairs, ripping them from my face. My hair had dried for twenty minutes before Mariette decided it was the perfect dampness to apply her 'specialty oils.' She dolloped a coin-sized amount of oil into each palm and gently rubbed them together. She then gently ran her hands through my hair, applying the oil from root to tip. I shut my eyes at the relaxing feeling of her fingers massaging my scalp. It felt like every tug on my hair relieved the slightest tension.

"That," Mariette flicked at the opal stone around my neck, "needs to come off."

My eyes flung open. Mariette was hovering above me, a finger still resting on Dayne's necklace. I swatted her hand away but didn't move my body, knowing she would just push me back down.

"It stays on," I looked at her, eyes already welling with tears at the thought of taking it off—of losing that tiny speck of him.

"No." She clicked her tongue at me and started towards the necklace's clasp at the back of my neck.

I stood now, the water dripping from my naked body. I was taller than Mariette, but standing in the tub, I towered over her. I locked my eyes on her as hers flicked to that opal stone around my neck. I shifted as the light in her eyes —the fight in them snuffed right out. She backed off, flicking her wrist at me, which must have been her picking her battles with me. She wrapped a warm towel around my body and pulled me out of the tub and into the central part of the room. Aeryn was still in bed but awake. He watched, holding in laughter at the scene before him. Mariette dragged me to my bed, sitting me down and hurrying back to the washroom chambers to grab her stool.

"Do you think someone will come in and make me all pretty too?" Aeryn joked, stretching his arms about his head.

I shot him a steely look, watching his face grow into a deeper smirk. Mariette hurried out of the washroom with her stool and was immediately seated before me. A table full of assorted items, some that I did and did not recognize, stood near my bed. Vials and bottles of various colors and shapes were messily strewn on the top of the small table. I looked back to Mariette, a weary look on my face.

Eevy A.

She didn't deign to return a glance and began slathering on an assortment of thick feeling gels and lotions, fanning my face after each one. As the gels and creams dried on my face, it felt like they were tightening my skin, latching on to me, and pulling my skin taut. It was uncomfortable, but it didn't hurt.

"What exactly are you doing?" I asked Mariette in a not-so-nice tone.

"Shhh, my beautiful canvas."

Aeryn burst out laughing harder than I have ever heard him laugh. I would have sent daggers through him if Mariette had let me turn my head. She rustled through the bags on her table and pulled out even more items, placing them in specific spots on her small portable table. She took my face in her hands and adjusted the angle of my head ever so slightly. She picked up a spongy-looking item and began dabbing it into an assortment of products.

"I will make you glow, girl," Mariette cooed at me as she began dabbing, rubbing, and smearing things onto my face. It felt like way too much, yet somehow, my face never felt heavy.

She pulled at a chain around her neck, a small vial of black emerging from between her breasts. She held it between us, allowing it to swing and glint in the twilight.

"What is that?" I asked, watching the pure black liquid slosh around inside the tiny vial.

"Cold-pressed fury's blood," Mariette spoke in a voice that thrummed with excitement. I shivered. "Sourced from the Twilight Grove itself, the most expensive liquid on the continent."

"And what do you plan to *do* with it?" I asked.

"It lines your eyes, dear."

Great. I thought about the poor souls who were likely sent out to gather the liquid that hung so closely to Mariette's body. Such a trivial use for it.

"Close your eyes."

I obeyed. I felt slight pressure touch the corner of my eye. In a swift swipe, the pressure was gone, but a cool sensation remained where Mariette had put the fury's blood. Mariette did the same swipe on my other eye and asked me to open them. She gasped. I wanted to see, but she wouldn't let me up. She continued adding powders to my face, showing them and explaining where they were sourced before patting them onto my skin.

288

Mariette stood back from me, clasping her hands to her face. "Beautiful," she breathed.

I opened my eyes, blinking as they adjusted to the twilight-lit room. Aeryn's bed was empty, meaning he had slipped out at some point during my torture.

"Can I see yet?" I asked Mariette, but she was already ushering me toward the washroom.

I sucked in a breath as I beheld myself in the mirror. Mariette had accentuated every delicate and fine detail of my face perfectly. My eyes glowed before, but now they had intensified into a different kind of beast. The type of beast that looked like she'd seduce and kill you. And then my lips... She had stained them a natural-looking blushing rose color that was harmonious with my skin tone. It matched the blush on my cheeks.

"I—"

"You're beautiful," Mariette interrupted, a dainty smile creeping onto her face.

I smiled at the bossy female and embraced her with an arm.

"The Goddess has a dress for you," Mariette ushered me back into the central part of the bedroom. "You keep this towel on until I'm back." She looked at me sternly, shaking a finger in my face before hurrying out of the room.

I sat on the edge of my bed and considered the day to come. The meeting of kings. I would meet the four kings: Theon, Jules, Galen, and Erix. I shook at the thought of taking in the King of Olvidare, knowing he would look even more similar to Dayne than Nicodemus did.

I stood and wandered the bedroom, with nothing better to do. I took in the ornate designs along the dressers and other furniture in the room. I wondered if Gaia and Idris were getting as prepped and pampered as I was. Goddess help whoever was tasked with assisting Idris to get ready.

Mariette shoved through the door after a moment of me wandering the room. She held a long bag above her head to keep the contents of it from trailing on the floor. "I don't want you to see the dress until it is on you," she sang from the other side of the room.

I remained in the bathroom, eyes shut as she maneuvered behind me. I felt

Mariette remove the towel from my body in a swift swipe. She led me a step back, placing my feet in a particular spot. She then grabbed the dress on the floor surrounding my feet and pulled it up my body. She cinched the top part of the dress tightly and pulled me into the bedroom. She finally allowed me to open my eyes once she had me situated perfectly.

"Open, dear," Mariette nearly squealed.

My eyes fluttered open. I clasped a hand over my mouth at the beauty of the dress. It was sheer, apart from extra layers of fabric concealing my breasts and the spot between my legs. But the rest... the rest left no mystery beneath the see-through material. Thankfully, the entire dress was adorned with beautiful white pearls of various sizes. While the fabric was sheer, the glittering pearls helped create the tiniest barrier between my skin and wandering eyes. I turned in the mirror. The entire back of the dress was the same pearl-covered sheer material. My whole backside was exposed in this dress. I spun back around to the front to take in the silhouette of the dress. It was cinched tight through the waist, with beautiful beaded straps on each shoulder. The dress flourished from my hips subtly, falling into a pool of starlight around my feet. I was still thankful for the pearls, even though it offered little coverage.

"An elegant temptress," Maritte whispered. It was quite the contradiction, but I understood why the Goddess put me in this dress. It was stunning—*I* was stunning. I allowed my hands to run along the pearls as I took one last look at myself in the mirror. If there was a dress for the temptress of an Ice King... this was the one.

"The others are ready," Mariette told me before packing the things she had brought.

Mariette and I proceeded through the sanctum's grand corridors, retracing our steps to the throne room that had served as our initial introduction to the Goddess's sanctuary. I looked up in awe and memory of the gleaming crystal walls that refracted the ambient twilight from above. It almost felt eery being in such a grand space with no one but Mariette.

With a casual flick of her wrist, Mariette divulged our next destination—a remote, neutral island nestled in the heart of Lake Xoro, where a gathering of kings was to take place.

"It is a secluded isle, serving as the main common ground for rules. It has been used throughout history for kings to convene to negotiate, forge alliances, and host grand parties."

"I see," was all I could say. The eeriness of the room weighed on me, bringing out the nerves that already roiled within me. I would be sleeping in a new bed tonight in an unfamiliar place. I shivered at the thought of being alone.

"Holy Goddess, Selene, what is that dress?" Aeryn strode into the room, looking well-kept himself. His eyes trailed up my body, taking in the sheerness of the dress. My nerves fluttered away the moment my eyes rested on his familiar auburn bearded face.

I shrugged.

"You look great," He smiled, and my heart fractured. I was going to miss him.

"You too," I breathed, scanning him. He was wearing black creased suit pants with a black button-up shirt. It fit him well in how it hugged his body and made him look regal. If I hadn't already seen the male naked, I knew I would have blushed to see him in such exquisite clothing.

Idris strode in next, with a nervous-looking female who had to be the one who helped her get ready. I gave her a sympathetic smile.

Idris was glowing beneath her vibrant crimson dress. It hugged her body and was short, like a cocktail dress. She strode to me, drinking me in as well.

"Wench," Idris spat at me with a smile.

Aeryn belted out in laughter at the irony of the name she had called me.

"Says you. Put those legs away," I spat back with love.

Gaia walked in next, snapping Idris's attention from the playful conversation to her lover. She wore a flowing green dress made from layers and layers of chiffon. Green floral appliqués adorned the entirety of the dress. She looked like Mother Nature herself. Gaia spun for us, the long sheer chiffon pieces that fell near her arms twirled around her. She was breathtaking.

Mariette cleared her throat, and the four of us snapped our attention from Gaia to her.

"I will notify the Goddess that you are ready." She bowed and left the room.

Not even a minute later, that same feeling of when Dayne flexed us over-

291

came me. There was a moment of fleeting darkness before I was thrown into a new location. I blinked, adjusting to the sunlight that streamed around us. The room was thin but long, with ceilings even taller than the enormous length of the room. Tall, narrow windows ran from floor to ceiling, allowing sunbeams to radiate into the grand space. Sunlight. I sucked in a breath, finding myself walking toward it. I let the warmth of the sun take in my entire body. I basked for many long minutes as my friends wandered the building we found ourselves in. I turned to the center of the long hall, eyes falling upon the lengthy table that mimicked the shape of the room. Some of the Fae dressed in blue from the sanctum bustled around it, moving chairs and adding placemats and other things to the long oak table. I stalked over to it, taking in the stunning goblets, silverware, and centerpieces. Everything about the event would be grand.

I stopped a black-haired female to ask how much time we had until the meeting and learned that the guests would arrive within the hour.

The four of us walked around, taking in the sights through each tall window around the room. I looked out at the expansive lake that surrounded us. I spotted the Twilight Grove in the distance, its gnarled trees a symbol of what it was. I knew on the opposite side of the hall, I would find a red mountain range where Idris would be going. I learned from Orphic that Lake Xoro was a massive lake with the Kingdom of Fire bordering its north and Twilight Grove to its south. The Kingdom of Nature was to the east. Seldovia was the farthest from the lake, meaning I would have the farthest to travel tonight after the placement ceremony.

"Isn't it risky for the Goddess to stand before the kings?" I turned from the window, eyes falling on Aeryn, thinking he might've considered this already.

"I'm not so sure she will physically be here today," he answered. I raised a brow at him. "I think she may allow herself to be seen but remain in the sanctum; I agree it would be far too risky for her to make a physical appearance."

I nodded, wondering how the Goddess planned to be involved in today's meeting of kings. I knew this was a meeting that had been planned for decades. I shivered at the thought because *I* had been just as planned.

The bustling helpers filtered around the room, bringing it to life. Giant white flower arrangements adorned the long oak table in the center of the room. I counted seventeen seats at the table, one at the head of it and eight on either side. The entire building seemed to be built from smooth sandstone. It made me think of Avalon. I wouldn't be too upset if I never saw sand again. I trailed a finger along the smooth stone, admiring the silken texture. It was strange to imagine that most people didn't get to see inside this grand building, yet here I stood. I shook my head and jogged to meet with Gaia, Idris, and Aeryn, who were headed to a set of double doors at the back of the room.

The doors were propped open, leading to a lengthy hall with several rooms running down it. I shrugged but decided to open one of the doors to peek in. Inside, I found a humble bedroom with a bed and minimal furniture adorning it. I shut the door quickly. Odd. Perhaps some meetings here took days, weeks even.

"Welcome, welcome!" A familiar voice boomed from the other room. The Goddess. She was welcoming someone to the 'Hall of Kings.' The name sounded familiar from one of Orphic's lessons, but I couldn't say he mentioned this place.

We worked our way back through the hall doors, joining the Goddess and the first guests to arrive. Aeryn had been right. The Goddess sat at the head of the oak table in an obscure, sheer form. As she waved at the first guest, her petite body shimmered an iridescent blue. I wondered what kind of magic allowed her to stand before us while her body was entirely elsewhere.

"Children," The Goddess cooed at us as we approached the center table. A large, round male with dark skin and snow-white hair stood proudly before us. Two thin males with the same bronze skin tone stood at the king's side.

"I am Galen of Belgar, the Kingdom of Nature. These are my sons, Kian and Gylo."

They looked nearly identical. However, the one he called Gylo seemed to be slightly taller. The looks on their faces gave me the sense that they may just kill everyone in this room. It was a stark opposite to their jolly-looking father.

"Do I get the pleasure of knowing your names?" Galen spoke to us, but the Goddess interrupted.

"In good time, Galen dear. Do find a seat. The Meletrix Girls will be here to entertain shortly."

I raised a brow to Aeryn, who looked as confused as I was. Around ten females clad in sensual black dresses filled the room as if in answer. They carried an assortment of wines, foods, and musical instruments. The twin sons, Kian and Gylo, broke from their father's side and began eyeing up the women like prey. My stomach turned at the realization... and the bedrooms. I felt these females were not here to serve only food and lively music. I wondered who they were... if they were employed or forced to do this. They seemed to move around the space gracefully, with no fear in their eyes.

The Goddess beckoned Aeryn and me to stand on her left, Gaia and Idris on her right, waiting for the remaining kings to arrive. I touched the opal stone around my throat and wondered if I would see Dayne tonight. It was a thought that hadn't crossed my mind until Galen showed up with his two sons.

The next king to arrive was Jules of Krakata, Kingdom of Fire. He only brought his wife, Klarissa. They were both tan with dark brunette hair and blazing ashen eyes, similar to Idris's. Their scowling faces told me enough about how they felt about being here.

We remained uncomfortable at the Goddess's side as the kings and their companions eyed us. Did they know why a meeting was called? Did they know who we were? I doubted they had been given much information at all.

A thin male with onyx hair shoved through the doors next. He kept his eyes on the sandstone floor as he strode in. Everything was silent apart from his heels clicking as he strode forward. Erix. He, unsurprisingly, arrived alone. I took in a deep, shuddering breath. So it begins. I straightened my spine.

As Erix approached the table, I studied his face. His eyes were distressingly somber with deep plum-colored bags beneath them. His irises were an enchanting shade of icy blue, but the horror and grief that swam in them was haunting. His cheeks were gaunt, but a slight blush radiated through his pale skin, giving him at least a hint of life. His onyx hair and beard were both unkept but not shaggily so. Despite the horror that consumed him, he was one of the more beautiful males I have seen since being on the Fae continent. Some, like Dayne, I found to be handsome and ruggedly attractive. It was the strength that radiated from them and their strong features that called to me. But Erix was... he was elegant in a strange, unkept way, like an old ship... Still beautiful but weathered from a lifetime of waves.

He glanced up for only a moment, eyes falling on the Goddess. He tilted his chin in a quick nod before slipping into a chair at the end of the table. He ignored the other two kings entirely while running a hand through his unkept ebony hair. It fell in loose strands and waves by his ears. The only rugged quality about the male was the short but unkept beard he wore on his face. He slumped in his chair, looking wholly and entirely exhausted with life—*with living*. My eyes were torn from Erix as a familiar face strolled through the sandstone archway ahead.

My heart stopped. Dayne. I was hot and cold at the same time. I willed him to look up, but he kept his eyes on his father. He strode a few more steps before finally scanning the room. His eyes first fell on Erix, bouncing to Galen and his sons. He nodded toward King Jules and his wife before finding the head of the table. His eyes began flicking up to the Goddess but were pulled from her as if I were a magnet attracting his gaze.

Our eyes met. My heart picked up speed beneath his heavy gaze. His red-rimmed eyes went wide and filled with panic and confusion. He struggled to keep a neutral face as he beheld me. I couldn't begin to guess what was swirling in his mind as he studied us all next to the Goddess... As he beheld me in my full Fae form. Every feeling I had ever had toward him, from hate to grief to adoration and lust, all slammed into me at once. His eyes dropped to my neck, the opal stone I still wore. The look on his face had me reaching for the necklace. The stone I fought Mariette to keep on. His face—posture—*aura* radiated with relief. His shoulders slumped, eyes finding mine again. For a moment, just a fleeting heartbeat, it was just us in the room. I shifted, suddenly finding it difficult not to launch myself at him. Tears welled in my eyes as the weight of missing him began crushing me. My heart wanted to burst into a million pieces at that smile. I had no idea how I would get through this day with him so near. I watched him carefully as he stalked to the table, eyes drifting down my body and my sheer dress. His once deep, evergreen eyes lit in a blazing crescendo of lust as they trailed my body. He sat on the side of the table where I stood, leaving two chairs near the Goddess. He was hoping picking that spot would land him next to me. I broke my eyes from him only to watch his father and Nic fill the two seats to Dayne's left. I looked back at Dayne. Goddess, he was handsome. Even more so than I remembered. His dirty blonde hair was longer than when we parted at the Hideaway, but I liked it. His lips quirked up in a small smile, and I realized I was still holding the opal stone around my neck. I dropped my hand to my side and felt my cheeks blush.

"Welcome, kings," the Goddess spoke to everyone. Her ghostly form rose from her chair. Everyone at the table mimicked her, rising to their feet. Theon, Dayne's father, looked exquisitely angry as he drank in the sight of us four standing beside the Goddess.

The sight of Dayne's father had me scanning Dayne for any sign of healing injuries or scars, but I found none.

"It is no mystery that the relationships between you have been somewhat," the Goddess paused to think, "somewhat strained over the past decades." The kings all grumbled indistinct words from their places around the table. All but Erix, who kept his eyes set on the oak table before him. "I felt it was time to bring in a set of peacemakers."

The room erupted.

Theon slammed his fists against the table, knocking over the few flute glasses near him. "You will not put a peacemaker in my kingdom," he roared.

"Silence," the Goddess snarled, making me jump. Aeryn steadied me by putting a hand on my back. I could feel Dayne's eyes before I looked at him. He looked away the moment our eyes met. My stomach turned.

"Since *none of you* want to get along, I took things into my own hands." The Goddess looked around the room furiously, eyes landing hard on Theon. He was the worst of the bunch. There was no doubt about that. I glanced at the King of Nature. The jolly male who signed his death sentence by being too lenient, too fearful of war and pushback. The irony was painful.

"Now, you will not disgrace me with another argument. You will listen and welcome these lovely peacemakers of *yours*." She gestured toward us on both sides.

Dayne's eyes were wide as he watched the Goddess. I knew he was trying to understand something that he just never would. I was betraying him by not telling him. He looked back to me, eyes lingering on where Aeryn's hand still steadied me. I refocused my energy on Erix. He had been the only king not to react at the mention of peacemakers. He hardly managed to keep his attention on the Goddess. It seemed as if he found the oak table very, *very* interesting.

"I will introduce them now if you don't mind," the Goddess said to the room before her.

The kings grumbled but sat once the Goddess gestured them to do so.

I resisted the desire to watch Dayne, to drink in his face and body. Instead, I kept my eyes focused on Erix—on my task. Every reaction was critical; Every muscle twitch or eye quiver. All of it was important.

"Idris, peacemaker for Krakata, Kingdom of Fire." I glanced away from Erix to King Jules. His face lit with rage as he took in my beautiful little fireball. Ice coursed in my veins. Aeryn's hand stiffened against my back, but he kept it there, thumb gently stroking me.

"Gaia, peacemaker for Belgar, Kingdom of Nature." I looked at Galen, his face neutral as he nodded toward Gaia. Thank the Goddess, my sweet Gaia was going with him. I tracked my eyes back to Erix, who had not looked at us.

"Selene, peacemaker for Seldovia, Kingdom of Ice." I bowed, keeping my eyes set on Erix. He finally lifted his eyes and met mine. Those beautiful, sad eyes roamed my face for half of a moment. He flicked his icy gaze down my body, taking in the dress that was picked for me—or, more, picked for *him* to see me in. The corner of his mouth twitched upward slightly as his eyes returned to my face. I returned the slight smile, not that he was even actually smiling. He looked away at that, back to examining the oak table before him. I let out a long, slow breath, focusing on Aeryn's steady hand at my back. I might've fallen beneath Erix's gaze if his hand had not been there.

"Aeryn, peacemaker for Olvidare, Kingdom of Wind." I heard Theon grumble some form of a curse in Aeryn's direction.

"Sit, children." The Goddess beckoned us to take our places at the table. Aeryn walked ahead of me, taking up the spot by Dayne before I could. I sent a heated glance in Aeryn's direction but didn't want to make a scene. I slipped into the seat between Aeryn and the Goddess.

The Goddess spoke, "Enjoy yourselves, Kings and guests. Take a room if you so desire. We will regroup at midnight for the placement ceremony." Her image was gone in a flash.

The females dressed in black began swarming from the double doors that led to what I assumed was the kitchen. They began setting an assortment of foods before us. Erix drank in a particularly beautiful blonde female who already seemed partial to him. He wasn't apparent about his lingering gaze upon her but looked back a little too frequently for it to be nothing. I wondered if they had met before by the way she kept finding herself near him. The kings and their guests slowly fell into conversation around me. I glanced around Aeryn to look at Dayne. All I wanted to do was touch him—devour him and get drunk off aspen and honey.

I breathed deeply and prepared for a long, long evening ahead.

Chapter Twenty-Nine

Selene

Throughout the meal, I did my best to focus on Erix, taking in his mannerisms and studying his face. At this point, he had slipped the blonde female onto his lap and was whispering something into her ear. He had an uncanny look, a solemn, sad face, and melancholy yet lustful eyes. It was a strange mixture. I felt the two would disappear into one of the back rooms until the placement ceremony. Galen's twin sons, Kian and Gylo, had watched many of the females clad in black throughout the meal. The way they looked at them made my skin crawl.

Gaia, Idris, Aeryn, and I sat uncomfortably at the table, unspeaking, even to each other. None of the kings wanted to be here, and they most definitely seethed with rage over our very existence, so we kept quiet, picking at our food.

Erix was the first to push away from the table. The moment he did, the Meletrix Girls, who had been playing slow, relaxing music, switched to more upbeat, jovial songs. The change in atmosphere had most guests rising from their seats and finding new spots around the Great Room to sit. I tracked Erix and the blonde female walking shoulder to shoulder toward the hall with the bedrooms. I settled the urge to roll my eyes. It was likely the last I would be seeing of him until midnight. I sighed and slumped in my chair.

Kian and Gylo had taken up twin armchairs, both adorning beautiful females on their laps. Their hands roamed their bodies, up their skirts and torsos. I looked away, disgusted at the sight. Dayne, the four of us, and Galen remained seated at the table. We had hours to kill.

Gaia and Idris glanced at each other and simultaneously rose from their seats. I watched them closely but did not speak. The chatter died down at their movement, everyone in the room now watching them. We were warned that we would have all eyes on us tonight, our every smile or wince tracked by these cunning individuals. I forced a neutral face at the thought.

I watched my two friends walk to the back hall, likely headed to spend their last hours together in one of the rooms. It was an act that Orphic would surely slap them on the wrist for, but... there was no way I was stopping them. They needed this time. I watched them disappear in the same direction Erix and the blonde female had, down the lengthy hall with the bedrooms.

Galen and Dayne pushed from the table at the same moment. They exchanged a brief chuckle over their shared action. Aeryn and I awkwardly rose from the table, the last to do so. I scanned the room. The kings were scattered about the hall, most near the guests they brought or grappling at a beautiful Meletrix Girl. My eyes flicked to Nic, my stomach clenching into a tight knot. He had a brunette female atop his lap, brushing his lips against her neck. But it was his eyes, hard and lustful upon *me*, that roiled that unease. He smirked and tore his eyes from mine, turning his attention back to the female on his lap. I shuddered but swallowed my apprehension.

Aeryn and I found a somewhat secluded spot to sit, making sure not to sit too far or too close to the other guests. Dayne had taken up a seat near his uncle and father and repeatedly glanced between the floor and me.

"This is weird," Aeryn said to me. I elbowed him. If anyone in the room wanted to hear any other conversation, it would be easy enough for them to. I had no doubt we had many ears trained on us. I had no doubt that Dayne's ears were trained upon us.

"They truly seem to love us," I told Aeryn, deciding I could speak that way without Erix in the room. I watched as King Jules flinched, surely listening in.

Aeryn only huffed a laugh but scanned the room with me. About twenty of us were in the Great Room, so it was bustling with conversation, but the air remained tense.

300

A few of the Meletrix Girls came around with what seemed to be a white version of their Faerie wine... A more refined version for grand events, no doubt. Nearly every person in the room took a glass, including Dayne. I watched as some girls began dancing in the center of the room. They called on some guests, but only Kian and Gylo joined them in dance. Even though their mannerisms disgusted me, I smiled at the Fae males dancing before the other kings. They looked fun in a way, but I doubted they would give me the same gracious words.

"Do you suppose we should try to talk to any of them?" Aeryn sighed while leaning back.

"Probably." I shrugged, getting comfortable in my chair. I watched Dayne wave over a Meletrix Girl, his empty glass in his hand. I snorted, unsurprised by the sight.

"I see Erix didn't waste any time escaping this," Aeryn gestured to the party around us.

The black-haired Meletrix Girl who poured Dayne a new glass of white Faerie wine had on a short black dress that looked like she would be entirely exposed if she bent over even an inch. I glanced away and toward the group of dancing females and males.

"What?" I asked Aeryn, realizing he had spoken to me.

"Erix..." he narrowed his eyes on me.

"Oh." I shrugged, "I didn't figure he would have much to say to me," I answered Aeryn regarding Erix leaving with the blonde female.

"Are you considering taking a room?" He asked.

I thought for a moment. "I was thinking—"

My eyes found their way back to Dayne as I spoke. He had pulled the black-haired female to his lap. Aeryn tracked my eyes after my sudden drop off of conversation. Dayne wrapped a firm hand around her waist and pulled her in tightly to him. Her back lay flush against his abdomen, a position I had been in many times before. Heat coiled in my stomach. Not the bright red heat of lust or passion but the disgusting dripping black warmth of jealousy. It stung my insides as I watched him swipe the female's pin-straight onyx hair from the side of her neck, leaning in to whisper something in her ear. I could tell from here that he allowed his lips to brush against her ear as he spoke.

What was he doing?

"What?" Aeryn started, watching Dayne with nearly as much intensity as me, maybe more. "I'll kill him."

I shot daggers at Aeryn at his uncontrolled words, hoping that no one else was listening. I scanned the room. Thankfully, everyone else seemed busy with their conversations, even King Jules. Theon was speaking to Nic while the female atop Nic ground against him, her arms latched around his neck. Aeryn scooted to the edge of his chair as if he planned to rise to his feet and launch himself at Dayne.

"It's fine," I said. But my insides were coiled with a revolting jealousy.

Dayne stood and pulled the female to his side. My eyes dropped to his hand that clasped hers. He nodded to his father, who laughed pridefully before clapping his son on the back. Heat rushed to my cheeks. Dayne began walking back toward the bedrooms, that female nestled into his side. No. No. No. Why was he doing this? Did he think Aeryn's hand on my back meant something?

Aeryn shifted even further off the front of his seat, ready to rise. I rested a cool hand on his shoulder. He knew how much pain I had gone through over the past months. Hells, he had seen it in my mind the night the howler attacked us. For Dayne to be here and be doing *this?* I understood Aeryn's anger. If the roles were reversed, I would be launching myself upon the wench crushing his heart, too.

I closed my eyes and willed the tears away as Dayne and the female disappeared into the hall. Aeryn and I shared a look that said so much while saying nothing. His eyes were wide and glossy, 'Are you okay?' His eyes seemed to ask. I frowned. 'No.'

Aeryn tore his eyes from mine as a flicker of motion took our attention. Theon approached us, walking with an unmistakable swagger. It felt as if a hot metal ball seared through my insides as I beheld the spitting image of Dayne approaching me. He looked older, of course, but had the same green eyes, the same dirty blonde hair, and an angular face. I kept my focus trained upon him, shoving the sight of that female on top of Dayne out of my head. I knew this moment would be critical for Aeryn. For us all.

"Greetings," Theon boomed above us. We did not rise like he expected us to.

"Greetings," Aeryn and I mumbled back. Aeryn's posture was straighter with the male he was to kill standing before him.

"It is my understanding that you know my son," Theon looked at me. I winced, not just at his stare but at the thought of Dayne again.

"I do," I kept my voice cool and unbothered.

"He is a fine boy, is he not?"

Out of the corner of my eye, I watched the black-haired female who had gone to the rooms with Dayne scamper back into the Great Room. Her hair was now tied up, so she looked different, but only slightly. She made intense eye contact with me and gave me the slightest nod. I kept my face neutral, but I knew what it meant. Dayne had used her as a decoy to get back to the rooms. The jealousy vaporized in a heartbeat.

Aeryn bumped me, and I whipped my head back to King Theon. "What? Oh, yes, he is."

Theon's eyes narrowed on me. He looked to be the same age as his brother, Nicodemus. His beard was fuller, and his green eyes were aggressively more vibrant.

"I am sure King Erix is overjoyed you will be placed with him."

I snorted a breath out of my nose at that. The king only smiled, noting that I understood his sarcasm. Erix didn't feel joy. Theon raised his arms to Aeryn. "My boy, I'd love to speak with you."

Aeryn stood, waiting for me to incline my head for him to go. He strode off with the king, who was clasping an arm around Aeryn's broad shoulders as they walked. Undoubtedly, Theon's good nature just now was a ruse. I stood and walked as casually as I could to the back hall containing all the bedrooms.

My heart pounded against my chest as I strode through the open double doors and into the hall. I exhaled deeply when I was out of sight from the rest of the group. My nerves spiked as realization set in. I was going to see him. I was going to see Dayne. Feel him, kiss him. I stared down the hall, the length of it filled with doors on either side. How would I know which one he was in? I began walking down, glancing at each entry as I walked. Nothing. I was near the end of the hall before I noticed one of the doors was cracked open slightly. I swallowed, praying I wasn't about to walk in on either Erix and his blonde female or Gaia and Idris. I nudged at the door, holding my breath as it cracked open. I peered through the crack, a flash of dirty blonde hair coming into sight.

Thank the Goddess.

I nudged the door open the rest of the way. Dayne stood from where he sat on the edge of the bed the moment I came into view. We stared at each other for a moment, me standing in the hall, him at the foot of the bed. He didn't dare move in my direction as I entered the room, closing the door behind me. I could smell him already from ten paces away. I stood with my hands and back still pressed against the door. My hands were shaking. Hells, *all* of me was shaking. He took a step forward, and I echoed it. Another step, and another. We stood only a few paces away, the smell of him wafting towards me.

"You're Fae," he croaked his first words to me. He looked hurt but somehow still at peace with being here with me. Alive.

"I..." I stopped myself. There was so much I couldn't say.

"Apparently, I always was." He looked confused but didn't press. His eyes fell to the opal stone around my neck. I reached up and touched it. "I haven't taken it off."

The green in his eyes deepened, his face turning lustful as he trailed his eyes from the stone to the rest of my body. "That dress," he said.

I rotated for him and heard him suck in a breath at the exposed backside of me.

We remained a few steps away, unsure how to indulge ourselves. Neither of us was entirely sure what was okay. The lust was overwhelming, but I wanted to hear his voice... To have him tell me everything that had happened since we parted. I wanted the sweet kisses and the ones that burned hotter than Idris. I wanted everything from him all in the same instant. He took a step forward, now towering above me. All of me quaked, aching for his touch. He slowly reached his hands forward and gripped them on my hips, pulling me against his body. Everything snapped. I flung my arms around his middle and buried my face in his chest. He held my body against him with one hand and stroked my hair with the other.

"I missed you," he leaned down to whisper against my hair. My heart lurched, threatening to leap from my chest.

I missed him, too. So much so that it threatened to burn me from the inside out. I had hardly allowed myself to think of how much I missed him during my time in the sanctum. It all came out now and crashed down on me. I missed him so sodding much that touching him wasn't enough.

"Kiss me," I leaned back from his chest, peering up at his shining evergreen eyes.

A chuckle rumbled from Dayne's chest. I wanted to cry at the sound–at his laughter. I wished I could replay it in my head over and over and over. "I see my princess is still quite demanding." My breath hitched at the term I hadn't heard in so long.

I jabbed him in the ribs. I needed his lips against mine. He released the hand that was pressing my body to his and led me to the bed. We sat on the edge of the bed, hand in hand, looking at each other as if we weren't even sure what we saw was real. He brought his hand up to my jaw and gripped it. I was burning for him. I placed my hand on his chest as he leaned in, touching his nose to mine. My lips began quivering at the nearness of him.

"I need you," I breathed.

Dayne leaned in then and pressed his lips hard against mine. My head exploded with sparks of fire. Goddess, I missed this, the feeling of him beneath my palms—my lips—my body. The kiss turned feral in moments. Dayne's hands were in my hair, grabbing my head and pressing my lips against him hard. I gripped his shirt, pulling him toward me with just as much need. I broke free from his lips for a moment, but before I could speak, his mouth was at my throat, kissing and biting it gently. I tried to shift my body atop his, but my dress was too heavy with all the pearls adorning it.

"Take it off," I told Dayne, who, up to this point, had hardly let me undress in front of him. How his hands roamed my body with urgency told me today would be different.

He fiddled with the zipper at the back of my dress for only a moment before slowly moving it down my spine. He stood me up then, zipper partially unzipped, and the dress slumped against my body. He turned me around and finished unzipping the dress. It fell easily in a heavy heap around me, leaving my bare backside fully exposed to him. I heard his breathing become ragged. I waited for him to turn me back around, but he only began pressing sweet kisses along my shoulders and down my spine. I started turning, but he stopped me with a hand.

"Wait," he said.

I heard him begin taking articles of his own clothing off. I was suddenly so thankful for the male he was; he wouldn't allow me to feel uncomfortable in any way. I knew without turning that he stood as bare and exposed as I did. I felt his hand wrap around my shoulder as he beckoned me sweetly to turn and face him. I began shifting slowly in the direction his hand gently tugged. Before I had fully come face to face with him, he was sucking in a shaky breath at the sight of me.

His eyes dropped from my face and trailed down my neck to my breasts. They lingered a long moment before dropping lower, down my abdomen, and to the part of me that I could feel well with heat and wetness. His eyes lit with desire and hunger as he took in that tender part of me. He continued down my legs before bringing his eyes back up to my face.

"You are..." Dayne breathed. "There are no words for what you are, Selene."

My insides were boiling at his words and handsome, strong face. I hadn't dropped my eyes from his yet, but a part of him beckoned me to look down. I inched my eyes down his broad shoulders and chest, down his muscled abdomen that formed into a smooth muscled V as if pointing to what I knew I wanted more than anything. I hovered my eyes just above his length for a moment. I could feel his eyes on me, beckoning me to look just an inch further down.

I flicked my eyes down. I sensed his chest heave forward from my peripherals. His entire body shifted as he took in the devilish smile that crept across my face as I beheld that part of him. I ached for him, for the part I now took in. It was bolt upright, begging me to come closer, to wrap my hands around it once more. He had not allowed anything between us to go this far yet, but... a prick of fear stuck with me. Would he stop it again, like he had so many times before? My eyes flicked to his face, finding nothing but pure desire there. I wanted him—needed him more than I needed air. I was against him in a heartbeat. We stood still, allowing our bareness against each other to fully register. Dayne

306

threw his head back the moment my bare body met his. The feeling of my breasts against his bare chest was nearly enough to bring me to my knees.

He threw me to the bed and away from his body, ripping the breathtaking sensation away from me. I wanted him against me. I peered up at him, standing over me. I trembled at the sight, his eyes roaming my body again. He lunged toward me, hovering himself above me as if wanting me to beg for him to lower it against me.

A whimper escaped my throat, and Dayne let out a deep, throaty laugh.

"What do you want, princess?" He nipped at my ear.

I grappled at his length, but he only raised his hips away from me further, keeping that part of him just out of my reach.

"Say it," Dayne was licking up my neck now, forcing the burning feeling inside me to heat so hot I thought I would combust right here before him. Kissing–touching–licking, none of it would be enough.

"I want you in me," I whimpered as a sound that resembled a snarl ripped from Dayne's throat. He lowered his hips and chest back to mine, propping himself up at his elbows. His hardness pressed firmly against my abdomen. I writhed against him, trying to lower him to where I wanted to feel that part of him. We kissed again, his teeth not asking for entrance but biting my lower lip down and slipping his tongue into my mouth in a single fluid movement. He ground his hips against me, and we moaned in sync into each other's mouths. The sound of him–the sound of me, it fueled us both. The kisses became urgent, as if they were necessary to live. Dayne ripped his mouth from mine and began kissing down my neck and chest. He placed a kiss between my breasts. I arched hard against his lips.

I was burning for him, more than I ever had before. He began licking soft circles around my chest, careful never to pass over my nipples. I arched in silent begging for him to take them into his mouth. He continued teasing my chest as he dipped his hand low, taking in the wetness of me. The moment he felt it, I sensed his undoing. He slipped one of my nipples into his mouth, twirling his tongue over it and nipping gently. His fingers slipped inside of me in sync. I couldn't help the breathy moan that slipped from my throat.

Dayne pumped his fingers into me, sucking my breasts into his mouth further. I gripped his hair, his back, and his chest. Anywhere I could touch him, I gripped and squeezed with manic passion.

"Please," I begged him.

He rubbed his fingers against my wetness while sliding his teeth against a nipple. He then trailed his mouth back up to mine. He kissed me deeply and slowly. I forced my mind to slow, to take in the sweet and sensual kiss. I couldn't contain the heat and urgency that ripped through my body. I broke from the kiss with another plead.

"Please."

We locked eyes. He kissed my lips and stroked a thumb against my cheek. I locked my arms around his neck as he brought a hand down and began guiding himself between my legs. We watched each other silently, neither of us breathing. I felt the tip of him nudge my entrance, my whole body arching at the feeling. His face went from sweet to devilish the moment his tip began nudging forward inside of me. I echoed his sinful stare. He hesitated with only the tip of him inside of me for a moment, as if giving me time to shift away if I needed to.

A smile crept across my face as I inched my body down, allowing more of him to slip into me. Dayne's eyes rolled to the back of his head in pure pleasure. In a swift thrust, he sunk the rest of his length within me. I gasped as he opened his eyes to meet mine. They were sad and sweet as they roamed my face, falling to my lips. He leaned in to kiss me softly, his length buried within me.

I was roaring on the inside. The sweet kiss was sensual, but I needed to release the heat furling within me. He began slowly thrusting his hips against me, pumping himself in and out. I clutched the back of his hair tightly, pulling and begging for more. The hair-pulling fueled him as he began pumping faster and with more force.

My back was fully arched from the bed, and my hips bucked into the air against him. He wrapped an arm around my back with one hand, still propping his body up with the other elbow. He pulled me tightly against him, allowing him to pump even deeper within me. He started thrusting and rotating against me fast. I was nearly panting from the feeling of him sliding into me. We both breathed heavily, locking eyes as he continued thrusting. I rotated my hips against him, moaning at the feeling the rotation brought. I couldn't get enough. I needed more. I needed him to be deeper. I shoved him forward with a hand. He stood then, his knees resting against the side of the bed while he remained inside of me.

He pulled my hips closer toward the edge of the bed and thrust. He was able to get so much deeper from this angle that I couldn't help the moan that ripped from my throat. I didn't realize that this could feel this good. I moaned his name in sync with the deep thrust, and his eyes went wild. He tugged my hips against him tight and thrust hard, sending him deep inside of me. Deeper than he had been yet. He continued rocking forward into me until I felt the edge appear. The urgent look in his eyes told me he felt it, too. He kept the pace, making sure the edge stayed there for us both, but he wouldn't approach it, not quite yet.

I was ripping at the bed sheets as he thrust forward, watching me with those feral green eyes. Sweat glistened on his face as he held my hips against him tightly. He moved his hands from my hips up to my waist and flipped us both around in a swift motion without even removing himself from me. Dayne was now seated on the bed, me atop him. I didn't think he could get any deeper. Still, this position, my weight atop him, had my body sprinting for the edge, needing the sweet euphoria of release.

I ground my hips against him now, twisting and rotating around him. I threw my head back, exposing my throat to him. Dayne held my arching back as he kissed down my throat, taking my breasts in his mouth. The feeling of him, his tongue swirling against my nipple, and his sheer size inside me... I whimpered his name. We both began rocking and bucking our hips against each other. The edge was near. Dayne and I wrapped our arms around each other. He pulled my chest tightly against his as we thrust our hips together. It was coming, the edge, the explosion of love and lust, and that sweet release of heat.

I bit my cheek, holding back for Dayne to go first. I wanted to feel him within me—I needed to feel him pulsating inside while I straddled the edge. Three more deep thrusts, and it was here. The edge. Dayne allowed a deep, throaty moan to rip from his chest as he threw his head back in sweet release. I still rocked my hips against him and felt for the feeling I wanted most. It was there. I could feel that subtle feeling of him pulsating within me, and I let go. The heat ripped from me in one swift moment. I squeezed Dayne tightly as my legs shook and spasmed at the release. Sweet spirals of euphoria wafted through my core as I closed my eyes and got drunk on the feeling. The heat fizzled from my core while bubbles of pleasure popped slowly. Once every pleasurable bubble had burst inside of me, I released the tight grip of my legs around Dayne.

We slumped against each other in utter satisfaction.

After our breathing had recovered and the euphoria of release dissipated, Dayne removed himself from me and wrapped his arms around me in a sweet embrace. He stood and carried me to the washroom. He sat me on the tub's edge as the water filled behind me.

"How are you feeling?" He pressed soft kisses all over my cheek and neck.

If I was honest, I didn't know how I was feeling. My head was spinning with so many different things. It was hard to put into words. I was happy to see him, more than happy. I was drunk off how he had made me feel, yet I was horrified at the fact we would be separating in a matter of hours, yet again.

"I don't want to leave you," I frowned.

The tub had filled, so Dayne scooped me in his arms and stepped into the warm, welcoming water. He lowered us gently, him resting against the back of the tub, me nestled between his legs, my back resting against his chest. He wrapped his arms around me, warm water flowing all around us.

"I thought about you every day," Dayne whispered. Guilt flooded me; I had spent the past months shoving Dayne deep inside, not able to bear the weight of it. If a memory of him scraped the edge of my mind, I shoved it down.

"I told you we would see each other again," I opted to say, trying to lighten the mood.

"Can we promise it again today?" His voice was sad.

"Of course," I leaned my head back, and he nuzzled his face against my cheek.

All I wanted was this. Every day of this. I didn't want to leave here with Erix. I didn't want to try to get the sad male to fall in love with me, and I didn't want to have to kill anyone. I wanted Dayne. I wanted to wake up in his arms. I wanted to spend the day walking his gardens and riding his horses. I wanted to bathe with him, lay in his bed, and do *that* repeatedly until it was morning, and our day started anew.

But it didn't matter what I wanted. It would never matter. I wasn't created to do what *I* wanted.

"What are you thinking about?" Dayne brushed a finger against my cheek.

"Wanting to spend every second with you."

He chuckled, and it warmed my heart. He kissed the back of my head and pulled me even closer to his chest.

"I want you to know," I began telling Dayne, "If this wasn't my life, if... I didn't have to go to the Kingdom of Ice." I choked on my words. "I would be spending every moment with you."

"I know," He breathed against my ear as he stroked my hair.

It wasn't fair.

We lay against each other in silence, Dayne holding me tightly against him. We had so much to say but not enough time and not enough reason to talk about most of it. I wanted to tell him everything about the draves, my explosion of magic that shattered the iron, Gaia and Idris, and my friendship with Aeryn. I sucked in a breath, Aeryn.

"Dayne," I spoke suddenly, turning my whole body so I was now face to face with him. "I need you to promise me something."

He took my hand in his. "Anything."

"It's Aeryn... he... well, he is going back to Olvidare with you." I paused.

"Yeah?" Dayne asked, confused where I was headed.

"I need you to keep him safe. Don't let anything happen to him, please, Dayne." My voice was desperate and pleading.

Dayne cocked his head at the tone. "Did something happen between you two?"

"No... I... he... he's a really good friend." I stumbled through my words. Something *had* happened between us, but the circumstances were too strange to mention it to Dayne. It still made guilt coil inside of me.

"Not an... old friend?" Dayne's eyes scanned me. I understood what he was asking. Thoughts of Mairda and the dark-haired female from the Hiareth Inn flashed in my mind, a jealousy bubble cracked open within me at the thought of him with them. I shook my head.

"No. When we had to leave each other... and I thought." I choked. "I thought your father would do something terrible to you... he... He helped me through a lot. Nothing can happen to him. Ever."

"I promise," Dayne said, eyes locked on mine.

"Thank you," I turned around and nestled into his chest again, satisfied with his response.

"I know there is a lot I probably can't know," Dayne started, "But if you need me, Selene, I will come to you. I don't care about anything that happens–anything you do, I will always come to you."

I began weeping softly at that. At all that I couldn't say. I was angry at my life. I wished he could be my life, yet... if this wasn't my life, I would have never met him. I would have never experienced what it was like to be with him. Dayne kissed the top of my head over and over, squeezing me to him in a tight, warm embrace. I wished he was my home. I didn't have a home.

"Let's get into bed," I began, standing before him and helping him rise.

We crawled into the bed clothless and spent the next three hours talking, weeping in each other's arms, and making love again and again until we didn't have the energy left to do anything but hold on to each other.

Chapter Thirty

Selene

"Are you sure you can't tell me anything?" Dayne peered down at me. He was helping me back into my sheer pearl-covered dress. He slipped the thin straps over my shoulders, resting his hands atop them. All Dayne knew was that I was a part of the Goddess's plan to create peace between the kingdoms. Of course, the plan to create peace involved my closest friend butchering his father. Would he hate me for it once all the kings fell, and he knew how much I had known? How much I didn't disclose to him now, at this very moment?

"I can't." I frowned. If I wanted any chance of a future with Dayne, I would have to complete the Goddess's requests. Even then, Dayne would have to leave Olvidare to be with me. Telling him anything now would damn it all. Not telling him now might damn it all, too, if he never forgave me for it. His words echoed in my mind; 'The stars will align.' So, I would bite my tongue.

The stars would align. One day.

"How do we..." Dayne started and stopped himself. To him, this parting had no end. This parting meant I was being sent off to the Kingdom of Ice with King Erix. It meant he would return to the Kingdom of Wind and... and what? "Will you send word to me whether you need my help or not?" His eyes were teeming with pain.

"Of course," I stepped forward, pressing my cheek against his chest. We hovered before the door of the room we had spent the last few hours holding one another in.

"I don't want to say goodbye," He stroked my hair. "I don't know how long this goodbye will last." I could hear the frown in my voice.

I nuzzled into his chest. In some ways, I knew. If all went to plan, I could see him again in a few months. There was no way that I could give him that seed of hope without telling him everything I had vowed to keep secret.

"In three months, if we have not heard from each other..." I trailed off, not entirely sure what it was that came next. I would be a queen at that point. I would have a kingdom to run... People to tend to.

"Three months then," Dayne repeated, understanding why I couldn't finish the sentence. Whatever it was we could manage to do, we would do it in three months' time.

It took thirty minutes for Dayne and I to break free from our parting hug. I made him promise again that he would keep Aeryn safe before stepping out into the hallway to head back into the Great Room. As I strode into the room, many eyes looked up from their conversations. Kian and Gylo had two entirely different females with them now, as if they were tired of the others. Moonlight now streamed through the enormous windows lining the length of the Great Room. The once inviting space held an entirely new ominous aura. I scanned the room for Aeryn, finding him seated on an enormous fabric loveseat, a shy-looking Meletrix Girl beside him. I glanced around the room as I strode to Aeryn. No sign of Erix yet. I slid onto a cushioned ottoman that matched the loveseat where he and the girl sat.

"Hey," Aeryn gave me a devilish smile. I rolled my eyes at him. "This is Flora; she was just telling me about her harp."

The shy-looking strawberry-blonde female held her harp up in my direction. Of course Aeryn was having a normal conversation and getting to know her–the female brought here to offer entertainment and sex.

"She's really amazing. Will you play something for her, Flora?"

Flora blushed but nodded and began stroking her harp. I watched her fingers move about the harp's strings, creating soft humming sounds that came together in a beautiful song. I closed my eyes and let the song wrap around me.

In a way, its beauty added to the ominous tone of the room. A haunting tale of a faint light fighting its way through the darkness. When she was finished, she smiled at the two of us.

"An honor to play for you." She bowed her head.

"That was beautiful," I smiled at her. So many questions swarmed me as I watched the enigmatic female. I wanted to know who they were and why they were here. "Are you... Can you leave this place?" I wasn't sure why I asked it, but the females seemed far too comfortable here.

Flora glanced around the space before rising to her feet. She bowed to me first, ignoring the question I had asked. She turned to Aeryn. "Thank you, Aeryn, for your kind words and company." She bowed again, only to Aeryn this time, and left us alone.

I furrowed my brows before turning to Aeryn. "Of course you befriended the Meletrix Girl."

"What else was I to do? You left me."

Dayne walked back into The Great Room with the black-haired female from earlier. I hadn't even noticed her slip back down the hall for him.

"So?" Aeryn raised a brow at me, a sinful smile blooming on his face. "We're not mad at him anymore?"

"We're not," I couldn't help the smile that blossomed onto my face. Aeryn winked at me and shifted back to rest against the back of his seat. I got up from the ottoman and collapsed into the loveseat beside him.

Aeryn and I lounged together as we waited and watched the clock tick down. If we didn't have royal Fae ears trained on us, we would likely be saying our final goodbyes before the ceremony. Instead, we spoke the words with our eyes. 'I love you,'... 'I sodding love you too,'... 'We are going to be okay,'... 'I'm going to miss you.'

It wasn't until the final minutes before midnight that Gaia and Idris walked shoulder to shoulder from the back hall. Gaia looked composed, but Idris... Idris looked like she was barely holding it together. They took up the large square ottoman I had been sitting on earlier. I smiled at my friends, sadness overwhelming me. We had all seen enough sadness for one lifetime. Maybe even two. I was so tired of being sad.

My peripherals registered motion in the direction of the back hall of the bedrooms. Erix strode out, alone and swaggering into the Great Room. It was an uncaring sort of swagger—nothing self-absorbed about it. He was still fixing the collar of his shirt as he walked to take up a seat far from the rest of the kings. He glanced at no one, keeping his sad eyes trained on the floor. I wasn't sure what my first move would be with him. Orphic's voice boomed in my mind. Leverage *everything*.

The Goddess appeared, snapping my attention to the center of the room. Her ghostly form was even more eery in the dim lighting, haunting all of us. "I'm glad to see you all in one piece," Grumbles sounded from Jules and Theon, but the rest of us remained silent. "Orphic will be helping me out today, as I sadly could not be here for this momentous occasion."

My eyes lit up at his name. I was about to be thrown into a world without familiar names or faces. The familiar male strolled out of the double doors that the Meletrix Girls had been using all night. He waved hello to all the kings, careful not to disturb the navy ribbons in his hand.

"If you would all line up before me, next to your respective peacemaker..." Orphic trailed off.

Galen rose first, looking over toward Gaia. She rose to meet him. The rest of the kings stalked before Orphic. I stood, patting Aeryn on the shoulder before striding towards my mentor. I lined up, waiting for Erix to find his place beside me. It wasn't until all the other pairs had lined up that the brooding male shuffled in line next to me. He didn't acknowledge me or even remove his eyes from the ground. His very presence was dark and cooling. It threatened to make me shiver, even though ice ran through my veins. I kept my head straight forward, only glancing at him in my peripherals. I could smell the Faerie wine that seemed to seep from the male.

"I will begin the ceremony now." Orphic walked to the end of the line, standing before Gaia and Galen. He brought a small blade from his pocket and asked for their palms. He held the diamond-studded silver dagger in a way that made me wonder if he had ever wielded a weapon. He sliced Gaia's palm first and then Galen's. Crimson as deep and pure as Idris's dress welled to the surface of each line. "Clasp your hands together, let your blood run as one."

Gaia rested her palm atop Galen's, her hand looking like a child's in his. Orphic began wrapping the ribbon around their two hands all the way up their

316

forearms. The Goddess in her ghostly form stepped before the two and blew a gust of glittering silver dust that encircled their hands. A thin, tattooed band appeared on Gaia and Galen's pinky fingers, sealing their bond as peacemaker and ruler.

"Your peacemaker has been placed; go in peace," the Goddess nodded to the two, dismissing them, but they remained unmoving. I blinked. Was that... it?

Orphic moved down the line, continuing this process until he stood before me and Erix.

"Hands," He beckoned. I stared at my instructor as I extended my palm for him, waiting for Erix to do the same. After a moment had passed, I glanced over to Erix, who stood only a foot to my right. Both his arms hung at his sides, his eyes drooping and glazed. The bastard wasn't even paying attention. Orphic cleared his throat, snapping Erix's attention back to him. He glanced at my outstretched hand, eyes falling upon the milky white skin of my palm. He let out a nearly inaudible huff of air before extending his own palm forward. He hovered his hand a few inches from mine.

Orphic braced a hand beneath Erix's as he touched the dagger's tip to his palm. I allowed one more glance up at him before Orphic slid the blade across his skin. His jaw was now set, eyes more alert, yet he paid no heed to me. By the time I glanced back down, a crimson line was forming. I knitted my brows together. Had he not even flinched at the cut?

Orphic mimicked the action, gently bracing my hand before allowing the sharp silver blade to run along the skin of my palm. I winced at the pain, awarding me my second-ever glance from Erix. It was short-lived.

"Clasp your hands together, let your blood run as one." Orphic repeated for the fourth and final time of the night. Erix hovered his hand closer to mine, waiting for me to place my palm atop his. I turned my palm over and gingerly set it against his hand. I curled my fingers around his hand, waiting for him to do the same. He kept his hand flopped open, the pads of his fingers facing the grand ceiling of the hall. A flare of ice snapped within me at that.

Orphic quickly wrapped the navy ribbon around our hands up to our elbows. The Goddess stepped before us, blowing the same glittering dust around our hands. I eyed our pinky fingers, waiting for the tattooed ring to appear. When it did, I brought my attention back to the Goddess, uncaring of where it was Erix was looking. It was probably at the floor anyway.

"Your peacemaker has been placed. Go in peace." The Goddess nodded to us and then vanished without even a goodbye.

"You are all dismissed from the meeting of kings. If you have any concerns about your peacemakers, please direct them to me," Orphic waved his goodbye and strolled back through the double doors he had come.

Erix began unwrapping the navy ribbon from our forearms and hands. I removed my palm from his, feeling the wetness of our mingling blood on my palm. I held my palm before me, taking in the red X of smeared blood that formed after our two diagonal cuts merged. Erix let the navy ribbon flutter to the ground between us. The other pairs began shifting from where they stood in line to meet back up with the guests they had brought. I began dropping my hand to my side, hoping that the blood wouldn't get on my white dress. Erix reached out a quick hand, catching my wrist. I nearly took a step back in shock at the swift movement. I didn't dare look at his face; I only watched as he slid a finger across my palm. The cut was already half-healed, but it closed up entirely with a flick of his finger. A moment later, water enveloped my palm, washing the blood from it, leaving once more that unscathed milky white skin. I couldn't help but stare wide-eyed, not only at the action but also at the healing. Erix dropped my wrist lazily and turned from me. I couldn't even register a thanks before he was striding down the center of the Great Room toward the arched sandstone doorway all the kings had entered.

A wave of panic coursed through me as I experienced those last breaths with the people I loved so dearly. I turned, taking in each one of their faces one last time. Gaia and Idris could not return my glance, but Aeryn held my eyes for a fleeting moment before turning back to Theon. I took a step in the direction Erix was headed, eyes falling on Dayne. His evergreen eyes had dulled, yet he mouthed. 'I will see you again'. I was only able to nod and brush a finger against the opal stone around my neck. Saying anything, mouthing anything could cost him. I ripped my eyes from the face that I adored so much and turned to follow Erix out the door.

Part Three

Fates Entangled

Chapter Thirty-One

Selene

ERIX SHOVED THROUGH THE SET OF THICK WOODEN DOORS AND away from everything I cared about. He strode through, uncaring whether or not I was able to slink through before the doors swung shut behind him. I wasn't entirely sure he cared if I followed him or not.

I blinked to adjust my eyes to the intense darkness that surrounded us now that we stepped out of the sandstone Hall of Kings. I took a few steps forward, nearly tripping on the steps that suddenly appeared beneath my feet, leading down from the entrance to the Hall of Kings. Erix jogged down them, hands shoved in his pockets. I squinted ahead; the only light I could see was from the moon reflecting off Lake Xoro and a few flickering lights from what looked like the shadow of an enormous boat. I kept several paces behind Erix, half wondering if he hoped I would wander off, get lost, or perhaps purposefully leave him. We neared the edge of the small isle, the ground shifting from packed dirt to sand. Erix walked straight for the water's edge, the boat now towering above us. I stopped walking, wondering how we would board the massive watercraft. There was no dock... there was no—

"Oh," I whispered quietly, watching Erix ascend a set of stairs made entirely of water. I supposed having magic for hundreds of years taught you all the quirky ways to use it. Erix jogged up the steps, swung his leg over the edge, and boarded the boat. I stood at the base of his water stairs, tapping my foot on the top step. It held. I glanced up at the several stairs ascending far over my head. I shrugged and took the first step. The water vanished the moment both of my feet stood on the step. I fell the foot drop into the shallow edge of Lake Xoro.

"Really?" I snarled quietly. I trudged back a step, yanking the bottom of my dress, now soaking wet, out of the lake. I rolled my eyes and made my own steps just as the boat began shoving off from shore. I bounded up the steps, heart racing at the thought of being left—of failing within minutes of walking out of the hall. I reached the top of my water stairs and threw myself over the edge with about as much grace as a peglin. I toppled to the floor, the wet bottom of my dress sloshing against my face. I scrambled to my feet to assess the new space. Erix stood, leaning against the ship's mast, chin tilted down, staring right at me.

"You could've left the stairs," I grumbled at him but bit my tongue in self-punishment.

Damnit, Selene.

I had to seduce this male; I needed to keep my anger leashed. I smoothed my hair and scanned the rest of the ship. It had three masts, with several low-mounted torches that offered a peaceful glow around us. Being on a boat again reminded me of the boat Dayne had taken me. The day we crossed the Onyx Sea. This was everything that the boat was not. I looked back at the barely illu-minated Hall of Kings, seeing it now from the outside. I didn't care to take in its grandiosity or the way its sprawling sandstone peaks reached for the sky. I could only stare blankly at it as we set sail further and further from those I loved so dearly.

The ship picked up speed, sailing forward, my friends becoming distant cries of home. I finally broke my eyes from the dark horizon behind us, finding it difficult to set my eyes on that endless darkness, an echo to what fluttered in my soul.

I stalked to the edge as Erix remained cross-armed against the mast. The breeze picked up, sending my loose curls flowing wildly behind me. I sucked in a deep breath, allowing my lungs to fill so deep that it began to hurt. Fresh air. I sighed. I hadn't realized how damp and musty the air had felt below the

322

Twilight Grove until this very moment. The moon, too, was a stately sight. In the grove, or rather, beneath the grove, it was strange. There was twilight, but the source of it, you could never see. Here, the moon stood proudly in the sky, a song of ancient stories plastered above us all—seeing all. I shivered, wondering how many atrocities had been committed on this magical land with that same moon watching. I winced, finding myself, once again, pitying the sun and the moon.

* * *

WE DOCKED WITHIN MINUTES, pulling up to a dimly lit peninsula of land. I assumed we were sailing east, meaning this would be Belgar. We would be leaving the neutral grounds of Lake Xoro and entering the Kingdom of Nature.

I turned to watch Erix stalk to the opposite edge of the boat I was leaning against. He swung his leg over the edge. His head slowly bobbed down until it disappeared below the lip of the boat and out of sight. The silent treatment, then. I jogged to catch up with him, peering over the edge. We had pulled up to a raised dock; thankfully, the steps were wooden this time. I mimicked Erix's motions but faster to keep up with him.

He headed down a dirt path that was lined with flickering lanterns. In the distance, I could hear the city roaring with life. We were on the western edge but seemed to be walking toward the booming heart of the city. The closer we got to the center of Belgar, the more firelight lit up around us. I was no longer squinting to keep an eye on Erix's turns and could keep a good distance behind him. He took a swift left turn that seemed to put us onto a crowded cobblestone street. The source of the distant noise came into clear view as I took in the swinging sign on the only building down the street. It read 'Pub'. I snorted at the straightforward name.

Fae, both male and female, spilled out of the pub into the cobbled street. Most of them had deeply bronzed skin, indicative of their roots. I felt entirely too naked to be walking down such a crowded street with such drunk Fae bastards. The whooping that stirred up as we made it halfway to the pub secured that feeling, driving it even deeper. Erix kept his head ducked low, the

Eevy A.

collar of his shirt nearly touching the bottoms of his ear lobes. Many glanced at him as we passed, but my dress took the attention off the king. Or perhaps it was my exposed backside. Probably both.

Once we reached the quaint pub, Erix strode up the two small steps before the swinging slatted door. This time, when he shoved through, he held it open for a few moments, allowing me time to slip through. I noted the contradictory actions, not knowing or understanding how I could possibly use that to my advantage.

The pub was an eruption of noise, with laughter and brawls. Males sloshed their drinks wildly, uncaring that they spilled on the wooden floor at their feet. I stepped into the pub, feeling the slight tension with each step as the tacky wine-covered floor stuck to my shoe with each step forward. I winced, finding both serenity and pain in the scene before me. It reminded me too much of the Hideaway.

We strode through the pub's foyer, a small entry space that still had several small round tables jammed within it. We had to squeeze past many others into the larger back room. The bar containing all of the drinks was on the backside. It, of course, was even rowdier than the entrance. Erix didn't stop to scan anyone or anything. He only stalked in like he knew exactly where he was headed. I wasn't entirely sure why we were here, but it didn't seem he was in the mood to tell me. It didn't seem he was in the mood to talk at all.

As I scanned the room of bronze-skinned nature Fae, my eyes found two individuals seated in the far back of the pub. Their light skin tone stuck out in the crowd. At that moment, I knew they were who we walked toward.

We approached the tiny round table they sat at, the milky-skinned female's eyes darting up to us first. The male beside her had a tanned complexion, but not like the luxurious chocolate skin of the nature Fae. His hair was long and the same shade of ashen brown as Idris's. He had it slicked back, falling just below his ears. A fire affinity, no doubt. He said something to the dark-haired female whose electrifying eyes were pinned on me. He tracked where she was looking, his eyes landing on us, only a few paces from their table now. A wicked grin bloomed on his face at the sight of Erix. The female was the spitting image of the king. Her straight onyx hair fell past her chest. Her eyes were a vibrant icy blue, the same snowy core as Erix's. Aven and Ynette. I was sure of it.

Aven jumped up, nearly knocking over their table, and approached us. He slapped Erix around the back. "Brother," Aven said in a playful voice. The male seemed like he could not stop smiling. It was an intoxicating smile that provided his rugged face with some added charm. He was very handsome, in the same way that Dayne was.

"Hells," Aven eyed me, "So the Goddess wanted to give you something sexy?" Aven pushed past Erix and stood before me. I realized then that no one knew about the peacemakers.

"Aven," he towered over me, grinning. "I'm basically the king around here since this prick won't do anything but sleep and screw."

I stifled a laugh and glanced at Erix. He was rubbing his eyes with annoyance as he strode to stand next to where his sister sat.

"Selene," I said, looking at the remarkably alluring Aven in his deep brown eyes.

"She even has a hot name." Aven clapped me on the back, leading me to the table that Erix now sat at with Ynette.

"We're not staying, Aven," Erix grumbled to his friend.

I was taken aback upon hearing his voice for the first time. It sounded as regal and elegant as he looked despite the rugged beard. I wondered then if he and Ynette were the spoiled, snobby type. I suppose it didn't matter either way. There was only one outcome in all of this. I returned my attention to my task, finding it hard to focus beneath Erix's sister's gaze.

She watched me with pure, unrelenting interest. It wasn't a harsh gaze but an intense one. It made me want to shrink or run to a mirror to ensure nothing was out of place. It felt a little too thoughtful as her eyes roamed my face.

"It sure looks like you're staying." Aven swung a chair from an empty table over for me. "My lady."

I hesitated, watching Erix. He sat there rubbing his eyelids and temples, eyes squeezed shut. I took the seat and scooted up closer to the table. I was surprised at how inviting Aven was, considering he had no idea who I was.

Aven plopped into the chair next to me, throwing an arm around the back of my chair. I found myself liking the male, not because he called me hot, although that helped, but because he could keep the air around us light. It was refreshing.

325

"Do we get to know why you grace us with your beautiful self?" Aven wiggled his arm from behind me. I kept my eyes glancing between Ynette and Erix, finding only Ynette's eyes trained on me.

"I am the Kingdom of Ice's new peacemaker," I spoke confidently, eyes brushing over all three of them for their reactions. Erix kept his head down, unchanged in any way. Ynette and Aven both became wide-eyed and curious. The term peacemaker didn't have a particularly great connotation amongst the Fae. I'm sure it helped that I looked rather frail and like I could never overtake a kingdom as the last peacemakers had. I winced, but only internally, wondering if we, as peacemakers, actually did what the job title sounded like, if things would get better with much less... violence.

"So, how long are you in for? One century, two centuries?" Aven joked, making my body relax slightly.

"Three," I batted my eyelashes at him.

"Funny and hot? She's a keeper, Erix, I tell ya."

I had a sudden urge to banter with him, so I dug into my slumbering ice and allowed frost to form on my fingertips. I flicked a finger at Aven, the smallest pebble of ice bouncing off his nose.

Aven raised a brow. "Okay, okay, not hot... just funny." He winked at me, and I smiled back.

Guilt roiled in me at the feeling of my lips spreading into that unfamiliar smile. What was I doing? I'm not supposed to like them. I slunk into my chair, trying to distance myself from further conversation with Aven.

"Is the carriage still on the edge of town?" Erix asked no one in particular.

"It is," Ynette answered in a sweet voice.

Erix and I had yet to speak a word to each other. I could leverage that. Make the first conversation worth his while. He would have to be interested in it, right?

Erix pushed back from the table and stood. I guess he had just wanted to sit for a minute. Ynette rose an instant later, echoing his movements.

"Aw, come on, guys," Aven cried at Ynette and Erix. The two ignored him and started off toward the pub's front door.

"Sodding lightweights," Aven grumbled and pushed to follow them. I scampered behind, the last of us to exit the pub.

Ynette and Erix walked side by side along a dimly lit dirt path. Aven followed while he sang and did some sort of air-punching dance behind them. I hung back, following in the distance. It sounded as if we were headed to a carriage. I already missed Dayne and his flexing.

"Comin', Sel?" Aven shouted to me.

Great, a pet name.

I just shoved a thumbs up in the air, and Aven flipped back around, back to his singing and air punching.

We approached what looked to be the carriage we were riding in. It was extraordinarily lavish. I had expected some sort of horse-drawn carriage with bare wooden benches, but no. A giant majestic silkie was hooked to the front of an all-black cabin on wheels. While the carriage lacked color, it made up for it in intricately carved designs on the corners and walls. There were glass windows on either side of the cabin. The cushions within the cabin were a deep crimson red with swirls of silver throughout. Half of the seats were set into a semi-reclining position for sleep. I swallowed, hoping I wouldn't have to sleep with the three of them in such tight quarters.

Erix and Ynette hopped into the carriage, but I followed Aven once I noticed he was approaching the silkie. He began scratching it beneath its jaw like a house pet.

"Stacia," Aven spoke to me, telling me the giant pet's name.

I approached them, taking in the beautiful silken striped coat. The only silkie I had met was during my training in the sanctum. That silkie had looked similar to Stacia; only she had much darker fur on her. Stacia was almost entirely white, with lighter grey stripes around her torso.

"Can I..." I started to ask, but Aven grabbed my hand and brought it toward Stacia's forehead. My hand disappeared into the furry beast's face when I set my palm there. Her green eyes lit as I trailed my fingers beneath her chin, where Aven had scratched. I smiled as she stretched her face forward for more scratches.

"Erix tamed her. We've had her for seventy years." Aven looked lovingly at the creature.

Seventy years. About the same time, Leyola and their unborn child had passed.

327

Eevy A.

"He cheated, though, found her as a cub; if we're lucky, we will have her for a couple hundred more years." He scratched her jaw as I continued working on her chin.

Aven sighed, dropping his hand, "After you." He gestured at the cabin.

I stepped into the cabin and cringed at how small the space felt. Erix and Ynette were seated on the same side, so I opted to sit across from Erix. I reclined my seat into a partially lying position as Aven swung himself next to me. Aven started poking Ynette with his feet to get her riled up, but she shook him off and told him to sleep.

"How long is the trip?" I asked no one in particular.

"A bit under two days," Ynette answered me, her blue eyes searing into mine. I nodded back to her, hiding my annoyance at the length of the trip. Perhaps I hadn't realized how spoiled I was getting flexed everywhere by Dayne.

Stacia tugged the cart forward, and we lurched into motion. I sighed, settled into the crimson velvet cushions, and allowed the subtle sounds of the wheels crushing on gravel to lull me into a sort of semi-twilight state.

* * *

WHEN I WOKE, Ynette informed me we were three-quarters of the way to the Kingdom of Ice, meaning I had slept an entire day away. Somehow, I was exhausted, likely from oversleeping. I stretched and forced myself to take in my new surroundings and companions. Erix and Aven had swapped seats at some point; perhaps they stopped and never woke me.

I glanced at Erix, whose hands were placed casually in his lap. He wasn't staring out the window as I had thought. No... he simply stared ahead at nothing. Sad. Empty. I tried to picture the male with a fraction of happiness on his face, but couldn't. Weirdly, the sadness suited him. I studied his face, even though I could only see part of it. It seemed like he had permanent dark bags beneath his eyes and red rimming the edges of his eyelids. His brows were always set low as if in a constant state of uncaring. As if he didn't care to access the muscles in his face to show any form of emotion. His unkept onyx hair had length, but it wasn't as long as Aven's. My eyes trailed Erix's cheek and down his neck. That skin was sparkling white, nearly as pale as mine, but it had a

328

warm, blushed undertone to it. No freckles adorned his cheeks like mine, only skin as smooth as buttercream.

I brought my eyes back to his face. His scraggly beard went down the lengths of his jaw, allowing for only a bit of length around his chin. It connected to a faint mustache on his upper lip. He and Aven had similar beards, but Aven's was much thinner and more discreet. They both looked good with their facial hair, yet there was something so sad about Erix's. It was as if it was only there due to the state he was in. I looked away, not wanting to keep my attention on him for too long.

We continued for many more hours, Ynette nodding off to sleep, leaving Erix and me to stare silently out our respective windows. Aven had an arm tossed loosely around Ynette. She was nuzzled into him comfortably. They must be a tight-knit group. I looked back out the window on my side of the cabin, finding nothing but sprawling plains to stare at. The irony of it was that to many, the view was plain—boring, but to me, it was worlds better than the sand I was used to.

A drip of water hit the window. Then another. Soon, faint sprinkling sounds filled the air as the world began raining around us. I tensed, turning from the window now as drops of water streamed down it.

Of course. Of course, it had to rain.

I chewed on my lower lip, controlling my breathing as the rain picked up, hammering down on the top of the cabin. Stacia continued forging forward despite the heavy drops that I knew peppered her from above. I shifted in my seat, finding it increasingly hard to get comfortable now that everything I hated about my time in Avalon showered me in a torrential reminder.

You're not good enough. Never good enough.

The synchronous raindrops seemed to speak the King of Avalon's words to me with each patter against my window. I shifted from the window slightly, putting a few more inches of distance between me and the downpour.

A moment later, the rain stopped, all of it. Yet, the way it had stopped was uncanny. One moment, the carriage was being peppered with loud, endless drops of water, and the next, nothing. I narrowed my eyes at the window, trying to look past the drips of water that still slid down the outside of the glass. It was still raining… just not *on us*. I glanced around the cabin, Aven and Ynette still snoring despite how loud the sudden storm was.

Erix continued staring ahead, yet his face had an ounce of rigidity to it. He seemed like he was focused on something, yet he did not look my way. I turned back to the window, staring at the rain that fell in the distance but no longer touched the cabin. I shook my head in shock at both the unusual scene and at the king, who I knew was stopping the rain. I didn't dare think he did that for me; how could he have known anyway? I was certain he had his own reasons, yet still, I found myself thankful I no longer had to sit in tense, anxiety-ridden silence as the cart tugged forward through the rain.

We hit a sudden bump, jostling the carriage, shaking Aven and Ynette awake. I watched the two stir and decided it mustn't be out of character for them to have slept that way, considering their lack of awkwardly exchanged words.

Ynette pulled herself away from Aven and stretched.

"You can still cuddle." Aven waggled his eyebrows at Ynette, who was rolling her eyes and scooting closer to the exterior window of the cabin. I had to physically will myself to look away from Ynette's sleepy eyes. She was mesmerizing.

Aven kicked a foot out at me, nudging it against my knee. "How ya' holding up, kid?" He yawned, waiting for my response.

I shrugged. "It's a beautiful day," My voice was hoarse after not having used it for so long. Aven looked out the window to take in the cloudy afternoon; the rain in the distance had died down but sprinkled enough for me to know the king still gripped it with his magic.

We were still in The Kingdom of Nature, but the terrain told me we would be crossing into the Kingdom of Ice soon. The grass came in sparse patches now, and the once rich dirt was now an ashy brown. I pressed my cheek against the window, looking ahead. I could make out mountains in the distance. The Kingdom of Ice… Seldovia. The city was surrounded by mountains as if planted in the center of a dome. Given all I had heard about the city, I wasn't excited to see it. Homes falling on families… crushing them—killing them. I glanced at Erix, his eyes hollow and distant.

"How often does it snow?" I looked around the cabin. The word was unfamiliar on my lips.

"In the Kingdom of *Ice*?" Aven emphasized the word ice but shot me a playful look. "Often, but not constantly," he said with a shrug.

"It's beautiful there. You'll love it," Ynette chimed in, her vibrant eyes locking onto mine.

She reminded me of Gaia, with her composed nature. Orphic had told me that Ynette would not be a problem until after I took out Erix. She was respectful and kind, and apparently, she was the only reason Seldovia hadn't revolted. He said it would be a shame if I had to also 'take care of Ynette.' I shivered at the memory. It was much harder to stomach when they sat mere feet from me. I turned from them and watched out the window. Everything lush about the Kingdom of Nature became duller and more sparse the further east we traveled until, eventually, snow littered the ground. The cabin wheels rolled through the powdery white, leaving tracks in our wake. I had never seen snow before... not in person anyway. I supposed, in some ways, it was a lot like sand. I had seen enough sand to last a lifetime.

I scanned the vast white-littered space around us, finding so much beauty there. It sparkled as we rolled forward, the sunlight catching on the flakes at every angle.

Stacia pulled the cabin along a path that had been cleared of snow. I was thankful the silkie didn't have to trudge through it. I rested the side of my face against the already chilling window, resting my eyes for the last stretch. After all this time, Erix had still managed to say no words to me. Good. Let him be that way. I could break him anyway.

A violent wind ripped around the cabin, jostling it. My eyes flung open. "Is it usually..." I trailed off, seeing the concern on all three of their faces. "Windy?" I finished.

Another gust of wind smacked the side of the cabin, teetering it. Stacia let out a bellowing that sounded like a warning. Both Erix and Aven were to their feet in an instant, scanning the outside of the cabin. I was surprised to see so much quick movement out of Erix.

Stacia snorted. Aven called out for her to halt, lurching the cabin to an

Eevy A.

immediate stop. I looked around outside and saw nothing. If it hadn't been for Aven and Erix's reaction, I wouldn't have thought anything of the wind.

Erix hopped out of the cabin first, Aven right behind him. They both strolled around slowly, scanning the vicinity around us. Every step they took left a print in the snow behind them. I watched both of their faces, studying them. Aven's was hard and focused, unlike the normal smiling, laughing male that he had been ten minutes ago. Erix looked the same despite the circumstances.

A wind picked up around us again, but it was slight.

I looked to Ynette. "What are they looking for—"

The cabin was hit with what felt like a massive boulder thrown at us. It toppled over on its side, sending Ynette and me flying from our seats. We hit the side of the cabin hard, glass crunching beneath our bodies. The windows had shattered entirely upon the impact of the frozen ground. I looked around, reorienting myself with the space.

"Are you okay?" I asked Ynette, now scanning her. Blood peppered the broken glass beneath us, staining the pure white snow that now found its way into the cabin. She nodded, holding up her hands to show a few minor cuts. I stood, the glass crunching beneath my feet. Hot panic coursed into me, but I tempered it with angry ice. I rose to my tiptoes, trying to reach above my head for the other window, but it was too far out of reach.

Stacia was shrieking, probably still hooked up to the cabin at the front. I tried to hear past Stacia's cries, but it was difficult as the beast howled so near and so loud. I could hear yelling but could not distinguish any voices. I looked around again, now jumping up to reach the window above our heads. I looked down at Ynette, still huddled on the broken glass.

The side of the cabin with the door was pressed against the snowy ground beneath us.

"We have to climb," I urged Ynette, hoping she'd follow me. I searched for a place to put my foot closer to the windows above us. More sounds erupted outside, puncturing the wall of Stacia's cries. Fighting. The sounds that broke through, the grunts, and yells and clashes of swords. That was fighting. I wedged my foot onto the side of the cabin and heaved myself up. I pressed my bloody palm against the glass above my head. I punched the window hard. It

332

didn't budge. I took a deep breath and willed ice to form around my fist. Ynette was finally up, trying to get into the same position as me but on the other window above our heads. I swung hard at the window, shattering it beneath my icy fist. I looked to Ynette, whose face was paled in horror. She looked to her fist, yet no ice formed there. I remembered what Orphic had said about her not using her magic.

"Let me--

The cabin was again hit hard by another violent gust of wind. I lost sense of where my body was within time and space as it toppled again, this time rotating more than the first hit. I shook my head, feeling my body in the places I felt pain. I was okay. I scanned Ynette, who was strung out haphazardly in the corner of the cabin that now stood on its ceiling. I winced, hoping Stacia had been ripped free from her harness. I listened for her cries but heard none.

Ynette and I scrambled to our feet, reorienting ourselves. I breathed a sigh of relief, taking in the door that was no longer flush against the snowy, frozen ground.

I shoved through the door, Ynette on my heels. I pointed. "There"

Aven was fending off two horribly violent-looking masked males. Their gold swords with gleaming opal stones told me enough about who sent them. My throat formed a lump with what felt like a hot metal ball slowly burning its way through my insides, working down into my gut. If Theon had sent these males, was Aeryn all right?

The violent-eyed males lunged toward Aven in motions that seemed perfectly synced and prepared.

"Goddess," Ynette breathed. Her eyes were on her brother, who sent a violent ice storm upon a group of more gold sword-wielding males. I counted. There were six of them, including the two that Aven fought. I sucked in the harsh wintery air, letting it's frigidness call for my magic.

A soldier lunged for Erix, breaking out of his ice storm that was pelting the others with endless razor-sharp blades of ice. Digging within that vat of mine, I sent a thick ball of ice forward, knocking out the soldier at his knees. It was ironic to save the King of Ice, considering my task. But he couldn't die yet. I thought of the tattooed line that would disappear, sending my friends into a panic. Six weeks, I had to give the others. Six—

Eevy A.

Ynette screamed as the two males leaped atop Aven, sending him sprawling backward into the snow.

Six trained males would be too many for these two to take on. I looked at Ynette, who was shaking in fear. Despite the high Fae magic in her blood, I knew she wasn't a fighter. Ynette's scream had all six males' attention snapping at us.

Oh. Goddess.

A wave of confusion consumed me at the ominous shift in the air. As if all at once, the attackers began trying to break free from the magic being thrashed upon them by Aven and Erix. They were no longer engaging them in battle, simply fending their attacks to get to... me and Ynette? I stumbled a step forward, unsure of how to help now that the fighting had shifted tones.

Erix's vicious ice storm had two of the four males he was fighting bleeding out on the snowy ground. The contrast of crimson blood against the sparkling white snow made me sick.

Erix fought off the remaining two males, yet one of them broke free. They were all clad in white, but I took in this male as he blended in with the snow, running straight for me. I looked down at my own white ensemble and laughed.

I flung into my vat of magic, already teeming at the surface, trying to lick its way out. I took hold of it and set my body ablaze with freezing white flame. I barely heard Ynette's gasp at the sight of me, but I did not care. I trudged forward through the snow, straight for that attacker in white.

Erix sent a spear of ice through the center of another male just before he was knocked backward by an enormous wind. I took a step toward him, unafraid. The male slipped his sword from his back but thrust his other hand before him, sending a huge wind in my direction. I was sent flying backward into the snow, my white flame snuffing out on impact. I ground my teeth, annoyed that he had tricked me by unsheathing his sword. I turned to rise from the ground, finding the male already upon me. He lunged for me but with his hand rather than his sword that remained in hand at his side. I didn't have time to think or react at the unusual sight of him reaching for me. Instead, I slowed time in my mind, ice swirling angrily. I focused on the male's dominant right hand, the one clutching the sword he should be extending out at me. I allowed

334

everything around me to cool into silence. I became an embodiment of the soft, somber snow that surrounded me. That hand became the only thing important to me. I blocked out the rest of the world.

As if real-time was slowed, he took another hard-lunging step toward me. Ynette's scream broke through the icy wall I had built within me, distracting me for a fleeting moment.

His hand. I blocked out her scream. His hand. His hand. I blinked, watching as the male's hand lost all color as it gripped even tighter around the sword he held. I still remained in the snow, now nearly beneath the wild-looking male. His paling white hand gripping his sword with such intensity that I thought his fingers might shatter. I cocked my head at him as he retreated his other hand and slapped his sword hand repeatedly. He began attempting to pry his fingers from it, but they would not budge. My eyes widened at the picture before me. His hand would not budge from the sword and not from the position I knew I forced it to remain in. I narrowed my eyes upon that hand that gripped his sword.

Any commotion around me had gone wholly silent. It was only me and that sodding hand. I drained it even further of color. I almost screamed as I willed the white flames of me to consume my body. My mind—my brain, felt like I was flexing—morphing into that hand. I tilted my head to the side, and his hand tilted slowly. I met the male's eyes, a smile spreading across my face as we both realized what I was doing. I didn't understand it, but I knew.

In an instant, I lunged a hand forward, not touching the male but forcing his right hand to turn on himself and slice right through his throat before me. His blood spilled forward in a momentous outpour. His cut was true and deep. My once pure white dress was eternally stained a deep, blushing crimson red. I allowed his sword to drop from his hand with a blink and wasted no time in picking it up and plunging it deep into his heart. A mercy, I thought, instead of laying here choking on blood and snow.

I slumped, dropping the bloodied golden sword as I suddenly found it too heavy to even hold. I had never felt so entirely drained. My legs wobbled as I stepped, trying to refocus on the grunts and sounds of fighting.

Whatever I had done, that kind of magic... it seemed to have drained me almost entirely. I did my best to control my breathing as I forced the world around me to come back to life. It did, but just barely. Ynette's screams scraped the edges of my mind, the scent of burning flesh and bloodshed... the clashing of ice and fire and wind in an eruption of elemental rage... I shook my head, trying to clear the foggy vision. I stepped toward who I thought was Erix, yet he was only a blurry figure with dark hair. I glanced at the ground around him, making out bodies dressed in white that were bent and contorted. Bright red stained all around us. I took another shaky step in his direction, but my knee buckled beneath me. I heard Aven curse and cry out in warning. One of the two males he was fighting was now running toward me.

I tried to push off my knee, but it only wobbled. I took in the male barreling at me, twin gold blades like Dayne's in his hands. Even through my blurring vision, I could tell he was limping, blood covering his body as if gravely injured already. I ground my teeth together as I forced the burning sense of fear deep within me. Somehow, I felt that if they were tasked with killing me, they would not stop until I was down. I shoved a hand into the snow, forcing the icy burn of it to clear my vision. I could sense the horror in my peripherals but could not take my eyes off the male that barreled forward. His eyes burned with fury as he hobbled over to me, still in a run but a clumsy one. I was strangely calm as I watched him approach, unable to do anything. Unable to save myself. I tried again to push myself off the ground before accepting that I had failed the Goddess before entering Seldovia. Whatever that magic that I had used had not only drained me but doomed me. It had felt like my salvation only moments ago. Now... now it was my downfall.

A small whimpering sound bubbled out of me as I forced my arm to rise. Even that simple act was difficult. I shoved my hand in the male's direction, and my ice only sputtered. It took everything in me to keep from collapsing backward into the snow. I sucked in a breath, hoping the ice in my lungs would help. He would be to me in seconds. I glanced at Erix, who had finally downed the last male he was fighting. He was turning to me before his attacker had fully fallen, taking in the scene before him. His eyes grew wide, and ice sputtered from his fists.

I looked back to my attacker, his eyes having softened now. I barely registered the confusion that blossomed within me at his softening face. He lowered his sword like the other male did as he took his final steps toward me, extending his hand forward instead of the sword. I opened my mouth as if to speak before a brick of ice connected with his body, sending him tumbling into me.

I saw the blood before I felt the sword that had ripped through my chest and abdomen. My vision went blurry once more as red-hot heat erupted from my chest. Pain. That was pain. I could hardly register it due to the state of exhaustion I was in. I turned back to the crazy-eyed male who seemed to have *fallen* and thus impaled me. He had toppled to my side, now a frozen block of ice. I looked down at my chest. Mistake. His sword protruded from my gut. It hurt before, but the moment my eyes landed on that wound...

My dress was cut down the center of my belly, my intestines clearly visible from the deadly slice. My blurred vision started to turn black around the edges. My head lulled to the side. I hadn't any energy to even scream. This would kill me. I knew it would. A laugh bubbled out of my throat, sending shocks of electrifying pain through my chest. The assassin was assassinated before even making it to her destination. My body writhed against the pain. I could feel it trying to heal, but it was unable to. My body didn't have the energy, and my guts spilled out before me. It couldn't heal even if I had the strength to do so.

I felt my head grow light from blood loss. It was dancing in clouds, like when Dayne and I drank Faerie wine. Dayne. I smiled at the thought of him. I allowed my eyelids to flutter shut the same moment that my arm gave out. I fell backward into the snow. The icy powder caressed me, promising to put me to sleep soon. So soon.

"Open your eyes," Erix growled above me. I barely heard him, but the shock of his first words spoken to me had my eyes fluttering open to meet his. We were moving... but all I could see was his face and the sky above him. He cradled me in his arms as he ran.

"It hurts," I rasped, my voice weak and hoarse. His eyes darkened as he clutched me against him harder.

"I know, sweetheart, I'm going to make it stop."

Chapter Thirty-Two

Aeryn

"SIX MALES ARE UNACCOUNTED FOR," I GROWLED AT THEON. HE sat with nonchalance at the other side of the small breakfast table. I didn't care that I was interrupting the king's leisure.

"Take it up with Mairda," He waved a hand at me indifferently.

"I know you want me dead, Theon, but we have to work together. I didn't have a choice in coming here, as much as you don't have a choice in having me here." I narrowed my eyes on him, watching him spear a berry with his table knife. He lifted it, examining it before his face, the red juices sliding down the blade. I grumbled some form of a goodbye before stalking out of the king's room. I trudged into the white marble halls of the Olvidare Manor.

It was my priority to keep track of every soldier who left Olvidare. Having six missing was... more than unusual. Theon had too much history of edging the borders with his troops. I worked my way down the long hall, the clack of my heels echoing down it. I stood before a white door, hovering my fist before it.

"Come in," Mairda said sweetly before I could even knock. I rolled my eyes and shoved through the door.

Her office was quaint, reminding me of the library Orphic had used for his office in the sanctum. It was a warm space amidst the coolness that was the rest

338

of the manor. Books, both tattered and new, bordered the walls of the room. It was a little cluttered but 'organized chaos' as Mairda liked to say.

"We're missing six soldiers," I cut straight to the point, plopping into the chair across from her. Fake people weren't particularly enjoyable to be around, and Mairda was the fakest person I have ever laid eyes upon.

She looked at me over her reading glasses. I ignored the playful shine in her eyes as she watched me. She looked unusually scholarly when she wore those glasses. Yet, the low-cut shirts she was always clad in negated the glasses entirely.

"Did you check with the others?" She spoke indifferently, yet her voice was still as if she was reading poetry.

"None of them know. The king sent me here," I tapped a finger against the desk in annoyance.

She narrowed her eyes at me and removed the glasses from her freckled face. She was quite beautiful, in a chilling sort of way. Her bone structure was out of this world. I'd heard of females taking extreme measures to change their faces to become even more beautiful... Mairda's face was the type those females all begged for. "I wish I had more information for you, my dear."

I grunted in disapproval but rose to stand. "Isn't this your *job*?"

Mairda leaned over her desk and was in my face in an instant. She pressed a finger against my chest, poking hard, "*You... are* hardly welcome here. But because you're a peacemaker, we can't slice you up into tiny pieces and throw you off a cliff," she spat at the word cliff.

I didn't move; I only watched her angry face slowly fade back into that sweet Mairda smile. I grabbed the hand that was still poking me in the chest and threw it back at her. "Glad to see that you do have real emotions." I turned on a heel and was out the door before she could reply.

She would be a problem. I strolled through the halls of the Olvidare Manor, running a hand through my hair. I took in the change of scenery. The marble around me cooled the air, keeping it clean, airy, and crisp. Mairda's office was entirely different from the rest of this place. I often wanted to escape the harshness of it. Maybe I would take Mairda's office once I took down the king. I'd likely have to deal with her as well. I sauntered to the front of the manor, wishing I could lay down in that dark, cozy office filled with smells of old books and chamomile tea. I hated it here.

Eevy A.

I wasn't sure what to do about the missing soldiers. Perhaps ask around more... pester the king again. His son, Dayne, and Selene's lover seemed to avoid the king at all costs. While I didn't see Dayne often, he was usually alone or with Nicodemus or Mairda.

I made it to the grand entrance of the manor and shoved out the front doors to the sprawling front garden. I blinked, adjusting to the sun. I could wander the streets hoping to run into a soldier... not that they'd know of their comrades or even tell me anything. Quick footsteps sounded on the steep marble steps that led to where I stood at the face of the manor.

"Oh hey," Dayne said casually as he bounced up the final step.

"Hey."

"I'm sorry I haven't been able to welcome you yet. I hope you are enjoying Olvidare."

"Between the death threats and the side eyes, I'm not sure which I am enjoying more." I knew I spoke with a clipped harshness that made Dayne uncomfortable.

He let out an awkward laugh that was tinged with sadness. "Let me know if you need anything," was all he said back to me before jogging up the final stairs to the manor.

I huffed a laugh aloud, unsurprised that Selene's lover was the first to truly welcome me to the city.

I hoped she was doing okay. I hoped they all were.

Chapter Thirty-Three

Selene

I OPENED MY EYES TO FIND AVEN SPRAWLED OUT ASLEEP ON AN armchair, his legs and body contorted so strangely that I had no idea how he was sleeping so soundly. That fit him, though... of course, he was the type to lay like that and sleep like a dog. I looked around, my eyes adjusting to the room. It had a dark, gothic feel, with dark gray stones covering the walls and floor. The silver curtains were pulled shut, but I could see a sliver of moonlight peek through. It was a small room, only a few paces between the bed and the door.

I shifted on the overly plush bed that was shoved back in the corner of the room. A mound of pillows was stacked at my back, keeping me half upright. I felt beneath the covers to my chest and stomach. I winced at the pain that shot through me beneath where I pressed on the bandage. To my surprise, it wrapped from just beneath my breasts to my belly button. How was I alive?

I bit my teeth down hard as I slowly swung my legs off the bed. I pressed my bare toes against the cold gray stones. I slipped out of bed with little to no grace. I shivered at the cool air that wrapped around me and opted to pull the top sheet from the bed around my body. I was wearing a cloth brassier, my abdomen fully wrapped, but my bottom felt too exposed in the skintight cloth shorts. I tiptoed out of the room silently, checking to be sure Aven didn't wake.

Eevy A.

The coldness of this place soothed both the pain from my wound and my mind. My body reacted the same way to cold as others. I shiver and want to seek warmth for my body, while at the same time, the cold fuels my magic like kindling. My magic and the cold air around me were like toxic lovers. They'd beckon each other, use each other, and from time to time be a harmonious pair that filled me with strength and power.

I stuck my head out of my already ajar door, propped open with a large stone. My door opened to a lengthy hall. A grand open-concept room lay to my right, the length of the rest of the hall to my left. Beautiful gray gothic stone adorned every part of these rooms as well. I looked up. Iron chandeliers hung from the hall's ceiling, offering a faint glow of firelight. I cocked my head at the chandeliers. Iron. They must have a purpose for having iron so near... perhaps it strengthened us over time. The chandeliers swung high enough that my magic did not buck to escape it.

I wandered down the hall and into the large room that had to be the main attraction of the castle. I gasped at its beauty. The room was sprawling, with vaulted ceilings that came to a point at its apex. Intricate designs and appliqués adorned the ceiling. It was a work of art on its own. I turned to the rest of the room, shuffling in, careful not to trip on the sheet I had wrapped around me. There was some seating sprinkled throughout the room, but it seemed the front of the room offered the best seat. Moonlight streamed through the enormous windows that stood from floor to ceiling. Black diamond-shaped panes ran through the glass, offering a unique design to the space. I found myself giddy to see this room with sunlight streaming through those massive windows. I hadn't seen anything so grand in my life.

I shuffled to the center of the room, where a half-moon-shaped bar stood with a glistening quartz countertop. I peeked over the edge and was not shocked to see it was, in fact, a bar stocked with an assortment of barrels and bottles full of what had to be Faerie wine. I pushed off from the bar to the smaller seating area illuminated entirely by moonlight. The space was similar to what we called a living space in Avalon. It was a rounded off-shoot from the main room. The enormous windows stood proud before this room. I glanced at the seating; black cushioned couches and chairs were all facing toward the center of the room, where a short but ornate table stood. It felt eery standing here. I wondered how many had stood in this very place looking out this very window. I strode through the sitting room to the window. I couldn't help the gasp that escaped me as I took in the moonlit snowy mountains before me. I was in the Seldovia castle. I knew it was tucked away in the mountains, but nothing could prepare me for the view. It was as if the castle was built, putting this window aimed directly at the best view of the land. Large distant peaks sprawled before me, while even more enormous ranges jetted up so close I felt I could reach out and touch them.

"Enjoying the view?"

I jumped, flipping around, allowing the sheet I held draped around me to swoop like a cape.

Ynette.

Her eyes glowed an even more enchanting shade of blue as the moonlight danced in them.

"I... yeah, it's nice," I told her. She strode toward me, extending a hand.

"Let me see,"

I unwrapped my arms from around myself, giving the female access to my abdomen.

"Good," she said, only touching it lightly. "The blood has been seeping through the bandages."

"Oh." I looked down at my stomach. "Who—"

She cut me off, "We have healers, some of the best from Belgar."

"Do they not want to live in their own land?" I asked her with an edge.

Ynette smiled sweetly at me. "We pay them well and offer their family to accompany them."

Of course. They supply themselves with what they need as their city starves. I only nodded in reply. "Who can I thank for... saving me?"

"One of our best healers, Odessa," She paused, "and well, Erix."

I swallowed hard, hoping she would continue.

"As peacemaker, you will learn that Erix and I..." She hesitated, eyes darting from mine, "We have an unusual history... It provides us with many unique forms of magic."

I thought of Erix healing my hand at the placement ceremony.

She went on, "Erix kept you alive until he could get you to Odessa. Thankfully, we weren't far from Seldovia when we were attacked."

Shame bloomed within me. I had been prepared to die. I was okay with it, too. I remembered the male barreling toward me. The strange way he dropped his sword to his side, extending his hand as if he wanted to grab me.

I was prepared to die once before... on my eighteenth birthday. Then I met Dayne, and at some point, I decided I wanted to live. Yet this life, this destiny the Goddess had created me for, had me look death in the face once again and not shy away. Perhaps that meant something. Perhaps dying was the only route out.

"Olvidare soldiers?" I croaked.

"I'm looking into it," Ynette said, worry blooming on her face.

We stood in silence for a moment. She shouldn't waste her time on it. The city... those people should be a priority. I could handle my own.

"You won't see much of him, you know." Ynette was referring to her brother. "That means it will be you and me," She smiled softly at me. But I already knew that. I had trained for it.

She looked relieved someone was finally here to help her shoulder the weight of ruling this kingdom. I found the irony to be comical; the rest of the kings were furious at the placement of their peacemakers, yet this small female stood before me, thankful that someone–*anyone* was here to help her. This would be monumentally harder for me to do than I thought it would be. The Goddess made us with compassion to rule a kingdom. Compassion got in the way when it meant killing for that place upon the throne.

"You should probably rest..." Ynette trailed off.

"Why don't you use your magic or fight?" I suddenly found myself asking her.

Her blue eyes flared at the question, but not in anger.

"Erix was taught by our father... and he was," Ynette stopped to think, "a traditional male."

She didn't have to say more. I, of course, knew of the previous King of Seldovia. He was struck down by his own son. Many assumed Erix had done it for the crown, but Orphic had told me the truth. The previous king of Seldovia forced the mother of his children to be just that. She was no more than a castle keeper, abused in many ways by him. When she fell in love with a healer, he struck them both down. Erix took his father's head the next night. I shuddered at the thought of having such trauma. I kept finding myself being reminded how minuscule my heartbreaks were.

I finally replied to Ynette, "I can teach you how to fight," I shrugged.

Her blue eyes narrowed on me. "That's not necessary," She waved a hand toward me, "You should get back to bed."

I wanted to stay and talk to the female. She was strangely comforting, and it was better than being alone. She was wise and intelligent like Gaia, but there was something different about her. Ynette seemed more curious—more eager.

I slipped back down the hall I had come from earlier. Aven was in an entirely new position on the chair, head tilted back in a snore. I wondered if he was told to stay here or chose to stay on his own. I crawled into bed and listened to Aven's soft snoring that came in an almost hypnotic pattern. I allowed the timeliness of the snores to become a metronome to my thoughts. I couldn't *like* any of them. I had a plan, a duty to fulfill. If I failed, the Goddess would send me back to Avalon. Tomorrow, it begins.

Chapter Thirty-Four

Selene

AVEN WAS ON THE FLOOR WHEN I WOKE TO A STREAM OF SUNLIGHT bouncing off my face from the gap in the curtains. The healing slice down my center hurt less than earlier, so swinging out of bed was easier this time. I glanced around the room again, seeing it in a new light. My eyes fell on a door I hadn't seen before. I shuffled over to it, opening the door to a closet. I gasped at the bag and assorted items that sat within. It was the bag Dayne had packed for me. I bent down, touching it. His golden sword lay sheathed behind it.

"How..." I trailed off in a whisper. I nearly hugged the bag. It was so good to see something familiar. I began rifling through the drawers in the closet, hoping for clothes. I knew my task was to be as desirable as possible, but this closet didn't give me much to work with. I opted for a loose-fitting white dress with short sleeves that covered my shoulders. It had a square but low neckline, and fell loosely to my knees. I slipped it on over my head with only a few winces in pain before walking to Aven.

I nudged him with a foot, but he didn't even move. I kicked him again, and he shifted slightly, but nothing more. I gave up and wandered back into the large room I had been in last night. Erix was nowhere to be seen, but Ynette was in the small round sitting room with a mug of something hot in her hand.

"What's that?" I asked her, making her jump at my entrance.

"Peppermint tea." She sniffed her cup, letting her eyes flutter shut at the scent. She wore a skintight navy dress that hugged all her curves and accentuated her blue eyes.

"You look nice," I said to her. She whipped her head to me as if she had never been complimented. I cocked my head in surprise, holding her eye contact for many moments. I wasn't sure what swam in those eyes, but somehow, I felt she needed to hear that.

I smiled and tiptoed to the sitting room, wincing at the chilly stones beneath by bare feet. I took a seat in the sitting room near the towering windows and took in the view during the daytime. The sun was still low, its beams bouncing off the snow-capped mountains, dispersing its glittering rays beautifully.

"I am willing to guess the Goddess wants you to fix him?" Ynette asked before sipping her tea.

"Basically." I shrugged, turning away from the exquisite view to face her. She was just as exquisite.

"And you're equipped to do so?" She raised a brow at me. I didn't miss the urgent hope that tinged her voice.

"I am," I said slowly, but I couldn't stand to watch her as I lied. I turned back to the mountainous horizon. She felt too naive to lie to—too trusting. It felt so... so wrong.

"I can take you into the city today so you can meet some of the people."

"I'd like that, thank you, Ynette." I kept my eyes on the horizon ahead.

"They want to revolt," she said. I turned to her then.

"I am here to help. We tackle this together."

The same relief that Ynette had on her face last night bloomed on it again. "Later then, I'll take you into the city later."

I nodded. "How do I get one of those?" I pointed to the peppermint tea in her hand.

She laughed and called for someone named Valeria. A pretty female with the skin of umber scampered into the room. Her black hair was braided loosely down her back. Valeria stood next to Ynette, who was still seated with a mug in her hand.

"Valeria, this is Selene, our new... member."

347

I wanted to laugh at the term member. I waved a hello to Valeria instead.

"Selene, Valeria is one of many castle keepers, but she stays here with us." She patted Valeria on the back. "She is family."

Valeria beamed at the words and nodded. I was used to servants in Avalon, but none were treated with such... common decency. I stood and walked to the girl, reminding myself not to shake her hand like I had Mairda's.

"I'd like some peppermint tea," I started, "But if you don't mind, I'd like to help you."

"Of course," Valeria answered and ushered me toward the bar in the center of the room.

I kept the female company while she made me the tea; she swatted my hand at anything I attempted to touch. Ynette only laughed and said they all tried the same thing with her, but she refused to let anyone help. Valeria beamed at me as she extended the tea. I took it from her with a slight bow in thanks. I scooted onto the tall chair at the bar and set my tea down. It smelled heavenly but was entirely too hot to drink. I could cool it but decided to allow it to rest.

"What is good, ladies?" Aven strode into the room, stretching his muscled arms above his head. "At the bar already, Sel? I knew I liked you."

I rolled my eyes at him and gestured to my tea. Aven swaggered into the sitting room, making sure to ruffle Ynette's hair before flopping himself on the couch. I watched Valeria scamper down a set of rounded stairs that must lead to the castle's first floor. I would have to explore that later.

"How sweet of you to wear my favorite color," Aven said to Ynette before kissing the air in her direction. "The ladies are looking perky this morning," he gestured towards Ynette's breasts.

Ynette threw her now empty mug at Aven, but he caught it before it could smash into his face.

"Feisty," he purred to her.

Ynette turned to me. "I have a headache by the name of Aven. Would you care to see the city now?"

I laughed as Aven made a dramatically hurt face toward Ynette. I looked down at my piping hot tea but shrugged. "Sure." I felt bad leaving it but needed to get my foot in the door with Ynette. If she trusted me, she may speak to Erix about it. I could leverage that.

I stood and followed Ynette, who strode toward the stairs Valeria had just scampered down.

"Bring me back something sweet," Aven called after us.

"Where did you find that one?" I laughed, asking Ynette about Aven as we descended gray cobbled stairs. The ancient steps unfurled like a spiraling ribbon, their weathered surface bearing the scars of centuries. I wondered then how many had walked these very steps.

"Goddess. The poor fool was part of Krakata's troops when he found himself staked and left for dead after he pissed off the wrong people."

"Really?" It didn't surprise me that he pissed anyone off, but to be staked... to have your body hung to a stake to die...

"Yeah," Ynette frowned. "They traveled to The Kingdom of Ice, leaving it up to Aven's body to decide if it wanted to die of cold or blood loss first. If neither took him, dehydration would."

Poor Aven. I frowned.

"Erix found him. They were both just in their teen years at that point. He brought him back to the castle, and Aven hasn't been back to Krakata since."

"Wow," I said, truly horrified and amazed by Aven's story.

"He's a good boy, most of the time," Ynette smiled, and it was contagious.

"Once we leave the castle, we walk the path to the city. They may say things and shoot looks but won't touch us." Ynette was referring to the people of Seldovia. "No violence... yet," she grimaced.

We finished descending the stairs and strode out of the front castle doors. We stepped onto the stone platform with only a few steps leading to a dirt part below.

I took a moment to stop and stretch as a burst of wintry air embraced us. The brilliant sun was enough to warm our skin, even as delicate flakes of snow fell around us. I flipped my palm to the sky, letting a few flakes fall there before examining them. Ynette stood silently by, allowing me to gawk at the snowy world I now stood in.

It was like rain, but... it brought me no unease. The flakes were made up of the same components of rain, yet they were changed in the best of ways. I cocked my head, dropping my arm to my side to take in the graceful, floating flakes as they wafted around us. A smile crept onto my face as I realized I was

349

no different from what fell from the clouded sky. Once trapped in a form, like a droplet, now everchanged by a force of nature. I sucked in a breath, the chilly air spearing my lungs in a painful but refreshing way. Snow can only form if changed. I blinked at it, the almost rain droplets, changed by the frigid temperatures of the Kingdom of Ice. The snow was stunning. The snow was... me.

I breathed in a long and deep breath of air, feeling the unease from seeing the city flutter away.

"Just this way," Ynette brought my attention back to her. She began to lead us down the winding slope toward the city. Pines towered over us, casting shadows and blocking the warm sun as we trudged down the path. I shivered beneath the shadows, wishing I had brought a jacket.

The distant silhouette of a city formed up ahead. Even in its rundown state, its architecture whispered tales of long ago—of a time when every building stood tall and proud. Beneath the scent of pine and snow, I picked up a whiff of smoke that was carried on the delicate winter breeze. The dirt beneath our feet turned to stone as we neared the city's edge. We crested the last turn before a small stone bridge stood before us, leading directly into the city. A loud, bubbling brook rushed beneath the bridge as we skittered over it. We slipped down a thin alleyway and entered into what seemed like a common space. Broken stone mingled with dirt beneath our feet as we clung to the city's edge. Several people passed us, giving Ynette horribly disgusted glances, some to me as well. No one spoke to us. Walking silently, I noticed each wooden building we passed held a molding stench. Many had collapsing or rotting walls that fell in different directions.

There weren't many people in the streets, but I found myself catching the eyes of a few through broken glass windows. We walked out of the round, sprawling common space to a strip of what looked like shops. Signs swung in the wind, many of them no longer legible. Most shops were boarded up with signs that read things like 'SELDOVIA, LAND OF THE UNWORTHY' or 'CLOSED UNTIL THE KING IS DEAD.'

Ynette flinched at the signs, but they didn't seem to surprise her. We passed a fabric shop, the name of it entirely washed away from time and misfortune. I peered inside, a frail-looking younger female sitting at the front spinning a ball of yarn. I gave her a sad smile. Her lack of reaction told me enough about her broken spirit.

The city was covered in dirt, but the people kept themselves clean. Every time we passed someone, I tried to keep from looking at them but found it difficult. I wanted to see their pain. I wanted them to know that I saw it. I thought to the Goddess's words. She had said that once I saw the state of the city, I may find myself trudging back to the castle and sliding a sword across Erix's throat. I shook my head. The city was a wreck, and I knew it was his fault, but I did not have that urging feeling to kill him. I wasn't sure I would ever feel compelled to kill anyone.

I began looking at every person I passed, feeling their sorrow. We looped back around to the town square we had first entered. A crumbling fountain stood holding no water in a city of Fae with water affinity. It was a testament not to their abilities but to their broken spirits. I filled the fountain with only half a thought, a small symbol to the people that I was here to help them. Some people looked at me in shock, but most glared as I climbed atop the fountain that was now splashing with clear water. Ynette only watched wide-eyed.

"People of Seldovia," I shouted. I yelled it three more times before a crowd began forming around me. Many shoved from their homes or shops while others peered out their windows. I wanted to shrink back at the sight of their angry faces, but I couldn't. This place... it was their entire life—their whole *world*. I shook my head as more and more faces poured into the town square.

My whole life, I always wanted to live. I selfishly wanted to live through that curse that would end me on my eighteenth birthday. I selfishly wanted to be able to pick *life*. I hadn't realized until this very moment that maybe it wasn't so selfish. Maybe someone out there needed me to. I scanned the crowd before me. That a whole city—a whole kingdom needed *me* to survive. To prevail. I scanned the faces before me, finding some twisted in disgust... finding faces that cried... faces that couldn't even bring themselves to look up at me. But it was the faces that held a glimmer of curiosity—of hope that branded my very soul. I survived. And I would keep on surviving... For them.

"The Goddess has heard your cries. *I* have heard your cries." People started turning to leave. "Wait. I am Selene of..." I paused. "I once was Selene of Avalon." I stood taller. I am here to help you. Help you rebuild," I gestured to the dirt, rubble, and rundown buildings around us. If I could glance at their broken spirits, I would have done so, too. "I am here to listen to your woes and offer solutions to them," I spoke to them with strength, not allowing any form of weakness to crack in my voice. Some of the faces softened, but most remained hard and annoyed.

"I will stand here. Write down your concerns, bring them to us," I gestured to Ynette, who now climbed up on the fountain's edge with me. "I promise you, people of Seldovia, that we will read each and every one of your concerns. Be patient, as you have been. We will come through."

It was not a grand speech. It did not seem impactful, but more faces softened at the words, which was enough for me. The group that had gathered broke away just as quickly. Many grumbled and found their way back to their homes or shops. I found it concerning I saw nearly no children in the crowd.

Ynette and I slid to sit on the edge of the fountain. I wondered if even one person would bring their concerns to us.

"You're not shy," Ynette stated.

"I..." I started. "Not really, but I was trained for this." I gestured around me. I was, in many ways, trained for this. To lead and rule with compassion.

"Do you think they'll bring their concerns to us?"

I gestured behind Ynette, where a mother, clutching a baby to her chest, held a small slip of paper. I stood and approached her. "My baby, it has been hard to get her proper food. The shops keep closing, and the ones that stay open have strange hours." She extended the paper to me, and I took it from her.

"We hear you," I said as many more people lined up behind the female.

Ynette and I took turns taking the papers from the people of Seldovia. By the time the last person stood before us, it had been hours, and our pockets and hands were overflowing with papers.

A young girl who looked to be thirteen skipped up to us with a green satchel that had assorted flower patches sewn onto it. She looked behind her to what looked to be her father. He gave her a loving smile and beckoned her forward.

"For your papers," the young girl said, extending the satchel to us.

Ynette got down on one knee before the girl. She accepted the satchel from her and discreetly placed a handful of coin in the girl's palm. It looked to be twenty or more coin, far more than the satchel was worth. The girl scampered back to her father, showing him her handful of coin. Ynette remained in a kneeling position as we beheld the girl's father, tears streaming down his face. He mouthed the words thank you. Ynette nodded and rose. We shoved all our papers in the green satchel and looked back at the father and daughter, but they were already gone.

Ynette trembled at the interaction. I placed a strong hand on her back to settle her.

"That was..." She started.

"I know," I agreed with her. We let the unspoken words waft in the crisp air around us.

* * *

YNETTE and I spread the papers out on the rounded bar top in the center of the castle's main room. Sunlight streamed in from the window. It took everything in me not to leave the notes and bask in the beams. I had missed the sun and the shifting from day to night.

"So, what does everyone do all day..." I trailed off, organizing the papers into groups of concerns.

Ynette laughed, "Aven... who knows, maybe getting drunk, taking Stacia out, helping me if I beg him..." She trailed off, not mentioning Erix. I looked back to the papers, setting aside the fourth one that read "KILL THE KING" into a separate pile to later destroy.

"Everyone seems the most concerned about the buildings... the state of the city." I shifted a few papers in front of me, squinting at them. They had every right to have these concerns. The buildings were crumbling, falling down on them in their sleep. Lives had already been lost. A spurt of ice flared as ice anger twitched within me.

"Or shops closing," Ynette shoved a pile before me. I flipped through them, reading different variations of people being concerned there were no shops left to buy things they needed or some that were forced out of business and had no way to make coin.

"So many people have left the city over the past decade," she shook her head. "They can't sustain life here."

I nodded, unsurprised at the loss of patrons in Seldovia.

"I have a few worried about King Theon and his soldiers patrolling the border," Ynette twisted to read the few papers in my hand.

"I hope that bastard rots," She seethed. I didn't have the heart to tell her that her own brother created just as much heartache, maybe more than King Theon did.

We shuffled through the rest of the papers, finding an interesting theme.

"They want to be taxed again," I breathed, shocked by the forwardness of many of the concerns that included taxation. Orphic had explained that the people of Seldovia were once taxed fifteen percent of their wage. It maintained the city, the troops, and the paths into the Kingdom of Belgar. Now, there was none of that. Only rotting buildings and rotting souls.

"How long has it been since they have been taxed?"

Ynette's eyes deepened into a dark shade of cerulean, "The year Leyola died. No one could manage to plan the events where we collected tax. It became the new norm after the first year of not collecting."

I sat back in the high-top chair, my legs dangling beneath me. It felt wrong to stay in such an enormous castle. I knew that the high Fae maintained their wealth as it was passed down from generation to generation, which, when you were immortal, meant a *long* time. It was why they could afford to keep the best healers and castle keepers.

"Are we in agreement that reinstating taxes is a priority?"

Ynette nodded, scribbling it down on a sheet of paper.

We spent the rest of the day finding themes within the concerns and jotting down notes on how to help the citizens of Seldovia. I wanted each concern to be heard equally. We would not let even one slip through the cracks. By the time Ynette and I finished, slumping against the bar top, it was well past dark. Ynette retired for the night, thanking me at least ten times before scampering down the hall to her room. I glanced down at my ankle, taking in the three inked lines. Orphic made it clear: I would seek out Erix every day. Whether the interactions were pleasant or not, Erix would slowly expect the company, maybe even look forward to it.

I thought of the female that had come and gone from his chambers while Ynette and I sorted through the slips of paper. A mere hour later, a second female had gone in but had yet to leave. Both of the females sharing his bed today were beautiful. Many Fae were beautiful regardless, but the ones that found their way here... there was always something about them. I did note neither was blonde, and neither looked anything like me. I pinched the bridge of my nose. Had Orphic and the Goddess considered that when they created me... what his *type* was? I rested my elbow against the bar top, annoyed that I would have to stay up and wait until the female left his room.

I sat for another half hour, reviewing the notes Ynette and I made before the female finally slipped past me through the main room and down the stairs to leave the castle. We exchanged glances and smiles but otherwise shared no words. I slid off the bar stool, my feet hitting the stone floor beneath me. I curled my toes at the sharp, cool temperature that pricked the bottoms of my feet. I slipped from the bar and strode for the back hall toward Erix's room. I turned the corner quickly, finding myself nearly bumping into someone's chest. I let out a slight 'unf' sound as I took a half step backward in surprise. Erix glanced down at me, but my presence didn't change his trajectory in the slightest. He stepped around me without a word and strode right for the bar. I turned from the hall to face the main room as Erix slid into a stool.

"Can't sleep?" I asked, keeping my face neutral. I glanced at the clock on the wall. It was two in the morning.

Erix shoved all of the piles of papers that lay on the bar top out of his way. The irony of the action was not lost on me, considering what concerns lived on those sheets of paper.

"Are these important?" He mumbled, picking a paper off of him where it had clung to his shirt. The irony was rampant tonight.

"Just official peacemaker business," I kept an edge to my voice.

"I see."

He leaned over the bar, grabbing a bottle and a glass before uncorking it with his teeth. He poured the white wine into the stemmed glass and wasted no time swallowing the first pour in one gulp. He set the glass down and poured another, his jaw clenched tight as he poured. He wanted to be alone, no doubt. He always wanted to be alone.

Too bad.

I walked to the bar and slipped into a stool beside him.

"I'll have that one." I extended my hand. Erix looked at my extended hand, unclenching his jaw. He pressed one finger on his glass and slid it across the bar top to me. I took the glass, taking a long drink as Erix settled his eyes on my face. I set the glass down and locked eyes with him. Those terribly sad eyes. He broke from the stare to lean over the bar again for a new glass. This time, he stood to grab the bottle and didn't even pour it before tucking the full bottle beneath his arm and setting off for his room.

"I'd like company," I said to him. He scoffed but didn't miss a beat walking away from me.

"Why do you always go back to your room?" I asked, all the sweetness drained from my voice.

Erix stopped.

"Come back," I demanded.

He turned but didn't approach. Anger bloomed on his sad face. I wasn't sure I had ever seen anyone look so sad *and* so infuriated at once, "I don't need saving," he growled.

I had expected him to yell or tell me not to order him around, so his response shocked me enough that he was able to turn on a heel and disappear down the hall before I could respond. I sighed. He would make this harder than Aeryn had, but that was no surprise.

I finished the glass of Faerie wine he had poured for himself and returned to my room. No sleeping Aven this time, thank Goddess. I nudged the large stone out of the way so I could close the door before stripping down to my undergarments. I slowly unwrapped the bandages on my abdomen. I touched the red line that remained, still healing slowly. I shuddered while looking down at it, replaying the image of my intestines hanging out of me.

"I don't need saving," I repeated out loud, thinking.

His life had been tragic from beginning to end. It was not surprising to me that he assumed I was here to 'save him.' I imagined sliding a cold blade against his throat and those sad blue eyes turning grey. I shivered at the thought. I would do it, though. "The lesser evil," I whispered into the crisp darkness of my room. After seeing the people of Seldovia, their homes falling down around the children that they were barely able to feed, I could do it. I *would* kill the king.

Chapter Thirty-Five

Selene

THE NEXT NIGHT, I SAT IN THE SHADOWS OF THE SITTING ROOM, waiting. I rested a plate of bread and ham on my knee that Valeria had put together for me. I peered at the night sky through the sprawling glass. My eyes scanned for the three links I always searched for. When I couldn't find them, at least not from where I sat looking out the window, my heart rate rose. Being unable to see my stars when I searched for them created an awkward weight within me. I peeled my eyes from the night sky, wondering if Dayne or even Aeryn sat and stared at the same sky. Maybe they could see my links. I shifted the plate from off my knee to the cushion beside me. I wouldn't let the thought of Dayne or Aeryn run any deeper. Not as I sat here in the shadows, a predator in wait.

Like clockwork, a thin brunette female scampered through the main room from the hall, hugging the wall furthest from me. She skittered down the steps and out of sight. I slumped in my chair now, becoming one with the shadows. Had I not scared him away yesterday, I expected the king any moment now. I set my eyes on the hall.

It took him twenty minutes, but the sorry sap came sauntering out, two wine glasses lazily held in one hand. They both had a slight puddle of wine left in the bottom that sloshed around as he strolled into the room. My

358

muscles tensed, hands shifting to the cushion in preparation to shove from it.

Erix set down the wine glasses, their rounded base clinking on the bar top. He would pour another. I waited as he shifted to the back of the half-moon-shaped bar and bent to rummage around. Muffled glass clinking filled the air as I rose. Having staged the bar with no white wine, I grabbed the bottle I had planted on the cushion next to me and held it behind my back. With quiet precision, I tiptoed to the bar. Erix remained bent and searching. I reached the bar's edge and leaned on one of the high bar stools, allowing it to shift forward, letting out an awful screech as it slid across the stone floor.

Erix bolted upright, smacking his head on the bar top with a loud thud as he rose.

"For the love of—" his eyes focused on me in the dark moonlit room. He grumbled a noise I couldn't quite distinguish before ducking back below the bar to continue his search. I pulled my arm from behind me, still clutching the neck of the wine bottle. I set it atop the bar with emphasis, letting it clang loudly against the quartz bartop. While the echo reverberated through the grand room, Erix slowly rose. This time, his eyes fell on the only bottle of white Faerie wine I knew existed in this room. The rest was tucked away in my closet.

I waited, almost excitedly, for what the poor bastard had to say. He flicked his eyes from the wine to me and back to the wine a heartbeat later. Without a word, he reached for the neck of the bottle. But I was faster. I lunged, wrapping my fingers around it before he could. I gripped it tight, cradling it against my chest.

His nostrils flared, but he remained hovering wordlessly behind the bar. My own temper flared at that.

"Why don't you talk," I growled at him.

The moonlight that streamed from the vaulted windows caught on Erix's milky white throat. I couldn't help but watch his throat bob, swallowing.

"Why don't you *talk*," I repeated the question with more venom. I spun the navy bottle by its neck carelessly, watching him eye the way my wrist contorted.

"Where is the rest?" The male finally spoke, gesturing to the single bottle of white wine I held.

Eevy A.

I shrugged, "If you don't answer my questions, I don't answer yours."

His nostrils flared again, eyes locking onto my rotating wrist. I continued spinning the bottle before me, slight splashing sounds filling the air between us.

"Please," the king ground his teeth together, his words taking me by surprise. "Where is the rest?" His voice was desperate. A male looking for his escape. A female, holding the key to it. I smiled, knowing I had positioned him for this—knowing Orphic would be proud.

I took a swaggering step forward, finally pausing the casual rotations with the wine bottle. I set it on the bar top between us and leaned closer. Our faces were close now, and I could nearly *smell* the bastard's desperation. My stomach churned. "Please?" I mocked him... Actually *mocked* the Fae King of Ice.

His eyes dipped to my hand, now grasping the barstool as I lifted myself into it. I sat for a moment, watching him watch me. I left the bottle of wine untouched for a moment before grabbing and casually popping the cork out. The crisp popping sound had Erix's eyes dropping to it. His escape. My key. I brought the bottle to my lips and tilted my head back, taking a mouthful of the velvety wine. It drained into my mouth and down my throat with ease. I removed the bottle from my lips, allowing a drop of wine to spill down my chin. Erix's hardened gaze dropped from my eyes to the single bead of liquid that dribbled down and then slid off my chin into my lap below.

"Delicious," I mused, now wiping my chin with the back of my hand. "Want some?" I smiled, making sure it looked sickeningly sweet.

Erix's face dropped into a deep scowl as he beheld the bottle I extended to him. He shifted before reaching out for it. I quickly snatched it back, tipping my head back in throaty laughter.

"Sod off," Erix grumbled, yet he did not walk from the bar. He did not turn back to his room. I was waiting for him to lower his standards... to break a little. He ripped his steely gaze from me and bent to grab a red glass bottle from beneath the bar. My eyes lit up for this challenge. I knew he wasn't willing to fight for it.

I cleared my throat and shifted in my seat so my knees were pressed against the cushion, and I was no longer sitting. I propped my hands atop the quartz before quickly lifting myself to the bartop. I shifted around so my legs dangled

360

off the other side of the bar, right in front of the king's face, who was still half-bent over. The quartz was freezing against my bare thighs, but it fueled me with icy rage as I beheld the King of Ice. I glanced at his hand, gripping the bottle of red Faerie wine. He rose from his bent-over position.

"A drink for an answer," I whispered, knowing that he could feel my breath upon his face. He glanced between my face, the white wine I gripped, and then at the bottle of red in his own hand.

"Why don't you talk," I repeated in a neutral but inviting voice.

Erix sighed and allowed his shoulders to sag a fraction of an inch before setting the bottle of red wine atop the quartz.

"Because others do for me," his thick voice sliced the air as he leaned his forearms against the bar's edge. It was still so unusual to hear his voice. I waited, letting his words sink in, wondering if they held a truth about him. Had he implied that others speak on his behalf? I narrowed my eyes on him, glancing at the nearness of his forearm to the side of my thigh. I weighed the idea of shifting so our skin would touch but decided against it.

"That doesn't entirely answer my question," I waited, now taking another swig of the wine he so desperately wanted. His jaw clenched in my peripherals as I knocked back another smooth swig.

"Listening has more advantages," he spoke with a strong voice but kept his eyes set on his fiddling fingers before him. I thought of my training and the reason I was forced to seduce him. He was cunning, apparently. According to Orphic, he was more cunning than he wanted anyone to know. I wondered then if Erix would be the one to best me... If he had his own plan. If he was watching my every muscle flick and movement. I took in his sad face and the deep purple bags beneath his eyes. A pang of relief coursed through me. He didn't care enough to do any of that. That much was clear.

He turned to me then, expecting me to hand him the drink. I shrugged but knew I would not be handing the king his escape so easily. I shifted again, this time putting my knees beneath me against the cool quartz counter. I rose above the king, watching his face morph into confusion and surprise.

"Want your drink?" I shook the bottle in front of his face. He shoved his forearms against the bartop, no longer leaning against it. His eyebrows knitted together, but I could see the hunger in his eyes. I scooted forward until my knees met the edge of the quartz. I was mere inches from the king. I brought my hand to his face, and with as little delicacy as possible, I squeezed his cheeks until his mouth opened. Without giving him a moment to react, I poured a mouthful of wine into his mouth, watching with pure delight as he fought between shock and sweet relief. More moonlight streamed in, dancing on the king's bobbing throat as he guzzled as much wine as I was willing to pour into his mouth. I ripped my hand from his cheeks and rocked back, resting the heels of my feet against my rear. I remained perched atop the bar before the king, preparing for my next question. I clutched the half-drunk bottle to my chest as his eyes roamed me wildly.

"Isn't it lonely?" My words weren't a knife. They didn't carve out a part of the king as I had hoped. He didn't even flinch. His eyes only dropped to the bottle I clutched as he weighed if this was worth it... If this conversation was worth what I held.

"You have the females that come and go, sure," I whispered now, "But isn't it terribly lonely in that room all day?" I glanced toward the hall where his room lay at the very end of it. My words missed their mark once more. His eyes did not flash in challenge. His jaw did not clench. He did, however, cock his head, if only a half an inch.

"Where's the rest of the wine?" his voice was unforgiving and cold.

I shoved forward, no longer rocked back against my heels. My knees dug into the hard quartz as I towered above the king. "Should you beg, I may tell you," I knew my smile was more of a sneer.

It looked as if the king seemed to actually ponder my words.

"I have kept my bargain thus far, have I not? A drink for an answer." My words echoed loudly around us.

Silence, yet the king still had not left for his room. Not even with a bottle of red wine. "Isn't it lonely?"

"You don't even know what loneliness is," Erix snapped, nearly cutting me off. His eyes blistered with rage as my words finally knifed him in the gut. It would have been satisfying if his words hadn't stabbed me all the same. I shrugged, swallowing the pain that glowed within me as the fight I had moments ago winked out. I forced the bottle of wine into his chest, watching it slosh out of the top, sprinkling his shirt with dark specks of liquid.

I shoved my face before his, allowing my breath to curl around his lips, "You didn't have to beg after all, *king.*"

Chapter Thirty-Six

Selene

I STOOD BEFORE ERIX'S DOOR, WAITING FOR HIM TO ANSWER MY knock. Last night was not how I intended, and I needed the poor fool to open up to me. I shifted on my feet and knocked three more times. I pressed my ear against the door but didn't hear any movement from within the room.

Bastard.

I rested my hand on the handle of the door to his room. I would be annoying and relentless if he wouldn't talk to me. It had been nearly a week in the castle by now, yet I could probably count the words he had spoken to me. I took a deep breath, unsure what I would find or see on the other side, and opened the door.

I poked my head into the room, eyes scanning it. His room was enormous, with the same gothic feel as the rest of the castle. The same silver curtains adorned the window to his room and were pulled shut, keeping the space dark. My eyes fell on Erix's bed on the wall furthest from me. He was tangled within the sheets, eyes glaring right at me. My eyes dipped to his bare torso; only a white sheet thrown lazily over him was keeping him from being exposed.

He didn't move. "Out."

Every part of me heated as I took him in. One of his legs hung out of the sheets lazily as if he couldn't decide whether he was hot or cold. Only one part of him was covered; the rest of his milky white skin was bare and exposed to me. I leveraged the moment, sliding my eyes across his abdomen for just a little too long. He would notice it. I was sure of it. I slid into the room and closed the door behind me. Erix glowered at me but remained in his disheveled position beneath his sheets. His dark hair was the messiest I had seen it, dark strands waving in all directions. I took a step forward toward his bed. The room was mostly bare, aside from a small desk. Nothing hung on the walls. No firelight lit the space. It was one massive room; even the wash-room was a part of the bedroom. I cocked my head at that, the large square tub and toilet that stood in the corner of his room, exposed to the entire space.

I turned my attention back to Erix. "So, you lay in here all day?"

"Were you hoping to join me?" His blue eyes twinkled, but that scowl remained on his face.

It was too soon to jump on the sensual joke, especially after my lingering eyes.

"I have Olvidare soldiers hunting me. What are you going to do about it?" I tapped a foot. Erix groaned and rolled himself deeper into his sheets, pulling a pillow over his face. "It is your job as king to protect your peacemaker." I was hovering over his bed, pulling the pillow from his face.

"I got you here alive, didn't I?" He snapped at me, now sitting up in a huff. He remained covered by the sheets, but barely. I wasn't sure he cared whether or not he exposed himself to me.

I kept my eyes from dipping to his chest and abdomen, if only because I felt the urge to. "What if they come after me again?" I whispered in as scared of a voice as I could muster. I wasn't frightened, though. Not of the Olvidare soldiers, and not of him.

Erix eyed me and cleared his throat. "You're not my problem."

"Oh, but I am." I smiled.

"Can you leave?" Erix began getting out of bed, the white sheet slipping free from his body.

I turned before the sheet fluttered off him and back to the bed. So he didn't care if I saw all of him, then.

He shuffled his feet against the stone floor. The sound of water flowing broke the silence, and I knew he was filling the tub. My face was burning hot as I stood facing away from the now-naked Erix.

"Ynette and I need you today. We are reimplementing taxation. Any time you can bless us with your appearance would be great." I waited. I only heard the slight splashing sounds of Erix getting into the tub and groaning.

I turned to face him now. His head was leaned back against the tub's edge, eyes piercing through me. The dark bags under his eyes were even more prominent in the dark, shadowy room.

"Get out."

I stalked over to the tub, standing on the opposite side of where he sat submerged. Angry ice flitted in my veins as I beheld him. Thankfully, there was forced air in the tub, creating bubbling water to hide him beneath it. 'Take things easy at the start,' Orphic's voice echoed in my head as I took in the bathing king. I blinked at him, shoving Orphic's stern tone from my mind. I gripped the bottom of my shirt and stripped it off over my head. I kept my eyes set on him as I bent to drop my bottoms, too. His scowl turned to raised brows as I stripped before him. It may have been the first time he allowed his brows to rise, even if only slightly. I kicked my pants off my ankles and stood before Erix in black, less-than-sexy cotton undergarments. The once red line on my abdomen had faded to pink. His eyes flicked from my face to that line.

Odessa had promised it would fade to nothing in a few short days. Before stepping into the tub, I waited until his eyes were back on my face. I stood for a moment, towering over where he sat submerged in the large square tub that likely could fit six. The bubbling water licked at my thighs as I stood, staring down at him. I allowed the corner of my mouth to twitch up slightly before I sunk down into the warm bath water. I rested against the opposite side, holding the king's eye contact with neutrality. I gave him absolutely nothing to read on my face. His jaw was clenched tight in challenge.

"So this is what we're doing today, then?" I asked him.

"This is what *I'm* doing today," Erix grumbled, finally looking from my face. His eyes settled on the bubbling surface of the water.

I shrugged at him and reclined further against the side of the tub, shutting my eyes.

I kept my eyes shut as I spoke. "Your city is suffering, you know, the buildings are falling down around them. *Killing* them."

Erix only grunted a reply. My eyes flung open, my body filling with rage. I hadn't expected the sudden shift in mood... yet... something about his nonchalance filled my entire being with a rage so cold I had half a thought I may freeze us both into a brick of ice.

"Why don't you care?" I splashed him with water. It was childish, but I didn't care. I waited for a reaction.

He blinked, water dripping from his face. I snorted air out of my nose at his disheveled look. He let the water slide down his eyelashes and cheeks as he pinned me with an icy stare. He could kill me right now, with a blink, as I likely could him. My eyes dipped to his throat. If only I had a dagger. If only I didn't have to wait six weeks. I could do it. Right now, I could launch myself at the sodding bastard and—

"I am the king. Get. Out." He pointed a finger at the door.

I laughed. "No, you're not."

His glare burned through me at that.

My tone became wholly serious. "You've spent nearly a century pouting. It's time, Erix."

A smile crept on Erix's face at my words. The look of him, wild-eyed and smiling, made me feel small. Weak. I forced myself to sit taller.

"If you think," Erix began in a menacing voice, "that just because the Goddess sent you means you will be able to do *anything* for me, you are sorely mistaken." He spat the last few words.

Goddess, why did I have to seduce *this* male? He was hateable enough; why couldn't my task be 'creep into Erix's chambers at night and cut him open with a dagger.' I forced my scowling face to neutralize.

"I think you should see your city." I held him with my gaze until his face softened, and he reclined further. His eyes fluttered shut as he rested his head against the lip of the tub. My eyes once again found his exposed throat. If he allowed such a compromising position now, I should have no problem fulfilling my task in six weeks. The thought soothed me to my core. I sunk into the water until both of my shoulders were fully covered.

Neither of us had more to say to the other, so we remained silent. After about twenty minutes, Erix shifted, bracing a hand on the tub's edge. He slowly began hoisting himself out of the still-bubbling water. A small squeaking sound escaped my lips as I covered both of my eyes with my hands. Erix let out a deep, throaty laugh. I could hear the water move as he stepped out of the tub. My hands remained covering my eyes. Blood and heat rushed to my cheeks. I had just given away so much of my naivety with that squeak. I silently reprimanded myself.

"You can look," Erix grumbled. I was surprised he had spoken at all. I slid my hands from my face and beheld him dripping wet, a towel tied *very* loosely around his hips.

He walked over to the tub and stood above me with crossed arms. This time, I fought to keep my eyes from trailing down his dripping wet body. "It was a pleasure, sweetheart, but if you don't mind, I have moping to do."

Sweetheart. I wanted to scoff but refrained.

I stood, meeting his height, thanks to the tub that was raised up above floor level. I turned to mimic his crossed arms and pouty lips. His scowl deepened at that. "Out." He pointed at the door.

I leaned forward, shoving my face right up to his.

What a rotten sodding male.

My eyes bore into him. "You're not the only sorry male that had a bastard of a life. But *your* actions made you king." I shoved a finger forward, digging it into the center of his still-wet chest. His eyes dropped to that finger and then back to me.

"If you can't shoulder the burden, you shouldn't be standing here right now." His face showed no reaction to my words. I wasn't surprised. He truly did not care. "And," I removed my finger from his chest, "if you don't mind, I could use some help getting out." I held out my hand with a dainty flick of my wrist.

A muscle in his neck tightened at the request, but he offered his hand anyway. I plopped my hand atop his and allowed him to help me rise and exit the tub. I grabbed my clothes from the ground, wadding them up in a ball I cradled to my chest. I stalked to the door but stopped just before it. "Will you see the city with me," I asked Erix without turning. "We can go at night," I added.

A long moment of silence with tension so heavy I nearly swayed on my feet. I could feel him studying me, even though I did not face him.

"Ten tonight," His voice was harsh and cold. I heard him shift and shuffle toward his bed.

I nodded, even though he likely didn't see. I was thankful I faced away from him, as I couldn't keep the shock of his reply off my face. I wasn't sure why he had agreed, but I wasn't about to ask.

I slipped out of his room, closing the door behind me. I rested my back against the door for a moment. That was a win. I heaved in a deep breath. Perhaps it was his mood or my pushy forwardness, but he agreed to see the city. It was a good step... a great one.

I peered down the hall, hoping to sneak back to my room unnoticed. Erix's room was at the far end of the hall, meaning I had to walk dripping wet back to my room on the opposite end. I crept down the bend in the hall, my door finally coming into view when Aven came around the corner. He burst into laughter at the sight of me.

"Damn, Sel, you've been here for like two minutes; whose room are you coming from?" He glanced at me and then behind me, his eyes lighting up. He lunged forward, wrapping an arm around my shoulders. "No way you came from his room." He jostled me around in excitement. "In the tub, too?"

"Nothing happened," I said flatly, trying to push from Aven, but his grip on me was strong.

"Your outfit begs to differ," Aven laughed and released me. "Let me walk you back to your room."

He walked ahead of me, shielding my body from any of the castle keepers who may be walking through. Given the way Aven talked, I was surprised at how respectful he was in not looking at my body in such an exposed state. I slipped into my room and found a set of dry clothes to change into before meeting Ynette in the main room. We worked on structuring a new taxation system for Seldovia, pausing only to roll our eyes at what Aven said as he passed through.

The ten o'clock hour rolled up on us before we knew it. I had told Ynette I got Erix to agree to see the city. She was so surprised that I had to tell her to close her mouth three different times. Out of fear of ruining anything, Ynette was sure to be anywhere but the main room when Erix came out.

I sat at the bar top where we had been working, thinking they needed a table in this space. I flicked through some of the stipulations we had written while I waited for Erix. Would he even show? My mind drifted to Idris as I thumbed through the tax law. It wasn't that long ago we had joked about appropriate taxation, and now look at me. I sighed. My little fireball. I hoped she was doing okay.

"Official peacemaker business?" Erix spoke from above me. I jumped, surprised by his presence and ability to walk in so silently. I couldn't lie; I was a little surprised he had shown up at all.

"Yeah, would you like to join in?" I asked a little too eagerly. Erix only stared blankly at me.

Okay then.

He was dressed in all black, shirt unbuttoned slightly. It suited him, complimenting both his onyx hair and pale complexion.

"Ready?" I asked him. He grunted in reply. What good company he was.

We walked down the stairs silently as I racked my brain on what to say and how to act for peak temptress performance. What would make Orphic proud? "There are some signs that... say some not-so-great things," I decided to say as we walked down the last steps exiting the castle.

"I know what they say," his voice was bitter.

When was the last time he left the castle, other than for the placement ceremony? Or the last time he had been in the city?

"When were you here last?"

Erix chuckled, but it was cold and distant. I swallowed hard; it had probably been with his wife. I knew then that he wouldn't answer me. We walked down the path to the city. He didn't speak to me, even ignoring my side comments on our winding walk into the city. There was a chill in the air, and I wished I had worn a coat. I started down the final steps that led into the streets of Seldovia. Erix cleared his throat, nudging me in a different direction. I cocked my head at him but followed silently.

We walked along the city's outer edge for a moment until we came across a set of stairs tucked into the back of a stone building. He walked up them slowly, and I followed. We went up a few flights of stairs before we came to a wooden hatch above our heads. Erix shoved at the two wooden doors, allowing them to swing open. We climbed the remaining steps and exited the hatch, closing the swinging wooden doors behind us. I took in the building we stood; it was tall and on the far edge of the city closest to the castle. It overlooked much of Seldovia, even the row of shops with those horrible signs. I walked to the edge of the stone balcony we now stood. A few people were still walking the streets, but it was otherwise empty. The city was a pitiful sight during the day, yet at night, the darkness covered those imperfections. The run-down shops, the broken glass... it was all masked by the cover of nightfall. I turned to watch Erix's face, to discern what he was feeling... why he had agreed to come here with me. I hadn't thought the male would be an enigma. Orphic made it out that he would be straightforward... An easy read. I cocked my head at him, finding myself surprised on many levels, Not just because he came here, but for saving me from the wind soldiers. I cleared my throat.

"Why did you save me that day?" I leaned against the stone balcony.

He shifted his weight but kept his eyes on the flickering lights in the city below us.

"You could have let me die. You said it yourself, I'm not your problem—"

"Do you wish I had?" He turned to face me now. His face was neutral but bordering on a frown. "You gave up," he spoke it with such nonchalance it took me a moment to realize what he meant. The image of the male barreling toward me flashed in my mind again. I had felt overwhelming peace at that moment. Time had slowed... I had agreed to go—to fall. I felt a flash of anger and embarrassment bubble. I hadn't wanted him to see those things. I hadn't planted them as perfectly executed manipulations intended for my target. He had seen them in the raw. But he wouldn't know the difference. I let my eyes become glossy.

"You uh..." Erix shifted uncomfortably, "Don't have to talk about it." He turned from me now, clearly uncomfortable by my tearing eyes.

Shit.

That was not the intended outcome. Erix's attention was no longer on me but on the starry night sky above our heads. I turned to face forward now, scanning the sky for my three links. My eyes fell upon it. It was different now. I was

371

Eevy A.

seeing it from an entirely different location. My breath caught in my throat, and I couldn't help but wonder, as I had many times before, who else was looking up at these stars at this very moment? My hand inched its way to the opal stone around my neck. With every ounce of my being, I hoped Dayne was.

I pointed into the sky, "Those," I breathed, "The links, do you see them." Erix's head snapped from the sky to my face.

"What?" I scrunched my nose at him before again squinting at my constellation. Somehow, in this new orientation, the links in a straight vertical pattern were even more beautiful than what I saw in Avalon.

"You know Aeternus?"

I dropped my arm to my side, "What now?" I raised a brow at him.

"That constellation," he pointed now to my three links of stars, the brightest shining in the center link. "It is called Aeternus."

"Oh," I looked up at it, the memories of all I had told it flowing into me at once. "How do you know about it?"

He shrugged, but I could tell there was much more to it than he would be willing to share.

"What does it mean?" I asked

Erix shifted on his feet. "Eternal..." he paused, "light. Eternal light."

"Eternal light," I repeated, tapping a finger against the stone balcony. I broke my eyes from the constellation to find Erix watching me carefully.

I felt a rush of heat flood my cheeks at the attention. I suddenly found myself saying, "I fixed the fountain the other day," I looked at the half-crumbling fountain. It still had lively bubbling water bursting from the top, trickling down to the basin below.

Erix's head whipped to me with such force I turned to him. His eyes became two pools of sorrow. "It wasn't working?" He asked.

I shook my head. His head dipped, and his eyes shone against the moonlight. I didn't understand his reaction but waited, giving him an opportunity to speak. I didn't hold my breath in wait.

"It was her favorite part of the city," he mumbled.

Leyola. He meant Leyola.

I took a small step toward him. "You have to let her go," I whispered to

372

him. He tore his eyes from the fountain below us. Instead of finding something new to watch, he let his eyes dull and unfocus on the horizon.

"I have," he whispered back to me.

I didn't understand, but I allowed silence to hang in the air between us.

"I've only lived eighteen years," I started, and Erix turned to watch my face as I spoke, "but every year has been terrible. Every year, except this one." I hardened my eyes upon his. "I know it doesn't compare to seventy-five years, but for what it's worth, I think you should make this year your first good one, too." I waited for his reply, sure that he would stay silent.

"It's not them I grieve anymore," he bowed his head, "I lost myself; I don't know when it was, but I... I can't feel myself anymore." He shook his head. "I don't even know where I could start in finding that person again."

I rested my hand atop his; surprise fluttered through me that he spoke so freely, but I paid it no heed. Somehow, I forgot about my task and everything I was told I must do.

"Let's start by saving your people."

Chapter Thirty-Seven

Aeryn

I was crouched, watching Dayne from a distance. He was stepping through the thick brush and trees scattered through the forest that lay at the Olvidare Manor's back. I had followed him out here on behalf of the king, his father. I assumed when asking the king if there was any... *business* I could take care of for him, trailing his son to learn 'What the damned boy does all day' was not on my radar.

I crept back from a distance as he trudged through the brush, bending every now and then to examine something. He used his wind magic to shift branches and brush out of his way as he walked. I squinted at him, trying to figure out what the hells the male was doing. He bent over again and shoved something into his pocket.

"Who is following me?" Dayne suddenly whipped around.

What? I hadn't made a sound.

He sent a massive gust of wind in my general direction, knocking me to my back. The twigs and brush around me snapped in ways that I knew his precise hearing would zero in on.

Sod.

He was hovering above me instantly, his brows set together in anger. His face slackened a moment later when he realized it was me. I shifted a hand from where it connected with the ground, rocks and twigs jutting into my skin.

"What are you doing?" I asked Dayne.

"Funny, I was just about to ask you that," He offered a hand to help me up. I gripped it and allowed him to pull me to my feet. I bent to brush off the remaining pebbles from my pants, hoping Dayne would explain himself without further prompting.

He dug around in his pocket before opening his palm. Several rocks and pebbles of various sizes sat atop his hand.

"You're... collecting rocks?" I glanced from his hand to his face.

I was taken aback by the grief that swam there. "I promised Selene eighteen years' worth of gifts," he frowned.

"So you... got her rocks?" I raised a brow, trying not to laugh at the poor sap. I ignored the anxious weight that hovered above me at the sound of Selene's name.

He shoved me, noting the laughter building on my face.

"My room is filled with gems, daggers, crowns, and anything else I could already manage to buy," he sounded embarrassed. "There was nothing left to *get*."

I understood him then. It wasn't about the gifts or the rocks. It might not even be about getting her eighteen years of presents. He was keeping himself busy, trying not to succumb to whatever demons he fought inside. I winced, feeling bad for him and hoping Selene was doing better than he was.

"Do you want to grab a drink tonight?" I shoved him back.

He raised a brow. "You never told me why you were following me."

"Honestly, your father asked me to," I grinned at him.

He snorted a breath of air. "No surprise there," he shrugged, shoving his rocks back in his pocket.

"You want to go now?" I inclined my head toward the city streets and began walking that way.

He only nodded and followed.

* * *

Eevy A.

THE PUB IN OLVIDARE WAS... not really my style. Too many snobby females and males with something stuck up their asses. The air about the place was off, but the style was worse. It was too clean, with polished stone covering most of the floors and walls. Delicate round tables were spaced out in the large open space before the bar. Dayne and I found a booth with a cool, slick white cushion to slide into. I didn't like that, either. I second-guessed my heritage, as this *was* the land of wind.

"So you miss her then?" I asked Dayne over our two large goblets of Faerie wine.

"I do," He nodded but didn't seem to want to talk about it.

"Me too," I said. His head snapped up to mine, and I realized that hadn't been the smartest thing to say at that moment. I could see he didn't trust me, and I only half-trusted him because of Selene.

"Do you think we will see her again?" Dayne leaned back against the cushioned backrest, sad but contemplating.

I had to kill his father, likely kill Nicodemus, and then take the crown as King of Wind. Assuming Selene completes her tasks, I will definitely see her again... I would make sure of it. But him... What would happen to him? I doubted he would be a problem when it came to Theon's death. I can't say he would be my number one fan, but...

Dayne leaned into the table, snapping my attention back on him. "Are you going to kill my father?"

It took every ounce of training not to spit my drink all over Dayne's face. I forced my face to contort into a sort of confused look. But Dayne's eyes only narrowed.

"I'm a peacemaker; would that not be the opposite of peace?"

He considered my words. "I'll help you if you are." He took the risk in saying, which meant he already had to be fairly certain that I was going to kill his father. I had no idea how he got that idea into his head in the first place. But if he wasn't certain, he wouldn't have risked offering his help.

I watched him for a moment, gauging his sincerity. It would be risky to trust the male, yet everything within me told me I could. I trusted Selene's judgment too, maybe even a little too much... Maybe I shouldn't hold her to that high of a standard, considering she screwed the first male she laid eyes on.

376

"She made me promise to keep you safe," he whispered.

His words were like a hot stake to my gut. I thought back to the meeting of kings. They had taken a bedroom together. They shared their last moments before she set off on her Goddess-chosen task. Yet she still thought of me. She still looked into her lover's eyes and tried to secure my safety. In a way, I was offended that she thought I needed to be kept safe, but... we all knew the risks of our task. I almost shook my head in disbelief at the bond Selene and I had formed so quickly in the sanctum. That friendship... it was unbreakable.

"Okay," I whispered back to Dayne, holding my breath for something terrible to happen.

Dayne only smiled sadly, "Okay."

And the deal was made.

Chapter Thirty-Eight

Selene

"YOU HAVE GOT TO STOP PICKING AT YOUR NAILS." I SWATTED Ynette's hand. We sat side by side at the bar, trying to focus on the never-ending list of *things* we had to do.

"Agreed." Aven chimed from the couch in the sitting room. He was lounged lazily, tossing a small ball of fire up in the air while we worked.

I turned on the spinning bar stool to face Aven. "You are one of the most disgusting people I know; you have no room to judge Ynette's habits." I laughed while saying. He only gave me a vulgar gesture as I turned back to the papers strewn before us.

- Reinstate taxes
- Get a list of people who can help rebuild the city
- Find people to be apart of the Seldovia troops

The list went on and on and felt overwhelming, to say the least. Ynette's anxiety was evident, but she was happy not to be in this alone. I was, too.

"Do you think Erix would come out of his cave if I knocked?" I asked Ynette, "Or does he have a lady friend in there?"

I hadn't seen a single female come through since the night Erix and I had gone to the city. I wasn't entirely sure if it was because of the fleeting moments we had spent together or something else. Either way, I sat in secret triumph at the feat.

"I'll check." Aven shoved off the couch and jogged the hall to Erix's room.

Ynette rolled her eyes in sync with me. I felt bad for Aven, though; his friend—his brother had lost himself entirely. Despite how his life ended up, I gave Aven a lot of credit for staying so... chipper.

Banging and shouts rang out from the end of the hall. I winced as the sounds grew louder and louder. Aven rounded the corner with Erix's neck squeezed tight in the crook of his elbow. A cheesy grin spread across Aven's face as he dragged the King of Ice into the room and up to the bar where we sat. Ynette and I laughed at the sight but quickly stopped as Aven released Erix, his enraged face now coming into view. He stood there glowering at us all as he rubbed the back of his neck where Aven had him squeezed tight.

"My ladies requested your presence," Aven said, bowing to us at his performance. Despite the anger that radiated from the king, he gave Aven a playful shove, love shining in his eyes. An unfamiliar sight, given how minimally I saw these two interact since I had come to the Kingdom of Ice.

"Sel's wearing black for you," Aven waggled his brows at Erix. The slightest red flushed into Erix's cheeks, but he did not glance my way. "Her legs look sodding bangin', don't they?" He elbowed Erix, who only kept his eyes set on the ground. Aven shoved him again. "Ahh, you're no fun."

Erix looked up from the floor, his eyes falling on his sister. He gave her a curt nod before turning on his heel.

"Stay." Ynette beckoned her brother to the seat beside her.

"I don't think—"

"Please," I added, glancing at Ynette to see her approving smile.

We all watched him, waiting to see what he would do. Even Aven stayed quiet as if sensing Erix contemplating being anywhere but his room. Erix let out a shallow, huffing breath before dragging himself over to the stool next to Ynette.

"Oh, I see," Aven cooed at Erix, "If I need you to do anything, I just have to get Selene to say please and bat her pretty eyelashes at you."

"Wine," Erix grumbled back to Aven while extending his hand.

"Of course, your sodding royal majesty."

Ynette and I both let out a small yelping laugh.

The four of us sat and drank and talked for hours. Well, Aven did most of the talking, and Erix did none of it. Ynette eventually got up to head to her room, Aven scampering after her, asking if she needed 'someone strong and sexy to cuddle.'

I looked at Erix, swirling half a glass of white wine around in his cup. It was a miracle he hadn't left during the entire exchange. His face looked somber and thoughtful, but he did not speak, even as we sat alone in the room. "I'm going to make you come out and help Ynette and me one of these days," I spoke with hesitant neutrality. Erix grunted a reply. What a delight he was. I glanced down at my ankle, finding three navy lines there. I stood from the stool I was on and slid into the one next to Erix. It was still warm from Yenette's recent departure. "I've seen your room; it is *not* interesting enough to stay in all day.

Still no reply.

"You do know it is generally perceived as rude to ignore people?" I raise a brow at Erix, who stopped swirling the wine in his glass.

"And what is it you would like me to say?" His face was neutral, but his eyes shone with challenge.

"Oh, Selene, you are so smart, beautiful, and talented. I would love to help you take care of the tasks that I'm already supposed to be doing." I narrowed my eyes slightly but wore a slight smile.

He turned to me then, studying my face. He cleared his throat and echoed me in the most monotone voice he seemed to manage, "Oh, Selene. You are so smart, stunning, and talented. I would love to help you with all the tasks that I am already supposed to be doing." His face was smug.

"I said beautiful, but I'll accept stunning, too." I forced a bright smile, flashing my teeth at him.

"You are very annoying, you know that?"

"I know," I smiled, "and you are very stubborn." I poked at his bicep at the word stubborn.

We watched each other for a moment before turning back to our drinks. I slumped in my chair, finding my mood lifted from these past few weeks. While every shred of my soul wished Dayne could be here with me, I still felt some sense of normalcy. Whether it was the planning with Ynette, the sunshine, or even the pesky conversations, I found myself looking forward to with Erix... it had been *fun*. Such a simple word, a simple feeling. One I hardly remember feeling at all in my time in Avalon. I propped my elbow on the frigid quartz bartop and rested my cheek against my knuckles. Erix stared intently into his glass of wine, eyes concentrated but lacking that crushing sorrow I normally saw there.

My heart lurched, a pit forming in my gut at the sight of him. I was both excited and triumphant at his shift in mood. It meant that whatever I was doing, it was working. The other half of me, the half that sent warning bells off in my mind, was crushed by seeing him this way. If he could come this far in a matter of weeks, what could we accomplish in months? Could he crawl out of that darkness entirely? Had this been a hasty solution from the Goddess, one she chose because it was *easier*?

For the first time since stepping foot in the Kingdom of Ice, guilt shredded my insides. It wasn't fair. Not to Aven, to Ynette. Not to Erix.

Not to *me*.

"Are you okay?"

I felt the tears. I wiped them away and willed them to stop. "Yeah, yeah, it's fine." I was so stupid. Crying in front of him.

He scooted his chair closer to me, and I froze. My whole body pulsed with conflicting emotions. The push and pull of guilt and motivation to complete my task coursed through me. Do I use the moment and get closer to him? I knew what Orphic's answer would be. Erix cocked his head at me. I could hear Orphic's voice in my head. He was screaming at me, 'Look at him, LOOK AT HIM.' I couldn't do it. I shifted my head away from Erix, looking straight ahead.

Erix reached out a hand, hesitating at what to do with it. It didn't matter. I shoved so hard from the bar that the stool toppled over backward, clanging to the stone ground behind me.

I didn't even look at him before I ran from the main room back to my bedroom and slammed the door behind me. My heart was racing. What was I doing? All I could hear was Orphic and the Goddess screaming at me. Telling me I was a failure—telling me that I needed to go back out there and use the moment to my advantage. It *was* the moment I had worked for. I shrunk within myself, cringing at the feeling of making myself smaller. I didn't want to feel smaller. I began hyperventilating, chest rising in clipped, uneven motions. Everything seemed to be crashing down around me. Not just this but everything from the past few months. I pressed my back against the closed door and slid to the floor. I pulled my knees to my chest and cried.

* * *

THE NEXT MORNING, I slipped out of my room, silently praying that I would find Ynette and only Ynette in the castle's main room. I wrapped a sheer flowing cardigan around my body tightly as I crept around the corner of the hall to the spacious room.

Sodding Goddess.

I nearly cursed it under my breath as I beheld Erix, for the first time ever, sitting at the bar while the sun was shining. It was almost unusual to see him during the day. He looked exhausted and sad again, holding a small steaming cup of tea. I could smell the peppermint the moment I walked into the room. His eyes roamed over me, but concern did not bloom there as I had expected. Perhaps he didn't care, then.

"Hi," Erix said to me. The male spoke to me first. I narrowed my eyes, assessing him. I glanced at the sitting room, sensing movement there.

Aven and Ynette sat on the black cushioned couch, watching Erix with wide eyes. The fact that he was out here at this time was a miracle, but talking?

"Hi," I said back, embarrassed about the night before.

He cocked his head at me but didn't say more. I hadn't wanted to bring it up but felt obligated, "Sorry about last night, I was... just embarrassed from crying."

Erix shifted at the conversation we were having. Or perhaps at the lack of privacy. I glanced at Ynette and Aven, who weren't even trying to disguise themselves as uninterested.

"It's fine." Erix breathed and brought the mug to his mouth.

I hadn't addressed the crying but rather the dramatic sprint to my room... I didn't plan on saying more. I nodded to him and joined Ynette and Aven in the sitting room.

"I have news," Ynette spoke, making me concerned. I found my eyes dropping to my ankle, three lines. I relaxed.

"What is it?" I asked, taking up an armchair across from both of them.

"I was sent word that Krakata's peacemaker resigned and was officially exiled from the Kingdom of Fire."

I gripped the chair. No. Idris. No. My hands began to shake even through my tight grip on the armrests.

"Where... do they know where she went?" I tapped my foot, unsure of how to still my body. Holy Goddess, Idris. What was she thinking?

"Only a rumor, but they say she was seen in Belgar this morning."

With Gaia. I took a deep breath in. She was with Gaia; it would be okay.

"The Goddess will have to appoint them a new peacemaker."

I nodded, but my head was spinning at the news. Resigned? How could she resign? What the hells was she thinking? The Goddess would be furious. I knew the threats she had gracefully bestowed upon me, and I can't imagine Idris's threats were lenient. I resisted the urge to nibble on the skin of my fingernails. I thought about how low I had felt last night. A flicker of hope sparked within me. I don't know how, but Idris had just changed everything.

Chapter Thirty-Nine

Selene

I HAD COME TO TERMS WITH IDRIS'S RESIGNATION AFTER A FEW days of shutting myself in my room. The weight of my existence seemed to crash around me after the news. Pulling myself through the thick of it was excruciating. Had Dayne been here, I felt everything would've been okay. I would've had someone to lean on. The reality was that Dayne was not here, and I only had myself.

I looked down at the pros and cons list I had scribbled out over the course of about three days. It was crumpled and tear-stained but legible enough. The only pro I managed to come up with for allowing the king to live was that he *may* turn his life around. My hands shook at the reality of everything. That it just wasn't enough. I wadded the paper up and shoved it beneath my bed. I hoped my days of avoiding him hadn't hurt my position with the king.

I strode toward the full-length mirror resting against the wall of my room. I began braiding my hair over my shoulder, steadying my breathing as my fingers twisted through my locks. One step at a time, I reminded myself. Even if I had to work back to where I was with the king, there was still time.

I turned from the mirror and began searching for a pair of socks to slip on. The castle was kept cold, and the stones of the floor were like ice beneath my toes. I grabbed a pair of white ankle-high socks and flopped onto the bed, bouncing up and down just slightly. I would find Erix. I slipped on the first sock. I would open up about the night I had run from the room in tears. I lifted my other ankle, resting it on my knee. He had seemed so concerned that night that he would surely be interested in the conversation. Right? I began slipping the other sock onto my toes. Tonight, I would make big moves. I tugged the sock up higher, breath catching in my throat. I dropped the sock, allowing it to hang off the end of my foot. I traced the lines on my ankle.

One. Two.

My heart gave no warning before it erupted into a gallop, thundering so hard against my chest it was nearly painful. I sprung from the bed, sweat already forming on my brow.

"Shit, shit," I rubbed my eyes as I paced my room. Who was dead? I had to cool my buzzing mind to make heads and tails of anything. Idris had resigned, so Jules would still be alive. Which left Galen or Theon. My breathing became ragged, all of this now feeling too real. Death. Dead. A king was *dead*. And I had one week. I was hot and cold at once, my body sweating, but my mind a frigid block. I wasn't far enough with Erix. I surely should have *kissed* him by now.

Think. I needed to sodding think. I forced myself to sit, taking in deep, cooling breaths. My body slowed, the sweat cooling on my skin into nothing. I glanced at the gold gleaming from my closet. Dayne's sword. I took a deep breath. I could do this. I would do this. I just needed my next moves.

Chapter Forty

Selene

I spent the next day pacing my room and waiting for Erix to leave his. This was a tall ask, of course, given the male had barely left it over the past seventy-five years. I told Ynette I wasn't feeling well today, which wasn't a lie. I couldn't even look at Ynette or Aven without feeling sick to my stomach.

It wasn't until nearly 8 in the evening that Erix left his room for a fix of Faerie wine. I knew that would be the reason he left his room unattended and that it would offer me only a fraction of time.

Even though I had a week, I needed to start—I needed to do something. I pressed my ear against my door, listening. I heard Erix asking where I was. It was all I needed to confirm the male had left his room. I slipped out of my room, holding Dayne's sword against my abdomen. I hurried down the hall to Erix's room. I slipped in, shuddering at the gothic aura that enveloped me. It was strange being here alone. I stalked to Erix's bed and climbed atop it. I stood and found my way to the headboard of his bed, leaning to look behind it. I reached into my pocket, pulling out several pins. I forced the pins into the grit between the stone wall behind the headboard, forming a line of protruding points. I took a deep breath before quietly sliding the golden sword behind the headboard. It rested gently atop the pins. I sighed and hurried off his bed, careful not to make it creak.

I bolted out of his room and back into mine. I had made it undetected. My heart was thundering out of my chest. I began pacing again. Occasionally, I would press my ear against my door to listen. Aven was flirting with Ynette, making Erix retire early for the night. I held my breath as Erix's heels clicked toward the hall. The sounds came in a smooth, easy pattern until they reached just before my door. They stopped momentarily, forcing my already air-free lungs to squeeze even tighter. I counted the seconds.

One. Two. Three.

His heels began clicking down the hall away from my room and toward his. I cooled my thoughts and body, forcing my lungs to fill with air. I needed to calm down before I spiraled.

I sat on the floor, willing a dome of cool air to surround me. I closed my eyes. My mind drifted to Orphic and to the Goddess. I breathed the cool air deeply and held it until my lungs burned. The image of Seldovia flashed in my mind. I pictured a wooden home falling, crushing a family beneath its splinters. My icy rage spiked at that. I could do this. I felt stronger then, more confident, and sure of myself. I waved a hand, dissipating the cool bubble of air into nothing.

I waited for Aven and Ynette's voices to disappear before I began the next step of my plan. I dug in my closet for the sheer robe I had taken from Ynette's room weeks ago. It felt like the right piece of clothing for when the time came. My past thoughts were confirmed as I held it in my hands, moonlight glinting off the shimmering black fabric. It was a stunning piece I wished I could wear for Dayne. I slipped off all of my clothes and stood naked in front of the mirror. I touched the opal stone around my neck, hoping Dayne was safe. If it was his father... I sighed. I hoped he was okay.

I slipped into the sheer robe and tied it loosely in front of me. Everything was visible through the robe, even in the dark lighting of my room. I walked to my door and waited many more minutes to be sure I didn't bump into Ynette or Aven on my way to Erix's room. If things went poorly, I had already stacked clothes and other items to grab and go. I twisted the doorknob silently and tiptoed out of my room. Cold air enveloped me, forcing a shiver to run up my spine. I hurried down the hall, clinging to the wall. It wasn't until I stood before his door that I realized I hadn't been breathing. I took in several deep breaths, calming my bucking nerves. I rested my hand on Erix's door and turned the knob. I walked into his room, closing the door swiftly behind me.

I kept my back pressed against his door as my eyes adjusted to the darkness of his room. Erix was sitting on his bed, his back fully rested against the head-board. He held a half-drunk glass of white wine in his hand. Shadows were cast on his face, making him look intense. His jaw clenched as he took in the inter-ruption. His eyes hovered on my face before dropping to the sheer robe that hung on my nude body.

I trailed my eyes down him sensually, finding it more than easy to take in the male's beauty. Even after seventy-five years of rotting away in this room, everything about him was still fit, as if carved from stone. My eyes trailed down his muscled core to where he was covered only slightly with a thin white sheet messily strewn on his lap. I took a step in his direction, then another and another. He did not shift, keeping his eyes on my face. As I took easy, calcu-lated steps forward, I tried to understand the look he wore. It was mostly neutral, with a wild sort of hunger in his eyes.

I stepped forward until I stood at the left side of his bed. What I did right now was forward. So forward that I had to pray Erix didn't see through it. I only hoped that he would give in to the temptation. That it would cloud his mind, muddling all of his curiosities. I brought my hands to the delicate black ribbon that was just barely keeping the front of the robe in place. His eyes dipped to my hands as I fiddled with it, allowing the ribbon to fall in a plume to the floor. The front of the robe sagged open, offering Erix a nearly unob-structed view of what lay between my legs. My breasts remained mostly hidden behind the sheer fabric and my hair.

I kept my hands hanging at my side, waiting for him to do something—say something. Erix's eyes roamed that spot between my legs. A plume of heat puffed in my core. I brought my hands to my shoulders, gripping the robe on either side. His eyes were on mine now, an unmistakable lust burning there.

Yes. Yes.

I flicked my wrists, allowing the robe to flutter the ground around my feet. He did not break my eye contact even as I stood bare before him. I inched my body forward until my thighs brushed against the side of his bed. My heart was thundering out of my chest, but I maintained a steady stream of ice to calm my nerves. I could do this.

I shifted my leg slightly, lifting it so my knee rested on his bed. His eyes shifted then, turning feral as they lowered to my breasts. He was chewing the inside of his lip as he slid those enchanting eyes over me.

I was close enough for him to reach out and touch me. I shifted forward, allowing most of my weight to shift to the knee that was on his bed. His eyes flicked from my peaked and annoyingly aching breasts to my face. They were his sad eyes, still filled with lust and desire but glossy and hollow. I nearly gasped at how much shone there. It was as if I could read the male perfectly at this moment. I leaned forward and crawled my body the rest of the way onto his bed. He still only watched me in the same position as when I entered. I rose to my knees and lifted my leg over his center, straddling him. I remained on my knees, the spot between my legs hovering inches from the part of him I could feel was pulsating heat.

I reached out, plucking the wine glass from his hand. His jaw clenched as he watched me tip my head back, swallowing the remaining contents of the glass in one gulp. When I finished, my eyes fell back on him; his eyes had already broken free and were roaming my chest again. I tossed the wine glass, not caring that it smashed into pieces on the other side of the room. Erix flinched at the sound but otherwise did not shift or speak.

I lowered my hips then, settling atop him. The hardness that twitched beneath me was evident in how the king felt. I forced my eyes to droop slightly, the corner of my mouth twitching into a seductive smile. Only the thin sheet of fabric remained between those two parts of us. I reached a hand down and ripped the sheet out from between us. I hadn't realized the wetness that had built there until I rocked my hips against his length. I slid forward and backward with ease. My chest tightened at the feeling. It was good... pleasure sparking in my core. Pleasure though. Not desire. I bit the inside of my cheek, shoving down the hot feeling roiling beneath my skin. I continued rotating my hips against him, sliding that wet part of me up and down the clearly generous length of him. Erix's eyes closed, jaw clenching and unclenching in sync with my hips. Ice, I needed ice. A flourish of cold fluxed throughout my body. He kept his arms at his side. I furrowed my brows slightly. Why wasn't he touching me? His eyes fluttered open, still sad but full of need. He trailed those icy eyes up and down my body.

I leaned forward, pressing my hands against the top of his headboard above his head. My breasts hung in the king's face, and he sucked in an uneven breath at their nearness. I slowly walked my fingers up the headboard, preparing to feel for the sword I had planted. I wasn't close enough. I shifted my hips forward now. My breasts became flush against the king's lips. Heat burst through me at the feeling of his breath curling around my nipples.

Focus.

I needed to focus. But I needed to see his face. Oh, Goddess, I wanted to see him squirm. I inched back, allowing myself the moment of indulgence. He ran his tongue over his lips, wetting them. Instead of holding it in, I let the whimper bubble from my lips as I arched my back, feeling the tip of him between my legs. To my delight, Erix's chest jumped in response to the sound. He shifted slightly now, sitting up taller.

I inched my body forward again, wetness sliding off his length onto his abdomen. I again braced my hands high above his head, nipple pressed against his blushing lips. I threw my head back, surprised by how my body reacted. Yet he was not reacting, not touching, or speaking.

It didn't matter.

I inched my hand up the headboard again, finally feeling the top of it. Erix's lips twitched against my nipple, sending a spiral of heat through my core. I chewed my lip, biting it hard to recenter myself.

I slid my left arm down from the headboard, wrapping my fingers around the king's jaw. This offered me the ability to reach even further behind the headboard with my right hand. I walked the fingers of my right hand to the top of his headboard and began feeling. I groped for the golden sword I knew was there. I gripped Erix's throat tighter as I extended my body forward, pressing my chest harder against his face. Reaching for... I groped again. Nothing. My body went rigid. It wasn't here.

"Your sword," Erix croaked. I didn't need to hear another word before I was flinging myself off of him, scrambling off the bed. I took careful steps away from him, shifting into a defensive stance but wholly naked. Erix didn't move.

He hadn't moved since I had slipped into his room. This whole time... Goddess... This whole time, he knew. While I sat there and... and...

Oh, sodding hells.

I bent down and threw the robe around myself, tying the ribbon as tightly as possible. It didn't provide much coverage, but it was something.

"How—" I whispered, keeping my eyes trained on him.

He smiled. I wasn't sure how he could smile at a time like this. Despite his lips, everything about his face was teeming with sorrow. The shining lust remained but dimmed from moments ago.

"I'm a king, Selene, and multiple hundreds of years old. I can sense more than you think." I shifted before him, wrapping my arms around myself. "The Goddess?" he asked, sadness consuming his face... no, his entire being. I nodded, wringing my hands together before me. "Do it, then." Erix lifted his chin high in the air, offering his throat to me.

My whole body began trembling. We stood like this for many minutes, Erix with his chin tilted high, me trembling before him.

When I didn't step forward, he asked, "Do you want to?" His eyes sparkled in wait.

I considered the question for a long while. "No," I whispered. I couldn't bear to look at him, so I looked to the floor in shame.

"Do you want to be..." he thought for a moment, "here?"

I somehow knew what he meant. He didn't mean here in his room. He didn't mean with him. He meant here, in The Kingdom of Ice, saving it. I chewed on my lip at the thought of all the work Ynette and I had done. The attachments I had formed in such a short amount of time. The Goddess's warning echoed in my mind.

"I..." I stuttered.

"Either do it now," he tilted his chin even higher, "or pledge your allegiance to me. You can't stay otherwise." Erix sunk his teeth into his wrist and bit down until blood welled at the surface. My eyes went wide at the sight of him.

His eyes teemed with craze as he waited, either for a killing blow or... or what? He lay there before me, throat offered and bloody wrist extended.

It clicked. Orphic taught us about the Fae mating bond. It can only occur between two Fae if they drink each other's blood; even then, only about thirty percent actually forge the bond. Anyone can choose to test for the bond, but whether or not it is forged is entirely up to a higher power.

He was giving me a choice. Kill him now, or try to forge the bond and become mates. Blood dripped from the king's wrist onto the white sheet below. I knew the wound was already healing itself. I shifted in thought.

After sucking in a quivering breath, I stepped toward the sword that lay atop his desk, keeping my eyes set on his bleeding wrist. Erix tracked me as I moved closer to it. He kept his chin high, bloodied wrist extended.

I wrapped my fingers around the cool hilt of the golden sword. I tiptoed toward the bed, hovering before it for a moment. I gripped the sword tight before climbing into the bed and positioning myself before the king. I rotated the sword in my hand, watching the silver moonlight glint off its blade. I looked back at him and lifted it to his throat. Echoes of the Goddess's threats boomed in my ears.

Yet something louder called. Something sweeter. Choice. It was like a breath of fresh air. A flicker of hope in an eternity of predestined darkness. I pressed the sword against his throat, watching a bead of blood form there. I locked my eyes on the king, and the world went silent.

A single tear fell down his cheek. I tracked the tear as it slowly dripped, a memory flashing in my mind. Avalon. I knelt in the sand. Golden sword at my throat. A tear had rolled down my cheek then, too. I blinked, freezing Erix's tear, watching it fall easily from his face to his lap.

Why did I have the right to kill him? The Goddess had damned me. She let me kneel in the sand, awaiting my death. I had been cursed by the sodding Goddess herself. Look at me now, following her orders so loyally. Bile rose in my throat. I was utterly sick at my actions. I lowered the sword from Erix's still-bleeding throat, bringing the blade to my palm. I wanted to be here, not with him, but with Seldovia. I wanted to complete that part of my journey. I would, too.

I slid the blade over my palm, and a thin line of blood appeared. I offered my palm to Erix. A different sort of light flashed in his eyes as he watched me extend my hand to him. He lowered his face slowly, eyes darting back up to mine as if waiting for me to stop him. He pressed his lips against the slice and drank the blood that welled there. His eyes fluttered shut for a moment before he released his lips from my palm.

His blue eyes were feral as he returned his palm to the blade to re-open the healed wound from earlier. I shoved his hand away from the blade, eyes falling on the line of blood still at his throat.

He didn't need to be cut anymore in this lifetime.

I leaned forward toward the king, his shallow breaths becoming a metronome to my swirling thoughts, settling them. I wrapped my hands around the back of his neck and tugged him toward me. He lowered his throat to me as I approached with my lips. I could smell him then, with the soft skin of his neck so near. The scent was sweet but twisted with a bite of something harsher. Honied mint. I breathed him in for only a moment before pressing my lips against his throat. I could feel him swallow and tense beneath my lips. I closed my eyes and ran my tongue against him, his blood coating my mouth. It was sweet and alluring, but I did not desire to drink too much. I closed my eyes and released my lips from his neck. I sat back and watched the king as he, too, watched me with soft, wide eyes.

The heat started in my chest first, a delicate wisp of it. It quickly spiraled out of control, becoming a vortex of destruction within me. I opened my eyes, locking onto Erix's face. We both clutched our chests as that *thing* spun and turned inside. Without warning, the spiraling heat combusted within my chest, chipping off a piece of me for only a fleeting moment. Then it was gone. I doubled over, feeling around on my chest. It felt as if the heat had taken something from me, replacing it with... with... I looked at Erix, unsure of what the feeling meant.

Did it forge? I didn't understand; it was so quick. My eyes scanned his face. I poked at that new piece inside of me. I waited, unbreathing until he poked back.

Chapter Forty-One

Selene

I COULD FEEL MY BODY TREMBLING, MY MIND TRYING TO WANDER to every problem I had just made worse with one tiny choice. I felt myself smile. But it was a choice.

Finally, I was done dancing with fate. Fate wasn't a very good dance partner anyway.

I shifted before Erix, feeling the urge to run from his room. I felt entirely too bare now that the intense moments had passed. The sheer robe left nothing to the imagination, and now... sitting in this bed with this near stranger... I wrapped my arms around myself, sliding my legs off the edge of the bed to rise.

Erix kept his eyes on my face, either out of respect or... well, there wasn't much left of me for him to see. I shifted my weight before him, yet he remained stoic and sad, resting his back against his headboard. I couldn't help but feel a prick of annoyance at the sorrow that remained in his eyes. The bond changed nothing... For either of us.

I cleared my throat, "Well, I'll go back to my room then." It was almost comical: Standing here after nearly assassinating the king. Now I walked out... mated to him? My mind bucked at the thought. The new issues I formed from the single decision to stay here. To not kill him. To save them.

"Okay," Erix breathed, glossy-eyed. Sorrow consumed him. He looked sadder than he had in days.

"Okay," I echoed and slipped from his room.

I ripped off the robe the moment I closed my bedroom door behind me. I balled it up, threw it into the corner, and turned to the closet. I flung the door open, eyes falling on the slumped canvas bag. Dayne's bag. I flipped open the top and quickly found a long-sleeved shirt to slip on over my head. His smell was there. Aspen and honey. I pressed the too-long sleeves to my face and sniffed deeply. Goddess, what had I done? I crawled into bed, the high from the mating ritual wearing off.

I felt off. Not in a bad way, but it wasn't good either. I brushed against my magic, finding nothing out of the ordinary. What was different was so much deeper. It was untouchable without making it evident to the king that I was toying with it. I shoved myself into the corner of the room, pulling my knees to my chest.

My feelings for the king were the same... mostly, even with this new string that connected us. Orphic told us that while all mating bonds are intimate, they weren't always romantic. The difference I felt was not in emotion nor, love, or lust. It was a shifting of heart... Of loyalty. Something so raw and primal that only existed because of that bond. I knew it was why Erix had asked for the bond. What forged between us was his way of ensuring I could not kill him. I let the thought float for a moment, realizing all it meant. It meant he *wanted* to live. It meant that he might just begin caring if only a little at a time.

I shivered. My room was cold, but I refused to huddle beneath my covers. I allowed my body to tremble as the cool serenity washed over me–through me. I had a mate.

I kept thoughts of Dayne barricaded from my mind. I wasn't ready to think of him just yet. But the Goddess... thoughts of her swarmed me. My body reacted physically to the fear I felt of her wrath. My trembling became full-on shaking as I thought of her forcing me back to Avalon. Everything I had done since coming to the Fae continent had changed me. My feelings had always been a puppet on a string. I had never been in control. Hope glimmered within me then. It was a faint flickering light that I would protect at all costs. I would fuel it with my dreams until I had every sodding thing I wanted.

Eevy A.

I would not be afraid of fighting for happiness—for hope.

I breathed in the thoughts of the Goddess one last time before exhaling them out.

The shaking in my shoulders subsided as I slumped against the wall. Dayne. It was time to think about Dayne. I lifted the sleeves of his shirt to my face once more, breathing him in deeply. I wished he was here. Stinging wet shame coiled in my gut at what I had done. Of course, I didn't regret it. But I knew there was a third alternative that Dayne would have wanted me to choose. Walk away from the Kingdom of Ice. Walk away from the mating bond and the king drowning in his own sorrows. Seek Dayne. I chewed on my lip. Even if that alternative had crossed my mind at the moment, I wouldn't have picked it.

I wouldn't have been able to leave, knowing what would continue to occur in Seldovia. I pulled my knees tight to my chest, praying that he would understand. I hadn't known Dayne long and Erix an even shorter amount of time. I knew that Dayne surely should have been the one if I were mated to anyone. I wished it had been Dayne. I wished that things were different. That I was born a happy child without an expiration date. I wished I wasn't fated to kill the King of Ice. I wished that so many things had gone differently. But they didn't.

I searched for the faint flickering light that was hope, finding it nestled within me. Hope did not look back. Hope was about the future. What we can and will do. Dayne would forgive me.

My mind was calm, fueled only by that subtle light that glowed within me. I could deal with the Goddess, I think. Everything else would fall into place. Dayne would forgive me. Gaia will succeed with Idris at her side. I somehow knew it was Aeryn who killed his king first. I smiled at the thought of him sitting triumphantly on the king's throne. He deserved it. He deserved everything.

Chapter Forty-Two

Selene

I STALKED TO THE MAIN ROOM THE NEXT MORNING, FEELING ON edge, the serenity of the night before having worn off. Ynette sat in an armchair in the sitting room, a book in her hand. Aven lay on his back on the couch and was surprisingly not talking. Light bounced in from the window before them, illuminating the space around them.

"Hey," I tried to stroll into the room as casually as possible, as if I didn't try to kill their friend—their brother last night.

Aven sat up to look at me. His brows furrowed for a moment before he rose to his feet. Ynette turned, setting down her book in her lap.

"What?" I raised a brow at Aven, wishing he would talk. It was unlike him to just *stand there*. My heart raced as the moments ticked by with him watching me. I shoved down the feeling of guilt. There was no way he could know about anything that had happened last night. Had Erix spoken to him? I let out a quivering breath, knowing that something was off.

Aven's face twisted from neutral to skeptical, a look he did not often wear.

"You—" Aven started, but he was cut off by the heels that began clicking down the hall, stalking for the main room. I swallowed the lump forming in my throat. I was all too aware of the sweat that pricked beneath my underarms. I didn't need to turn to know my mate stood behind me.

"You're sodding joking." Aven was walking toward us now. His mood seemed to teeter on anger, yet it wasn't quite that far. I turned to Erix, who was stepping around me to meet Aven.

Ynette stood now, too, but remained in the sitting room, watching. Aven stalked right up to Erix and shoved a finger into his chest. Centuries of brotherhood flowed between these two males.

"You mated with *her,* but not Leyola?" Aven pressed his finger harder into Erix's chest.

I hadn't even had a moment to be offended by Aven's words as the reality of last night crashed into me. The sad look in his eyes. Was it because of this?

Erix growled, swatting Aven's hand away. "You know damn well she didn't believe in mating bonds."

Aven shook his head, taking a step back from his brother. He turned now, looking past Erix toward me. It wasn't anger that swam in his eyes, but confusion—sadness. I hated every part of this... of seeing Aven, of all people, this way. I tried to force a smile. The confusion in Aven's face softened, slowly turning into indifference as he beheld me.

"Welcome to the family." He shrugged in a tone edged with sadness.

"It changes nothing," Erix said next, more to the whole room than to just Aven. I winced at the words, but they were true.

I braved a glance in Yvette's direction. Her blue eyes were already piercing through me. She was hurt and confused; both were evident on her face. Aven walked back to the sitting room where Ynette stood. He wrapped a strong arm around her and led her to the couch. Ynette nestled into Aven, allowing him to hold her. They were upset at us–both of us. They spent years dealing with Erix, and I come in here, and he is all of a sudden mated with me? I felt the sudden urge to tell them everything. I wanted to drop to my knees and explain it all, even if they could never trust me again.

"I'm sorry," I choked at Ynette. I understood her sadness; they loved Leyola, too. She was their family—their sister—his partner. This whole *thing*... It was a knife in a centuries-old wound that had never healed in the first place. I stepped toward the sitting room. I wished I could—

Valeria stumbled up the stairs that stood behind me, nearly toppling over herself. All of our heads snapped in her direction. The panic in her eyes was enough for both Ynette and Aven to rise.

"There's..." She took a moment to catch her breath. "There's a male at the gate." She took another few hurried breaths. "He said he's looking for you." Valeria pointed a finger right at me.

I shook my head. No one should be here for me. My heart sank. The Goddess. This had to have something to do with the Goddess.

I turned around, looking to Ynette, Aven, and Erix for direction. Do I go? Is it safe? What if it is more wind soldiers? I bit down on my questions, knowing the three may not even care what happened to me. They were a family. I was nothing but a disruptive outsider.

"I'll go with you," Erix snapped my mind out of its downward spiral.

"I..." I choked. What was going on? I turned back to Valeria. "I'll be right there." I ran for my room to slip on my boots.

Erix and I sprinted out of the castle, immediately turning off the dirt path that led to Seldovia. I followed closely behind Erix, never having been to the gates myself. Within minutes, the tall gothic gates came into view. I picked up my pace and squinted at the people on the horizon, too small to make out. There were a few of them... but they weren't dressed in white.

I forced my legs to shove off the ground harder and faster. My footing slipped, sliding on a patch of wet snow, twisting my ankle slightly. I bit down on the yelp of pain and kept pushing forward. Erix hadn't even glanced back. As I forged forward, I couldn't help but think about what Aven had said... About Leyola. She didn't believe in mating bonds? I watched Erix's onyx hair bounce slightly as he jogged before me. I had assumed they were mated, but... I ground my teeth together; the pain in Erix's eyes as he offered that bond to me suddenly made sense. I took more hurried steps forward, fear and exhaustion bubbling through me. I was tired of all of this. I just wanted *normal*.

I scanned before me, biting through the painful heat pulsating with every step forward. Something was wrong. I could see two males hovering over someone who sat on the ground, doubled over. I took three more steps forward, just enough to glimpse deep auburn hair.

No. No. No.

Eevy A.

I tried and failed to push forward any faster. What was he doing here? I was close, so close. His face, once too distant to make out, became visible as I sprinted forward. I didn't see any blood from here, but that didn't mean much. I closed the final stretch between us and nearly collapsed at Aeryn's side. I grabbed his cheeks in my hand, searching his eyes for answers. He looked defeated.

I dropped his face from my hands and launched my body at him, hugging him around his neck. "Are you hurt?" I whispered in his ear.

A pang of pain ripped through me as Aeryn tried to shove me off of him. I didn't care and kept squeezing him until he gave in and hugged me back. I rocked back on my heels, waiting for an explanation.

"I killed the king," his voice was flat.

"Nicodemus," his eyes locked onto mine. I held my breath, waiting for the news. Whatever it was... if Aeryn was here... it wasn't good.

"He has Dayne... he... I don't know if he killed him or..." Aeryn started coughing.

No.

"I think Nicodemus is holding Dayne captive," he choked out.

My heart. I clutched my chest, feeling pain ripping through me.

"How," I whimpered.

"It didn't go as planned," Aeryn frowned but said no more. I shook my head. I didn't understand. I needed more than that.

"Get a healer," Erix barked from behind me. My eyes scanned Aeryn's body, looking for injuries. When I found none, I looked up at Erix. His eyes were set on something behind me. I turned, my eyes falling on the short brunette female striding toward the gates from the other side.

I squinted harder. She was coated from head to toe in blood. It was caked in her...Oh, Goddess... in her short brunette hair. No. Idris. No.

"Go," Aeryn croaked, but I was already shoving off the snowy ground and sprinting for her.

My ankle wobbled beneath each lunge forward. My gate became unnatural as the limp set in. I didn't care. I charged forward through the pain.

The blood. There was so much blood.

I was close now, only a few strides away. I was screaming at her, "Idris. Idris. Idris. Idris..."

She didn't flinch or change her pace; she only walked slowly toward me. I reached her, taking her shoulders in my hands. I shook her violently, trying to snap her from this fog. Her eyes, once roaring with beautiful rage, were wholly dead. Not an ounce of life behind them. Not a flicker of that roaring volcanic ash. Her eyes were nothing but dust. I touched her all over her body for injuries. An unbearable pang of sorrow ripped me in half, as I realized. It wasn't her blood. Oh Goddess, Idris.

"Gaia," I croaked. Her eyes finally snapped to mine. All she did was shake her head, and I knew.

Gaia was dead.

* * *

I WANTED to fall to my knees before her. But I couldn't. Not my Gaia. No.

"What happened?" I was screaming... I think. My ears rang so loudly I could barely hear my voice. I shook Idris by the shoulders, but she wouldn't respond.

She stood before me, a living dead girl. I took her in my arms, not caring about anything but getting that blood off of her. I welled water to my hands and began furiously wiping at her face. She stood dead-eyed, staring ahead at nothing. I soaked all of her, washing away Gaia's blood. I didn't stop until every bit of her was drenched with water. She shook violently as she stood dripping wet in the snow. But she was clean.

I took her dripping wet face in my hands and held it.

"I'm going to carry you back to the castle." I didn't need to wait for a response. I knew she had none to give.

I took a shaky breath and limped on my injured ankle to her side. I bent my knees and cradled an arm beneath her legs and neck. Despite Idris's light weight, I wobbled as I cradled her to my chest. I took a step forward, grunting through the pain that tore through my ankle into my shin. I picked up speed until I was jogging, my little fireball cradled against me. I kept my eyes set on the gates. I couldn't bear to look at her, those dead gray eyes. All I could do was hold her tightly against me and run.

I didn't realize I was screaming his name until Erix stood before me. My vision had blurred at the edges from the shock—the pain. I wobbled, Erix's hand steadying me as I strode through the enormous gates. Odessa hovered by Aeryn, waiting. Unless she could mend a broken soul, there was no use for her.

Erix shifted in front of me and began taking Idris from my arms. "No," I screamed at him with as much fury as possible.

I pulled Idris against my chest protectively. Erix stepped out of my way, offering me a clear path back to the castle. He followed close behind as I half walked, half limped forward. Blood roared in my head so loud I couldn't hear anything but the crashing waves of it within my ears. I tried to pick up the pace, needing to get her into the warmth of the castle. I took a jog step forward, but my ankle protested. I couldn't run anymore. My legs wouldn't allow it. I screamed out in frustration but kept trudging forward. I hadn't heard his approach but felt it as Erix pressed a strong hand against my back. It strengthened me.

I forged ahead, taking Idris with me up the path, stairs, and the castle. It was a miracle I made it up the few steps into the castle. I looked up the several flights that now towered over my head, leading to the main room above. My legs trembled as I took them in. I tried anyway. My ankle rolled to the side. Erix caught me before I fell, and Idris nearly went down with me.

I screamed out in frustration. Without a word, Erix scooped Idris from me. I didn't have any choice but to let him. He held her against him with his left arm and wrapped his right hand around my elbow, hauling me up. He gently pulled me up the stairs while holding my sweet Idris against him. Aven and Ynette jogged down the stairs the moment they heard us.

Aven took Idris into his arms and turned to bring her the rest of the way up the stairs. Erix turned to make sure I was okay. "Get off," I screamed at him, shoving his arm off my elbow. I hobbled the final stairs to the top and made my way as fast as I could manage after Aven. He cradled Idris against him even more gently than I had. He walked a smooth gate to the sitting room and laid my sweet fireball atop the black cushioned couch. He sat and rested her head on his lap. I fell to my knees before her face. I pressed my forehead against hers, allowing my cheek to rest against Aven's thigh. I looked and looked at her, but she only looked through me. I stroked her face, tears streaming down my cheeks.

"I'm so sorry," I whispered. "I am so, so, sorry."

Chapter Forty-Three

Selene

I woke up on the floor of the sitting room and looked around. I looked out the large window at the starry sky. My eyes fell upon my constellation. The three links that I could now see from my positioning on the floor.

It had been the four of us. For so long, without even knowing each other. It had always been the four of us. I looked to the center of the links, the bright glowing star, and whispered one last promise. "You saved me," I whispered into the night, eyes locked onto that center star, "Now I avenge you."

I sat up and took in Idris and Aven. Moonlight encircled them as they slept. Idris's head still rested atop Aven's lap. His arm curled gently around her torso. Her eyes were closed, and her breaths were shallow but even. I turned to scan the rest of the room. I nearly jumped as my eyes met his. Erix. He held a glass of Faerie wine in his hand, but his attention was upon me. I pushed off the ground and crept over to him, careful not to wake Idris and Aven.

"Where is he?" I whispered.

"Odessa brought Aeryn to your room; he sleeps there now," Erix replied, taking the smallest sip of wine I have ever seen him take.

"Was he hurt?" We both kept our voices low and hushed.

A Dance of Fates

"Most of his wounds were partially healed from the time he spent traveling here. None were grave. He will heal properly."

I sighed in relief and took a seat beside Erix.

"I'm sorry," he whispered to me.

I turned to meet his eyes. We hadn't discussed anything since... well, since I almost tried to cut his head off. My eyes fell to his neck.

A hushed laugh escaped from me. "You're sorry? I almost *killed* you." His eyes were intense on mine.

"You didn't want to." He waited as if hoping I would reassure him of it. I only stared back at him.

"I had to offer the bond—"

"I know." I interrupted him, wanting to think of anything but that bond.

His eyes darkened, "Do you still want to help Seldovia?"

The question took me off guard. Of course, I did. I wouldn't have taken the bond otherwise. Even so, I considered everything: Gaia's death, which I had yet to allow myself to process... Aeryn's arrival to Seldovia and Dayne's capture. It overwhelmed me and rocked me to my core.

"Yes," I breathed quietly in answer to his question. "I want to help." His icy blue eyes bore into mine.

"We get Dayne first," I whispered, trying not to think of him chained to the floor in a dirty and dark cell beneath the Olvidare Manor.

Erix nodded.

I turned back to look at Idris. She looked distant and cold even in sleep. Ice seeped into my veins at the sight of her. I looked through the window toward the sky. It didn't matter who or what I believed in, but I spoke to her–to Gaia.

"I will kill them, whoever it is that did this... I will kill them."

Chapter Forty-Four

Dayne

NIC HOVERED ABOVE ME, A LOOK OF DISGUST SMEARING HIS FACE.

"Tell me how to get to her," He spat at me.

"No," I growled, shifting so the chains stopped digging into my ankles.

Nic raised the iron pipe above his head and brought it down to smash against my skull. My eyes rolled back into my head as the shock vibrated through me. My vision blurred.

"I will keep you here until I get her," Nic snarled and tossed the pipe to the corner of the cell. I barely heard it clang to the ground beneath the buzzing in my head.

"I can't even send six imbeciles to bring her back here successfully," He snarled to no one but himself.

I blinked, forcing the buzzing in my head to subside.

"What did you say?" I spat at my uncle.

He turned back to me, eyes glowing with rage. "Your pretty princess *killed* my soldiers."

I refrained from sucking in a breath of surprise. The six missing soldiers.

"Tell me how to get her," Nicodemus snarled at me one last time as he hovered by the door to my cell. He hardly gave me time to answer before he swung the door shut and locked it behind him.

I groaned in pain. He wanted Selene. The irony of it all was that he wouldn't have to seek her out. My entire body stiffened at that. She would come right to him.

Book Two in The Veiled Fates Series

A sneak peek

CHAPTER I
Selene

"CUT IT," Idris said, a bubble of heat rising in her tone.

"Are you sure—"

"Cut. It," she repeated, this time pinning me with her dulled ashen eyes.

I held her rich brunette hair in my hands, running my fingers down the length of it. Her velvety locks fell below her shoulders now, longer than she'd ever kept it.

I met her eyes in the mirror we stood before; a spark—no, not even a spark, but a whisper of fury danced there. She nodded to me as I brought the blade to her hair and sliced it. A plume of dancing brown strands swept to the ground beneath us. I hesitated, holding my breath for her reaction.

"More," Idris snarled at me. Her eyes were now set hard upon herself in the mirror. Had she had an ounce more life in her, she may have burned a hole right through the mirror. I frowned at the harsh gaze she held on herself. I wished she would burn a hole through that mirror because it would mean she was using her magic again. Idris shifted, forcing my attention back to the sharp blade I hovered near her head.

I let out a long breath and slid the blade across another handful of hair and then another. I cut it until it was at the length she usually kept it, falling just above her shoulders. Idris cocked her head to the side, taking in her typical hairdo. Darkness swarmed her eyes before, but now... now it consumed them. "More," she growled, eyes falling to her lap.

I winced at the tone, hesitating to cut more off. I knew it wouldn't release the pain like she thought it would... but if it could help her heal... if it was a first step—

Idris whirled around, snatching the blade from me and nearly slicing my palm. I jumped back in surprise and watched her wide-eyed as she began slicing through the hair in a near fit of rage. She had no pattern—no grace in doing so. She only grabbed a cluster of hair and snapped the blade right through it. I backed away another step, offering her space as strands of hair fluttered around us.

I should not–could not interrupt this. She was separating herself–her physical self from the past... from Gaia.

My heart lurched at the thought of Gaia and the raw pain radiating from Idris. It burned into my very bones... my soul. I clutched my chest, feeling the gaping hole that remained there. I had to be strong... For her. My eyes welled with tears, but I would not let them fall.

Idris's breathing became heavy and ragged, but she continued slicing anyway. Her arms blurred around her head in a fitful promenade. It was far from graceful... yet somehow, it was a heartbreakingly beautiful moment.

Once the final strand had been sliced and settled amongst the rest of her locks on the floor, I finally beheld my friend. My fireball.

"Goddess, Idris," I breathed, taking her in.

Her hair curled near her jawline, so short that it didn't have weight to hang freely. I flinched as she slammed the knife down hard on the table before her, shaking the mirror violently.

"There," she said, turning to face me with crossed arms.

I steadied my breathing as I willed my mouth to remain closed.

How... how the sodding Goddess could she look *this* beautiful after that whirlwind of violent stabs through her hair? I shook my head as I beheld her.

It was short but fell in swooping face-framing waves. This length... it worked on her. Goddess... it worked too perfectly on her.

"Idris," I started, "It's... beautiful." I meant it. I beheld my friend, her short umber waves flowing wildly around her head. It was a testament to what she was trying to become–to get back. That wild, free spirit that had only been trapped beneath the weight of her hair... the weight of her lover's death. *My* friend's death. My Gaia.

Acknowledgments

While I have many individuals to thank — my alpha reader, beta readers, ARC readers, etc., there is one individual who I feel needs to be spotlighted. Despite the time that passed since we were such great friends, this individual reached out to me when she learned of this book. Her very essence radiated with pride as she affectionately dubbed herself my "ultimate hype woman." She told me that she not only couldn't wait to hold my book, and read it, but to tell every person she knew about it.

Hannah, you never got the chance to read this before the cruel world took you from us. How full your words made me feel, empowering me to share my work with others. Your enthusiasm, pride, and steadfast kindness will forever live within these pages.

RIP to the feistiest, most loyal 'crazy horse girl' I ever had the pleasure of creating memories with.

* * *

Thank you, Gary Smailes, for taking this book on a wild developmental editing journey.